Praise for international bestselling author
RICHARD DOETSCH
and his electrifying thrillers

THE THIEVES OF LEGEND

"*The Thieves of Legend* stole my breath with the sheer audacity of its storytelling, proving yet again that this series gets better with every installment. Bold, richly told, and rollicking with adventure, here is a thriller that demands to be read in one tension-wrought sitting. Count me a fan for life!"

—James Rollins, *New York Times* bestselling author

"The tension leaps off the pages in this classic, ticking-clock thriller. Watch out. You'll grip the pages so tight your knuckles will turn white."

—Steve Berry, *New York Times* bestselling author

"Doetsch steps up his game with his fourth thriller featuring ex-thief Michael St. Pierre. . . . Plenty of action blends with interesting history and criminal trade craft for a satisfying read."

—*Publishers Weekly*

"Doetsch continues to demonstrate why he's one of the best thriller writers in the business."

—*Booklist* (starred review)

"[ ] well researched, in-
st

—*BookReporter*

THE THIEVES OF DARKNESS

"[A] masterpiece. . . . Richard Doetsch handles all the elements of a classic thriller superbly, and his characters are fleshed out and involving. He has earned his seat at the table with other A-list thriller writers."

—*Booklist* (starred review)

"Whip-smart and lightning-paced, *The Thieves of Darkness* left me breathless and awed by the scope and scale of its story. Truly a masterwork by an exploding talent."

—James Rollins, *New York Times* bestselling author of *Altar of Eden*

"Plenty of action . . . a most fascinating, page-turning thriller."

—*Mysterious Reviews*

HALF-PAST DAWN

"One of the best thrillers of the year."

—ABC News

"A shocking thriller."

—*San Francisco Chronicle*

"A gut-wrenching read. . . . The constant shocks and twists will delight the most seasoned thriller fan. A riveting and emotional journey filled with hope and faith, *Half-Past Dawn* is probably how late one will stay up reading this amazing book."

—The Associated Press

THE 13TH HOUR

"Brilliantly conceived, perfectly executed. Fresh, exciting, bristling with originality."
—Steve Berry, *New York Times* bestselling author

"A modern masterpiece . . . daring, original, and perfectly attuned to the pop culture . . . a devilishly orginal thriller."
—*Providence Journal-Bulletin*

"One of the best thrillers of the year."
—*Booklist* (starred review)

Also by Richard Doetsch

RICHARD DOETSCH

THE THIEVES OF LEGEND

POCKET BOOKS

NEW YORK LONDON TORONTO SYDNEY NEW DELHI

Pocket Books
A Division of Simon & Schuster, Inc.
1230 Avenue of the Americas
New York, NY 10020

This book is a work of fiction. Any references to historical events, real people, or real places are used fictitiously. Other names, characters, places, and events are products of the author's imagination, and any resemblance to actual events or places or persons, living or dead, is entirely coincidental.

First Pocket Books paperback edition November 2013

POCKET and colophon are registered trademarks of Simon & Schuster, Inc.

For information about special discounts for bulk purchases, please contact Simon & Schuster Special Sales at 1-866-506-1949 or business@simonandschuster.com.

The Simon & Schuster Speakers Bureau can bring authors to your live event. For more information or to book an event, contact the Simon & Schuster Speakers Bureau at 1-866-248-3049 or visit our website at www.simonspeakers.com.

Manufactured in the United States of America

10 9 8 7 6 5 4 3 2 1

ISBN 978-1-4165-9899-2
ISBN 978-1-4391-0967-0 (ebook)

For Virginia,
My best friend.
I love you with all my heart.

I did not tell half of what I saw,
for I knew I would not be believed.
—Marco Polo

Princeps legibus solutus est.
—The prince is not bound by the law.

I will show you fear in a handful of dust.
—T. S. Eliot

PROLOGUE
ITALY

The castle sat at the edge of the cliff looking out over the Tyrrhenian Sea, where dark waters blended seamlessly with the nighttime sky at the horizon. Constructed of stone, brick, and granite, the structure was built directly into the cliff face and seemed to grow out of the earth, as if it had existed for all of time.

When approached from the sea, the ancient building appeared as one with the rock, but now, in the depths of night, the glittering windows made it look more at home with the stars of the sky. Constructed in 1650 for the third Duke of Faronte, the castle had traded hands with the rise and fall of the region's fortunes, and had been most recently purchased by a man of vast wealth who was rumored to have made his fortune in some unscrupulous dealings in the Far East.

Michael St. Pierre stood on the edge of the structure's roof, his hand resting upon the stone battlement, feeling like a crusader who had breached the walls of Jerusalem. He took in the stars that filled the sky, the moon that had just begun its climb, the unusually heavy surf, a remnant of a forgotten storm, as it crashed like thunder against the base of the cliff face two hundred feet below.

Anchored a quarter mile from shore was an impressive ship, a 150-foot megayacht; the white Sunseeker belonged to the man whose home Michael stood upon now. He had been watching it for nearly an hour. A few hundred yards to its south, a smaller yacht had arrived about fifteen minutes ago, deploying a small tender into the rough water. Michael watched as the tender came closer and closer to the dock directly below him, and after battling the heavy waves, finally managed to secure itself. Now a group of six well-dressed men moving in single file climbed the narrow, steep stairs that had been hewn out of the rock centuries earlier. They paused several times along the way to catch their breath.

Michael clipped his harness to the rope that he had affixed to the metal scupper and threw it over the edge. It had taken him nearly fifteen minutes to scale the hundred-foot façade on the north side of the structure, bathed in shadow, hidden by the growth of forest that stretched up the coast. Due to the façade's knobby granite and stone design, climbing it had been like climbing the face of a mountain that had been dotted with foot- and handholds, making it one of the easier climbs he had done in the past few years. He had trekked five miles through the Italian forest, the rope on his shoulder and a small backpack of supplies giving him the appearance of a hiker. His phone was turned off. His girlfriend and Busch would be pissed if they tried to reach him and couldn't, but the idea of being discovered here by either the people coming to the house or the two people he was closest to was too terrible to contemplate. Explaining he hadn't actually gone to Chicago could prove to be a problem. An unfamiliar rush of guilt filled him, not for what he was about to do but for the deception he'd enacted and for the promise he had broken.

Only one person actually knew where in the world he was: his old friend Simon, who had hired him. He was probably sitting down to a nice meal in the town of Tramonti just a few miles up the Amalfi coast. Michael wasn't sure if it was Simon's persuasive argument that had brought him here or his own vanity and hunger for an adrenaline rush, but like an alcoholic who had lapsed, he knew deep down there would be a price to pay for giving in to temptation.

Michael pulled out a black stocking hat and pulled it down over his shock of light brown hair. He wore brown contacts over his slate-blue eyes and had rubbed his cheeks with eye black; it was a rudimentary disguise, but it would keep away the dogs if his image were caught on video.

Michael took one last look at the sea and stepped off the roof's edge. Falling through the cool air, he silently zipped seventy-five feet down the kernmantle rope. He released his hold on the Petzl stop descender, the self-brake slowing his descent until he came to a large double window that occupied the middle of the enormous stone wall. He hung there a moment, glancing down at the crashing waves two hundred feet below, the froth luminescent. It would not be a pretty death if he fell. He removed a knife from his waistband, guided it through the window sash, and with a quick burst of force slipped the lock on the leaded-glass window.

The castle was guarded by an impressive security

system. He had confirmed its presence twenty-four hours earlier with the installer, a man in Naples who was more than willing to talk shop with a fellow security professional. Michael had installed three similar systems in New York and knew that there had been no successful compromise of it to date. He also knew that the owner of the system had chosen not to incur the heavy expense of installing wiring through the stone façade that bordered the rear windows overlooking the sea; Michael understood his logic. Who would ever consider trying to scale the stone structure and risk death on the rocks below?

Michael slipped through the window into the study, a comfortable, dimly lit room with dark mahogany walls and a fire crackling in the stone hearth. A heavy antique desk filled one corner, and deep high-back wing chairs faced the blazing logs. The shelves were filled with antique books and religious artifacts. Michael recognized the painting above the mantel; it confirmed the rumors he'd heard of the castle owner's questionable integrity and his passion for the unattainable. Picasso's portrait of Dora Maar had sold for $23 million at auction twelve years earlier, but it had only spent one week aboard the yacht of the nouveau-riche Internet mogul who'd bought it before it had vanished in the dead of night. Michael thought of repatriating it and collecting the million-dollar reward, but that wasn't why he was here.

He turned and locked the study's heavy coffered door.

The security man in Naples had been forthcoming enough for Michael to hack his system and pull the security quotes for the castle. Beyond the alarms and the entrance cameras, three safes had been purchased and installed: a gun safe for the garage and two Helix 09 safes, one for the second-floor study at the rear of the small liquor closet on the far side of the room, behind a few boxes of eighteen-year-old Macallan scotch, and the second placed under the bar in the lounge of the Gentlemen's Den. Michael didn't know where the Gentlemen's Den was located, though he'd heard it was a bar not far from the castle. He knew the Helix 09 safe well: its modern design, its electronic keypad. He also knew how to override the lock in the event its owner forgot the code, something that occurred with 65 percent of its purchasers.

But as Michael opened the door to the liquor closet, his heart nearly stopped. The boxes of scotch were already moved to one side, and the safe door stood wide open, its interior light reflecting off the diamond bracelets and necklaces and the precious-gemstone rings that lay in black velvet trays. There was also a Sig Sauer and a faded black-and-white photo of a child in an old wooden frame. Nothing else. No file, no envelope with a family crest upon it, no small red Chinese puzzle box. None of the things he had been told would be here.

Michael stepped back from the liquor closet. The house was utterly silent, which gave him pause. The meeting was scheduled for nine. He'd seen the men arrive; he could smell the faint odor of food being cooked.

He suddenly heard voices through the open window, some sort of a commotion outside. When he looked out, he saw the six men on the dock below surrounding a seventh man, pushing him. The man in the middle looked older than the others, his body frail, the hunch of his back attesting to his advanced years. Michael could hear his anguished cries over the sound of the crashing waves.

Against his better instincts, Michael unlocked and opened the study door. He stepped into a dark paneled hallway, the carved rails and Persian rugs giving it a baronial feel. The hallway extended for a hundred feet at least, bordered on the left side by four doorways, all closed, while the right side looked out over a vast reception hall filled with gleaming modern furniture that stood in sharp contrast to the centuries-old castle. Michael pricked up his ears, listening, but there was only silence.

He glanced about, getting his bearings, noting every possible point of exit. And as he peered over the rail, he noticed something protruding from behind the couch in the reception hall that again gave him pause. He headed down the stairs to see if his worst suspicions were true.

Michael carried no gun—he hated them—only the knife at his waist. He was skilled with it, but it possessed no magical properties; it wouldn't protect him against anyone who might be lying in wait. He thought of the Sig Sauer he'd seen in the safe, but it was too late to go back and get it.

As he stepped onto the stone floor of the great hall, his eyes fell on the protruding foot he'd glimpsed from above, and with his next step the rest of the bodies came into view.

Bile rose in his throat, and his heart began to pound. Though he was prepared to witness death, he had not expected this. Despite his best efforts, he couldn't help but picture KC lying there, and it filled him with fear. And anger.

The three women he saw were of various ages, two probably in their twenties and one much older. And the child . . . the child was surely under five.

The gruesome sight was an affront not only to his senses but to his reason. Each of the bodies, the three women and the child, had been decapitated, their heads lying in pools of blood beside them.

"Absolutely not," Michael said.

"You didn't even wait to hear what I had to ask," Simon said, pushing his black hair back from his forehead. He stood up from the barstool, stretched out his body, still stiff from his long flight from Rome, and walked back to the pool table.

"It doesn't matter, you know I can't."

Simon nodded.

They were in the upstairs lounge of Paul Busch's restaurant and bar, Valhalla. It was Paul's private retreat, what his wife, Jeannie, affectionately called his man cave: a bunch of beat-up oversized couches and chairs, along with a pinball machine, a pool table, and a dart board. *Monday Night Football* played on the oversized TV on the far wall, while Busch himself stood behind the small bar, restocking the shelves.

The restaurant, which Busch had opened three years ago after he'd retired from the Byram Hills police force, had become a huge success. It was the destination of choice for not only the residents of Byram Hills but much of Westchester County. The food was typical American cuisine: steaks, fish, chicken, in generous portions, all served up by Chef Nick Mroz. Busch didn't believe in trends or in small portions, or in catering to the whims of some nouvelle cuisine food critic. He believed in making people happy.

"And whatever you were going to ask me, don't ask KC," Michael added, holding up his bottle of Coca-Cola for emphasis.

Simon threw up his hands. "I'm just—"

"Don't."

"But—"

"This is your fault, you know." Michael turned around on the stool, watching as Simon picked up a cue and began clearing the balls from the pool table with ease.

"My fault?" Simon said in his subtle Italian accent, keeping his focus on the table. "How is it my fault?"

"You're the one who said KC and I would be perfect for each other."

"And was I right?"

"Yes—no."

"You're still together," Simon said, holding up one finger. "She's actually living with you." Finger number two went up. "And I think you love her," he concluded as finger number three slowly extended.

"Don't you think it's time you bought her a ring?" Busch asked from behind the bar.

Michael looked up at Paul. "Why do I need to get married again?"

"Oh, I don't know," Busch said in his mocking tone. "Maybe because you love her, maybe because you want kids . . . and maybe it's what she wants, Michael."

"I was married before, and we both know what happened."

"What are you talking about?" Busch sounded genuinely puzzled. "I pretty much thought those were happy times for you."

"Well, they didn't last."

"They never do," Busch said quietly.

There was an uncomfortable pause.

"Look," Michael finally said. "You don't think I've thought about it? But I can't do it, not yet. I love her; for now that's going to have to be enough."

Michael turned back to Simon. "And you, the reason KC and I are together is not because of our backgrounds."

"I didn't introduce you because of your backgrounds," Simon said in protest.

"That's a load of—"

"Hey," Busch interrupted, his six-foot, four-inch body still squeezed into the small space behind the bar. "No swearing in front of the priest."

Simon turned to him and said with a smirk, "That never seemed to stop you."

"Or you," Busch said, running his hands through his blond hair, looking every bit like an oversized surfer. "Mr. Man-of-the-Cloth. I'm thinking my ride to heaven may be a bit easier than yours."

"Aren't you supposed to be closing up downstairs?" Simon asked.

"You two keep it down while I finish up," Busch said with a laugh as he grabbed his bottle of beer, headed out the door and down the stairs. "And Simon," his voice came floating back, "don't even think of trying to pull Michael into anything. He's going to be getting married soon. He needs to stay alive for his future bride."

"Can I at least tell you—?" Simon tried to say to Michael.

"No."

"Okay." He sank the last ball, turned around, and leaned against the pool table. "It's in Italy, a private residence. The owner's an attorney."

"I dislike him already."

"You'll like him even less when I tell you the rest. He worked the underworld circuit in Europe and Asia, dealt in every type of contraband: weapons, drugs, stolen art, whatever anyone needed. He had no qualms about who he bought from or sold to.

"Turned over a new leaf twenty years ago, raised two daughters, became the picture of a family man. Though that wasn't really the case. He just covered up his dealings, using middlemen, and continued to dabble in arms and artwork. He became a fanatic for ancient weapons, collecting swords, sabers, fancy pistols and revolvers, daggers, katanas. He bought most of them from the most unsavory people, tucking them away in his home.

"He also became a fanatic for rare books, sea charts, manuscripts—documents that gave him insight into the world of the past. Word came down that he found something very rare, something that combined his two passions."

Simon paused.

"What?" Michael asked.

Simon smiled, knowing he had his friend's attention. "Some secret that he was willing to sell to the highest bidder. And that bidder is about as dangerous as they come. Head of a Chinese Triad."

"Since when does the church care about the dealings

of a Chinese Triad? Are they interfering with Sunday Mass?" Michael half joked.

Simon hadn't performed Mass in all the years Michael had known him. Simon was in charge of the Vatican Archives. He was the keeper of the Church's mysteries, its secrets and history. He employed methods to protect the Church that didn't always align with a priest's job description, but then again, even God's laws were sometimes broken for the greater good.

"As hard as it may be for you to grasp," Simon said, "we care about everyone. And I happen to know a bit about what this man is selling."

"And?"

"It's a three-page document and a red Chinese puzzle box about the size of a brick, currently in a small house on the Amalfi coast."

"What's inside the puzzle box?"

Simon took a deep breath, then expelled it slowly.

Michael hated when he did that. It almost always meant that Simon couldn't say, but the matter was deadly serious. "Why don't *you* do it?"

"Because it's not what I do. It's what you do."

"Used to do, remember?"

"I know you, Michael. Playing the businessman—"

"Playing? I think I've done more than play."

"Granted. And you've built yourself a nice profitable business. But what I'm referring to goes beyond profits, balance sheets, and paychecks."

"Simon . . ."

"Michael, you know I wouldn't ask if this wasn't serious."

And Michael understood. Simon was one of the most serious people he knew. In the past, when he'd said something was serious, it had always meant that someone's life was in jeopardy, not just that some political powder keg was ready to blow, not just that some smoldering Church issue was causing his superiors at the Vatican to fret. When Simon said "serious" he meant it in every sense of the word.

"I can't help you," Michael finally said. "I promised KC."

Simon nodded. "I respect that." He held up his beer, leaned over, and clinked it against Michael's.

"Thanks," Michael said.

"Do you mind if I ask KC to do it?" Simon said with a half-smile.

"Simon," Michael said, holding up his hand.

"I'm kidding," Simon said, his half-smile becoming full-blown.

LATER THAT NIGHT, Michael ran his thumb over the electronic eye, slipped in his key, and opened the thick metal door of the two-foot-wide safe behind the desk in his library. It was filled with legal papers—his will, the title to his house and car, a half-dozen contracts—an unused Sig Sauer that Busch had given him, still in its box, and a file box for confidential work papers.

He took several documents off his desk and filed them away. He had arrived home after midnight, and instead of going upstairs to sleep, had opted to finish up a proposal he wanted to take to the office tomorrow morning. As much as he hated admitting it, he was becoming a bit of a workaholic.

What had started out as a small home security business had grown into a corporate consultancy with thirteen full-time employees who performed security installations for sensitive businesses and high-end private clients who needed to go to unusual lengths to protect their most valuable assets. The only client he did not take on was the government. His felony conviction precluded him from working for the federal, state, or local government. Truth be told, he had no desire to answer to bureaucrats who thought the best-qualified person was the lowest bidder.

Michael never tried to cover up the nearly three years he had served in Sing Sing Prison in Ossining, New York. The first and only time he was arrested. He'd been caught stealing diamonds from an embassy on the Upper East Side of Manhattan, the property of a corrupt ambassador. He had forfeited his success, his freedom, in order to save a woman from certain death. With his prize-filled satchel, Michael had been descending a rope when he'd caught a glimpse of a woman bound and gagged, her assailant standing over her, moonlight glinting off his knife. In Michael's mind, it was a fair trade.

His honesty about his past career more often than not endeared him to his clients, for who could understand security better than a man who truly knew how to compromise it? Michael's business had grown from a small alarm shop to a small warehouse in Byram Hills, New York.

Tucking the folder into the safe, he glimpsed a small

blue Tiffany's box on the rear shelf. It had been sitting there for months now, next to his old, battered wedding ring. He had worn the gold band on a chain around his neck for over a year, finally removing it when he met KC, when his heart began to heal.

He had bought the diamond ring at Tiffany's on Fifty-seventh Street in Manhattan. KC had quietly admired the ring every time they stopped by the store. She did not gush over it, or even ask to try it on. She simply gazed at it and became lost in her thoughts for a few moments. And that was all Michael needed to know.

He thought of Busch's words, of Simon's hints about marriage. It wasn't the first time his friends had brought it up. Michael didn't like being told what to do, or being backed into a corner. He knew his own feelings for KC and didn't doubt them. As he looked at his gold ring, he thought of Mary, thought of her death and what he had put her through, thought of the pain he'd endured when he lost her, and the fear he had of going through such a loss again. He looked at the blue box once more and closed the safe.

It was after midnight when Michael crawled into bed.

KC rolled over and looked up at him with her warm green eyes. She wore the red silk top Michael had given her the previous Christmas, the buttons loose, her long blond hair spilling around her.

"Hey," she whispered in her soft English accent.

"Hey back." Michael smiled.

Michael kissed her gently, running his hand along

her cheek. He settled in beside her, wrapping his arms around her, holding her as they both found a familiar position, their bodies pressed against each other, sharing their warmth. No more words were needed to convey their feelings.

KC tilted her head and kissed Michael again. In a single moment, passion rose up as he returned her kiss, deep and heartfelt, any thought of sleep slipping away.

IT HAD BEEN just over a year since Michael had met Katherine Colleen Ryan on the basketball court, an impromptu blind date arranged by their mutual friend Simon. She had almost kicked his ass, not only with her athletic ability but with her distracting long, lithe legs. Their month-long courtship had been interrupted when Michael learned that she, too, was a thief, and he'd rescued her from a man named Iblis, who had not only trained KC but had grown obsessed with possessing her, only to finally die at Michael's hand in the high mountain reaches of India.

They had returned to Byram Hills and had fallen not only in love, but into a natural friendship, listening to each other as much as talking, taking comfort in the silent moments when just the other's presence was enough.

Every night they would lie in bed and talk, warm in the embrace of the moment after, the sheets tangled about their feet. They had each experienced the death of loved ones and were aware of the fragility and preciousness of life. They revealed their pasts to each other, pasts that were filled with exploits that were slightly to the left of legal, slightly to the right of moral. Each was a thief who had found a moral barometer and had committed crimes that in some cases had served the greater good.

They spent their weekends reveling in head-to-head athletic competitions. While KC was superior in tennis and Michael had the edge in golf, their athletic passions ran more toward basketball and kayaking. They had competed in triathlons; he was the superior swimmer, leaving her behind, though she caught up and passed him on the bike, with the final leg, the 10K run, an all-out lung-burner to the finish line. No matter the sport, no matter the outcome, there was no question: Each was happiest when the other was around.

But with their type-A personalities, their occasional fights were spectacular. Usually they started over something mundane, like her forgetting to buy white bread or his blindness to the overflowing garbage in the kitchen, and ended with Michael's marching out the door to cool off at Busch's bar in downtown Byram Hills. The anger would usually last a day, sometimes two, but it would always resolve itself with apologies, warm embraces, and incredible make-up sex.

They told each other of their past crimes, sharing things neither had ever spoken of to anyone else. In an odd way, this, too, became a competition, as if they were trying to top each other: Michael's daytime theft at the Vatican, KC's evening grab from the Louvre, Michael's adventure beneath the Kremlin, KC's retrieval of a stolen painting from an African warlord. They had each secretly loved what they used to do: overcoming security and unexpected obstacles, outsmarting the establishment, sometimes feeling the satisfaction of righting some wrong—often at the behest of the man who would eventually introduce them, Simon Bellatori.

They would talk of hypothetical thefts—the White House, Buckingham Palace, MI6—pounding their chests, displaying their ingenuity, each correcting the other on the foolishness of their hypothetical plans.

It was on a warm fall day, two months ago in September, that they had headed into Manhattan to see all the sites the tourists see, the ones the locals rarely ever approach except to show to their out-of-town relatives.

They went to the top of the Empire State Building, looking down on the vast city, standing in the same place where Cary Grant and Deborah Kerr had stood. They visited the Statue of Liberty, Ellis Island, Central Park; they had lunch in Chinatown.

They finally ended up at the United Nations building on the East Side of the city. They took the ten-cent tour, shuffling along with a group of tourists as they were escorted through the General Assembly and ancillary spaces. Throughout the tour they were the couple in the back whispering, not paying much attention to the guide or their surroundings until they arrived at a special exhibit.

They looked in a glass case filled with artifacts and stones, a display of treasures and jewels from around the world representing what various cultures held dear. There were diamonds from Africa, emeralds from South America, rubies and sapphires from India, gold from Alaska, and in one corner, sitting in sharp contrast to all the glitter, a small black polished stone from a Pacific isle. It made

Michael think that what is precious to one person is but a rock to others. What one person finds alluring in a mate could be considered dreadful by another. An object's—or a person's—value was all a matter of perspective.

"You know," Michael said, as he looked around the room, "the security is pretty tight in here."

KC smiled. "You're not proposing what I think you're proposing, are you?"

"Don't you think this is a romantic place to propose?" Michael smiled, playing on her words.

"I didn't mean . . ." KC laughed, though his suggestion made her feel awkward.

Michael took her in his arms and looked at the case of jewels. "I'd steal all that for you."

"Really? I was thinking of something a bit more simple," KC said. "Besides, I don't need you getting caught. Conjugal visits just don't have the same appeal."

"Caught?" Michael laughed. "They'd never even know I was here."

"Really? And how would you do it?" KC said, taking Michael's hand and walking toward the exit.

"I could build a device that would—"

"Build? You don't always need to build something. What is it with men and their tools?"

"Oh? And how would you do it?"

KC smiled and paused a moment before answering. "I just need a pen knife, a pair of flats, and my feminine wiles."

ONE WEEK LATER they were back in the city. Michael took KC to lunch at Smith and Wollensky, and afterward detoured her over to First Avenue, where they found themselves once again standing before the UN under the colorful array of international flags waving in the breeze.

"Michael?" KC asked suspiciously. "Why are we back here?"

Michael simply smiled and led her to the tourist entrance, paid the fee, and joined a tour. As the tour guide yammered on, they once again didn't hear a single word. Staying at the back of the group, KC pressed Michael about what was going on but he said nothing until they once again came to the display case of jewels.

Michael looked at KC, reached in his pocket, and pulled out a small box wrapped in a white ribbon. He placed it in KC's hand.

"You didn't," KC said.

Michael laid his hand upon hers.

"Is this—?" KC stopped herself and looked over at the case of jewels.

"It's not a ring," Michael said softly, a note of regret in his voice. "Please understand—"

KC put her fingers to his lips. "I know."

"But do you know that I would do anything for you?"

"Michael, tell me you didn't pay a little nocturnal visit here? If you had gotten caught—"

"But I didn't." Michael stared at her. "And they don't even know it's missing. No one pays attention to that little black stone. To some it represents nothing, to people on that Pacific island it means wealth, but to me it means you."

"Aren't you sweet," KC said, mocking him. "And it meant a challenge. Were you showing off for me?"

"You never even knew I'd left the house."

"When?"

"Monday. You were out cold."

"I was tired," KC said. "Did you make one of your little contraptions to get in here?"

Michael tilted his head in the affirmative and looked at the small box. "I hid that in the back of my sock drawer all week."

"Really?" KC asked.

"I said I could do it."

"I can't believe you did it, though—kind of a stupid risk." KC challenged, "I would have done it with more style."

"Is that so?"

KC pulled the ribbon on the small jewelry box, gazing up at Michael, smiling. But when she lifted off the top and looked inside, she found it empty.

She looked up at Michael and saw confusion wash over his face. He took the box from her and stared inside. The moment lingered as his mind spun. And then KC smiled, a knowing smile. She took him by the hand and led him to the display case.

And there inside, among all of the precious jewels, was the small black stone in the corner as if it had never left.

"Thursday night," KC said. "You were out cold."

Michael stared at her a moment then laughed. "I was tired."

As they walked to Grand Central Station to board the train home, their conversation turned serious, both understanding their foolish ways.

"You know, for a minute there when I saw the jewelry box . . ." KC whispered.

"I know," Michael said. "I'm sorry."

"It's okay, but promise me something?"

"Of course."

"No more showing off. We can't be foolish."

"We'll make a vow then," Michael said. "To each other."

KC looked deep into Michael's eyes. "Agreed."

"WELL, NOW I'M awake," KC said, mock annoyance in her voice after they had made love.

"So sorry about that," Michael apologized with a smile.

"How was Paul?"

"He's good. Giants won."

KC nodded. "At least we won't endure a week of his Monday-morning quarterbacking."

"Simon's in town."

"Really? I didn't know he was coming. How long will he be here?"

"A couple days."

KC sat up suddenly. "What does he want?"

Michael stared at her, formulating an answer, knowing that he would have to phrase it just right; his face was a truth barometer that KC could read even in the darkness of the bedroom. "He's just saying hello, had a few work questions."

KC reached up and turned on the light. Michael sat up and stared at her. He always loved the way her blond hair fell about her face after they made love.

"Don't even think about it," KC said.

"I'm not . . ." Michael laughed; he was already back-pedaling.

"What does he really want?"

Michael stared at her a moment and then finally relented. He told her about Simon's request regarding the simple theft of an envelope containing a three-page document and a puzzle box from a home in Italy.

"And you told him no, right?"

"Of course I told him no."

"Michael, we made a vow, we both agreed—"

"That's right, we both agreed," Michael said as he gazed at her. "So when he asks you—I told him to not even think of asking you, but I know he will—-when he asks you, you better give him the same answer."

"You really think—"

"KC, I know you and forgive me for saying this, but it wouldn't surprise me if you ran off and did this behind my back."

KC smiled her get-out-of-jail-free smile that Michael always fell for. But he wasn't about to let her fall into danger.

"KC . . ."

"I made a vow to you, Michael, I gave you my word," KC said, kissing him gently on the lips.

ITALY

MICHAEL RACED UP the stairs of the castle, the sight of the three women and the child, their headless bodies on the floor, burning in his mind. He ran down the second-floor hallway and back into the library. He opened the liquor closet, thrust his hand into the safe, and grabbed the Sig Sauer. He ejected the clip, confirmed the bullet count, and tucked it in his waistband. Without hesitation, he ran to the window. He grabbed the second rope off the floor, tied it to the thick doorknob on the closet, and threw its two-hundred-foot length out the window. He clipped on and dove out the window, sailing down the side of the castle, his eyes darting between the ocean below and the six men on the dock who had shoved the older man into the launch and were heading out to sea.

Michael blew past the building's stone foundation, flying down the cliff face, his hands burning from the rope's friction, his feet bouncing off the sheer face as he descended. Nearing the water, he slowed himself and came to a stop. The dock was seventy-five feet to his left.

Michael angled back his body, his feet on the wall, holding himself nearly perpendicular to it, and began to run toward the dock. It was an odd sight as he struggled across the rock face, his feet scrambling along, slowly arcing upward until he could go no further. He turned his body and began to run in the other direction, his momentum increasing with the downward arc of his charge. He ran along the wall to the right until gravity once again stopped him. He reversed direction and this time ran with even greater speed, accelerating as he raced across the wall, but this time as he reached the apex of his charge, he released himself from his harness to fall into the heavy waves fifteen feet below.

He hit the frigid water and swam as hard as he could against the current, struggling against the waves, determined not to be smashed upon the rocky wall. He was only fifty feet from the dock but it felt like a mile as he pulled and kicked his body through the sea. He finally caught hold of the dock and pulled himself up. Without stopping, he jumped into the launch. He thanked God; it being a private dock, the key was in the ignition. He turned the key and pressed Start. The Mercury engine sputtered, coughing and choking, until it sang with life.

Michael looked out across the water and saw the other tender was heading not for the boat that had brought the men to the castle but for the megayacht and was nearly alongside it.

Michael turned the launch out to sea, grabbed the accelerator, and punched it. The boat skittered across the waves, jumping in the air only to land hard on the next wave. It was like a mogul run on skis, his bones jarring with every wave. Michael had no idea what to do. He knew the men had taken the file and the puzzle box from the safe, but they'd also taken the man and killed his family.

As he looked up again, the six men were already dragging the man onto his yacht, and it occurred to Michael that if they'd found what they were looking for, they would already be on their way and would have killed the man alongside the other four. As he drew closer, the wash of the aft light reflected off the rolling sea, illuminating the name stenciled in large gold letters on the rear of the boat, *Gentlemen's Den* . . . And Michael understood.

As he neared the Sunseeker, Michael cut the engine, allowing the launch's momentum to carry him to the yacht's edge. He set his boat adrift and slipped over the side, swimming around the back of the yacht, the heavy waves thrusting him up and down. The kidnappers' launch was tied to the port side, the boat fenders squeaking as they rubbed against the larger craft.

Michael grabbed hold of the rolling ship and slowly climbed up on the swim platform. He looked about. The yacht was much larger than Michael had imagined from shore. Three decks above the water line, climbing nearly thirty feet high, it was truly a mansion at sea. Her polished white hull was adorned with brass fittings and teak rails, her mass absorbing the roll of the waves far better than the flimsy craft he had arrived on.

He climbed three steps, kept to the shadows, and peered into the main salon, an opulent living room filled with all-white furnishings—couches, chaises, and leather chairs, even a white grand piano in the corner. Heavy soundproof glass doors were pulled tightly closed.

The old man was lashed to a chair in the center of the room, his face bloody and tear-streaked, his eyes filled with pain. Five men were scattered about the room, the man obviously in charge crouched down before their captive. His dark hair was pulled into a tight ponytail that hung over his tailored suit jacket.

Three of the men stood with pistols in hand, while a fourth held an elegant polished scabbard, the black leather hilt of a sword protruding from it. While Michael couldn't see the face of the leader, he could see the others; there was no doubt in his mind that he was looking at an Asian group: Yakuza, Triad, Tong, or Bangkok Mafia.

As Michael looked at the ponytailed man, he knew the man had slain the old man's family in front of him, and would no doubt use the same sword on the man once he'd obtained what he had come for. The old man struggled against his bonds, uselessly flexing his arms against the rope. The agony in his face, the tears in his eyes were not from physical pain, but from the sheer torture of his heart.

The ponytailed man held out a dark red lacquered box, turning it about in his hand. Michael caught a glimpse of a fearsome dragon entwined with a tiger etched into its surface and recognized the object that Simon so desperately needed him to steal. The ponytailed man held it before the old man's eyes and screamed in a language Michael didn't understand.

Michael had yet to see the face of the leader as he interrogated the old man, his body, his hands subtly moving with his demands. There was confidence in the ponytailed man's body language, in his actions, superior and exacting. He suddenly dropped the box to the floor and violently stomped on it, cracking it open. He picked it up and thrust it in the old man's face to reveal that it was empty.

The ponytailed man took off his jacket, tossed it aside, then unbuttoned his white shirt. He removed a lighter from his pocket and flicked it on, the flame dancing above its silver case. And with a powerful grip, he grabbed the man's left hand, bending it up against his constraints, holding the flame to the old man's palm.

The old man's face grew stern, hard like granite, as he locked eyes with his torturer, a test of wills as his palm blackened, as the smoke curled up. And the ponytailed man smiled. He pulled the lighter away, tucked it in his pocket, and pulled out a black box, similar in shape and design to the red one; a dragon engaged in battle with a raging tiger was etched in its top. He held it before the old man and whispered in his ear.

And Michael saw fear pour into the old man's face, an agony worse than flame upon his skin . . . and the old man finally screamed.

Michael averted his eyes and climbed the rear steps, keeping his body low within the shadows, quickly arriving at the second deck, which was far less formal, with a large teak bar, overstuffed couches, and a wide-screen TV on the rear wall. The rear deck was open to the elements, with lounge chairs and towels in the corners. No cost had been spared on the luxurious craft.

Remaining in the shadows, Michael looked about until his eyes fell on an oddly shaped form toward the far end of the room. As Michael's eyes adjusted, he saw the open door to the pilothouse, the glow of instruments casting a green haze in the ship's bridge, and realized . . . he looked again at the form, now discerning the crumpled body of the ship's captain.

A light three hundred yards off the port bow caught Michael's eye. It was heading toward the yacht. He didn't know if it was coincidence or something worse, and he had no intention of waiting to find out.

Michael ran to the bar, slipping behind it. He looked about: at the liquor bottles in their leather hammocks, at the secured glasses, the fully stocked wine cooler. He knew it had to be here. He finally looked at the ice maker; he saw the wide seams, slightly off angle, something incongruous with the exacting detail of everything else on the ship.

He pulled the ice maker out to reveal the other Helix 09 safe. It was listed on the sales quote: one for the study, the other for the *Gentlemen's Den*, the name of the yacht Michael was on now.

He knew the bypass code, the one used when the owner forgot the combination and needed access to his valuables.

Michael punched the numbers into the keypad and pulled open the door. He reached into the safe and pulled out a single manila file. Opening it, he found three pages, Xerox copies, but as he looked closer at the lettering, it was indecipherable. It was Asian calligraphy, Chinese, he believed.

Tucking the manila file inside his wet shirt, Michael stood and heard the sound of a footstep behind him. Without thinking, he dove to the right, just as the sound of a bullet exploded. Michael took cover behind the heavy teak bar, drew the Sig Sauer from his waistband, and peered around the corner to find the man crouched, his pistol double-gripped, moving with his line of sight.

Michael aimed and pulled the trigger. The man tumbled back, the bullet catching him heart-high in his chest. While Michael hated guns, that didn't mean he didn't know how to use them. Simon had seen to that years earlier.

Michael stood, and the sudden wash of a spotlight shone through the port window. He ducked for cover as he heard a flurry of commotion below. And before he could move, a firefight erupted. An onslaught of bullets pelted the side of the ship; Michael could hear the men below returning fire.

The windows were shot out and bullets flew over Michael's head as the second deck was sprayed with gunfire. The lights of the salon and the upper decks were shot out, sending the room into darkness.

The thundering crack of shotguns, rifles, and pistols filled the nighttime air. He heard the pounding feet of people boarding the ship, there were shouts and commands, a coordinated attack unfolding. He heard splashing as bodies hit the water, heavy thuds on the lower deck as people went down.

A giant roar cut through the cacophony of sound, an explosion not far off, the orange glow of flames pouring through the window. Michael could see the ponytailed man's yacht, the one the six men came in on, being consumed by the sea, flames hissing as she quickly disappeared beneath the surface.

Michael turned to see the small boarding craft bobbing off the port side. There was no one on board, though her lights were lit and her engines were running in wait.

And then there was silence. Michael held his breath, listening. He could hear the footfalls of only one person. He crawled through the salon, past the body of the man he had killed; he grabbed the pistol from his hand and tucked it in his waistband for backup. He continued crawling past the dead captain of the ship, who sported a bullet hole just above his glazed-over eyes. He came to the interior stairs and listened, slowly creeping down to the first deck. The lights were gone, shot out, but even in the shadows Michael could see the carnage.

There were bodies strewn everywhere. The old man was slumped over in his chair, his torso riddled with bullet wounds—he'd been trapped in the crossfire. The ponytailed man stood in silhouette, crouched, ready to strike, his left hand clutching his pistol, waving it about the room while in his right was the unsheathed sword, refracting shards of intermittent light off its honed edge.

A moan escaped the old man's bloody lips.

The assassin raised the sword as if in ceremony above the old man.

"Don't," said a deep, commanding voice that, surprisingly, sounded American. Michael caught a glimpse of the man: He stood in the deep shadows of the shattered remains of the door, dressed in black fatigues, his closely shorn black hair under a dark cap. He gripped his pistol in both hands, his eye lined up with the sight; there was no question as to his aim. Beside him stood two more commandos, each with a short submachine gun, their faces painted with black pitch.

The assassin lowered his sword and dropped his pistol on the deck. But then, with a sudden swiftness, he turned the blade over in his hand and thrust it through the old man. It slipped through the man's body without resistance, as if piercing water. And just as suddenly, it was withdrawn, with a wet sound of death.

The two commandos moved in, their guns raised, their fingers on the triggers. The ponytailed man lowered his sword, bowing his head in defeat.

"Drop the sword," the first commando said as he

circled around in the darkness. He moved behind the man while his partners remained in front, both guns aimed.

"Drop—" but the commando never completed his sentence.

In a single motion, the man dropped to a crouch, spinning like a dervish, his blade held out, slicing the air, through the first commando's throat, its speed increasing as it whipped around, slicing through the second man, felling them where they stood before they could even react.

And a shot rang out.

The ponytailed man was knocked back by the force of the bullet; he tumbled over an ottoman and fell to the ground. The American with the deep, commanding voice approached, his gun at the ready. "You're not going to escape this life yet."

"But you soon will," the ponytailed man whispered. "And there's nothing you can do about it."

"What have you done?" the American said.

"You will die," the ponytailed man said. "You may hold the weapon but I will be the one that will kill, and know this: You will not be the only one to die."

"Where's the file? The pages . . . ?" There was desperation in the American's voice. "Where is the box?"

"You are the last person I would tell."

"If they get out in the open, if anyone learns—" The man stopped. He pulled a black bag from his pocket and threw it at the assassin. "Put that over your head."

The assassin held up the bag, examining it.

"I could shoot you right now and end this insanity."

The assassin smiled as he slipped the black bag over his head. "Know this. You think you're in control here, but you're not. If I die, you die."

The man pulled zip ties from his pocket and circled behind his captive. "We'll see."

With control of the ship seemingly taken, Michael continued down the stairs, doing everything he could to avoid being seen. And he found himself belowdecks, where there was a host of bedrooms. Michael bypassed them all and moved toward the stern. He opened a door and found himself in the engine room, two enormous engines gleaming under the red night lights. Michael made his way to the rear door, and that's when he saw them. They were large and crude, thick chunks of C4, a radio transmitter attached to the detonator.

Michael grabbed the door but found it locked; he shook it but knew it was useless. Wasting no more time, he turned and raced forward toward the bow, past the bedrooms, the crew galley. He found a narrow crew ladder and quickly climbed up it through a hatch into the bridge of the yacht. He didn't know if he had minutes or seconds, but acted as if he were out of time. He took the central stairs back up to the second deck and stopped in his tracks.

The American commando was there now, his captive on the floor before him, his head encased in the black hood, his arms tied in front of him.

Despite his captive's binds and the bag over his head, the American kept his gun up, aiming it, holding it tight as he walked behind the bar. He crouched down and saw the open safe.

"Where is it?" the man shouted.

His captive said nothing.

"My men, before they were all killed, rigged the ship with C4."

There was no response.

"If you want to leave this boat, you'll tell me where those papers are."

Again there was nothing but silence from the prisoner on the floor.

"Know this, I'm going to invade your world, I will bring you all down. Starting with you." The man reached in his pocket and withdrew a small transmitter; he thumbed off the safety cover.

Michael turned in the shadows and quietly scaled the steps to the third deck. Thirty feet above the sea, open to the elements, it was an outdoor living room of lounge chairs and cushioned decks for sunbathing.

Without another thought, Michael reached within his shirt, pulled out the file, took the pages, and tore them down the middle. He tore them again and again and again, until he had nothing but confetti paper, and he ran to the rail of the boat, tossing the tiny remnants of what everyone so desperately wanted into the air. They fluttered on the wind into the high seas, where they were scattered and lost in the flotsam and jetsam.

Michael peered over the port-side rail to see the American, the lone survivor of his team, carrying the body of one of his men on his shoulder. He lowered him into his boarding craft and walked back in only to emerge with another body.

Michael looked about, but his boat was gone, drifted

off. The man carried out two more bodies. But this time he didn't turn. He simply stepped onto his boat and went to the wheel.

He was leaving the assassin to face his death. Michael couldn't help feeling satisfaction. The man had killed innocents, an entire family. He deserved nothing short of death.

Without another thought, Michael dove off the starboard side, falling headfirst thirty feet into the sea, the icy waters shocking him once again.

He turned toward shore, toward the brightly lit castle that was filled with death, and began swimming faster than he had ever swum before. He heard the engine of the American's landing craft rev up and speed away, the sound fading with the distance.

The explosion lit up the night, an enormous fireball rolling skyward. Michael could feel the heat hit his back, the shock wave rippling through the water. The ship groaned and screamed in protest as the sea poured in, the twisted hull turning about. And then, as if a giant hand had reached up from the depths, the giant yacht began to sink, slowly at first, but soon hastening its dive to its grave. Within a minute she was gone, the sound of steam and bubbles all that could be heard.

Michael didn't look back. He swam as hard as he could toward shore; it was only 350 yards away, but the heavy waves made every stroke feel like the effort of four. His legs had already begun to cramp, his joints ached with every kick.

Michael swam for his life.

CHAPTER I

T he stone-and-shingle house sat out of view of Banksville Road, secluded in the middle of twenty acres. It was the place where Michael could forget about the cares and troubles of his days.

He had bought the run-down house out of foreclosure two years ago as an escape from the world and the reality of the death of his wife. He had spent nights and weekends renovating the ranch-style home into a place of comfort. It had become his sanctuary, his refuge as he grieved. And as he worked upon it, as he brought the house back to life, so, too, did it bring him back to life, allowing the scars of his heart to begin to heal, helping him work through the cycles of grief: the pain and anger, the emptiness and rage, the sorrow and denial.

As Michael drove up the long driveway and parked in the gravel circle, Hawk, Raven, and Bear, his three Bernese mountain dogs, came running. They leaped upon him as he grabbed his bag from the rear of the Audi, fighting for attention, nuzzling and herding him until, with weary arms, he patted them as he did every night upon his return.

Michael was exhausted. He had crawled ashore in

Italy, his body hypothermic, his muscles barely functioning as he climbed the rock-face stairs up to the castle. The lights were on in the dead of night, the warm glow emanating through the castle windows masking the horror within. Michael raced through the forest for nearly an hour, his legs cramping, his heart pounding as his body fought off the cold.

Simon was waiting in the small Renault, parked in a gravel lot that overlooked the Tyrrhenian Sea. They drove through the night, arriving in Rome at dawn. Michael told Simon what had happened. He told him how he had torn up the three sheets of paper, scattering them at sea. He told him of the horrific deaths within the castle, the torture of the old man, and the subsequent death of everyone upon the yacht except the single survivor who sped away with the bodies of his dead comrades.

"I'm sorry," Simon said as he nodded in sympathy. "For the family . . . for those killed on board . . . most of all, I'm sorry for putting you through this."

Michael looked out at the moonlit sea.

"And the box?" Simon asked quietly.

"Broken open. It was empty."

Simon nodded.

"But there was another box."

Simon looked at Michael.

"Identical, but black, etched with dragons and a tiger," Michael said slowly. "He held it before the old man. It scared him far more than torture, far more than what they had done to his family."

Michael caught the first flight out of Rome, chasing

the rising sun for eight and a half hours. He tried to sleep but couldn't close his eyes without seeing the headless bodies of the three women and the young child. He tried everything from reading to music to movies, but the disembodied heads seemed to hang at the periphery of his thoughts, holding on, unwilling to let go.

As he stood in his driveway now, exhausted and aching, he admitted to himself what he had known before he had left. It had been a mistake to do this deed for Simon. He had a feeling it was a mistake that would haunt him for years to come.

And as he looked at KC's white Lexus in the driveway, the guilt of deception began to settle in.

He was startled from his thoughts by the ringing of his cell phone. He looked at the screen and shook his head as he answered. "Hey, Jo."

"Where are you?" Jo asked. Michael's assistant hated small talk.

"My driveway."

"Good."

"Why?"

"You have a two o'clock."

"No, I don't."

"You do now."

"Not a chance. I'm wiped."

"Take a shower, 'cause you're heading into the city."

"Absolutely not."

"A big contract. That will buy you a bigger bed to sleep in later. And provide all us serfs with a bonus. It's 300 Park, tenth floor. The guy's name is Lucas. I'll send the particulars to your BlackBerry."

"Dammit, Jo."

"If you were in the right frame of mind, you'd be thanking me, which you will do later." And with a mock cheery voice she said, "Good-bye."

While the exhaustion was getting the better of him, the thought of such a healthy contract helped to awaken Michael just a bit. He closed up the phone and looked at KC's convertible. She wasn't expecting him to return from "Chicago" until that evening and would understand if he had to run out for a quick meeting.

With the dogs trailing him, he walked into the house, dropped his bag by the door, and headed through the great room to the kitchen. "KC?"

Michael walked upstairs. The bed was made; the bathroom still held a touch of humidity from the shower. He checked their workout room in the basement, the laundry room. "KC?"

KC had become good friends with Paul's wife, Jeannie, and on more than a few occasions, Jeannie would pick her up unannounced for shopping, a quick lunch, or just company when she took her two kids to the park.

Michael thought of calling KC's cell, but as it was already after twelve, he decided to do it on his way into the city. He hopped in the shower, the hot water washing away the ache in his bones, quickly dressed in a suit, and grabbed a tie to put on in the car.

As Michael headed out of the bedroom, he finally saw her, sitting on the terrace in the back. He went downstairs and out the back door to the terrace where KC was sitting in a wicker chair, dressed in a heavy sweater, sipping tea, her blond hair glowing in the mid-day sun.

"I'm sorry; I didn't know you were back here." He leaned over and kissed her cheek, but she barely moved.

As she slowly looked up, Michael knew that she knew.

"Hey, Jo just called, I've got to run into the city for a meeting," Michael said, trying to start a conversation, but she remained silent.

Michael stood there a moment, knowing that a fire-storm was coming. He sat in the chair across from her, leaned in, and tried to look her in the eye, but she stared off at the rock gardens.

"Why?" KC finally whispered.

Michael took a deep breath and spoke quietly, "Simon asked me . . ."

"Simon asked me, too," KC said, still staring off into the backyard.

Michael rolled up his tie and tucked it in his pocket.

"That bastard asked me and I told him no. We made a vow." KC finally turned and looked at Michael. "Your words. 'A vow.' And you couldn't keep it for even two months."

Michael paused before answering. "You don't un-derstand—"

"Did you do this for Simon or yourself?"

"Since when did I ever go off and do it for myself?"

"Seriously? We both know not to go down that road. What if you were killed, arrested?"

"But I wasn't."

"Look at you." KC waved her hands up and down.

"You're exhausted. Why didn't you tell me? Why did you lie?"

"To protect you."

"To protect me? No, Michael, to protect yourself. How many other 'out-of-town meetings' were there?"

"KC, you know me better than that."

"Do I?"

The conversation fell to silence.

"KC?"

"No." She was fighting back tears now. "I can deal with you not being able to fully commit, I can deal with the ghost of your wife haunting your decisions. But I can't deal with being lied to, being deceived. And if you deceive me on this now, what else will it be? Didn't you think about me? Does Simon come before us? Does everyone come before me?"

KC paused, holding tight to her cup of tea as a tear ran down her face.

"You're so afraid of protecting your own heart, you forgot about mine. You know, a few months ago, when I found that small jewelry box in your sock drawer, my heart soared. I know I was being nosy, but for the briefest of seconds, I felt secure, I thought we had a future."

"We do have a future."

"I don't know about that. Maybe we were both kidding ourselves. Maybe our relationship is based on the wrong things." KC finally stood. "I think I need a break."

"What?"

"Where is my life, sitting around here waiting for you? Waiting to get married, waiting to have children, waiting while you're off trying to come to terms with your own heart, waiting while you're off stealing something?"

They looked into each other's eyes as if examining each other's soul, the moment dragging on until . . .

"I've got to go," Michael said, standing up.

"Of course you do," KC shot back. "Run away."

"I have a meeting," Michael said quickly.

"Where? Chicago, Italy . . . ?"

"Can we finish this when I get back?"

"No."

"I'll be back by six."

"I won't be here."

"What are you talking about?" Michael's anger rose.

"I'm going home."

"You are home."

"No, I'm in *your* home. It seems I was just visiting."

Michael couldn't look at her. So he looked at his watch. "I need to go."

KC walked past Michael into the house. "So do I."

CHAPTER 2

The man stood six feet, one inch tall in a sharply creased dark-blue suit. His shoulders were wide, his face deceptively young for its fifty-six years, and his short black hair had yet to know the color gray. He stood ramrod straight as he reached out to shake Michael's hand.

"Isaac Lucas." His voice was deep and he spoke softly.

"Michael St. Pierre."

"Please take a seat."

They sat in the small conference room of Braden and Associates, an executive suite for those who needed the prestigious Park Avenue address but couldn't afford the rent, a facility that presented the façade of success and power, but on an hourly rate as opposed to a ten-year lease. Michael didn't mind stretching his legs in the city for a change, riding the express train in—the ride giving him time to think, time to figure out how he would fix things with KC. He'd exited in Grand Central and walked up Park Avenue, among the skyscrapers that had so attracted him in his youth.

"You come highly recommended," Lucas said.

"Thank you."

"I understand you were traveling."

"Yes, a sudden business matter."

"You were successful, I trust?"

"Yes, very much so." Michael had trouble lying. KC could read his face like a children's book, but when it came to half-truths to strangers, words flowed far more easily. "I just returned, in fact."

Lucas didn't respond and allowed the seconds to tick by.

As Michael assessed the man, he ignored his body language, his lack of mirth; Michael stared into his eyes and felt a chill run through his gut. He saw something there—

"What was your last job, Mr. St. Pierre?"

"We upgraded the security systems and protocols for a Fortune 500 firm." Michael nodded. "And please, call me Michael."

"Do you do international work?"

Michael paused. He had done international work on several occasions, most recently twenty-four hours ago, but not the kind of work this man was referring to, and there were certainly no written contracts for it.

"What type of work are you referring to?" Michael asked.

"Your expertise, of course."

The warning bells grew louder in Michael's mind. He didn't need to be told that this man wasn't looking for an alarm system to be installed, for fortified security measures to be implemented.

"Specifically?" Michael prodded, trying to draw the man out.

"A security matter," Lucas said, as if it were obvious.

"I need specifics."

"Due to the nature of the matter, I cannot reveal specifics, but I will tell you the matter is complex, involves an existing system, and you will be rewarded very handsomely."

"I trust you know my résumé," Michael said, not so much as a warning but as a way out.

"If you're referring to your time in prison, yes."

"Are we talking installation, consulting, or design?" he asked in order to move the matter along.

"You may call it procurement."

The bells in Michael's head grew deafening.

"Understand, we are well aware of your activities beyond the norms of your business."

Michael stared at the man, his mind spinning.

"For instance, what you did in Istanbul was interesting. Not many people could survive that."

Michael stared at Lucas. No one but his closest friends was aware of what he had done in Istanbul.

"Do not be troubled," Lucas continued, his voice trying to convey the reassurance his eyes couldn't. "Your activities in the last several years are of no interest to the United States, but what they do show is that you possess the expertise we require for a certain job."

"You're with the government?" Michael said, concealing his alarm.

"We all hide behind façades, Michael."

"Don't you have whole divisions for procurement?"

"For security reasons, I can't say."

Michael took a breath and took the tactful approach.

"Well, thank you, it is an honor to be called on by you, on behalf of the U.S. But I must say no thank you."

Lucas sat there. He didn't move or fidget, he didn't reach for the unopened bottle of water in the middle of the table, he simply stared at Michael as if his force of will could make him change his mind.

"Well." Lucas nodded. "I don't think I made myself clear. We need you to do this job."

"You never mentioned what branch of the government you're with."

Lucas reached in his jacket pocket, withdrew his billfold, and slid it across to Michael. "It's actually Colonel Lucas."

Michael flipped it open and examined the official military ID of Colonel Isaac Lucas, U.S. Army. Michael felt his world spinning; this meeting was no coincidence.

"Is that the uniform of the 'new' army?" Michael said with a false smile, gesturing at the man's dark blue suit, trying to maintain his calm.

"Nothing draws more attention than an out-of-place military man on Park Avenue," Lucas said. "It makes those we work so hard to protect nervous."

Michael nodded in understanding. But uniform or not, Michael understood this man excelled at making people nervous. The man traveled alone, a rare thing in this day of corporate posses, and even rarer in the regimented hierarchy of the military. There was no attaché, no lieutenant to open doors, take notes, call out for sushi. This man was a loner—Michael could see it in his dark brown eyes, eyes that carried a hint of Asian heritage that had been watered down by some strain of European blood.

There was no doubt who this man was. It had been dark, Michael had never seen his face, but he recognized his voice, his body language, the way he carried himself.

But Michael was sure he hadn't been seen by this man or anyone else on the ship. Lucas had been the lone survivor and had been unaware of Michael's presence as he'd carried his dead comrades off the yacht. Though the chances of this meeting . . . this was no coincidence.

He had to get out of this room.

"I'm more than flattered to be considered, but my schedule is overbooked as it is."

"Your government needs your help." Lucas glared at Michael as if giving an order.

Michael couldn't believe he'd just said that: "Uncle Sam needs you," as if his patriotism would force his hand. Michael loved his country in his own way, the same way people believe in God, believe in the afterlife, in their own way.

"I help our government by paying my taxes. Way too much, I might add." Michael's joke fell on deaf ears. "You should move on to the next man on your list."

"You're the only man on our list, and I must insist." Lucas's tone grew deep, demanding. Michael could tell he was not used to being refused.

"Sorry, Colonel, thank you for considering my firm, but you'll have to find someone else." Michael rose from his chair, trying to keep his nervousness from showing. He shook the colonel's hand. "I really must be going; I've got some issues to deal with at home."

Michael walked out of the execu-suite, holding his anger in check. The colonel's demands and assignments were no doubt dealings the U.S. should not be dealing with. This man knew too much about Michael: He knew his life, his activities beyond U.S. shores. Was this really the same man on the boat? It had been so dark, he had worn a hat, his face never in the light. But the voice, the cadence of his speech sounded the same.

Michael decided he'd call Simon to see if he knew anything about Lucas, to see if his suspicions were true. It crossed Michael's mind that Lucas had known who he was all along, that he knew Michael had been on the boat, that he was just toying with him as he asked him about his most recent job.

Michael pulled out his phone and saw no missed calls; all thoughts of the colonel and the meeting disappeared as his mind jumped to KC, wondering if she would follow through on her threat, wondering if she was walking out of his life. He looked at his watch, thought of the train, but maybe it was better to call a car service. He'd get home before she left, he'd set things right, whatever it took.

Michael walked to the elevator and hit the button. He could hear the cab coming from the floors above, and hoped it would arrive before the colonel emerged from the office behind him—he was the last person Michael wanted to be with in the elevator. He began to dial the number for home.

And the elevator car finally stopped at his floor. As the doors opened, he stepped in and watched the signal on his phone disappear. He tucked it in his pocket and looked up to see a lone woman standing there in a dark pencil skirt, a dark checkered swing coat over a white silk shirt, and a large black purse hanging on her shoulder.

He couldn't help looking in her eyes, couldn't help reacting to her stare as she nodded a silent greeting.

She stood five-six, her jet-black hair styled in a short
severe bob. Her skin was pale and pure, her appearance
reminding Michael of Snow White, but this fairy tale
woman didn't seem to be pure innocence. She flashed
Michael an alluring smile that seductively came more
from her large brown eyes than her deep red lips. They
arrived at the ground floor, exited the cab, and walked
through the large lobby to the main exit. She nodded in
silent thanks to Michael as he held the door for her and
they emerged onto Park Avenue.

Michael stopped as she continued on. His eyes followed her into the afternoon crowd, her hips swaying
within her black Prada skirt. He briefly smiled as he
imagined KC hitting him in the shoulder for staring. Despite their fight, she still held his heart and was far more
alluring than the black-haired woman.

He was about to turn away when a kid exploded out of
nowhere, darting from the crowd. He tackled Snow White
to the ground, violently grabbing her purse, and took off.

In the sudden confusion, several women leaped to
her aid while others pointed and screamed at the fleeing
thief. Seeing Snow White helpless on the ground, the
shock on her face, tears welling in her eyes, Michael had
only one thought . . .

He looked at the escaping thief and gave chase.

KC STOOD IN the great room, looking around, her
hastily packed bag at her feet. It was just a carry-on. It

was difficult for her to figure out what clothes to take. When she'd moved in with Michael more than a year ago, she'd had a single bag of clothes. Now, after all this time, she had a closetful, but as she looked at them, she was too upset to focus.

She tried to temper her anger at Michael but couldn't stanch her sense of betrayal, realizing that we can only truly be betrayed by the ones we trust.

She placed a note on the dining room table and fought back her tears.

Her head was filled with confusion. After Michael had left, she'd questioned herself. Was she about to blow up her life? Was she about to take a step she could never take back? Relationships wax and wane, there are always highs and lows, but in order to ride those waves you must be able to trust the one you are with. She loved Michael but she knew him as well as she knew herself. When Simon had spoken to her she had felt the tug of risk just as Michael had, but she had been able to resist it. And if Michael couldn't, she knew he would end up dead.

For all of her adult life she'd longed for a relationship, to be held by a man who would love her and care for her, something she had never known, not from a mother, a father, or a sibling. She had been on her own since her mother died; KC had been fifteen, her sister nine. She had resorted to stealing for money, the only thing she could do to support her sister, to keep them together and out of the world of foster care. It had toughened not only her character but her heart.

But then she met Michael: a man with a past, a man

who understood her. She never knew her heart could feel the way it did, the way it soared, the way it skipped a beat when she saw him.

She had thought by this time they would be moving forward with their relationship, marrying, talking about having children, but Michael wasn't ready. Though she never doubted his love for her, she knew the memory of his wife still burned in his heart. She could forgive him for that; she couldn't imagine the pain of so much loss.

But lying to her, breaking a vow, a promise—it had hurt so deeply to be deceived. It had forced her to step back from the euphoria of love, to look at their relationship more objectively, and it made her realize she needed to get away to see whether she was blinded by her feelings, whether she was just kidding herself that their relationship could last.

She was leaving not only to gain some distance to look at them as a couple but to look at herself. She hadn't worked in fourteen months, leaving her former life behind. She needed to clear her head, to make a decision, and she wasn't able to think clearly while sitting around all day in the comfort of Michael's house.

She was thankful to get a flight out at ten; there was a direct flight tomorrow but she couldn't wait.

And now, to compound the matter, he hadn't called. She admitted that she probably wouldn't have answered, but if he had at least made the attempt . . .

CHAPTER 3

Michael ran at full tilt across Park Avenue. Brakes screeched as tires fought the pavement, car horns blared as he weaved in and out of the midafternoon traffic. For once, Michael was doing the chasing as opposed to being pursued. The punk was twenty feet ahead, his speed seeming to part the sidewalk masses in his way.

Michael had held the door for the dark-haired woman, exchanging smiles and nods as she walked out onto Forty-ninth Street. He had no idea who she was, and it didn't matter. There were just some things that he couldn't let happen and this was one of them.

They were already at Fiftieth and Park, running in the canyons of the city, the glass skyscrapers tickling the blue skies around them. The punk didn't seem so much a punk. He wore none of the trappings of a desperate junkie, of a kid looking for money for sneakers. He was running with focus, as if in a race, as if he were five minutes late to his own wedding. He was thin, broad-shouldered. His dark hair was full, falling just below the collar; he wore jeans and a J.Crew short-sleeve shirt, giving the impression of anything but a thief.

The kid was fast but Michael was gaining on him.

Only two car lengths back. They darted in and out of traffic with fits and starts to the sound of blaring horns and screeching tires.

The kid came upon a black Lincoln Town Car and, without missing a beat, leaped in a fashion that levitated his body onto the hood, his ass skidding along its surface as if sliding on ice until he landed without missing a stride on the far sidewalk, where he continued uptown.

Michael couldn't believe his eyes as bystander after bystander just watched, no one wanting to get involved.

Michael jumped over a chained-up bicycle like a hurdler and ran atop the hoods and roofs of three cars . . . and dived off.

With a bone-jarring tackle he caught the punk, pushing him down upon the sidewalk in a road-rash-inducing skid. Michael spun the kid around, wrapping his thick forearm across the punk's throat, and leaned back against a parked car, the young man practically in his lap as he held him tight from behind.

A crowd immediately gathered, oohing and ahhing but offering no assistance as the kid kicked and thrashed upon the sidewalk, trying to pull away from Michael's viselike grip. And through it all, the punk still held tightly to the purse. The sound of sirens grew. Michael wasn't sure if they were for his prisoner, sirens beings such a common sound in the city.

Holding the boy tight, Michael realized that the person locked in his grasp wasn't a kid but a man, the sinewy muscles of his arms flexing like rubber bands as he struggled for release. There was a hardness to the man's eyes, not the desperation of a kid. The girth of the man's arms was greater than Michael had expected, greater than Michael should have been able to handle. Michael was strong, fit, in far better shape at thirty-six than most men his age. But his prisoner was far stronger . . .

And then, much to Michael's surprise, she emerged from the crowd: the black-haired woman with the perfect skin, Snow White, the owner of the purse. Her dark, anger-filled eyes fixed on the thief. She leaned down and snatched the purse from the man's hands. A hush fell over the crowd as they began to understand Michael's heroics in his capture of the criminal.

Michael continued to hold tight to the punk, who no longer struggled. They sat on the sidewalk, the punk in his lap as he leaned back.

The woman finally looked at Michael and nodded. He wasn't sure if it was a nod of thanks or something else. She quietly reached into her purse and withdrew a small Beretta, its flat black finish the color of her hair.

"No," was the only thing Michael's prisoner said, fear filling his voice . . .

And without hesitation, she raised it and fired two shots squarely into the man's heart.

The force of the two bullets slammed the man against Michael, momentarily confusing him, causing him to believe that he himself had been shot. And Michael realized he would have been but for the man he held, who acted as a shield. Michael sat there in pure shock as the world fell silent and time slowed to a crawl. Crimson patches blossomed upon the young man's white shirt, the last beats of his heart pumping blood from two nickel-sized wounds into a pool upon the concrete sidewalk. Despite the dead man that he held in his arms, Michael couldn't help being thankful for the small-caliber bullets; any larger and they would have gotten two victims for the price of one.

The crowd screamed as chaos took over, jolting Michael back to the moment. People scattered in fear of the madwoman and her accomplice, who had held down the young man as she murdered him.

With a nonchalant motion, as if storing her makeup, the woman slipped the pistol into her purse, turned, and disappeared into the crowd.

And then Michael saw the barrels of two Glock 19s. The two young policemen were white-knuckling their guns as their faces expressed shock at the sight of the carnage, at the sight of the dead young man Michael clutched in his arms.

KC STOOD IN the driveway as the Town Car pulled up.

"Good afternoon," the driver said as he got out of the car and took KC's bag, placing it in the trunk. "JFK?"

"Yes, please," KC said as she turned back, looking at the house, wondering if she was making a mistake. And then she thought of Michael as he'd left two days earlier. She wondered if he'd thought the same thing as he'd gotten into the Town Car to head off to "Chicago," wondered what had gone through his head as he kissed her good-bye. Had he been feeling the regret she felt now? Had it occurred to him that he might be making a mistake?

"Will you excuse me for one moment?" she said

to the driver, who stood there holding the door open for her.

"Certainly," the man said.

KC turned and walked to the far end of the drive, where the three dogs were lying upon the large rock that overlooked the driveway, awaiting Michael's return. She quickly dialed his cell; maybe hearing his voice would give her pause. She didn't care if he was still in the meeting, he would answer.

But Michael's phone was off, the call going directly to voicemail. Michael never turned off his phone except in two circumstances: when he was on a plane and when he didn't want to talk to her. And she knew it was the latter.

She closed her phone and returned to the Town Car.

"Ready to go?" the driver asked.

"Yes." And KC climbed in.

CHAPTER 4

The interrogation room was twenty feet square, a dark Formica table in the center, surrounded by six hardback chairs. Thick carpet, tiled ceiling, and walls covered in segmented blocks of soundproofing all combined to pull the ambient noise from the air, leaving nothing but the sound of Michael's breathing in his own ears.

The small space was softly lit, no shadows, no windows. The heavy black door possessed no handle, making his exit difficult at best.

The cops who'd found him clutching the victim had cuffed him and led him to their car, locking him inside while they questioned the witnesses. An ambulance had arrived, but Michael was whisked away before he saw the outcome of their actions.

He had yet to be questioned, had yet to be charged, and had sat here for almost three hours without speaking to a single person.

The door finally opened and a familiar man stepped in. He held several large, thick files, which he deposited on the table, then he turned and closed the door. He took a seat directly across from Michael, pulled the first file to him. It was stamped *The Kremlin.* He flipped it open and quietly examined it, turning page after page of newspaper articles, eyewitness accounts, and police reports, each with an appended translation. He occasionally glanced up at Michael as if assessing him anew, condemning him with his silent appraisal. He closed it and reached for the second, this one marked *The Vatican.* He read through similar translations of news articles and police reports. For twenty minutes he worked his way down the pile: London, Brazil, Istanbul, Switzerland.

Michael felt the heat rising through his body. In all his years, he had been arrested only once and that had been here in New York. He'd served his time. But what he saw before him now . . . he had never been caught in any of his dealings abroad, had never even been named a suspect. Michael was thorough, compulsive in his preparation, in his actions and execution.

And yet here, against all reason, was a stack of files, each marked with a location he had visited for reasons having nothing to do with tourism. If he was convicted for even one of the crimes he'd executed in any of these foreign cities, he'd spend the rest of his life in prison.

His mind was a jumble. There were only three people who truly knew of each and every one of the jobs he'd pulled: Busch, Simon, and KC.

Busch was his best friend, Simon would never tell a soul, and despite the current status of their relationship, Michael knew KC would never divulge Michael's past dealings. His confusion and anxiety grew as the man before him continued to read, finally closing the last file and slowly placing it upon the stack for effect.

"So, Michael," the man said, his face devoid of emotion, except for a hint of martial triumph in his eyes. "Where did we leave off this afternoon?"

Michael just stared at Colonel Lucas, who was still in his dark suit.

"Have you ever been to Macau?"

KC WALKED THROUGH Terminal A at Kennedy airport, her long blond hair and lithe legs drawing the eyes of everyone she passed. At five feet, nine inches, KC had the appearance of a model, possessing the honest confidence that so many women lacked. No matter where she went she could not help exuding charisma, something that had proven difficult in her prior life, a life where remaining invisible, disappearing at will, was essential to success.

KC's earlier life had had a singular purpose: caring for her sister, Cynthia. Since the death of their mother, KC had taken on the responsibility of raising her while she was still a child herself. KC had imbued in her sister a moral compass, an understanding of right and wrong, lessons of the consequences of a less-than-honest approach to life, all of which were illustrated by their absent father, a man whose crimes ran from extortion to thievery to outright murder, a father who was ultimately consumed by the darkness within his own heart.

KC's accomplishment in raising her sister, seeing her off to Harvard, Oxford, and finally to her own private financial consulting firm in London, was not just admirable—much of it was illegal. That she had paid for her sister's education with money acquired through less than legal means was a secret she'd managed to keep until one year ago.

While both KC and Cynthia had grown up hating their father, hating his criminal way of life, KC knew early on she was following in his very footsteps. She had resorted to stealing to support her sister and had been taken under the wing of a man who imparted the kind of knowledge one doesn't find in books or schools. Iblis taught her how to pick locks, fence stolen artwork, hide the monetary fruits of her labor. He taught her how to use a gun and a knife, even though she refused—and fortunately had never needed to put her training to use. He watched over KC in a Fagin-like way until she realized he was obsessed with her and wanted more than a friendship with her.

Cynthia never knew of KC's "occupation," thinking that she was a consultant for the European Union. She never imagined that KC was a criminal like their father until Iblis, out of spite, anger, and jealousy, revealed the truth.

Once Cynthia learned KC was a thief, she lashed out, hating KC for deceiving her, despite the fact that KC did it not out of greed for herself but out of love for her. Only after they'd faced death did they reconcile, realizing that despite everything that KC had done, everything that Cynthia had said, they were sisters and shared a bond only sisters could understand.

KC hadn't been back to London in nearly a year, her mind, heart, and life so entwined with Michael's that she'd forgotten what she had left behind. And as she thought of England on her impending journey, she realized she missed Cynthia, missed her house in Essex, missed her old life where she could take off at a moment's notice to ski the Alps, to climb Mount Kilimanjaro, to scuba-dive the pristine waters of Fiji. She missed the freedom she had known for so long. But above all she missed the adrenaline rush she had grown so accustomed to. She loved the planning, the execution of penetrating a private museum, an embassy. Her targets had always been those she felt were deserving of some misfortune, those who had escaped judgment for less-than-moral deeds, whose money and power rendered them untouchable: dictators, unscrupulous businessmen, criminals . . . lawyers. She had never taken a life, had never physically injured a single person in her dealings. She would snatch her prize, selling it off quickly, and disappear back behind a façade of normalcy until the need for income returned once again.

KC arrived at the ticket counter and with a simple nod said, "Good afternoon, I have a flight to London via Germany." KC handed over her passport.

"I see you've only booked one way," the woman behind the counter said as she looked at her computer monitor. "Will you be returning?"

KC paused. The woman had inadvertently verbalized what she had been debating for the last few hours. She finally looked at the woman with sad eyes and said, "I'm not sure."

The atmosphere in the terminal was one of controlled chaos. People pushed and shoved and obnoxiously tossed about their large suitcases and overstuffed carry-ons. KC's bag was small and light. She had packed quickly: a pair of pants, a skirt, a blouse and some shoes, her sneakers, running gear, and a bathing suit. A simple carry-on over her shoulder was all she needed. In her past life she had grown accustomed to traveling light, formulating a short, simple checklist of essentials no matter how long her journey or how far it took her. She never bothered with toiletries, brushes, or hair dryers; she would simply purchase her essentials when she arrived at her destination. Not one for makeup, she only really needed eyeliner, mascara, and lip gloss; her good genes took care of the rest.

Amid the hustle and bustle in the busy airport, she didn't notice the woman with short black hair behind her who watched her every move.

MICHAEL SAT IN the interrogation room, staring at Lucas, doing everything he could do to restrain himself from diving across the table. The files on the table, the proverbial cards laid out before him, held his fate. They were proof of his past, deeds he had done for others, crimes committed to save lives, to save loved ones.

But now his past deeds and sacrifices were being used against him to force his hand.

"You killed a man to entrap me?"

Lucas said nothing.

"It never occurred to you to play the blackmail card before you killed that kid?"

"I didn't kill that kid, a stranger did . . . and you helped. I'm only here talking to you because this is a matter of *national security*," Lucas said, as if he truly believed it. "The feds can take the case over, pull jurisdictional rank, and I can make it go away, or . . ." Lucas laid his hands on the stack of files and pushed them toward Michael. "Or I can just give these to the New York City homicide detectives who are itching to get in here and investigate the death of that kid."

Though Michael was in an interrogation room, he felt he might as well have already been sitting in prison with a thirty-year sentence ahead of him.

"You do this one job for us and I'll make today's event disappear along with these." Lucas patted the files.

"You're playing a dangerous game," Michael said softly.

"There are many prices for freedom, Mr. St. Pierre, both for you and for this country."

"And this is the way you operate?" Michael could barely contain his anger. "You killed an innocent kid."

"Who said he was innocent?"

"How do you know I won't lawyer up and bury you? The press would have a field day with a story like this. Rogue colonel, death in the streets, lady assassin."

"Sounds incredible, right?" Lucas said. "All you have, though, is a story. I have this." Lucas patted the stack of files and then pulled out an iPad. "I figured you might not want to play this game, as foolish as you would be not to trade one simple act for the rest of your life . . ."

Lucas ran his hands over the iPad, a video quickly coming to life. Quick-cut images of a woman walking through the terminal of an airport filled the screen: KC, alone, carrying a single bag.

Michael's heart was instantly in his throat.

"You may think otherwise, but I get no pleasure from this." The colonel pulled out a file, pushing it toward Michael. It was marked in red ink: Katherine Colleen Ryan. Michael didn't need to open it to know that it contained a bio and "job experience" on KC similar to the one that the colonel possessed on him.

Michael's eyes were quickly pulled back to the image. Despite the crowds, the sea of people all running to escape New York, Michael could see KC within the masses. And with all of the emotions coursing through his body, he felt a pang in his heart, a regret for things he'd said . . . and left unsaid. And he wondered if he'd ever see her again. But he was quickly pulled back to the moment as Lucas paused the video.

"You're going to take a trip. If you need resources, I'll acquire them for you. If you need assistance, I will provide that, too. Just tell me what you require."

"Require for what?" Michael hated himself for even asking the question.

"There is a box."

"What kind of box?"

"Not large, gun-metal gray, about eighteen inches square, like a safety-deposit box."

"In a bank?" Michael had never robbed a bank and had no intention of doing so now.

"No, though the box is in a vault in a location whose security is far greater than any bank's."

"You said Macau. You can't conduct a military operation in China."

"No, we can't. It would greatly disturb the fragile relationship our government has with the country. Imagine the global implications. Imagine how Americans would react if the Chinese military were to conduct an assault on one of our cultural centers, one of our icons."

"There are no cultural icons in Macau."

"On the contrary, the largest—short of the Great Wall and the Forbidden City—and most profitable structure in all of China is there, and I need you to penetrate its security. I need you to retrieve this box before it falls into anyone else's hands."

"Or what, the world will end?" Michael said, his voice filled with derision.

"The balance of power in the world is more precarious now than it has ever been. The United States' lone superpower status is being challenged from all sides. Its greatness is in danger because of people like you who think that freedom is free, that the world owes you something. . . . Our fate hangs in the balance, and it takes just one event to push it down a path of no return."

Michael saw the fervency in Lucas's eyes, a fanaticism just short of madness.

He met his gaze and simply said, "No."

Lucas smiled. His hand moved back to the iPad and the image of KC came back to life.

"You remember Annie?" Lucas said, nodding at the iPad.

Michael had no idea what he was talking about, but a fear rose in him as he continued to watch the video. He could see KC's lips moving as she conversed with the airline employees, could see her turn—and then suddenly, there she was. Annie, her short black hair slicked back like that of a gangster from the forties, giving her the appearance of a rock star entering the stage, of someone who could grace the cover of *Vogue*. Michael continued to watch the screen. He watched as she smiled at KC, as KC unknowingly smiled back, a few words and nods were exchanged, and they fell into easy conversation, all surreal in the silent video.

Michael remembered the woman's smile, the same smile she'd given him when he'd stepped into the elevator—he felt such shame now for falling into her trap. The expression in her dark, glinting eyes as she engaged KC in conversation was the same expression he'd seen four hours ago, when she'd pulled the trigger, killing the young man.

The video suddenly paused.

"You will be leaving tomorrow, 9:00 a.m., Terminal A, Westchester Airport; we will provide you with the details of the mission once you're airborne. Gather what you need and don't be late. You've only got five days."

"What happens in five days?"

Lucas swiped his hand on the iPad. The video continued. KC and Annie now sat in an airline bar, sipping wine. As KC reached into her bag, searching for something, Annie turned and looked into the hidden camera, right into Michael's eyes, as if she were standing right there in the room . . . and she smiled, cold, emotionless, deadly. The image of her froze.

Michael stared back into Annie's eyes; her deadly intent was clear. He was trapped—free to roam, free to run, but held prisoner by his fear for KC.

Lucas gathered up his files, placed the iPad atop them, and tucked them all under his arm. Then a thought seemed to hit him . . . he grabbed the iPad and passed it to Michael. The screen was still lit; Annie continued to stare at him. "Why don't you keep this?"

Lucas gave three sharp knocks to the door and seconds later it opened.

With a military snap of his head, Lucas said to Michael, "You are free to go."

CHAPTER 5

"Hello again," Annie said as she sat on the bar-stool next to KC in the rooftop bar. The runways were laid out before them, planes landing and taking off, one after the other.

"Hi," KC said with a nod as she sipped her water.

"You don't mind if I join you, do you?" Annie said as she looked around at all the people. "You're the only one that looks safe."

KC smiled as she noticed the men in the bar looking at them. "Of course. Did your friend's flight arrive?" KC asked, referring to their brief conversation earlier at the ticket counter.

"Flight's delayed."

"Aren't they all?"

Annie turned to the bartender. "Could I get a white wine?"

The bartender nodded as he quickly filled a glass and put it on the bar.

"After the day I had," Annie said as she sipped her wine, "I can justify a drink."

"I think when you fly you can justify anything. It makes dealing with these delays a little more bearable."

"Are you from England?" Annie asked, noting KC's accent.

"London, but I live here in New York." KC caught herself, her response automatic.

"Do you travel often?"

"I've always had a bit of wanderlust, but I was hibernating for the last year."

"So where are you wandering off to?"

"Germany, then a connection to London."

"Really? That's an awkward way to go," Annie said.

"Last-minute. It was all I could get."

"I'm heading to Kent."

"Business or pleasure?"

"A bit of both. I'm waiting for my associate to arrive, then we're taking the corporate jet. You?"

"Going home to see my sister."

"Family is a good thing."

"Sometimes family is what we need when the world gets too confusing."

"It must be nice," Annie said, a touch of melancholy in her voice.

"No family?"

"Not really," Annie said. "I bounced from foster home to foster home."

"Sorry."

"Do you have a big family?"

"Ah, that would be no. Just my sister and me. But we're enough for each other."

"I had a foster brother for a while, it was nice."

KC nodded. "My mother died when I was fifteen.

My sister and I have been on our own ever since. It must have been hard to grow up in foster homes."

"No pity party." Annie smiled. "It made me who I am. It made me strong, appreciative of the little things in life."

KC was familiar with the wall that grew around the heart of a child who had no parents.

"Here's to being self-made women." KC hoisted her drink and cheered Annie.

"To self-made women." Annie clinked her glass in return.

"What do you do?" KC asked.

"Military consulting."

KC smiled, unable to contain her surprise.

"I know. I don't look the part. You should see me in fatigues. And what do you do?" Annie asked.

"Not much," KC said with feigned laughter in her voice.

"You don't look like someone who does 'not much.'"

"I was a consultant to the European Union," KC said, mentioning her longtime cover job of choice.

"Forgive me, but you look more like a model who'd appear on the cover of some fashion magazine."

KC tried not to blush. Michael had always praised her looks, something she had never experienced growing up; she had never gotten used to praise. "Thank you. I'm more the outdoors type: climbing, extreme skiing, BASE jumping; the more adrenaline-inducing sports."

Annie smiled a knowing smile. "That's why I joined the military; I loved sports, adventure-type things, none of this softball stuff. I couldn't sit behind a desk, and it's pretty hard to make a living being an athlete without a team."

She looked away wistfully for a second, then turned back to KC. "Married?"

KC held up her bare ring finger. "Always hoping. You?"

"I don't believe in marriage. I don't believe that we need to stand before God to declare our intentions." Annie paused. "And who's to say that love lasts a lifetime? Hell, for me, it rarely lasts a month," Annie said with a chuckle.

"It makes it easier, though, for the children."

"Do you have kids?"

"Always hoping on that, too. You?"

"Can't have any."

"Never say never."

"No, I mean I can't have any," Annie said, a touch of regret in her eyes.

"I'm sorry."

"I'm not." KC thought her eyes said differently. "If you really knew me, you'd understand: I wouldn't make a very good mother anyway. I enjoy what I do too much."

KC looked up at the departure board and her heart sank. Her flight was no longer delayed, it was canceled.

Annie followed her line of sight. "Oh, no."

KC stood and picked up her bag.

"Why don't you come with us?" Annie offered. "It's America's treat, taxpayers' money hard at work. Only two of us on a sixteen-seater."

"Thank you, but I'd better go find another flight."

"We both know that's not going to be possible until tomorrow. We're happy to help you out."

"No, that's okay." KC had no problem helping others, she just had an issue with people helping her. But KC began to realize if she didn't find another flight she would have to go home to Michael. And as much as she might have wanted to, her anger at him had yet to abate. She really needed to figure out where she was going, not just now, but with her life.

"I insist." Annie pressed her. "Kent is less than a two-hour drive to London. At the rate you're going, you might never get there. You don't want to disappoint your sister, do you?"

A tall man with buzz-cut black hair walked into the bar. He carried a green duffel over his broad shoulders, and his dark eyes scanned the room. He saw Annie and walked over to her.

"Rick Vajos," Annie said, "this is KC."

Rick nodded with a half-smile to KC. "We're fueled and ready, wheels up in twenty."

Annie turned to KC. "Please, come with us. You won't get a flight till morning, which means you won't arrive in London until tomorrow night at best. And have you thought about where you'll sleep tonight? The terminal floor doesn't look very comfortable."

KC looked up at the departure board as if somehow her flight would magically be uncanceled. And as she looked around, she wondered if she was doing the right thing, leaving Michael. The pain in her heart was telling her to stay, but . . . her mind was filled with doubt.

And this woman, there was something about her—she could feel a connection, the shared background of orphans. But there was something else; she couldn't put her finger on it.

THEY WALKED ACROSS the tarmac to the Bombardier jet that sat ready, the engines in a slow whine. KC followed Annie up the rolling stairs and entered the business jet to find a luxurious cabin that could have held at least sixteen passengers.

"Doesn't look very military."

"No," Annie said as she stowed her bag in the front closet. "Though our pilot is, as is our jet's call sign. It kind of sets tongues a-wagging when a military jet arrives. So these just leave the factory painted white."

Rick stored his green duffel, and without a word sat in one of the large white leather seats, reclined, and closed his eyes. KC and Annie sat across the aisle from each other. "Anything to eat or drink?"

"No, thank you," KC said as she took a seat.

As the door closed and the cabin became pressurized, KC couldn't help feeling as if she was somehow trapped, as if she had just made a foolish mistake.

PETE WILLIAMSON, A Navy pilot in full dress uniform, poked his head out of the cockpit and greeted them with a curt nod of his head. He did not know his passengers, he rarely did, as so many times their missions were above his security clearance. While he had seldom questioned his destination or what his passengers were doing, today was a bit different. The two women were not what he had expected. Annie Joss and her military companion, Rick Vajos, were cleared through military intelligence; he had been informed they would be traveling with a third passenger, an Englishwoman. But who she was and how she was connected to Joss and Vajos were things he would probably never know.

Williamson closed the cockpit door, strapped himself into his seat. Revving the engines, he dialed in their heading. He had overheard the two women discussing something about Kent. He hadn't been there in years; it brought back a taste of warm beer and undercooked fish and chips. He had no desire to return there and was thankful that it was not their destination; the heading he entered into the computer was far more appealing. He had never been there and the city had no connection to the U.S. military that he knew of.

As they climbed to twenty-five thousand feet, he wondered what the two women could possibly be planning to do in the ancient Spanish city of Granada.

CHAPTER 6

Michael burst through the front door of his home, his three dogs trailing him. He had exited One Police Plaza into the dark of night. No one paid him any mind as he stepped from the interrogation room. The desk clerk returned his watch, keys, and other personal effects without a word; not a soul questioned his departure. It was as if he was just a visitor as opposed to the suspect who'd been dragged in five hours earlier. He hailed a cab and gave the cabbie two hundred dollars to get him back to Westchester, to the North White Plains train station, as fast as he could. There was no time to waste.

Michael called KC's cell phone, but there was no answer. He called the house, but again, she wasn't there. He knew where she was, he'd seen the video, but still he needed more convincing.

As he charged through the great room, through the dining room, he saw the note lying against the centerpiece. He grabbed it and tucked it in his pocket; he didn't need to read it to know what it said. Without pause he continued through the kitchen, out into the garage and his adjacent office.

Michael walked in, closing the door behind him.

The office was far from typical for a man running a large security firm. Besides the mahogany desk, guest chairs, and couch, there was a full workbench littered with electronics lining the far wall.

Michael was a tinkerer, good with his hands, a talent imparted by his adoptive father, Alex St. Pierre, a man who, when he wasn't playing accountant, was in his garage building clocks, fixing cars, crafting whatever his mind could dream up. Although Alex was not his blood relative, Michael couldn't help feeling the skill had been passed down to him. He had taken a hobby of crafting and designing and turned it into a living creating security systems for business and industry.

Michael flipped on his computer, grabbed the phone on the table, and quickly dialed. It took three rings before a greetingless voicemail answered with a beep.

"What the hell was in Italy, what was supposed to be in that puzzle box, Simon? That envelope? And that black box, it scared the old man. And it scared you, too. I saw it in your eyes." Michael took a breath. "They took KC, dammit, this is your fault. You better find me!"

Michael hung up, calmed himself, and dialed another number.

"Hello—"

"Jo," Michael said. "Listen—"

"Good evening to you, too," Michael's assistant said, her voice forever cheerful and unfazed by the late phone call. "How was your meeting?"

"Just great," Michael said, unable to disguise the anger in his voice.

"Sounds like we won't be getting that job."

"Listen to me, the Jacobson contract has been canceled."

"Shit," Jo said, understanding Michael's code phrase for "the shit has hit the fan." "I'll take care of the paperwork."

"I'm going out of town."

"How long?"

"At least a week."

"All right, I've got it covered. Stay in touch."

He hung up the phone and plugged the iPad into his computer. After a moment, the video at the airport appeared on his monitor. As KC's face filled the screen, he did everything to keep his emotions in check.

"HEY," BUSCH CALLED out from behind the bar as Michael walked into Valhalla carrying the iPad and a file folder. The place was overflowing with men and women, drinks in their hands, their eyes scanning the crowd. Music came from the small stage in the corner with the singer Red Jon Doe cutting through a perfect cover of the Stones' "Gimme Shelter."

Michael squeezed his way through the crowd. Busch was like a musician playing his instrument: throwing glasses under the tap while mixing drinks, and stuffing cash in the register. At six feet four, Busch was like the quarterback running the game: people fighting for his attention, holding out bills as they made small talk to the strangers beside them. Busch slid three Cosmos to a group of women, two beers down the bar, and laid a bottle of Coke in front of Michael as he arrived at the bar rail.

All of the noise, the band, the crowd, the chinking of glass fell away. Michael didn't need to say a word; Busch could read his best friend's face as if it were a billboard.

"Shit."

THE TWO STOOD in Busch's lounge upstairs, the filtered noise from below droning in the background. Michael nervously paced as he quickly summed up the last six hours, from the purse-snatching to the blackmail to KC's unknown whereabouts.

Busch leaned against the bar in shock. His face was filled with concern as his mind processed KC's kidnapping.

Busch finally looked up. "What I don't get is why KC was at the airport. Where was she going?"

"She was leaving me . . ."

Busch's shock intensified. "What? A week ago at dinner you guys couldn't get enough of each other. Why would she leave you?"

Michael said nothing, unable to meet Busch's eyes.

"What the hell did you do?"

Michael remained silent.

Then it dawned on Busch. "You've got to be kidding me. Did you go off with Simon?" Busch's anger grew, his voice getting louder. "What did he do? What did *you* do? Dammit, Michael!"

"It was in Italy, on the Amalfi coast. And it was bad."

Busch turned away from Michael, trying to contain his anger. He pulled out a bottle of Jack Daniel's and poured himself a drink as Michael explained his trip and what had occurred.

"And KC found out?"

"Yeah, she figured it out. Simon had asked her to do the same job but she turned him down."

"That frickin' guy." Busch paused. "But you said yes, even though you told her you wouldn't?"

Michael nodded.

"You've got to be kidding me." Busch shook his head. "How could you fuck up something so good, so badly? You lied to her, and not a little white lie. She had every reason to leave you. And you lied to me, but we'll talk about that later."

"I don't need a lecture."

"Well, you're getting one. Do you know how hard it is to find love once? When Mary died, you died along with her; it took you over a year to pull out of that spiral, and then what happens? You meet KC. Bang, you're alive again. You guys should be married by now. You sat on that ring for too long." Busch paced the room, unloading on Michael as if he were his father.

"You should never have let her leave, you should have begged, pleaded, whatever it took, but you don't allow someone like her to get away."

"I know, Paul," Michael said, his voice filled with sorrow.

Busch could see it in Michael's eyes—he hadn't seen his friend so distressed since Mary had died—and finally stopped pacing.

"And where the hell is Simon?" Busch asked with renewed calm. "This is his fault, everything ties back to him."

"I left him a message. I can't find him."

"Of course not." Busch's anger was coming back.

"He'll turn up."

"What, when you're dead?"

"I could have said no to the job."

"Yet you didn't," Busch said.

Michael pushed the iPad across the table, waved his finger across it, and the video began to play. They both watched in silence. Busch's breathing grew deeper, steadier, focused with anger.

As the two-minute segment came to an end, they sat in silence, eyes fixed on the frozen image of Annie.

Busch sat there absorbing Michael's tale.

"How can someone be shot on the street in cold blood and it doesn't hit the news?" Busch asked.

Michael shook his head.

"What precinct did you go to?"

"Downtown, One Police Plaza."

"Why the hell would they take you down there?"

"You're kidding, right? How the hell should I know?"

"They process fed and state through there. It doesn't make sense that they would let you go with a man dead and no formal questioning."

Michael shook his head.

"Let's go." Busch headed for the door, not waiting for a response.

Michael grabbed the folder and iPad. "Where?"

"To get some answers."

MICHAEL SAT ON the couch in the office of the captain of the Byram Hills police department. The station was empty except for two duty cops and the desk sergeant;

everyone else was out on patrol or home sleeping at 11:30 on a Tuesday night.

"Well, this guy is the real deal." Busch walked in, already halfway through his sentence, and threw down a freshly printed picture of Colonel Lucas in dress uniform, his chest overflowing with medals. "Full-bird colonel, West Point, three tours of duty, a highly decorated hero. He's with military intelligence in the Far East and that is all we are going to get on him. He is otherwise buried in bureaucracy. As far as most people know, he doesn't exist."

"And yet you could find him?" Michael said as he looked at the picture. Lucas was at a formal reception standing among a retinue of military brass from all branches of the armed services.

"I didn't *find him*," Busch shot back. "Captain Delia's son is in the Pentagon on the Army Desk, and I burned my last favor waking up the captain to get this info. It would chafe his ass if he knew we were in here right now. But that wasn't my only call."

Michael could see the anger in his friend's eyes. Busch had retired three years earlier but still held the respect of everyone in his old department. Come tomorrow, not a word would be mentioned to the captain that Busch had paid the office a visit.

"Made some calls to some friends in the NYPD. There is no body," Busch said. "No police record of any shooting on Park Avenue."

"Bullshit, there were witnesses—"

"I'm sure there were, but the incident didn't happen as far as the NYPD is concerned. This guy made it all disappear. Do you know how hard it is to do something like that?"

Michael was lost for words.

"What the hell is going on? This is not the way the military conducts itself. They don't have jurisdiction on homeland soil." Busch was talking as much to himself as he was to Michael. "What is he trying to get you to do?"

"Steal a box."

"The U.S. military can't find someone within their own ranks to do it?" Busch threw up his hands in question. "Where?"

"Macau," Michael said. "That's all I know. Some huge high-security structure—"

"Macau? As much as we like to say we're friends, the U.S. and Chinese militaries don't get along; no joint war games with our Asian buddies. If the U.S. pulls an operation inside their borders . . ." Busch looked up at Michael. "Not a good thing. There's no paper trail with someone like you."

"Only a blood trail," Michael said.

"Macau's a backwater den of gambling and hookers, in the shadow of Hong Kong. There's nothing iconic there."

"He said high-security."

Busch sat behind Delia's desk and fired up his computer.

"You know his password?"

"The name of his dog and his birthday, two things he could never forget," Busch said without looking up. He worked the machine as if it were a shovel, digging, Googling, searching the Internet, pulling up anything and everything. It was only thirty seconds until he found what he was looking for.

"This is out of your league," Busch finally said, his voice filled with dread.

"What?"

Busch spun the computer monitor around; the screen was filled with an image, exotic, lit in bright lights. While his mind had been churning about how to get KC back either through compliance with the blackmail or something more devious, Michael realized now that the task at hand was far worse than he'd imagined. Before now, he'd had no idea the place even existed, but as he stared at the screen, he knew one thing was certain: Paul was right. This was not only out of his league, it was out of everyone's league.

"AND WHAT DO we know about Miss Merry Sunshine?" Busch asked.

Michael spun the iPad around and hit Play.

"Pretty safe to say, Annie is not her real name . . ."

They both watched the video, steeling their emotions, focused on Annie, on the terminal, on everything around the women.

"Well, we know there are at least two." Michael hit Pause, slow-moed the image, then stopped it. He pointed at the departure screen behind the ticket counter; when you mentally blocked out the LED readout, you could see the reflection of activity in the terminal. Behind the image of Annie and KC was a sea of people, businessmen on cell phones, young lovers more focused on each other than the line, crazed parents trying to control their kids. Among them was a man smiling, a bag on his shoulder, and for the briefest of moments, a red light could be seen flashing from the bag's side, the recording light.

"Our videographer," Busch said quietly.

Michael reached into his file and pulled out an enlarged photo of the man. "I've already pulled the images I think I'll need."

They both stared at the man: He was just over six feet, his hair buzz-cut short, a military air to his posture.

"I've looked at this thing multiple times, I don't see anyone else, but that doesn't mean there aren't more. That's Kennedy airport. KC didn't say where she was going when she left, and there was no indication in her note, but my guess is back to England. Her passport was gone. I tried her sister but there was no answer."

"Well, if these guys grabbed her, she could be anywhere now," Busch said.

Michael ignored the comment as he fingered the video, scrolling through as if turning pages, finally pausing at an image of the two women in profile, bags on their shoulders, lost in conversation. Michael pointed to the bag tag.

He reached into the file and pulled out an enlarged photo of Annie's bag tag, the word *Tridiem* emblazoned in gold on black.

"It means 'third day,'" Michael said.

"I remember my Latin."

"Kind of a small Blackwater-type company; elite soldiers cashing in on their spec op skills. But these people are far more selective, more specialized, pristine reputation, privately held. No record of any job, and the site only lists the chairman, Lee Richards. Based in Switzerland."

"She's a mercenary?" Busch asked.

"I don't know what to call her, but right now she answers to Lucas. And she's not a secretary."

Busch was silent, digesting Michael's words.

"I've torn through everything on this computer," Michael said as he touched the iPad. "It's brand-new, purchased with cash yesterday from the Apple store on Fifth Avenue. There's got to be a way to trace this woman."

"You can't go chasing windmills; she could be anywhere, and when I say that I don't just mean in New York."

"I know," Michael said, but his words meant something else entirely.

"If you do this gig in Macau, how do you know they won't kill you and KC anyway?"

"This colonel is so desperate for this box, if I get my hands on it, he'll trade. I guarantee it. And if he doesn't, not only will I destroy his box but I'll do it in front of his dying eyes."

Busch stood up and walked around the room, his gaze far off as he poured himself another drink. And then his gaze returned to Michael as if he had just arrived in the room.

"So." Busch slapped his hands together. "When do we leave?"

"Not a chance," Michael said in all seriousness.

"You listen to me," Busch said, his smile dissolving. "I'm with you whether you like it or not, and not for you, not for getting my yayas off or getting away from Jeannie. I'm going for KC."

CHAPTER 7

"She's sleeping," Annie said, the air phone held tightly to her ear to cut out the whine of the jet.

"The sedative hasn't worn off yet?" Colonel Lucas's voice sounded tinny through the small handset.

"Didn't need it, she came willingly."

"You told her what she had to do?" Lucas pressed her. "How did she react?"

Annie stared out the window at the moonlit Atlantic below. "She doesn't know yet."

"That's not what your orders were."

"And yet she's with me, on the plane. Sometimes there are ways to bend people to our will without the threat of violence," Annie said.

"Growing a conscience?"

"If you need to persuade someone to perform a series of unpleasant or difficult tasks, it's best to start with a subtle means of coercion. Fear, which you use so readily, can work for a time, but left to fester, it clogs the mind. Do you have St. Pierre?"

"I had him from the moment he saw KC with you," Lucas said. "But I still need to know that you can get this job done."

"That all depends on the skills of this woman." Annie glanced down the aisle at KC, sound asleep in her reclining chair. "Can she handle the job?"

"Trust me, she can."

"She doesn't look the part."

"Neither do you," Lucas said, ice in his voice.

"If she can't, or if she tries to pull some last-minute trick, it's my life that's in the balance, not yours."

"If the two of you can't get the job done, there will be far more lives at risk than just yours." Lucas paused. "And listen to me, if you fail, your orders are clear."

"I know what my orders are."

"Do you?"

Annie paused a moment as she looked back at KC's sleeping figure. "Of course."

KC AWOKE SOMEWHERE over the Atlantic. It took her a moment to get her bearings, to stretch the aches and sleep from her bones.

"Hi," Annie said, looking up from a thick file she was reading.

KC smiled, trying to focus as she shook off her dreams. "Hi."

"Brought you some dinner," Annie said as she put aside her file and lifted the lid off a warm dinner plate resting on the tray between them.

KC opened a bottle of water and drank half of it in one go, hoping to ward off the dehydrating effects of air travel. "Thank you. It smells delicious."

Picking up a fork and knife, KC took a bite, finding

the chicken dish far better than anything she would have encountered on the commercial flight.

"What time are you expected?" Annie asked.

"Expected?"

"Aren't you meeting your sister?"

"No. Yes." KC shook her head. "It's a last-minute trip. I'll go to my place in the country after we land, and then I'll call my sister from there. To tell you the truth, I wasn't sure until we took off if I'd change my mind and stay in New York."

"So you were really running away from something rather than running to someone?" Annie said sympathetically.

KC pursed her lips. "I'm having a moment of life-confusion."

"As long as you're not on a tight schedule, I've been thinking I might ask you something."

"Ask me what?"

"How would you feel about joining me on a little side trip? Someplace really special."

KC looked at Annie, unsure of what she was suggesting.

"Look, I know we've known each other for all of five hours, but I really think it would be fun. I don't have many friends. None, actually," Annie said, with no sense of self-pity. "But I completely understand if you need to get somewhere and can't take the time."

"I'm listening," KC said, growing a bit wary of Annie.

"It will only put you off by a day. What's one more day, when your sister doesn't even know you're coming?

Think of it as a girls' trip. You look like you could use a bit of fun, a distraction."

"Where would this distraction be found?" As much as KC wanted to go home and see how it felt to be away from Michael, she had never been on a girls' trip, never really had a close friend for that matter. She trusted only three people in her life: Cynthia, Simon, and Michael. Maybe a little spur-of-the-moment jaunt with a new friend would clear her head, help her see the world from a new perspective.

"I have one hour of business to take care of and twenty-three to have fun. We can get right back on the plane tomorrow and I'll drop you off in London."

"Where?" KC asked, trying to mask her curiosity.

"One of the most amazing places I've ever seen. Have you ever been to Granada?"

CHAPTER 8

"Good morning, Mr. St. Pierre," said the guard standing at the gate leading to the private jet terminal of Westchester Airport.

From his car, Michael stared up at the man, who was dressed in a blue blazer and gray slacks.

"Feel free to park in any of the available spots." The man pointed at the small, empty parking lot to his right. "Your plane is ready for departure. Almost everyone is on board. I've been told you are awaiting one more passenger who should be arriving any minute now."

Acknowledging the man with a curt nod, Michael drove through the gates and parked. Stepping from his Suburban, he turned and looked at the jet waiting on the tarmac. The white Boeing Business Jet was not what he had expected to see; he'd assumed his trip would be spent huddled in some noisy, oversized C-130 transport, not the luxury jet that sat before him. Michael knew the jet well, very well in fact, as it was a near duplicate of the one his father owned. The thirty-five-million-dollar plane was a luxury office in the sky, the sort of thing used by CEOs, billionaires, and Hollywood big shots.

He shook his head as he pondered the amount of government waste before him, a luxury jet shepherding military personnel. He couldn't stop thinking how much body armor could be purchased for $35 million.

"So much for slumming it," Busch said as he got out of the passenger seat and walked around to Michael, grabbing their carry-on bags. Michael always traveled light, preferring to gather any supplies he would need at his destination. Busch was different; he liked to be prepared and had a tendency to grab everything he thought he could possibly need—but not this time. He had told Jeannie that KC had walked out on Michael and he needed to take him away for some guy time, some golf, and maybe a little time to think. He'd grabbed two handfuls of clothes, tossed them in a bag, and headed outside.

After he'd thrown the bag in Michael's car, he'd turned and wrapped Jeannie in his large arms and kissed her. Finally pulling back and looking in her eyes, he said, "This is not about having fun." And as Jeannie looked at him, Busch knew that she knew. Seeing the look on Michael's face as he stared out the car window, she knew this wasn't about golf, it wasn't about cheering Michael up. It was something dangerous.

Paul had run off with Michael for "golf" before and they'd returned not with golf tans and stories but with banged-up bodies and sunken, tired eyes.

"Good luck," she said as she kissed him back. "Don't overstay your welcome. We've got the kids' award banquet next Saturday."

"I know. I won't miss it."

"And Paul, be careful on the back nine. That always seems to give you guys the most trouble."

* * *

MICHAEL WALKED UP the gangway, his eyes darting around the airport, wondering if this would be the last time he'd set foot not only in New York but in the entire United States. Busch walked in front of him as if he were a blocking tackle prepared to knock any and all comers out of his friend's way. Busch ducked his head under the entrance and stepped on with his left foot first: It was a habit since his first time on a plane, when his mother had told him to always lead with his best foot and it would ensure the safe flight of the plane. Busch loved his mother, though he always laughed at her superstitions: black cats, broken mirrors, and spilled salt. But despite the humor he found in her beliefs, he had always led with his left foot for more than twenty years, whether he was boarding a plane, a train, a boat, or an elevator, and had never experienced anything but smooth sailing.

As he and Michael boarded the jet, they encountered the pilot standing in the cockpit, lost in conversation with his copilot. The uniformed men turned, glancing at their new passengers, but quickly returned to the flight check.

The interior of the jet was large, three rows of wide leather seats seemingly more suited to some high-end screening room than to an airplane. There was a large conference table toward the middle. A door leading to the rear was closed, but Michael knew a private office and bedroom likely could be found behind it.

"Mr. St. Pierre." The man's voice was deep and direct, and he spoke with a self-conscious, unnatural diction, as if fighting to overcome an accent.

Michael nodded.

"My name is Jon Lei." Jon stood about five-ten, his thick arms stretching taut the fabric of the short-sleeved shirt he wore. His black hair was short, though not military length, as Michael would have expected it to be. "Please feel free to sit wherever you wish. We should be under way shortly. Our final passenger is running late."

Michael stared at him, waiting for him to continue. The moment dragged on into a noticeably tense situation.

"We will continue this *one-way* discussion once we are airborne," Jon said as he turned away and walked through the back door, closing it behind him.

Michael recognized him. He had seen his new traveling companion yesterday, a face in the crowd as Michael lay on the sidewalk, holding the kid who'd stolen Annie's purse. The faces of the onlookers had been burned into his memory. Like a bunch of rubberneckers, they'd all stared, murmuring about Michael's heroics, but then had cowered in fear and shock or fled as Annie shot the man. This man had blended in with the rest, looking much like any other New Yorker. His features were refined, a mix of Asian cultures; he had a strong jaw and cheeks, but it was the pair of cold, dark eyes that dominated his face and made it so memorable. Only now Michael realized the man hadn't just been a witness, but an accomplice.

Michael took the window seat, stretching out.

"Our stewardess seems like a real charmer," Busch said as he collapsed his six-foot-four frame into the seat beside him. "I can't believe Simon's not here. And he hasn't called back yet?"

"I left him three messages, sent him the video of KC,

and an email about where we're heading. I don't need to hear back from him to know that he will be doing everything in his power to help us."

"This is still his fault. Remember, you don't thank the guy who got you in trouble for getting you out of trouble."

Michael glared at Busch.

"I'm just saying." Busch settled back in his chair. "So who are we waiting for?"

As he said the words, a white van drove onto the tarmac and came right up to the side of the jet. Two men exited the van, ran around to the rear, and opened the double-panel doors, pulling out a long box. Two sets of wheels snapped into place below what Michael now saw was a dark, highly polished seven-foot-long rectangular case. Michael watched as they wheeled it toward the plane, the side-cargo door was lowered, and the case was slid inside the belly of the aircraft.

"Is that the passenger we've been waiting for?" Busch asked.

"I'm afraid so," Michael said as he watched the coffin disappear into the plane.

THE BOEING BUSINESS Jet tore down the runway, thrusting its passengers back into their seats until it finally leaped into the early-morning sky. Michael stared out as the world fell away and they climbed higher and higher. The jet circled once over Byram Hills and then headed north. They had an eighteen-hour flight ahead of them, and they would have to top off their tanks in Alaska before crossing the Pacific and riding the Asian coast down toward Hong Kong.

Michael's mind was spinning, and he realized it

hadn't stopped spinning since he had left for Italy. He reached into his pocket and pulled out the envelope he'd found on his dining room table—the letter KC had written when her wounds were fresh. What she had written was from her heart, and it had crushed him when he read it the first time. He slid the single piece of notepaper from the envelope and began reading.

> *Dearest Michael,*
>
> *I love you with all of my heart, with all of my being. The comfort you have given me, the home you have provided is like nothing I have ever known.*
>
> *And so it is with a heavy heart I write this letter. I can barely see through the tears in my eyes. For I know you are afraid of marriage, of recommitting, of being honest with me.*
>
> *But I, too, have decisions to make—time is fleeting at best, life is short. I long for children, and the security of a committed heart. I would give you my life, I would give you children, but I fear giving you things you do not want.*
>
> *Please do not follow me; I need time to clear my head, to think about life, to plan a future.*
>
> *Please know that I have never been in love before now, never felt so deeply about anything or anyone as I do about you.*
>
> *I will love you always and forever,*
>
> > *KC*

Michael read the letter twice through, a complex mix of emotions on the verge of overwhelming him.

Jon emerged from the rear of the jet, carrying several rolls of paper, which he dropped onto the conference table. Thankful for the distraction, Michael tucked the letter back in his breast pocket, rose from his seat, and went to the conference table. Jon unrolled a set of architectural plans, anchoring the corners with four heavy crystal glasses. The structure it depicted was enormous, bigger than any building Michael had ever seen.

"You're kidding, right?" Busch asked as he looked over the plans.

"Not in the least." Jon stepped back, allowing them to examine the design in greater detail.

They were looking at an entire city under one roof. There were man-made rivers and canals, a village square replete with shops, restaurants, and theaters, towers that climbed forty stories into the sky, subterranean levels that descended ten stories. The legend alongside the plan indicated that the structure contained ten million square feet. It was part palace, part pleasure dome, equal parts urban dream and nightmare. But to the richest people in the world it was known as the Venetian Casino Macau, the largest, richest casino in the world.

"You have three days to formulate and execute your plan."

"Three days? Lucas said five."

"Three days to execute, five until it's too late, five until he has KC Ryan killed."

Busch exploded, grabbing Jon and slamming him against the wall. "Listen to me, you little shit. If she is so much as scratched, I'll reach down your throat and tear out your lungs."

Jon stared at Busch, unfazed, offering no resistance. "Kill me and she will be dead in minutes, I assure you."

Busch glared at him, his body trembling with rage, finally releasing him in utter frustration. Michael put a hand on his friend's back, as if to calm him, then turned to Jon.

"I'm going into an unfamiliar world, facing not only language but cultural barriers. I know nothing of this structure, nothing of the goal, and you expect me to somehow pull this off due to the sheer force of my desire to save my girlfriend?"

"I understand she left you," Jon said.

"How the hell would you know that?"

"The same way we know everything about you; information not only rules the world, it's what allows us to rule you." Jon paused, in total control of the moment. "So, Michael, is KC worth saving?"

Jon reached for another set of plans and rolled them out on the conference table, too. "What we want is kept underground, deep underground. These plans will allow you to familiarize yourself with the various sublevels, but your main focus is the lowest level, where there is a safe containing a simple box, just waiting for you to liberate it." Jon paused. "You tell me what you require and I will get it. I have many different resources to draw from."

Michael glared at him. He hated relying on others; his survival had always been predicated on counting on no one but himself. Although he had allowed Busch and Simon into his inner circle, he wasn't going to expand it to include this man.

"And don't worry about the culture or the language," Jon continued. "That's why I'm your partner in this."

"Not a chance," Michael said. "I don't know you, and I certainly don't trust you."

"Why not?"

"That coffin in the belly of the plane. That's the man I chased down Park Avenue yesterday. He was one of your men, wasn't he?"

Jon nodded.

"You stood by as he was murdered. You watched Annie shoot him." Michael paused as he put the pieces together. "He had no idea what you and Annie had planned for him."

Busch watched as Michael's anger ratcheted up.

"Once you get your box, once we've served our purpose, you're going to kill us, just like you killed your purse-snatching partner."

"You are *gaijin*," Jon said. "*Wàiguó rén*."

Michael shook his head, not comprehending.

"You're a foreigner about to steal from a culture you don't understand. So you need me. And yes, I might kill you, but I can promise you this: You'll survive far longer with me than attempting this alone. You are stealing from some of the deadliest people in the world."

"What people?"

"A group who will not only kill you and your friend here, but who will reach into your life and kill everyone you have ever cared about, all in retaliation for the crime you are going to commit against them. So, yes, you need me. We will work together on this or I will kill you right now and then I will call Annie and she will end the life of this woman you claim to love."

CHAPTER 9

The house sat on the outskirts of Granada, in the foothills of the Sierra Nevadas, whose mountainous beauty stretched to the horizon.

Annie drove the Peugeot up a long, twisting road while KC looked out over the ancient city sprawled out below her, watching as it slowly came to life in the early-morning sun. The city was a sea of white, its buildings an amalgam of influences and cultures. Here, in the last Muslim city on the Iberian peninsula to fall to King Ferdinand and Queen Isabella, Moorish, Catholic, and Castilian strands merged to create a singular place, a medieval metropolis of sandstone churches, basilicas, and cathedrals, yet home to more ancient Muslim structures than the rest of Europe combined. Dotted with tall, thin evergreen and fragrant olive trees, it was truly a city that felt more like a lost fragment of the past than a part of the modern world.

As they crested the uppermost hill of the three-mile-long road, KC saw a single residence at the road's end sitting in splendid isolation with a commanding view of the city below.

What Annie had described to KC as a house was, in fact, a grand estate. Tall, imposing walls stretched as far as KC could see from either side of an iron-gated entrance. Annie drove up to the gate, rolled down the window, and held up a white security card to the electric reader attached to the gate's side. The black gates trembled and then smoothly swung open on silent hinges.

As they proceeded up a long drive, KC found herself looking upon a large yet somehow serene mansion whose design brought to mind the Alhambra, the ancient Moorish fortress on the other side of the river valley. Like that legendary castle, this red stone mansion was strategically located, able to view the world from every point of the compass.

Annie coasted into the circular drive, parking in the shade of a stand of fruit trees.

"I shouldn't be more than fifteen minutes," Annie said as she got out of the car.

She rang the doorbell and was soon admitted to the house by an unseen individual. The heavy wooden door closed behind her with a thud.

KC looked upon the enormous estate, a statement of power and extreme wealth, and wondered what she was doing here. She was determined to fight the sudden feeling of regret that she felt stirring deep inside her. She had run away, something she had never done before. Had she made a mistake in leaving Michael so suddenly?

"KC," Annie called out from the front door. "Come in."

KC rolled down the window. "What's going on? I thought you were just going to be a few minutes."

"Five minutes. Please, you've got to see a little of his house, it's not something many people have the chance to do," Annie said, beckoning KC to join her.

KC pulled down the visor and looked at her face in the mirror. She was tired; she not only felt it but could see it in her eyes. She quickly ran a brush through her hair, dabbed on some lip gloss, and exited the car with a sigh.

"I really should have waited for the next flight," KC muttered to herself as she walked up the wide slate front steps. The front door stood wide open, but there was no sign of Annie.

KC stepped into a large foyer, her eyes immediately drawn to an enormous crystal chandelier. There was no sign of Annie, no sign of anyone. The house was cold, devoid of anything that could have made it seem like a real home. No pictures or heirlooms were to be seen on the marble console tables along the back wall. It was too clean, too free of any sign of human habitation.

"Detener. Quién es usted?"

KC froze, fully understanding the order. "Stop. Who are you?" She spoke six languages, had a gift for them, acquiring them over the years. Raising her hands, she slowly turned to see a man standing there, a gun trained on her. His appearance stood in sharp contrast to the perfect, unaccented Spanish he'd just spoken to her. He was Chinese, appeared to be in his fifties, and had the slicked-back black hair of an earlier era.

"I'm here with Annie," KC replied in Spanish.

The man waved the gun, directing KC to proceed down a dimly lit hallway.

"This is just a misunderstanding," KC said in Spanish, though she already knew it was no such thing. Annie had lured her to this place for a reason. As she walked down the hall, she nearly tripped over a body, a single bullet hole in the man's temple, close range. The dead man was Chinese, too. It wasn't the first murder victim she had seen in her life, though the reality of her situation came crashing down on her.

Trying to keep her breathing calm and slow, she stepped over the body and walked into a sunny, open living room whose far wall was almost entirely made of glass and looked out over the city below. It unexpectedly reminded her of a house she had once visited in the hills above Los Angeles, but she quickly stopped herself from thinking about that and concentrated on looking for a way out.

The man drew out his cell phone and dialed.

"*Hola . . .*"

KC listened as he called the police and told them of not just one murder but three, two men and a blond woman. It would be only minutes before the police arrived; she knew if she didn't think fast she would be that dead blond woman the police were expecting to find.

The man directed KC to the center of the living room, which was filled with heavy furniture. An antique brass telescope was the only thing that gave the space any character.

"*En sus rodillas.*"

KC was filled with panic as the man pointed the gun at her, his thumb drawing back the hammer. She reluctantly complied with his order and knelt in the middle of the room.

The man stepped behind her. She was facing the panorama of the city, its white structures aglow in the morning sun, full of people so close and alive, yet unaware of what was about to happen to her. KC bowed her head and thought only of Michael. And she felt her heart die before the bullet had even struck her.

KC winced at the explosive sound of the gun. But she felt nothing. Inexplicably, the man fell down beside her, blood pooling beneath his prone body.

KC turned to see Annie standing in the doorway, knees bent, her gun held high in a two-handed grip. She knew exactly what she was doing.

"What the hell is going on?" KC said as she leaped to her feet.

"I'll explain later—"

"No, you'll explain now. You killed these men in cold blood."

"You heard what he said, the cops are on their way." KC continued to glare at her. "These men are members of the Snake Triad out of China. They are working with a terrorist group—"

"Bullshit," KC snapped.

"No bullshit. I came here to buy information but they had a change of heart."

"So you invited me in?" KC snapped.

"Not to have a gun held to your head. I need your help."

"How the hell can I possibly help you?"

Annie didn't respond. Instead, she led KC to the kitchen, into a small pantry where shelves full of canned goods and glass jars had been pulled away from the wall on a hidden hinge, revealing a metal door.

KC knew exactly what was behind the door: a safe room, a secure bunker in the middle of the house in which the homeowner could hide in case of a home invasion. She thought of the dead men in the house and realized these men had never had a chance to get there.

"The cops are coming," KC said.

"We've got maybe three minutes before they arrive. You can open this," Annie said, pointing to the steel door. "I know you can."

"And how do you know that?"

"Because," Annie said, "you have opened this type of door before."

KC's heart began to race. Beyond her sister, Michael, Busch, and Simon, no living person knew her background.

"You knew exactly who I was at the airport," KC said.

Annie nodded. "If I'd told you about this you never would have come. I've got three days to stop a madman; I didn't have the luxury to put up a help-wanted sign or convince you to help me. So, yes, I duped you, and I'm sorry for that. But if you give a damn about saving hundreds, even thousands of lives, you'll do what I ask."

"Why should I believe you?"

"You have no reason whatsoever to believe me," Annie said.

"You didn't bring me along 'just in case.'" KC's anger grew as she fully understood how she had been played. "You had every intention of killing these men when you walked through that door."

"Please help me," Annie said, almost pleading.

KC stared at her innocent-looking face, knowing full well this woman was lying to her. That this woman was more deadly than any woman she had ever known.

"If this matter was not of the utmost urgency, if this wasn't about something that threatens national security, do you think I could have procured a military transport to get us here?"

KC recognized the truth in what Annie said, and realized there was little chance of her surviving if she didn't cooperate, at least in the short term.

Her jumbled mind slowly cleared and she focused on the door, the hinges, the surrounding walls.

This was more Michael's forte; he was the one who could penetrate anything. She was the planner, and the jobs she had pulled in the past were generally in museums, private homes, and offices where the artwork was out in the open, not concealed behind walls of steel.

She had opened a door like this in Florence, in the home of a ninety-two-year-old industrialist. Salvatore Giannini had a painting that had belonged to the Church, a Fracetti that had disappeared from a Venetian cathedral during World War II back when Giannini was Sergeant Carmine Mattolo in Mussolini's army, collecting masterpieces for Il Duce's personal enjoyment. KC had studied the schematics of that door for weeks and knew its weakness lay in its safety measures.

That door, like the one before her, was six feet by three feet; its locking system consisted of six enormous rods, large deadbolts that, when activated, sank two feet into the steel door jamb, rendering the door impenetrable.

But KC knew it was not always tremendous force that was needed to penetrate such a barrier.

"I need an extension cord and a small knife," she told Annie.

KC turned her attention to the keypad, pried off the faceplate, and examined the circuitry behind it.

Annie returned with a long orange cord and a paring knife. Without a word, KC stripped the female side of the cord away, exposing and separating the two wires and the ground.

"Go plug this in." KC handed Annie the other end.

KC examined the circuitry wires and followed a blue and orange one that ran back into the wall separate from the main bundle.

Climbing up the shelves, she pushed aside the false ceiling tiles. Poking her head inside, she could see the thick metal walls of the safe room, walls she already knew couldn't be breached. She examined a steel ventilation shaft that ran into the concrete slab above. Again, its construction prevented any chance of access. KC ignored all that in favor of a small orange box that protruded from the air shaft where it met the metal wall. Two inches square, it was the Achilles' heel of the entire design.

She pulled off the orange cover to reveal a copper box, no screws, no visible way of opening it—but she didn't need to open it.

She gently pried apart the two exposed wires of the orange cord, ensuring they didn't touch, and immediately laid them upon either side of the small copper box.

Sparks flew and thin wisps of smoke curled up into the confined space.

The small copper box was the one fail-safe in the event the air in the small enclosed safe room became compromised. Fire, gas, lack of oxygen would spell certain death for its occupants. If it came down to either death or capture, the circuit within the small box would override the locks, sparing its occupants' lives.

With a deep metallic clang, the six bars in the re-cessed door below pulled back.

The sound of distant sirens began to reach them. Annie ran to the living room and looked through the telescope at the road entrance below to see a stream of police cars heading up the road. "We've got maybe two minutes," she yelled.

As the door swung open, KC leaped down from atop the shelves and realized the space she'd opened wasn't a safe room but an armory filled with guns and rifles of all makes and models, from pistols to sniper rifles, grenades, and Semtex. There was a metal shelf filled with stacks of money: U.S. dollars, euros, yen. Millions. And in the far corner sat a single safe, three feet square, the dial and handle in the center of the door.

"That should be easy for you," Annie said from the doorway.

KC held her anger in check and leaned down. She knew the lock well, rotary, three-number combo; the fifty-year-old safe was more than familiar. She had learned how to open it from her mentor, Iblis, when she was all of fifteen, practicing for hours that became days and weeks until she felt she could practically see through the two-inch metal as the tumblers fell.

"I need a crystal glass."

Annie returned in seconds and handed her a whiskey glass.

Laying the mouth of the glass just above the dial, she rested her ear on the bottom, allowing the crystal chamber to amplify the inner mechanics. She spun the wheel three times to the left. With her ears attuned, her fingers feeling for the slightest vibration, she picked up the click of the first tumbler falling into place. She rotated the wheel gently to the right . . . until she heard the second tumbler fall into place with the first, grabbing hold of its neighbor. Again to the left . . . *click*.

She turned the handle and pulled the door open. There were no jewels, no pots of gold, no priceless works of art, just two ordinary-looking items: a long tube and a single notebook.

KC pulled them out, glancing at the handwritten notations on each. While KC spoke six languages, this wasn't one of them; the Chinese characters were as unfamiliar as Braille.

"What the hell are these?" KC asked.

"That's classified," Annie replied tersely, as she snatched the items from KC's hands. "And we've got to go. Now."

They ran to the living room, but as KC headed for the hallway leading to the front door, Annie grabbed her by the arm. "Single-access road, cops have already sealed it off at the bottom, we've got to leave the car."

"They'll trace it back—"

"—to a fictitious company."

As the sirens grew louder, Annie turned to KC. "You're welcome to stay and try to explain all this . . ."

KC glared at Annie as the raven-haired woman opened the rear glass door and ran outside. The approaching sirens, one of the most dreaded sounds in her life, drowned out all other thoughts but the need to escape.

KC dashed out the back door without a backward glance.

CHAPTER 10

Colonel Lucas flipped open his notebook computer, and the image of a conference room with four officers sitting around a table came into focus.

Lucas looked into the camera on his laptop.

"How are you, Colonel?" a white-haired general asked.

"Alive." Lucas's tone was filled with shame.

"You should take some time off, Isaac."

Lucas sat forward, moving closer to the camera. "You know me better than that, General."

"I do. That doesn't mean I'm wrong, though. When this is done, you need to take a break."

"Understood, sir."

"Are you ready to give us an update?"

"The file was gone."

"And the puzzle box?"

"It was a counterfeit, it was smashed to pieces on the floor. Old man Marconi was trying to sell Xiao a fake and it cost him and his family their lives. But we know where the original file is."

"Why didn't you go for that first?"

"It's a bit more difficult," Lucas said. "My team is in place and active on it."

"Your team?" a bald, square-jawed general said.

"Captain Rogers and Captain Hendricks arrived back here from Japan without having received any explanation for their dismissal."

"With all due respect, four of my men were killed on that yacht, my best men."

"We know, Isaac," the white-haired leader said.

"Rogers and Hendricks are good men," Lucas said, "but I've assembled a new team, one whose loyalty, talent, and diligence I'm assured of. Each member is dealing with a specific task and unaware of any other aspects of the mission. I need to compartmentalize information."

"Outside contractors pose their own set of problems, Isaac," the white-haired general warned. "We can't afford another Blackwater situation."

"I need very specific skill sets," Lucas said. "And not to worry, I have these people's full cooperation and focus."

"You'd better be sure of that," the bald general said. "If Xiao has the Dragon's Breath—"

"Gentlemen, we all know we were compromised; someone on the inside assisted Xiao. I don't have the time to conduct an investigation at this moment to figure out who that person is. I'll leave that to you."

"Understood," the general said. "But we're walking a very fine line here, lives are at stake. If the Dragon's Breath gets out in the open, do you know how many lives—"

"I'm well aware of the implications and consequences, trust me."

"After thirty years, you don't need our confirmation on that," the white-haired general said.

"You think he survived the sinking of that boat?" the bald general asked.

"I don't know."

"How could you not know? A simple bullet would have given you the answer we all want to hear."

"I don't see how he could have survived. He was bound, the yacht was detonated and sank. But until I see his body myself, until I have that file and the Dragon's Breath in my possession, I'm acting as if he is still alive. I know what he has threatened to do. I've spent the better part of two years tracking him."

"And losing him . . ." the bald general said. "We are out of time."

"Not quite yet."

"In my book, five days is out of time."

The simple truth of the statement was followed by silence.

"When I get this file and the information it contains, the situation will be neutralized."

"And if you fail?"

"I do not have that option."

"Where is this file?" the bald general asked.

"Asia."

"Where in Asia?"

"Gentlemen, I shared my information about Marconi's yacht in Italy with you, the only people outside of my team, and now my team is dead."

"Are you accusing us of something?" the bald general exploded.

"Not at all, General. I'm just stating a fact. Xiao is manipulating us all. Somehow he knows what is going on. Somehow, I fear, he even knows about this conversation we are having right now."

CHAPTER 11

Annie and KC cut through the back garden and leaped the stone wall as the scream of police sirens approached the house. Not a word was spoken as they raced down the hillside, through the cover of trees, scrub, and bramble.

Annie had had her doubts about KC, but the intel couldn't have been more accurate. Under pressure this woman thrived; she had gained access to not only the safe room but the safe itself in just under two minutes. Annie experienced a boost of confidence knowing that this woman possessed an arsenal of unique talents that would be extremely helpful where they were headed next, a place where the security and the obstacles would be ten times tougher than what they'd just encountered.

They emerged on Avenida de la Montana, crossed the busy thoroughfare and headed into the Albayzin section of the city, the Moorish quarter that was coming to life in the morning hour, the sweet smell of sausage and spiced lamb wafting through its steep and narrow cobblestone streets.

Annie patted the notebook and the tube tucked under her arm and scanned the cafés from behind her oversized sunglasses. No one suspected the two women to be anything more than friends heading out to breakfast, their beauty not only turning heads but painting illusions, as people don't tend to think of pretty women as criminals.

Annie spotted Rick Vajos in a small outdoor café, sipping coffee, and quickly cut across the street to meet him.

"Would you ladies like some coffee?" Rick said as he offered them a seat next to him.

KC remained silent, her head slowly turning, expecting the police to arrive.

"You need to stay behind," Annie said to Rick, "see what kind of a hornet's nest we've stirred up in that house. Get some cameras on it, let Lucas know if anyone shows up."

"Where are you heading?"

"We need to get out of Granada."

"You be careful," Rick said as he took her hand, squeezing it to make a point.

He handed Annie a key. "A white Mini Cooper is parked in the lot around the corner."

"Thanks." She nodded as he still held on to her hand. There was more than professional courtesy in his gesture.

"And, Annie, remember: fate doesn't rule your future, you do."

ANNIE WAS BORN Annabeth Sandoval to Midiva Rajo and Carlos Sandoval, though before her first birthday, her fashion photographer father abandoned his young family and was never spoken of again.

They had lived a glittering life. Her mother was a fashion model whose beautiful face graced the covers of *Vogue, Elle,* and all the other top magazines of her day. Midiva was stick-thin with dark Mediterranean eyes that were mirrored in her baby daughter's face. Despite the birth of Annabeth, Midiva kept her figure and her source of income well into her late twenties when Annabeth was all of ten. She would likely have ridden the wave of success for many more years, if she hadn't fallen victim to what she called her family's curse.

They spoke of it as a curse—and with all of the evidence at hand it seemed it could be nothing but that. Midiva's mother had died at the age of twenty-nine, leaving behind twelve-year-old Midiva and her fourteen-year-old sister, Rose. Their grandmother had passed at twenty-eight, and it was believed that their great-grandmother had not lived to see twenty-five. Rose had died as a teenager. Each woman had been struck down in her prime by a different disease, alike only in their swiftness and cruelty. Not one ever knew the other side of thirty.

When Midiva died from pancreatic cancer, four months shy of her thirtieth birthday, there was no one left to care for Annabeth: no sister, no grandmother, no cousins, no father to magically appear and rescue her.

Annabeth fell into the foster care system in New York City, where she had lived for the last six months of her mother's life. She had spent the first ten years of her life in the glamorous cities of Paris, Milan, and London, eating the finest foods, sleeping in the finest hotels, safe in the warm embrace of her glittering mother. But now, all that became a distant memory, replaced by cold dinners from a can and sleeping in crowded bedrooms where she had to battle for a blanket. She was teased, taunted, and sometimes beaten up by the other foster children. Bouncing from home to home, she became in quick succession a member of two families who plagued the system only for the paycheck it provided, offering no love or kindness to young Annabeth.

That all changed when she arrived at her third foster home. The McGuinns were different; they had two young boys of their own and one foster child by the name of Enrique Vajos, who preferred to be called Rick so as not to stick out in the Irish home. Annabeth was given her own bedroom, the food was warm and comforting, they made her go to school and watched her do her homework. The McGuinns were by no means wealthy, barely eking out a living in the North Bronx as elementary school teachers. They had no intention of shuffling Annabeth off to another family, and they let her know they were committed to seeing her reach her eighteenth birthday and establish a life for herself.

But despite the reassuring comforts of this home, she feared she was preparing herself for a life that would never come to pass, that death would find her at a young age no matter what she did.

She learned the most from Rick. The seventeen-year-old boy was wise beyond his years; he had been a ward of the system since he was six, barely able to remember what his birth mother looked like the day she was arrested, never knowing his father, who was in prison for first-degree murder. With his family history of drugs and criminal activity, he understood how hard it was to fight against fate, especially when society seemed to judge you by your parents' actions. Like Annabeth, he understood how hard it was to be torn from your childhood reality and thrust into a bureaucratic system, but he was determined to have a different future. He told Annabeth that there was no such thing as fate, some kind of invisible force steering people's lives. He taught her that they lived in a world where people all too often believed that statistics were destiny, but that was far from the truth. Statistics said that no batter would ever get a hit in the bottom of the ninth with an oh-and-two count on a Friday night in May. Statistics said that if you weren't married by forty, you stood less than a 10 percent chance of ever saying "I do." That no airline stock would ever go up in value by more than 8 percent in a year, no matter how well the stock market was doing. It was all bullshit, Rick said. Men hit baseballs, people got married, and stocks rose and fell as a result of people's own actions, not fate. Statistics didn't rule her future; the only thing that did was her own actions.

Annabeth took what he said to heart. She was determined to outlive her mother, and every other woman in her family. She devoted herself to becoming as physically and mentally fit as she could be.

But her world crashed once again. She was fifteen when a gang of three broke into their small New York City house. They tied up the McGuinns and their two boys in the living room. They took Annabeth to her bedroom and tied her spread-eagled to her bed and left her there as they ransacked the place. But their goal went beyond a quick snatch and grab. They were gang initiates out to earn their stripes.

She heard the report of a gun four times, each teeth-shattering gun blast preceded by screaming, which finally ceased upon the final shot. She struggled against her binds, her wrists and ankles bleeding with her attempts. Tears flowed down her face as she imagined what had happened.

And then the three entered her room.

RICK ARRIVED HOME late from his after-school job; it was nearly midnight when he found the bodies. He looked upon the scene of the tragedy and ran to Annabeth's room to find her there naked, tied up, staring at the ceiling. Alive. The police had questioned the two teenage foster children, initially suspecting them of involvement, but they soon understood the true nature of the attack, especially when the evidence of Annabeth's rape was impossible to ignore. They told Rick and Annabeth that every effort would be made to capture the killers, but they could make no promises.

Rick, being eighteen and designated in the McGuinns' will as the sole heir to their small estate—all of thirty thousand dollars—assumed guardianship of Annabeth. He had enlisted in the Army and was scheduled to leave for basic training in three weeks, but they gave him an open-ended deferment in light of the circumstances.

Annabeth had become a shell, barely speaking, consumed with silent rage. She slept with the lights on, she triple-locked the doors and windows. She cried on Rick's shoulder for hours at a time, inconsolable in her grief, lost in her fear of being attacked again.

Rick picked her up one evening, forcing her to leave the house, and took her to a gun range. He put a pistol in her hand and had an instructor give her lessons on how to shoot. Three nights a week they would go to the range. And to Rick's amazement, as much as her own, she found she had natural talent.

Annabeth could hit a bull's-eye dead center from fifty yards. Each weapon she tried was like an extension of her arm, of her mind. Her fear slowly subsided as she learned how to protect herself, as she learned she could take charge of her own life. Rick then brought her to a martial arts class, where she learned the basics of self-defense, hand-to-hand combat, the simple moves a woman could use to ward off attack. The ability to protect herself without the use of a weapon. The lessons reminded her that she controlled her destiny, not some gang member, some thug on the street, some twist of fate.

WITH NO BREAK in the triple-homicide case and seemingly no effort on the part of the police to find the McGuinns' killer, Rick and Annabeth began to drive around at night themselves, hoping they might spot them and report them to the authorities. And one night, on 179th Street, they did. They photographed the killers, followed them, noted where they lived, and turned the information over to the police. But nothing happened: no arrests, no investigation, absolutely nothing.

Despite her newfound abilities, Annabeth's dreams were still filled with the horror she had experienced: the sound of the McGuinns being cut down, one by one. The images of the three killers walking into her bedroom that evening nine months earlier still filled her mind. She knew the dreams and the day terrors would never subside until she'd achieved some sort of resolution.

SHE FOUND THEM in a dirty three-bedroom apartment. There were six of them there that day: the three who had raped her and murdered her foster family, and three other gang members. She had watched them for a week, studying their patterns, their arrivals and departures, and noted that around 7:00 a.m. on any day was almost always when these nocturnal creatures finally put their heads down to rest.

She bought a gun off the street, a silencer, two boxes of ammo, and wore gloves when she loaded up. She parked outside the building and waited for sunrise. The three punks arrived home at 5:00 a.m., followed by three others. As the tenement's activity began to wane, she left her car and entered the building, taking the fire stairs to the second floor. She listened intently for sound or movement. She wore a stocking cap over her black hair, she had dirtied her face in an attempt to mar her beauty, and she dressed in rags, all in the hopes of being ignored by any passersby.

She stood in the hallway, the stench of urine and burnt toast filling her nose. She gave herself a ten count, stepped to the door, and kicked it in.

There were two men asleep on the couch; a single bullet to each split open their heads before they could move. She spun to the first bedroom and fired at the man who was coming out the door, gun in hand, never knowing what happened to him.

She found her three primary marks on the floor in the second bedroom, sleeping on dirty mattresses. She saw their sleeping faces up close, their images filling her with hate, churning her mind.

She paused, allowing the moment to wash over her.

She drew back her leg and kicked the mattress, waking them, watching as the reality of an assassin standing over them registered in their feeble brains.

As they leaped from their beds, reaching for their guns, she pulled the trigger. Without fanfare, without a word, she fired. Three quick shots, taking each of them down. In her mind, she was invincible. She had walked into the lion's den, stood over thieves, murderers, and rapists, and wiped them from this earth.

She emerged unscathed from the building as if nothing was wrong, climbed into the car, and drove off.

Annabeth had heard people say that revenge left a person with an empty, unsatisfied feeling, but that wasn't the case for her. She was filled with something she had never felt before. An elation, a freeing of her tethered, overburdened mind. The men who had raped her, who had killed the McGuinns, were dead by her hand, and she wanted to shout to the world of her accomplishment. Her ability, her demeanor, her fearlessness, they had all come to her naturally.

She arrived home to find Rick awake and waiting for

her. Without her saying a word, he knew what she had done; he saw the pain was gone from her eyes, saw her new sense of invincibility. He could see what he had created and it scared him.

Annabeth had found her calling. Following Rick's lead, she enlisted in the Army, quickly rising through the ranks. One of the first female spec ops, she honed her skills in hand-to-hand combat, tae kwon do, aikido. She became adept at using guns, rifles, excelling at whatever weapon she touched. She became an expert in counterintelligence, infiltration, and combat. An unlikely mix in an unlikely world. Her file was classified, and those who were privileged to see it found it redacted, more than 50 percent blacked out.

And in an unlikely congruency, one that proved an excellent cover, Annabeth had grown into a dark beauty like her mother. Cutting her jet-black hair short for convenience only enhanced her allure; her dark eyes and strong cheekbones would have been more at home on a runway than a battlefield. She wasn't sure if it was the murders of the McGuinns, her brutal rape, or the cruel death of her mother, but every time she killed, she relished it as an elixir that made her feel omnipotent. She felt no shame in her acts, each victim becoming a means to a righteous end and a way toward the restoration of her damaged heart.

But all things aside, her beauty, her childhood, her past, Annabeth was an excellent killer.

"How dare you?" KC screamed as the jet door was pulled closed. "You set me up."

Annie calmly took a seat, finally looking up as KC stormed up the aisle. "As I recall, you were happy to get on my plane, happy to go to Spain."

"All under false pretenses."

"Now you understand why I couldn't possibly have told you what I needed you to do."

"You put my life in jeopardy!" KC's voice grew shrill with anger. "You killed those people."

"You're not going to let this go, are you?"

"Let this go?" KC screamed, her face red with rage. "You just involved me in a robbery, a murder—"

"Relax . . ." Annie pointed at KC's face. "You're giving yourself a bloody nose."

KC wiped a drop of blood from her nose, ignored it, and continued tearing into Annie. "You killed them in cold blood, forced me to commit a major felony—"

"Come now." Annie smiled. "You can't possibly think I don't know everything about you, about everything you have done over the last fifteen years; about all of those thefts, those paintings and boxes and artifacts . . ."

The jet engines cycled up, the plane lurched forward, and it began to taxi. KC reluctantly sat, strapping herself in, dabbing her nose once more, confirming the trickle of blood had stopped.

". . . so please don't give me this phony attitude about what you just did."

"I never killed a man."

Annie nodded. "True, but I saw it in your eyes, you could do it."

"Never."

The engines' whine grew into a scream and the jet raced down the runway. KC stared out the window as the ground sped by, and in seconds, the jet leaped into the air, the nose angling upward as they climbed into the sky.

"All those things you did in your past," Annie said, "it wasn't just for the money, to support your sister. As much as you want to deny it, it was for something else, the thrill. I saw it in your eyes back in Granada, when you were thinking, opening that safe. It's your passion, it's your rush. It's the most alive I've seen you since we met."

"How do you know all this?"

Annie just smiled coldly.

KC glared at Annie. "Just drop me in London and stay the hell away from me."

Annie inhaled, unbuckled her seatbelt, walked toward the front of the plane, and entered the cockpit.

KC looked out the window as they climbed over the snow-capped peaks of the Sierras. She didn't know what to think. But she knew one thing. She'd seen it in Annie's eyes when she shot that man, she'd seen it as she'd tried to explain herself: Annie's smile hid her dark soul.

KC realized she was nothing more than a prisoner now. She'd been captured and was now being held at twenty-five thousand feet at the whim of her host. She couldn't believe any government would authorize the tactics Annie employed, and wondered just how much truth there was to her words. KC reached for and touched the delicate silver necklace around her neck and longed for this day to be over. Michael had given her the necklace when they'd first started dating, when they fell in love, when she was so sure of life and the direction in which she was heading. When she'd trusted Michael and was confident they had a future together.

As the plane leveled off, the late-morning sun in front of them was climbing into the sky. A shiver ran through her. They were not heading toward London. They were heading due east.

CHAPTER 12

Hong Kong was the most densely packed city in the world, but from ten thousand feet on final approach, Michael saw the city as the Chinese wished it to be displayed to the world: grand, spectacular, brightly lit in a rainbow of colors. Enormous skyscrapers reached to heaven, tickling the sky, a concentration of towers appearing as if ten cities were crammed together in the space of one. The giant glass structures rose out of the black harbor, silhouetted against the mountains, where the sun was setting behind them. Surrounded on three sides by the South China Sea, the historic metropolis sat at the Pearl River delta, the virtual capital of the Asian continent, the only city in the world on a par with New York.

The Boeing Business Jet touched down at Hong Kong International Airport and taxied to a private terminal in the far-side shipping area. Michael had never been to Hong Kong; in fact, he'd only been to Asia—India and the Himalayas to be exact—once, his leisure and business trips mostly having been confined to the Americas and Europe. He had always been fascinated by the ancient cultures of the Orient, but had learned of them through books, films, and television, where they were simplified and translated for the Western mind. While America was an infant at 235 years of age, European countries prided themselves on their cultures stretching back 500, 800, in some instances 1,200 years, but they all paled next to China, a 4,000-year-old culture with a rich, detailed recorded history from 1,700 years before the birth of Christ.

The jet finally came to a stop. Ground personnel threw chocks under the wheels as a set of gangway stairs was rolled up to the door. When Jon released the exit door with a loud hiss, Michael could feel the pressure release and smell the faint odor of jet exhaust as it invaded the cabin.

Michael and Busch grabbed their bags from the front storage closet and followed Jon down the stairs. They both watched as the coffin was rolled out of the baggage compartment. Two men in military dress uniforms draped a United States flag over it and rolled it over to an adjacent U.S. military cargo plane.

Jon stood next to Michael, his eyes on the coffin as it disappeared up into the belly of the aircraft.

"Where are they taking him?" Michael asked.

"He'll get a burial with full military honors."

Michael looked at Jon.

"Killed on a classified mission, at an undisclosed location." Jon's eyes were still glued to the coffin as the door closed. "He'll receive a hero's welcome back in the U.S."

Jon turned and walked away. Michael thought that he had heard a hint of emotion in the man's voice, though he wasn't sure if it was disgust, sympathy, or regret.

A shuttle van pulled up with Jon at the wheel. Without a word, Michael and Paul threw their bags over their shoulders and hopped in back. As the electric vehicle drove across the tarmac onto a service road, Michael glimpsed the enormous terminal, the third largest in the world. Built on an artificial island, reclaimed from the sea, it was accessed by the Tsing Ma suspension bridge and miles of tunnels. Planes came and went on the two runways with the frequency of taxis at a stand in the center of Manhattan.

Instead of heading toward the terminal, Jon turned left and drove toward a series of docks on the east side of the grand complex and pulled up alongside a sixty-foot dark-blue yacht. The boat was sleek and aerodynamic, with a salon, a rear deck, and a second-floor deck. Jon led them across the dock, up the gangplank, and onto the rear of the boat. Busch stepped aboard left foot first.

Jon walked through the salon, through the open door of the bridge, said a few words to the captain, and returned.

"Wait here," Jon said. "I need to fetch some things." And he ran down the gangplank back to the van and drove off.

Michael and Busch looked around at the luxury, at the teak and brass finishes, the leather furnishings; this was not military-issue. Without saying a word, they both knew Jon had connections.

Through open teak doors, Michael could see the captain, a man with dark eyes and tea-colored skin who sat silently in wait at the helm. Busch walked up and offered his hand, but the man ignored it, not even bothering to acknowledge his presence with a look.

"Nice," Busch said as he walked back through the cabin and out onto the rear deck. "Friendly guy."

"Not everyone shares your outlook on life," Michael said as he stared across Hong Kong Harbor at the Chinese junks, the sleek sailboats, and gleaming megayachts whose running lights seemed to stretch on forever. Michael rolled the fingers of his right hand on the rail as if playing trills on a piano.

"So what are you thinking?" Busch asked.

"Huh?"

"You drum your fingers when you're lost in thought. Did you look at those plans?"

"In case you forgot, I was standing right next to you." Michael paused a moment. "I have no idea how we're going to do this."

The two of them looked out over the water, lost in thought, until finally . . .

"Don't worry," Busch said with a smile, slapping Michael's back. "You're far better with the impossible than the easy. Let's get there before you consume yourself with doubt."

"Where do you think they took KC?"

Busch turned and looked at Michael. "If there is one woman on this planet who can stay alive in the worst of circumstances, it's her."

But all Michael could think about was Annie's eyes. It didn't matter how emotionally strong and resourceful KC was. Michael had seen Annie's eyes when she shot the man in New York. She had acted without remorse; it wasn't her first kill, nor would it be her last.

ANNIE POURED TWO glasses of wine. She walked up the aisle of the luxury jet and set a glass in the recessed cup holder of KC's chair.

"You proved yourself far more impressively than I thought you would," Annie said, "than any of us thought."

KC looked out the window at the cloudless sky, ignoring Annie.

"I had my doubts," Annie continued. "Extreme doubts, in fact. But the colonel was so insistent."

"Where are we going?" KC asked, still looking out the window.

"You did us a great service. Have a sip of wine," Annie said, tilting her glass toward KC's.

KC turned and stared at Annie. "Where are we going?"

"We will need your services, your particular talents over the next two days."

"Absolutely not," KC said as she shook her head.

Annie took another sip of wine. "The Granada police will take quite an interest in you."

"Until I explain how I got there, who shot those men. I don't think your country wants that getting out."

"I do like you, KC. You're unique," Annie smiled and nodded, "like me."

"I'm nothing like you."

"I disobeyed orders for you," Annie said as she

moved closer, bending down, her face within inches of KC's face. "I was told to be direct, brutal if need be, but I thought maybe—two loners, both unconventional, both smart—maybe we could be friends."

"Friends?" KC shook her head, smiling back, her eyes mocking. "I used to be alone in the world because I chose to be. You're alone because others choose to avoid someone like you."

Annie glared at KC. "I'd like to show you something."

KC turned away, refusing to make eye contact.

The TV monitor on the front bulkhead lit up with static until an image of the interior of a jet filled the screen. It took a moment for the two figures to become clear: Michael and an unknown Asian man.

"What the hell is going on?" KC looked closer. And as her question went unanswered, the sound of the jet engines' whine seemed to grow, portending danger, reminding her of her confinement at twenty-five thousand feet.

But unlike most women, KC didn't crumble. "Who is Michael with?"

"You're coming with us, and you will do exactly as we say. If you deviate from our directives, if you attempt to escape . . . one phone call and that man will snap Michael's neck like a twig."

THE DEEP SOUND of a ship's horn cut across the harbor as the dark-blue yacht backed up out of the dock, its large motor churning the water. Jon was on the bridge with the captain after taking nearly an hour to return with two large duffel bags slung over his shoulders. Without a word, he had carried them to the bridge and closed the teak doors behind him.

Clearing the dock, the boat turned about and headed into the open harbor. Paul looked out over the water, his thick blond hair whipped by the wind, and reached into his pocket, pulling out a battered brass pocket watch. He flipped open the clear glass lid and looked at the compass floating within.

Busch had grown up with boats, as his father had been a commercial fisherman. He had gone out on several occasions with his father, swabbing the decks, sitting up nights with the crew, listening to their risqué jokes and stories not fit for children. Those weeks off Cape Cod and the Continental Shelf had been a magical time. He'd been baptized into a man's world, bonding with his father only to lose him to the sea. One evening, he'd tucked him into bed, kissed him good night, and walked out the door never to return. The compass watch was his father's; his mother had given it to him at the funeral, telling him it would always point him in the right direction.

The yacht began to accelerate, picking up speed, twenty knots, thirty knots, until suddenly the bow of the boat began to lift out of the water on hydrofoils. And as it did so, the boat picked up even more speed, racing across the water faster than Paul had ever thought possible. As they cut across the Pearl River Delta to the island of Macau, Busch estimated they were traveling at nearly fifty knots and would make the thirty-seven-mile run in less than forty-five minutes.

The island of Macau was a former Portuguese port that had since grown into the gaming capital of the world, far exceeding the former leader, Las Vegas, in decadence. If "What happens in Vegas stays in Vegas" was their phrase, with a wink and smile, Macau's was "What happened in Macau never happened in Macau."

As the boat slowed, the craft settled down off its hydrofoils back into the water; slowing to twenty-five knots felt like they were crawling. The captain took a wide arc and pulled up to a modern dock aglow with light. Large ferry-sized hydrofoils filled ten slips to their left. Streams of people poured out of the ships, unleashed into a world very different from the city they had left behind.

Pulling up to the dock, Jon leaped off with the two large duffels upon his shoulders and headed straight into the ferry terminal. Michael came ashore right behind him and followed. And as Busch's left foot hit the dock, the boat and its silent captain raced away.

Busch caught up and the three climbed the terminal's stairs. A distant rumble began to fill the air.

"What the hell is that?" Busch said, looking around.

Michael heard it, too, but followed Jon without a word.

Michael emerged from the ferry terminal into a mass of people tens of thousands strong. All eyes were fixed, unwavering in silent anticipation, focused on a vacant strip of road fifty yards in the distance.

The roar of thunder approached, though the evening sky was crystal-clear. The sound grew, shaking the ground, strong enough to vibrate up through their bodies. The air was heavy with the smell of exhaust and gasoline.

And then from around the corner they exploded into sight, Formula 3 race cars, hurtling down the narrow streets of Macau. The roar grew, its pitch climbing from thunder to an otherworldly scream. Bright red, deep blue, traveling at over 160 miles per hour, accelerating down the straightaway, impossibly fast, and in the blink of an eye they were gone. But then more skidded around the corner, hugging the ground, their bodies painted yellow, green, white, their engines howling in pursuit of the leader. They were sleek, beautiful, with the heart of a beast as their drivers pinned the accelerators, white-knuckling the steering wheels with nothing in their eyes but the will to win.

The Macau Grand Prix was a race known the world over, attracting not only Formula 3 racers but motorcyclists and touring cars. The three-point-eight-mile track wove through the narrow streets, past the historic district, and through the heart of the ancient city.

The crowds overflowed the bleachers, the various stands; necks craned from behind concrete barriers, heads poked out of windows, a mass of people over fifty thousand strong.

Though the Macau Grand Prix didn't have the cachet of the Monaco Grand Prix's Triple Crown of Motorsport, it attracted not only the refined and proper but the young and hip.

Macau was the Monte Carlo of the East but on a far grander scale. Where the legendary Belle Époque Monte Carlo Casino, the standard bearer of glamour and prestige, was sixty-five thousand square feet, the casinos of the Cotai strip were high-octane versions with more than two million square feet of gambling. There was the Macau Jockey Club, a racetrack where thoroughbreds competed for Triple Crown–sized stakes, and handicappers spent days and evenings betting on their favorite horse. Michael instantly thought the city was like Vegas, Churchill Downs, and Indianapolis rolled into one.

With Jon in the lead, they made their way through the crowds, past the pit stops and enormous gas tanks, the fumes so thick they could almost be seen. Michael knew the fuel was high-octane, highly flammable. One of Busch's forever fears was burning alive, something that had haunted him since his youth, when he was burned on his father's boat, something that almost took his life years earlier, something that Michael knew still ran in Busch's veins.

Moving away from the noise of the race, the three walked into the heart of Macau. The Portuguese had arrived on its shores in the sixteenth century, bringing with them their vast culture, Christian religion, and diverse culinary tastes. For more than four hundred years the Iberian people and their customs had blended with the local Chinese and theirs, bringing about a unique world combining East and West.

Walking the cobblestone streets past the European architecture, the smell of cooking in the air, Michael felt transported to the other side of the world only to be reminded by the beautiful ancient temples and crowds that he was actually in the heart of Asia.

As they continued, the crowds began to thin out and

they found themselves in a decrepit part of town: run-down buildings, gangs milling at corners, looking for a target. They walked down old streets, rutted and smelling of urine and refuse, finally arriving at an unkempt brick building six stories high, curtains pulled in every window.

As they entered, Michael knew at once where they were. The brothel was tired and dusty. Women of various cultures dressed in colorful simple dresses sat about with far-off looks in their eyes. A glamorous hostess smiled at the group; unlike the other women, this woman still possessed an unmarred beauty and a clear mind. The woman smiled, nodding at Jon, her eyes never falling upon Michael or Busch.

Jon headed past the front desk, ignoring the hostess as if he owned the place, and walked through a curtain into a dark back hall. Michael and Busch followed him up a flight of stairs. The echoes of false passion reverberated through the stairwell and halls as they walked past a series of rooms to a chipped wooden door at the end of the hallway. There was no handle on the door; incongruously, a shiny metal keypad was shoulder-high next to the doorjamb. Jon pressed his thumb to a small pad, simultaneously punching a code into the keypad, and the door unlatched.

They entered a sparse apartment, the door slamming behind them. The living room had a couch and a host of chairs arranged around a long dining table. Against the wall was a large workstation covered in an array of electronic equipment; four monitors displayed images of the hallways and building exits. Upon turning, Busch could see that the wooden door was anything but, as the interior was made of pure steel; the windows were tempered, bulletproof.

"Nice safe house," Michael said to Busch.

Jon threw down the two duffels. Unzipping the first, he pulled a pistol from the small of his back and threw it into what Busch now realized was a bag filled with weapons, assault rifles, and pistols; he thought he glimpsed a grenade and a block of C-4 before Jon zipped it up.

Jon opened a double-wide door to reveal a filing cabinet, a safe, a gun rack stocked with an array of more pistols and assault rifles, and shelves stacked with clips and two-way radios.

"All the comforts of home," Busch said as he walked to the closet and picked up a 9mm Glock.

"Feel free," Jon said, pointing at the shelf. "Clips are up there."

Busch grabbed and slammed home a clip and turned the gun about in his hand. "Do you realize how badly I want to use this right now?"

Jon nodded, understanding Busch's subtext. "Wouldn't prove healthy to your friend's ex, though." Jon opened an adjacent closet filled with clothes and put on a sport coat. "No rest for the weary."

"I think he means wicked," Busch said under his breath as he ejected the clip and put the gun back. He opened his bag, removed a change of neatly pressed clothes, and changed into the preppy uniform of a blue sport coat and khakis.

Michael turned and saw Jon affixing a large gold chain about his neck, his fingers already adorned with rings, his wrist wrapped in a Breitling watch. Reaching into the armory closet, into a drawer built into the wall, he withdrew a large wad of cash and stuffed it in his pocket. The man on the Manhattan street yesterday morning was different from the man on the plane, who couldn't be more different from the man who stood before them now. Jon had not just changed clothes; it was as if he had changed bodies and personalities.

Michael threw on a dark jacket over a white shirt and dark pants, less concerned with his appearance than Jon and Busch. His focus was on the room, what was available, his mind cataloguing everything he saw, from the weapons and the money to the files and the electronics at the workstation.

Jon turned to the door, and as he thumbed another pad and punched in the number to open the door, Michael realized this room was not only difficult to access but difficult to escape.

They exited the brothel to a limo, the door held open by its driver. They climbed in and headed up the street. Michael stared out the tinted windows as they drove through the foreign world, committing buildings and landmarks to memory. It was a habit he'd established on his first job, and it was the first task he performed whenever he visited a new city. Since he had gone legal, whether it was a conference, a business meeting in a different city, or a vacation, he always spent the first hour getting to know the territory because the first rule of survival was figuring out your escape route.

Michael had traveled all over Europe, to parts of the Middle East, and had been to northern India a year ago, but in all of those places he'd felt as if he could move without drawing attention. Here he was truly a foreigner in a foreign land. He didn't know the language, the people, or the customs. The modality of thought between the West and East was different in many respects. Here it was about balance, about dark and light, strong and weak. There would be no hiding among the masses, no getting lost in a crowd; he couldn't blend in, and if he got lost, he might as well be on an alien planet.

As much as he didn't want to admit it, he would need Jon—his language skills, his understanding of the world they were in. He would need him like a child needs his mother if he was to survive. And it sickened him, for there was no doubt in Michael's mind that Jon had every intention of killing them once the task was done.

Within minutes, they hit the Sai Van Bridge, a two-mile-long span over the river, leaving the Macau of old behind. And as they exited the other side, it was as if they had entered Oz, a magical world where the sky was aglow with brilliant colors, where fountains filled the air in glowing cascades of water.

They finally turned in to their destination, a modern world replicating an ancient one, but there would be no old-world locks to pick, no simple walls to breach. This was a world ruled by modern security and death, a world Michael would have to penetrate if he was to ever see KC again.

CHAPTER 13
LOS ANGELES 1974

Jane Lei was sixteen years old when Jon was born. Having lived in Los Angeles since she was three years old, she embraced everything American and considered herself American and nothing but. However, others didn't see her that way; her parents considered her Chinese, and as much as she wished to be part of the crowd, her Asian appearance set her apart. Her parents had come from Hong Kong, her father a senior vice president for Hong Kong International Bank, her mother a homemaker trying to raise her two daughters in a distant land. If you were white with an American accent, you were American; if you were Chinese with an American accent, American habits and values, you were still considered Chinese.

It was a January night, and she was on her way home from basketball practice, the coach keeping them for an extra session after Wednesday's 45–20 loss. She was tired and knew that with all of the homework she still had to deal with she would be tired until the weekend arrived. Running up the stairs from the locker room, she bumped into Mr. Tanaka. She knew him as the quiet janitor, emotionless and silent, and she smiled as she passed him mopping the floors of the school at this late hour. She raced out of the school, walking briskly through the cold night, and arrived home to an empty house; her parents were still at her younger sister Carol's swim meet. Herkamer rolled around on the floor, belly up, begging to be petted, and as she rubbed the golden retriever, and looked into his tired eyes, at the graying fur about his mouth, her nerves calmed. He was fifteen, had been part of her life since she could remember, and while he had grown slow in his old age, their bond would never diminish.

Jane made herself a grilled cheese sandwich, grabbed a glass of milk, and took it to her room, where she changed into her favorite sweats, settled in, and began her homework.

THE MAN SAT in his car, watching the house. The girl had entered more than an hour ago, the parents a half-hour later with another daughter. There was no mistaking their Han heritage; it was in their faces, eyes, and builds. He wrapped his hand around his pistol, sliding it into the holster at his waist. He reached into the rear of the car and picked up the katana, the lethal sword his father had passed to him ceremonially at the age of eighteen before he went off to join the military.

Ichero Tanaka had tried to control his anger at the teenager since he had started his janitorial job a month earlier. They lived in this large home while he rotted in anonymity, in a one-room hovel on the far side of town, thousands of miles from the country he had sacrificed so much for only to have it turn its back on him. How had his life slid so drastically? How had this family achieved so much despite their inferiority?

He waited until after midnight, as the last of the house's lights was extinguished. He found the rear door unlocked, smiling at their false sense of security. He silently slipped in and found the dog asleep on the floor, and as he took a step, the dog raised his head, snarling, growling, his hair hackled, but before he could let out a bark, the katana split the air and severed the dog's head.

Tanaka walked about the home, looking at the Chinese paintings, at the porcelain figurines on the mantel. While the exterior of the house was American colonial, the interior was provincial Chinese, everything he hated in life. Nausea rose in him as his past came rushing in.

Less than twenty-four hours after Pearl Harbor, Japan began its assault on Hong Kong. Hailing from Nagasaki, where his family worked building ships for the Imperial Navy, Tanaka was part of the Japanese invasion forces on December 8, 1942. Seventeen days later, on Christmas morning, he and his fellow soldiers attacked St. Stephen's Hospital, torturing and killing the wounded British soldiers and medical staff, the final step in their capture of the city. Later that day, he and his garrison were present when Governor Mark Young surrendered to the Japanese at their headquarters in the Peninsula Hotel. The day became forever known as Black Christmas.

For the next two years, Tanaka was a member of a team known as the *Kin no yuri,* or "Golden Lily," a select group that raided museums, temples, homes of the wealthy, banks, and industry, confiscating any and all valuables, with a particular emphasis on gold. He traveled throughout Southeast Asia under the direction of General Yamashita and assisted in the amassing of treasure, helping to deposit it in caves and tunnels in the Philippines to await shipment to Japan. Two and a half years later, on August 14, 1945, a Japanese warship was loaded with thousands of crates with a purported value in the billions of dollars. Most of the *Kin no yuri* team were assassinated, along with all of the workers involved with loading the ship, in order to protect the empire's secret. The ship and the treasure, what became known as Yamashita's gold, headed out to sea, its destination Japan.

The following day, the Japanese surrendered. Tanaka, having somehow avoided assassination, at first didn't understand what had happened, but quickly learned that six days earlier, much of his home city of Nagasaki had been destroyed by a plutonium bomb that someone had crassly named "Fat Man."

With his parents, aunts and uncles, and younger brothers all dead, he was taken into custody, tried, and thrown into prison for war crimes. Ten years later, his rage at China and America festering in his marrow, he was released, a broken, bitter man.

And as he looked now at the young girl sound asleep in her bed, a child embodying the culmination of his hate, he thought of something far worse than killing her, than removing her head, than sliding the blade into her young belly.

JANE WOKE FROM her dream into a nightmare. She felt the cold steel against her neck, her eyes following the glow off the blade up to the man with malevolent eyes, his hand suddenly clamping over her mouth.

"If you scream," he whispered, "if you make a single sound, I will cut off your head."

Frozen in terror, she watched as the man pulled back the covers, exposing her nightgown, her bare legs and arms. She could smell the garlic on his breath and the rot of his teeth as he leaned in. And in that moment of terror, she realized she knew him. Mr. Tanaka, the quiet janitor from school.

And he raped her, all of his hate directed at this girl of Chinese descent. His loathing at this American child, at the country that had incinerated his parents, at the Chinese who had imprisoned him, the two cultures manifested in this lowly creature.

"If you tell anyone of this," Tanaka whispered in her ear, "I will come back and kill your sister in front of your eyes."

As Tanaka stepped back into the hall, he saw the parents standing there in their nightclothes in shock at the sight of the man brandishing a sword. Without hesitation, he swung the blade, severing the mother's head. But he stayed his hand against the father, the Chinaman. He had done far worse than killing him. He had imprisoned him in grief, a grief that would haunt him for the remaining days of his life, just as he himself had been haunted by the imagined vision of his own incinerated family.

Tanaka was never caught. No leads were found; the papers screamed of a madman who had decapitated his victims running loose in the city. But Jane and her father told the police nothing. They feared for Jane's sister, for their own lives, as they knew the ruthless man would live up to his promise if the police came calling.

Nine months later, Jon was born. His teenage mother was cold and distant. He didn't realize that he lacked a mother's love, because he'd never been loved. He never understood that she saw his Japanese father every time she looked at him, never understood that Tanaka had not only raped her physically, but raped her soul for eternity.

When Jon was ten, his mother finally took her own life.

His grandfather took him and his aunt Carol back to China, to Hong Kong, and raised him, teaching him of his heritage and history. He schooled Jon in language, philosophy, and mathematics. He taught him of China's myths and legends, tales of princes and emperors, admirals who sailed enormous dragon ships to mystical lands; stories of talismans, swords, and death. He taught him about balance and the Eastern mind, schooling him in wushu, writing, and art.

As Jon entered his teen years, he pressed his grandfather for information about his father: who he was, why he was never around, where he might be. But his father remained a mystery, as if his grandfather had forgotten all about him, as if his existence had been wiped from memory.

Jon finally learned the truth two days after his seventeenth birthday. His grandfather was on his deathbed when he told Jon what had happened, of how loving and strong his mother had been for sixteen years, and how it had all been stolen from her by Tanaka. He pled with Jon not to seek vengeance, to understand that out of something so evil could come something as special as himself.

With his grandfather's passing, Jon and his aunt were left a modest inheritance, one that would allow Jon to attend college, to educate himself and build a life. His aunt thought it best that they return to the United States, and made arrangements to move to Colorado, far from L.A., a city filled with too many harsh memories. And while Jon railed against her, she was his guardian; he had no choice.

With his head filled with such confusion, such tragedy, such thoughts of revenge, Jon grabbed his passport, several thousand dollars in cash, and walked out of his grandfather's house, disappearing into the night.

But Jon did not race back to Los Angeles to seek vengeance. Instead he went to Japan, finding work as a cook, in construction, as a gardener, earning enough money to live in a one-room apartment. And he began to study Japan, everything about it, absorbing the culture, learning the people's ways, studying life from their Nipponese perspective, understanding why they had invaded China, their expansionist views in World War II, their financial strength in the eighties. He studied and mastered kenjutsu, ninjutsu, and aikido; he mastered their language and culture and ways. He never told his aunt where he was, only sending an occasional letter informing her that he was alive and on his own, and that some day he would return to her.

He stayed in Japan for four years, then boarded a jet for Los Angeles on November 12.

* * *

IT TOOK JON a month to track down Tanaka. He was amazed that his father was still alive. He had researched the man, everything about him: his war record, his involvement with *Kin no yuri* and Yamashita's gold, and his criminal record in Japan, where, after his release from prison, he was a thief, a gang member, a thug, convicted three times, and imprisoned once again for ten years. Jon discovered he had immigrated to the United States in the 1960s, occasionally falling off the grid. He worked at Jon's mother's high school for six years after her murder, with no one ever realizing that a monster lurked on the school grounds among the children. Living off welfare for the last few years, Tanaka was found in a third-floor apartment in a run-down section of Los Angeles.

Standing in the center of the three-room unit, Jon looked at the small shrine in the corner, a table covered in candles. There was the Japanese imperial war flag on the wall, its red rising sun with sixteen sun rays as offensive to the Chinese as the Nazi swastika flag was to the world. Jon's eyes fell upon the display that hung to the right of the shrine, the two items resting there upon a wooden rack. He drew down the katana and its scabbard; the sword was magnificent, with a craftsmanship that exceeded anything he had trained with or even seen in Japan. As he examined it closely, there was no mistaking its vintage, the blade folded thousands of times by a craftsman centuries earlier.

Silently stepping into the bedroom, he saw a figure asleep in bed. Tanaka was nearly seventy, decrepit and old beyond his years, an oxygen tank at his bedside, its plastic hose running to the tube strapped beneath his nose. The rhythmic sound of his labored breaths was the only sound in the dark night.

Jon studied the man, the creature who had raped his mother, killed his grandmother, mentally tortured his grandfather and aunt for all these years. Jon's self-loathing swelled; that he shared this man's blood, his DNA, filled him with shame. That he was the product of an innocent's torture, his mother's torture, set his mind on fire.

Jon removed the tube from Tanaka's nose; he refused to ever think of him as his father again. He watched as the man's chest rose in distress, watching as he began to gasp.

And Tanaka's eyes snapped open, staring up at Jon, who stood there with his ancient katana in hand.

"Who are you?" Tanaka wheezed.

"I am your son," Jon said in Japanese as he pressed the katana to the man's throat. Then switching to Mandarin, "the embodiment of everything you hate." Switching to English, "A child of America, of China, of my mother, whose soul you stole when she was just a child."

Tanaka looked up at Jon, his face filling with confusion as he realized who this man was, his eyes registering the fact that he had created his own killer. Pain and anger overwhelmed him as he struggled to breathe, as he attempted to focus on his son.

In a slow ritual, Jon raised the katana above his head, ensuring that this man saw and digested his every move. That he understood death was seconds away, brought down on him in revenge for the heinous acts he had committed twenty-one years ago. And with a flick of his wrist, the blade screamed down through the air, shards of light exploding off its honed edge, severing Tanaka's head from his neck with surgical precision.

JON LEI MOVED into his aunt's small apartment in Colorado, attended Colorado State, then entered the Navy at the age of twenty-six.

While American, Jon acknowledged his heritage for what it truly was. From his grandfather's upbringing, he thought like a man from the East though he was from the West, a dichotomy that allowed him to walk in two worlds. He had mastered the languages, cultures, and martial arts of China and Japan, countries that had been enemies; enemies that had fathered him.

His language skills and modality of thought were immediately embraced by the Navy. He spent three years as a lieutenant in the SEALs and left to be stationed as an Asian liaison in Japan. He left six months later for the Tridiem Group, the allure of the pay and the challenge too great to pass up. He was still military, still loyal to the U.S., only on a pay scale more commensurate with his abilities.

He had denied himself the modest luxuries he had grown up with: the nice home, the nice car, the never wanting for anything. Living on his own in a one-room apartment in Japan helped to shape him, to teach him to distinguish between wants and needs; continuing that lifestyle through college and the military gave him an appreciation for what was important in life. But all that aside, he much preferred having money in his pocket, having the means to taste life, so Tridiem allowed him to walk in both worlds. He was paid handsomely yet still performed the job he loved.

He had performed eleven jobs in the four years he'd been working for the Tridiem Group, and had built up a substantial bank account. Unlike the old mercenary model, he never had to perform tasks that ran counter to his morals. Tridiem allowed him to accept or decline any job that was offered to him, and none held more allure for him than the one offered only days earlier. For what was in the box they had to steal, and what it revealed, held far more allure than a paycheck or saving lives. His grandfather had spoken of it as a fairy tale, as a legend. But as far as Colonel Lucas and the U.S. government were concerned, it was very real.

CHAPTER 14
PRESENT-DAY MACAU

The world was awash in light. An artificial day that never ended. The Cotai strip was Asia's answer to Las Vegas, a gambling mecca that provided a vast array of entertainment, shopping, amenities, and decadence. Built over the last five years, it had become the destination of millions, the flow of money surpassing that of its U.S. counterpart, making it the number-one gambling destination in the world. Whereas oil-rich sheikhs used to race to Vegas, they now headed to Macau with heavy purses, charging into the Venetian with dreams of winning.

Heading down Estrada do Istmo, the driver turned into the large circular drive and pulled up to the portico entrance, where smiling valets greeted Michael, Jon, and Busch with smiles of welcome.

Enormous doors were held open by nodding doorman as the three walked into a world Busch had never imagined existed. He had been to Vegas on more than one occasion, and while he had always had an exceptionally good time, he did possess a pretty detailed memory of the Wynn, the Mirage, the MGM, and the Bellagio, grand palaces where no expense had been spared.

But the Venetian Macau dwarfed them all, wrapping the senses in pure luxury. The soaring entrance included hand-painted ceilings in the lobby and along the colonnade, seemingly rendered by Michelangelo after he'd warmed up on the Sistine Chapel.

The staff was enormous but unobtrusive, blending into the background only to arrive at your side when they read your mind's questions or divined your unfulfilled desires. Gaming tables numbered more than 750, though nothing seemed crowded.

There were actually four casinos within the Venetian: the Phoenix, the Golden Fish, the Imperial House, and the Red Dragon. The four enormous spaces were located around the Great Hall.

The crowd was surprisingly upscale, men and women of all races and nationalities dressed in their finest clothes as if attending the opera or a presidential dinner. It was unlike Vegas, where people arrived in shorts and T-shirts. There was a sense of class here, as there had been in the Casino at Monte Carlo in the sixties, where tuxedoed men stoically lost fortunes while their gowned wives and mistresses stood behind them ready to offer consolation sex.

They stopped at the hotel desk, where Jon engaged a strikingly beautiful woman with black hair and almond eyes.

"Welcome to the Venetian," the woman said.

"Thank you," Jon said as he handed over a credit card and ID.

"This place has never been robbed, never had an incident," Busch said to Michael as they stood off to the side, watching the groups of people at the various gaming tables. "Every place has *incidents*: casinos, delis, car washes. You can't tell me nothing of a criminal nature has occurred here in four years."

"They must have a great PR rep who shuts it all down, keeps it out of the press," Michael said.

"Or some kind of 'special' help that is a great deterrent," Busch responded ominously.

THE THREE SUITES were adjacent to each other. More than eighteen hundred square feet, with a living room, a separate bedroom, and an Italian marble bath, each suite had a full complement of office equipment, a fully stocked bar, and a balcony overlooking the artificial canals.

After checking out their rooms, they gathered in Busch's.

"We can sleep in our rooms," Jon said. "The safe house is for staging. I'll have your bags brought over, but may I suggest you each purchase some clothes from the on-site stores. You can have a tailor visit you and tailor the clothes. It will enhance our ability to blend in if you do so; charge it to your rooms."

"I hope they have my size," Busch said as he flexed his arm in mock vanity, his statement more of an allusion to his six-foot-four frame.

"We need to make our presence known," Jon said as he handed Michael and Busch each fifty thousand in chips.

"Happily," Busch said with a smile.

"Who's funding this?" Michael asked.

Jon ignored Michael's question. "We have a private tour of the lower level scheduled for midnight. We can take as much time as we need."

"Is that so we can get our faces on their security cameras?" Michael said. "So we can make it easier for them to capture us before we even get near our goal?"

"You asked to see the lower levels, the area you need to penetrate," Jon said without emotion. "I'm providing that opportunity."

"And laying the groundwork so that after I have stolen what you need, you can direct everyone to a midnight video of us casing the area," Michael said, his voice filled with annoyance.

Actually, Michael wasn't annoyed because of the camera situation. He did need to see the lower level, needed to confirm the space was constructed as the plans had indicated. He was angry because he was being forced to do this, to partner with a stranger he didn't trust, and mostly for being forced to rely on someone else. Michael had a trust problem. He could count on one hand those he trusted with his life, and Jon wasn't on that list.

BUSCH HAD AN affection for poker, always had. He had fancied himself a bit of a card sharp in his teens, fleecing his friends on Friday nights, explaining to his mom that all the extra cash came from tips he got while working at the gas station and the deli. And while the games had fallen by the wayside, except for an occasional game with Michael or Simon, he still fancied himself sharp and attuned to reading others, to knowing when to fold, to knowing how to win.

He took a seat at the poker table in the Red Dragon casino, the red ceiling, gold accents, and elaborate dragons painted upon the coffers imparting a true Chinese feel. The chair was soft, rich leather, the table a dark walnut. He loved the green felt, the way the dealt cards would glide upon it. As if out of nowhere, a gorgeous waitress appeared and whispered in his ear, asking what he would like to drink; he whispered back for a Jack Daniel's and turned his attention to the others already engrossed in a game.

There were six at the table: three well-dressed Chinese businessmen—or at least that was the appearance they hoped their pinstriped suits would convey—a Japanese man dressed in a black polo shirt and dark pants, and a blond woman who kept glancing Busch's way.

As a new game began, they all anted up as the young dealer threw everyone five cards. Again, as if the job description called for beauty, the dealer was exceedingly beautiful: dark hair, deep eyes, a mix of cultures combining into a sensual woman who knew how to gamble.

The game was five-card stud. Busch's initial hand was nothing. An ace, a jack, a five, a three, and a seven. The Japanese man threw in a hundred, which was matched by all at the table. Within two minutes he won with a pair of queens.

To Busch, the first few hands were about reading faces, reading tells and quirks. With the second hand, all had folded except for a Chinese man and the blonde, who ran up the pot until the man called and lost.

Busch played the next hand aggressively, building up the pot, drawing three cards, watching to see who was paying as much attention to him as he was to them. With two pairs, Busch scooped in his winnings with a smile.

Four hands in, he could read all but two of the Chinese. The Japanese man's face never changed, but his right thumb subtly rubbed his next finger's knuckle with unbridled excitement when his hand was strong. The blonde was easier. While most men would become distracted by her beauty and flirting eyes, thinking they would be scoring with her after the game, Paul never lost his focus. Little did she know that though he returned her smile, he had no eyes for her: He had been with Jeannie forever and had no intention of ever breaking his vow.

Twelve more hands, four small losses, four huge wins, and Paul had tripled his money.

CHAPTER 15
BEIJING

KC and Annie walked into the large hotel suite, dropping their small luggage bags on the bed. Annie picked up a card and read it out loud. "'Welcome to the White Pearl Suite . . .' We are not the type of women who wear pearls," Annie said.

KC glared at her.

"Oh, we can wear them, probably make them look better than most women, but we are not the type, no matter how much we want to be."

The Crowne Plaza Beijing was on Wangfujing Street, one of the most famous streets in China, in the heart of Beijing. It was known for luxurious accommodations that were designed to meet the expectations of Western travelers while imparting a subtle flavor of the East.

Annie set about putting her clothes away, meticulously folding them as she took them out of the bag, laying them in the drawers, her military background shining through.

"Are you going to tell me what we are stealing?"

"No," Annie said without looking up. "But come tomorrow, I will show you."

Annie finally looked up at KC. "You think me despicable, but you don't know my motivation, why we're here."

"Maybe if you told me . . ." KC said.

Annie pulled out the tube and the small book they had stolen from the safe in Granada. She opened the tube and dumped a set of architectural drawings on the bed. They were detailed schematics of a modern facility. KC studied the plans closely. Though she didn't comprehend the Chinese writing, she recognized advanced environmental controls, fire safety mechanics, and an elaborate security system. In the upper left-hand corner there was a room circled in red marker, the number 9296273 written in the center.

Annie opened the small book; it was leather-bound, worn and stained by age. She quickly turned the pages, searching for something. As KC turned her attention to it, she was glad to recognize the language and realized she was looking at a ship's manifest written in English.

Annie paused. "There's a small crate from World War II. It was stolen by the Japanese only to be returned to China by the United States at the end of the war. Tomorrow you will see what it contains, and then you will understand.

"If you help me," Annie continued, "if we succeed, everything will be all right; we'll let you and Michael go. I promise."

Annie flipped open her phone, checking for messages, but there were none. "Have you ever known someone who unconditionally had your back, who had absolutely no obligation to do so, yet was always there for you?"

"You seriously think we can just chat?" KC said. "That I can look past what you are doing to Michael and me?"

"Obviously, it's Michael," Annie continued as if they were friends. "And you walked away from him."

As much as KC tried to ignore Annie, her words cut through her. KC couldn't believe the woman who had kidnapped her was helping her to put her life in perspective.

"So were you planning on spending the holidays alone?" Annie asked, a crack showing in her tough exterior. "Do you know what that's like?"

KC could see the hurt in Annie's eyes . . . and felt a wound open up within herself. She had loathed the holidays until last year.

The tree stood twelve feet tall, larger than any Christmas tree KC had ever seen, wrapped in white lights. It was covered in ornaments of all shapes and sizes, crystal and glass, detailed Santa faces, colored balls, and ceramic angels. It was in the middle of Michael's great room, whose mantel was adorned in garland and poinsettias, the tables displaying a collection of Santas of all shapes, sizes, and styles from the world over. There was holly at the entrance and mistletoe hanging in every doorway.

And sprinkled throughout the house were pictures of her and Michael at the beach, in the yard, with friends, and with Michael's dogs.

KC had never loved Christmas until last year. Growing up poor with only her mother and sister, there was barely enough money for food and rent in their small

two-room apartment in London. There was no Santa
Claus, no stockings or tree, no Christmas dinner, though
KC would awaken to find a single present on the end of
her bed, usually a scarf or a sweater, sometimes a dress.
Her mother had forgone her lunches at work, had saved
what little she could to at least give her girls one gift. And
as appreciative as KC was, the single gift, the lack of holiday decorations in their apartment, was made all the
more painful once she walked outside to see the streets
aglow in Christmas lights, carolers singing on the corners, parents rushing home with numerous bags under
their arms.

Over the years, KC would take solace in Christmas
Mass, sitting in the rear pews with her mother and her
sister, the strains of "Silent Night" filling the rafters; it reminded her of the day's true meaning. She loved the
choir's angel-like voices, the peaceful smile on her mother's face as she mouthed the words. It always brought
tears to her eyes, for it reminded her that they had each
other.

When their mother died two days before Christmas
when KC was all of fifteen and Cynthia was nine, the
holiday became almost too much to bear. They were two
children alone.

KC, looking far older than her fifteen years, convinced the child welfare officer that she was twenty and
could raise her sister. She had convinced the kindly
woman not to take Cynthia away and place her in foster
care, not to separate the girls, for they only had each
other.

As Cynthia cried herself to sleep that Christmas Eve,

KC quietly left the house. Walking the streets among the lights, laughter, and songs of those who rejoiced in the holiday, she'd felt as if her heart were breaking. She was overwhelmed with desperation not for herself but for her sister, alone in bed with dreams that should be anything but nightmares.

To escape the cold, KC walked into the large department store, open late for last-minute shoppers. She looked at the jackets, the beautiful dresses and shoes, things that she and her sister had never had. She looked at the TVs and stereos, pink pillows and posters, items that people took for granted but that she and her sister knew nothing of. There was a red cashmere sweater, softer than anything she had ever felt. She placed it to her cheek and closed her eyes, pretending for just a moment that she was someone else.

She held it up and looked in the mirror and a small smile escaped her lips, it was far too small for her. But the feel of it was something she would always remember. Seeing the revelers leaving with gifts and wreaths, heading home to be with family and friends, she realized that the only person she could rely on, whom Cynthia could rely on, was herself. There were no friends, no family to turn to; if they were to survive, it was all on KC's teenage shoulders.

When Cynthia woke on Christmas morning, it took a few moments for reality to sink in, to remember her mother was dead, to remember that it was Christmas. And the tears she had cried for two days returned.

But as she got out of bed, she saw the gift at the end

of her bed. She looked at it, confused, picked it up, and read the note.

Happy Christmas, Love Mom.

Cynthia tore open the package to find a beautiful red sweater; it was softer than anything she had ever known. She held it up, quickly putting it on, feeling it against her skin.

KC had watched through the crack of the open door and smiled.

The sisters bundled up and went to Mass, Cynthia so proud in her sweater that her mother had gotten her before she died, her young mind believing in the miracle of Christmas. They sat in the rear pew, the same one they had always sat in. KC knew how they would survive, she knew how to get money, and in the days to come she took the steps into her new life.

But as the choir began to sing, as the first words of "Silent Night" filled the cathedral, tears washed down KC's face, for she knew that she was truly alone.

Last year, the holidays had changed; they had taken on a true meaning. She and Michael had celebrated Christmas Eve at the Busches' house. Jeannie had fixed a turkey and a standing rib roast. Simon was there, visiting from Rome, laughing and poking fun at Paul as he always did. Busch's children could barely contain their excitement. New friends arrived with gifts and bottles of wine, laughing and talking about all they were thankful for. It was magical; she was no longer an outsider, observing others' happiness. With Michael she had found not only love but a life.

KC had awoken Christmas morning in their large

bed, the snow falling, the smell of bacon filling the air. She quickly threw on a robe and went downstairs to find a roaring fire, the sounds of holiday music pouring from the speakers, Michael sitting there in wait with a broad smile on his face. Beside him were gifts, dozens of them, all shapes and sizes, beneath the enormous tree. And though KC was well past the age of believing in Santa, she believed in the miracle of Christmas; it was something out of her dreams, what she had always imagined.

And as the strains of Harry Connick, Jr., filled the air, singing "Silent Night," KC had softly wept tears of joy, for she wasn't alone.

Within the Beijing hotel, a sharp pain filled KC now, an actual pain that ran up her side and hit her heart; she was devastated that this past Christmas might be her last.

CHAPTER 16
MACAU

Michael walked through the Imperial House Casino within the Venetian, past the poker, roulette, and blackjack tables to a large waiting area, his mind absorbing the room as he walked. He poked his head into a beautiful theater: Cirque du Soleil was dancing on the walls, tumbling and flying about the stage to the joy of the audience, who were fixated in wonderment at the impossible feats being performed before them.

Michael turned and headed through the Golden Fish, the Phoenix, and the Red Dragon casinos, each one's decor reflective of its name while the gaming was nearly the same if not identical. The crowds were equally spread out, no pattern evident in demographics, winners, losers, or staff. He continued past an array of shops: Tiffany's, Gucci, Prada, all bustling as if it were the day before Christmas. There was a business facility the likes of which he had never seen, and a spa, manned by a staff of masseuses who looked as if they had stepped off a movie set.

Any and every need could be met with a vast array of restaurants, catering to every imaginable taste, and shops and services to ensure that the clientele never needed to pass through the main doors to the outside world until either it was time to go home or they were flat broke.

Michael marveled at the business model. The house edge on slots was anywhere from 3 percent to 15 percent; for every ten-dollar wager the house would gain thirty cents to a dollar-fifty on average. Craps, poker, and blackjack varied, but on the whole the casino's average was an 8 percent to 11 percent edge. And for those lucky few who finished ahead, the traps were set behind the doors: gleaming shops where they would give that money right back, spending it on gifts, clothes, massages, food, and alcohol.

Michael changed his focus and walked outside into the cool night air. It was like being in the middle of Venice: 350 shops, cafés harking back to the Italian city's heyday, and it was all brought to surreal life by the grand canals.

Michael examined the wide canal, the water blue and clear, far cleaner than Venice had known in centuries. He boarded a black gondola and had the gondolier take him through the meandering waterways twice. The Asian man was dressed in black pants, a red-and-white striped shirt, and a straw hat wrapped with red ribbon about its crown. He guided the long and narrow craft with gentle strokes while music drifted on the night air. As Michael closed his eyes, he felt as if he were in Italy.

The canals wound their way for over a mile. Michael had noted the drainage and piping on the plans Jon had provided; he knew there were access ways, tunnels connecting the various canals that were used for cleaning and maintenance. He estimated there was more than 100 million gallons of fresh water with no perceptible smell, a dramatic improvement on the occasional stench and murkiness of Venice's signature feature.

As the gondola completed its final loop, Michael looked up at the five-year-old "ancient" city; in his estimation, the facility generated more than $10 million a night. And the amount gave him pause. While gambling had always been part of the culture of Macau, it was only in the late nineties when the new-age boom began, when the big corporate entities came with their Las Vegas designs, their Middle Eastern grandiose desires, when the island's old-world casinos were swept away to make way for a new dawn that would bring a potential for profits that would exceed the GNP of a small nation.

But Michael knew that this dream came with a price. No one gave up business to a foreigner, particularly the Chinese. And as the Triads had controlled the old world with an unspoken understanding, so, too, they had their fingers in every casino on the Cotai strip.

The public relations firms had wiped any mention of their existence from the shores of Macau, but like a shadow cast on a moonlit night, they were always there. The corporate world was in partnership with them, there was no question. Much as Vegas was initially controlled by the Mafia, the Triads controlled Macau. And where corporations used the law to deal with thieves, the Triads took a much different approach.

CARL WANG WAS impeccably dressed in a designer suit, his hair perfect, his nails manicured, but Michael knew that despite the man's metrosexual appearance, he was much more. Wang had two features that were difficult to disguise: a jagged scar that poked up through his white-collared shirt, haphazard and obviously not from a surgery, and tattoos that peeked out of the sleeves of his shirt.

Michael wasn't sure if he was a former or a current member of a Triad, though his presence and position spoke volumes. For where they were headed, the security was rumored to be at such a high level that no man should be venturing there unless he was in a position of power, unless he was on the board of directors, unless he held the keys to heaven.

Wang and Jon spoke in Chinese, quick words accented by sharp nods as they headed down the central hall of the four casinos like old friends. Michael and Busch followed them past a bevy of guards, arriving at a large door where two guards stood at attention. Nodding to Wang, they slipped their keys in the doors and opened them.

The rear section was a staging area where people raced about like bees in a hive, each with a task to be performed quickly and accurately. There were two armed guards standing beside a tall cart filled with chips ready to be deployed into the casino. They accompanied a steward whose sole job was to ensure that there was never a lack of chips to be gambled away by the patrons, gambled right back into the casino's possession. There were pit bosses and croupiers ready to hit the floor at the staggered shift change, and three security types watched several monitors that scrolled images of the high-end tables—a tertiary security point, it was surely one of many.

Jon turned to Michael and Busch. "Carl is part of

the security detail and will be taking us on our subterranean security tour."

THEY RODE DOWN through six sublevels in one of the two freight elevators, each large enough to hold an SUV with room to spare. Glancing up, Michael noted the standard service hatch, but unlike most, this one had a McKellan lock on it.

After a thirty-second ride, the doors opened to reveal a subterranean anteroom, a small vestibule with a single door, a camera affixed above it, and additional cameras in the uppermost corners.

"Carl and I decided we'd start at the bottom and work our way up, if that's all right with you."

Michael nodded, as if he had any choice in the matter.

Without requesting it, they were buzzed through into what could only be described as a vault room, another antechamber. This one was much larger, the ceiling soaring up thirty feet, the room equally deep, designed to accommodate its single feature: a solitary door.

The twenty-five-foot circular door hung on enormous four-foot hinges. The polished-steel access was open, revealing a vast space that stretched on for two hundred feet, where twenty-five more vaults stood, each one ten feet in circumference. They were equally spaced, architecturally beautiful, like an art deco design from the 1920s.

There was a central desk where a large, broad-shouldered man with piercing eyes sat at attention. If the main level was staffed by those with beautiful faces sculpted by angels, the lowermost level required appear-

ances that instilled fear. Rama Schavilia's face had been noticeably broken on more than one occasion: His nose was
askew, his right eye socket slightly off, giving him a preter-
natural appearance. He looked at the four men without a
hint of welcome, glaring at them as if they didn't belong.

Ignoring the man's glare, Michael looked around,
examining the vault doors, all Crains; he knew them and
their impenetrable reputation. Iron frames seated in
concrete, three-inch steel rods running crosswise
through the door into the frame, traditional interior me-
chanicals operated by key and combination wheel, no
new-age computers or electronics that could be hacked
or disabled by a thirteen-year-old runny-nosed genius.

The overall space was designed in a way that exceeded his usual protocols. Michael's security firm was
known for the belts, suspenders, and parachutes approach, redundant backups to redundant backups. What
he saw before him surpassed what he would have recommended for the world's greatest riches, for the secrets of
life, for the gates of hell.

Michael turned around and looked at the subterranean room—at the floor, noting its metal construct; at
the single guard, who was both intelligent and deadly; at
the twenty-five-foot vault entrance door—and felt panic
rise within him. Beyond that lay the elevators and the security measures above, a setup that left little to no room
for compromise.

Michael's eyes finally focused on vault door number
sixteen. It was Colonel Lucas's goal, and now it was Michael's goal. He had no idea what the interior of the vault
looked like, no idea what the mysterious box he was to steal

contained, but he knew that what lay within the impossible-to-breach space was the only key to KC's salvation.

SUBLEVEL FIVE, ONE floor up from the vault space, contained more than two billion dollars' worth of chips. Sublevel Five's sole purpose was to warehouse, maintain, distribute, and monitor the token chips, which, in the world of the Venetian, were as good as cash.

"The Fort Knox of chips," Busch joked to no one's amusement as they stepped from the elevator and walked into a small holding area.

A large cart, five feet high and deep, three feet wide, was escorted into the holding area. A man stood at the door with an electronic wand and waved it over the departing cart, checking the readout: $3,250,000; an exact match to the tag on the front. With a nod, the escort boarded the freight elevator and headed upstairs.

Tokens at the Venetian contained small electronic chips called RFID: Radio Frequency Identification. The pinhead-sized device identified the denomination of the individual gambling coin, its location within the facility, and its age.

The sophisticated system allowed the casino to know how much money was at a table, on the floor, in the rooms. The system analyzed the patterns of gambling, extrapolated the success rate of the house, and rendered a detailed report at the push of a button. It prevented people from introducing and playing with counterfeit chips. It deterred the staff from slipping chips into their pockets so their friends could cash them in later.

While chips would leave the casino as souvenirs, as items forgotten in pockets, they would be deactivated after thirty days. And in the event a large volume of chips left the premises at a single time, security would be called in.

It was estimated that this system saved the Venetian more than $100 million a year.

Carl flashed his ID and the four were waved into a large room filled with carts, cages of chips, and a centralized computer station. Two guards stood watch over a staff of fifteen, each employee busy at his workstation, stocking carts and reading monitors.

"Is Rene here?" Carl asked the lead guard.

"Gone for the night," the guard answered, his eyes focused on the room.

Rene Clauge not only was in charge of chip security but was the designer of the Venetian's custom RFID. The chip's built-in encryption was like a Defense Department firewall. It made the technology of the metal strip within the U.S. hundred-dollar bill look like a book of matches in the nuclear age.

The reader of the RFID was equally complex. Its multifaceted programming not only evaluated location and denomination but could track any of the ten-million-chip inventory for its life from table to table, from croupier to gambler to machine to safe. Through his design, Rene knew precisely how much money was on the casino floor, at the exchange windows, in the vaults on Sublevel Five, even in the pockets of the clientele. Rene's scanners were not only handheld, like the ones the guards used, but built into the tables and the slot machines, each wirelessly linked to his mainframe. His system protected against counterfeiters who, instead of creating U.S. dollars and euros, had gone into the business of creating gambling chips. It was a battlement against unscrupulous gamblers and thieves: an electronic shield worthy of the NSA, the CIA, the U.S. military—but those agencies could never pay him enough for his brilliance.

Carl explained that Rene had designed the space on Sublevel Five like a bunker to protect not only the chip warehouse but the system. The entire space was built within a Faraday cage, a system that shielded the main-frame and its ancillary components from outside inter-ference.

While there were breaches in accounting, guest suite security, and cash management—all of which was never shared beyond the senior staff—his division had yet to know an incident.

Currently, the system showed $137 million on the floor: $11.5 million within the slot machines, $90 million at the various tables, and $25 million at the windows, with the balance in people's pockets. On their busiest nights, the number would climb to nearly $250 million. There was close to $900,000 in unaccounted-for chips, but as more than 75 percent of the denominations were five and ten dollars, this number was attributed to souvenirs taken by guests, nearly pure-profit souvenirs as far as the Venetian was concerned, unless someone came to cash them in.

"Great plastic money—where's the real money?" Busch asked as they rode the elevator up.

"Cash is handled on Sublevel Four, but we don't

have a prayer of getting near there; it's more restricted than Sub-Six," Carl explained.

There were only five people who handled the cash. No one knew their process or how much actually flowed through the casino. It was rumored that skimming was anywhere between 10 and 50 percent. Though this was denied, it was suspected it was used to pay off various Triads, officials, and contractors, and to line the pockets of certain VIPs—things that were never spoken of but necessary in a world that had been controlled by organized crime for decades, in a place where the local government was in constant flux as various officials were on constant parade before a judge for corruption.

The elevator arrived at Sublevel Three, where the lobby was far more welcoming than those on the lower levels.

The heart of the Venetian's security lay within a twenty-thousand-square-foot space dedicated to protecting the clientele, the ownership, and the facility, monitoring everything within the walls of the vast structure short of people's thoughts—though they had experts on staff who some swore could read people's hearts and minds.

The security staff was not composed of the off-the-street, minimum-wage, rent-a-guard types that most industries employed to protect their most prized possessions. These men and women were highly trained, highly educated experts in gaming, security, investigation, and criminal procedure, with senses attuned to those looking to take advantage of the Venetian. They could spot the nervous first-time cheats, and the cool and calm con artists who excelled at sleight of hand, card counting, and all of the newfangled ways to tilt the impossible odds of gambling in their favor.

And while there were no reports of any incidents at the Venetian in the press, that didn't mean that people weren't caught. Those suspected of cheating were politely surrounded and escorted to a rear section of Sublevel Three, which contained four interrogation rooms, a crime lab, and twenty-four jail cells.

The security staff included individual guards, who manned various stations and stood imposingly at strategic locations, and an entirely undercover contingent of personnel who wandered the site with keen eyes and earpieces attuned to both their commanding officers and the security teams who watched from the cameras above.

Michael walked around the central security room; the volume of personnel was staggering. There were nearly a hundred manned monitoring stations in an enormous corral that surrounded a circular command desk.

There were monitors for the card tables, the slot machines, roulette, boule, sic bo, fan-tan, keno, and craps. Images of thousands of people gambling away unaware that God was watching; people who wished to remain anonymous, who didn't want to be seen, were being scrutinized, their manner studied, their behavior evaluated. And not only being watched but recorded, preserved on a server for months and years to come. It was much like Vegas. Society had no idea how on-camera their lives really were. Though no one ever realized it . . . what happened in Vegas was recorded in Vegas, archived and forever available.

Not only the gamers were being examined; so, too,

were the guests arriving, the guests departing, the staff moving among the tables and the guests. For those checking in, a video image was attached to their account; for those checking out, an assessment was made of their luggage and bags.

In the center of the room, upon a circular dais elevated two feet above the floor, were three men, headsets on their heads, tablet monitors in their hands. Above them were four huge arena-worthy TVs, where the feed from any camera could be isolated and enlarged to four feet high for all to see.

There was no sense of complacency in the personnel, no tired eyes or room for fatigue; a single loss of focus could prove financially disastrous. No individual ever sat at a monitor for more than forty-five minutes without a minimum fifteen-minute break. The personnel in here were some of the most highly paid staff onsite. And those who caught someone, who provided information that captured an individual who was trying to take advantage of the casino, received a million-dollar bonus. As a result, it created the most diligent crew of workers the industry had known, and a quiet reputation for being an impossible mark for those who had even the smallest plan to steal from the casino.

A deep sense of dread filled Michael; until now he had not fully grasped the scope of what he would be attempting. If he was to have any chance of success, he would have to literally blind every person in this room.

Carl led them to the server room. The enormous space was nearly a thousand square feet. Banks of computer servers and communication interfaces filled aisle upon aisle of racks, all of it kept at a chilly forty-two degrees Fahrenheit for optimum performance and protection. The wires entered the room via large bundles within steel conduits that were embedded within the concrete slabs. Without asking for clarification, Michael spotted the video server, a five-foot-tall self-contained computer system; the wires feeding into it came from a video junction box where hundreds upon hundreds of video cables terminated. Michael didn't need to examine the server. He knew it well—he had installed two himself.

He saw circuit breakers and fail-safe switches; there were massive surge protectors in place to guard against power surges, lightning strikes, and electrical mishaps, whose jolt could render the system useless. There were two backup generators in their own rooms to supply power for a week before requiring a refuel; an additional central station room filled with hundreds of static monitors in the event of a sectional failure in the other room. Every potential obstacle, failure, and disaster had been taken into account and protected against.

"In the event of a failure down here," Michael said quietly to Carl. "Standard protocols?"

"The entire sublevel, all six floors, lock up tighter than a nun's legs. Interior doors seal, the elevators are recalled to the main floor, even the fire stairs seal up. Everything is locked down and contained until the all-clear is given and the system is up and functional."

Michael nodded, hiding his fear, for the task he had to accomplish was truly impossible.

CHAPTER 17
THE FORBIDDEN CITY

KC stood in the middle of Tiananmen Square, staring up at the sweeping thirty-foot red walls on the far side of a moat that encased the royal compound known as the Forbidden City, a palace-city frozen in time, a world from antiquity in the middle of modern-day Beijing.

The red fortress was nearly a half-mile wide, dwarfing everything around it. On each corner were large, deep-red guard towers that looked like palaces in their own right. They were like nothing KC had seen standing in front of any European palace. Not clunky and utilitarian-looking, these three-story buildings that sat atop the high wall were elegant, with stacked, multitiered roofs capped with golden yellow tiles, their corners crowned with dragons.

A cold wind whipped through the open area, the crowds pulling their jackets tight as they moved en masse toward the entrance on this cold morning.

"She's late," Annie said. She stood beside KC, dressed in a long black coat and dark Dolce & Gabbana sunglasses.

"What are you going to do, shoot her?" KC said with a false smile. "We take the public tour instead—"

"Not a chance. We are on a timetable. You have no idea of the number of lives that are depending on our success."

"If you're so concerned about saving lives instead of taking them, then we only get one chance at this. I need to know what lies within those walls. Or maybe you can just let Michael and me go and find someone else to help you."

Annie glared at KC as they joined a group of tourists, European and American, an overly friendly guide before them. He was Chinese but spoke perfect unaccented English. Dressed in blue jeans and a North Face jacket, he looked no older than fifteen, but he spoke like the grad student of Chinese history that he was.

"In a dark time, the Forbidden City was a world of richness and opulence, a beacon in the center of a war-torn country. Rectangular in shape, the Forbidden City is the world's largest palace complex: Measuring 961 meters from north to south and 753 meters from east to west, it covers an area of 720,000 square meters, or 178 acres. It is the largest ancient palatial structure in the world and is recognized as one of the five great palaces, in the company of Versailles, Buckingham, the White House, and the Kremlin in Russia.

"Surrounding the enormous perimeter is a 150-foot-wide moat, the first of many fortifications to ward off attack from ancient enemies. Within the embrace of the moat, the red outer wall stands over thirty feet high, twenty-five feet wide at the base, nineteen wide at the top. It was specifically designed to withstand attack by cannon, marauder, and anything else hurled against it in ancient times. The twelve million bricks of the outer wall are made of white lime and rice, while the cement is glutinous rice and egg whites—materials some may laugh at, but they are of extraordinary strength. And to protect against those that might attempt to tunnel into the city, the paving is fifteen feet deep.

"Each of the four sides is pierced by a gate: the Meridian Gate before us, the Gate of Divine Prowess to the north, and the Eastern and Western Prosperity gates. On the four corners, the intricately structured watchtowers provided a sentinel view over both the palace and the world outside in feudal times."

"This kid is going to make me crazy," Annie said. "He's an actor regurgitating a script."

Two blue-haired older women turned to her and scowled.

"The Forbidden City was home to twenty-four emperors of the Ming and Qing dynasties. In ancient times, the emperor was considered to be the Son of Heaven, and therefore heaven's supreme power was bestowed upon him. The emperor's residence was built to mimic God's home in heaven; a divine palace forbidden to ordinary peasants, which is how the Forbidden City was named. To represent the supreme power of the emperor given from God, and the place where he lived as the center of the world, all the gates, the palace, and other structures of the Forbidden City were arranged about the south-north central axis of Beijing, while the emperor's residence was aligned with the Pole Star, which they believed to be at the center of heaven."

Annie pulled out her cell phone and dialed. She listened as the call went straight to voicemail. "You're late and overpaid. Where are you?"

"Excuse me," the tour guide said. "We ask that you turn your cell phone off during the tour so as not to distract from my discussion."

Annie slammed the phone closed and glared at the tour guide, who smiled, nodded, and continued.

"The walled area of the Forbidden City served as the residence and office of the imperial family and their household staffs, as well as the offices of the ministers and favored officials. The compound housed administrators, concubines, eunuchs, maids, and soldiers. The population numbered over 10,000, with some 2,000 women and 410,000 eunuchs at the end of the Ming Dynasty. Today it is considered not only an imperial city but also an imperial museum, hence it is also called the Palace Museum.

"It was built from 1406 to 1420 by the third emperor of the Ming Dynasty, Zhu Di, the Yongle Emperor, who, upon usurping the throne, determined to move his capital northward from Nanjing to Beijing. In 1644, it was sacked and the Ming Dynasty fell to the Manchu troops under Doergun. The succeeding Qing Dynasty emperors restored the buildings, and the palace was further renovated to its unique beauty.

"In 1911 the Qing Dynasty was overthrown by the republican revolutionaries. The last emperor, Xuantong, continued to live in the palace after his abdication until he was expelled in 1924."

"Are you sure you had the time and meeting place right?" KC whispered to Annie.

"Of course. We need to get away from this guy and hire someone to take us below."

"That area is restricted," KC said. "Your friend was our only means of getting down there."

"Not my friend," Annie spat.

A woman suddenly arrived at Annie's side, her mousy brown hair having not seen a brush in hours, the windy morning spinning it into a tangled net around her face. She was plain, shorter than Annie and KC, and Caucasian, though with her mode of dress, a short brown jacket with a mandarin collar, she blended in with the masses.

"Where have you been?" Jenna Nilan said, annoyed, as she adjusted her dark-rimmed glasses. "We need to hurry."

"You're late," Annie said, staring down at the woman.

"Actually, I was here an hour early. I told you to meet me here at the Meridian Gate entrance."

"You said—"

"She's here," KC cut Annie short. "Let's just go."

The three women approached the grand and imposing entrance to the Forbidden City, the Meridian Gate, which was far more than a simple gate. Like the surrounding walls, it was washed in red, grand and imposing, thirty-five feet high and surmounted by five pavilions that resembled a phoenix.

Enormous red doors were propped open, dotted with eighty-one large gold nails, their heads the size of tennis balls.

"You will see that the number nine is very significant throughout the imperial palace, nine being as close to divinity as one could get," Jenna said, sounding every bit the tour guide as she walked briskly, Annie and KC keeping pace at her side.

"Do me a favor," Annie said. "I don't need to hear a dissertation. I made it clear what we are here to see. You're being paid to show, not spout trivia."

Jenna was taken aback as she looked at Annie. "I'm sorry, I was told—"

KC reached out and touched Jenna's arm, smiling. "Please, I would like to hear."

Exiting on the far side of the Meridian Gate's tunnel, they emerged into an immense courtyard more than six hundred feet wide and five hundred feet deep, the grand size creating a sense of imperial majesty.

Running through it on a meandering course was the Golden River, its bed and sides paved with white stone, which enhanced the beauty of the water. Five bridges stretched over its center, decorated with marble balustrades carved with motifs of dragons and phoenixes, imparting a tranquil sense in an immense world.

"The Golden River," Jenna said, "serves as a fire hydrant as well as adhering to the principles of feng shui. According to these principles, the ideal location for a home is facing south with water in front and a mountain or hill behind. The five white marble spans represent the five Confucian virtues of humanity, sense of duty, wisdom, reliability, and ceremonial propriety."

"We don't need to know every detail," Annie said.

KC shot a glare at Annie. "Jenna, she's having a bad day."

In point of fact, KC wanted to hear everything she could, since she needed every detail, every nuance she could absorb to develop an intimate understanding of what she was being forced to undertake if she were to have any chance of success. Annie had outlined her plan to KC, the location beneath the Forbidden City where the object of their search rested, and the route they would take to get there. Annie already knew the palace grounds and spoke fluent Mandarin. That, coupled with her demonstrated lethal skills, made it obvious to KC why she had been assigned this particular mission. But Annie didn't know the ebb and flow, what made the palace operate without incident, what unassuming hidden detail could prove deadly.

Jenna was earning her Ph.D. in Asian studies and had done her dissertation on the Imperial Palace; she was a far greater expert than any tour guide they could hope for. With knowledge of not just its history, but its intricacies, she knew what lay behind the façade and what lay underneath it. Jenna possessed the more intimate information they would need to achieve their goal and had access to a world that was hidden from the world, a place that held the key to saving Michael.

Recommended by the U.S. embassy, she was honored to give a private tour to members of the U.S. military. Though, truth be told, when she met them there was no disguising her suspicion: The two women seemed more like the type found on Page Six of the *New York Post* than military personnel.

Crossing the bridge, they stepped into the huge courtyard, more than 130,000 square feet. And despite the chill in the air, tourists abounded, taking pictures, following tour guides, standing about looking at maps.

"Across this enormous courtyard lies the Gate of Supreme Harmony," Jenna said as she pointed to the large building in the distance. The red structure was the focal point, the center of a series of buildings, flanked on either side by two minor structures. "That is the main gate to the Outer Courtyard."

Jenna hustled KC and Annie across the remaining seventy-five-yard expanse.

As they approached, Jenna pointed at two enormous green patinated lions that stood guard on either side of the three sets of stairs, representing imperial dignity. "The west one is female," Jenna said. "The lioness's front left paw rests on a lion cub, indicating a prosperously growing family and the succession of the imperial lineage. The east lion's front right paw rests upon a pomegranate, symbolizing the world and imperial power."

They walked up the left set of stairs to the large red building, the Gate of Supreme Harmony, which had a two-tiered sloped roof of yellow tile and seven arched openings supported by tall red columns. Light blue and yellow accent bands wrapped the arches and the molding section between the first and second roof lines.

Passing through the building, KC did not understand why such an elaborate structure was called a gate, but as they exited the rear and stood upon the terrace, it all became clear.

The overwhelming scale and grandeur before her took her breath away. The courtyard was enormous, more than 370,000 square feet, the size of nearly eight

NFL football fields, a vast, wide-open space that could hold tens of thousands of advisors, subjects, and soldiers. The designers had created a powerful and heart-stirring atmosphere that overwhelmed visitors while creating a feeling of imperial grandeur that was sacred and revered.

All of it lay as if in worship before the Hall of Supreme Harmony. Sitting on a seven-meter-high three-tier marble terrace, the grandest building ever built in China was truly overwhelming, soaring nearly ten stories into the open sky. KC found it incredible that the entire complex was built for a single man.

"The Court of the Imperial Palace is referred to by some as the sea of flagstones," Jenna said as she led them down the stairs to the gargantuan courtyard. "You'll notice there are no trees or obstructions, as ancient Chinese emperors considered themselves to be Sons of Heaven, born to reign over the country, so they should occupy the highest position. Nothing was allowed to overwhelm the Hall of Supreme Harmony, the highest building in the Forbidden City.

"The Chinese believed their country was the center of the world—"

"They still do," Annie jabbed.

"The Chinese name for itself," Jenna ignored Annie, "Zhōngguó, means 'middle kingdom.' And the center of that kingdom is right here: the Emperor's Palace, the Forbidden City.

"The Hall of Supreme Harmony, along with this courtyard, is the Chinese symbol most depicted to the world." Jenna pointed at the enormous hall before them.

"It's the one shown in movies, television news programs; it communicates the enormity of China's culture and China's history."

They walked through the courtyard past hundreds of tourists as Jenna pointed to a series of low-rise red buildings that bordered the east and west boundaries of the courtyard three hundred yards away on either side. "Those structures—there are hundreds of them throughout the grounds—served as warehouses for storing items such as furs, porcelain, silver, tea, silk, satin, and clothes. Today, they house exhibitions, offices, and tourist facilities."

A group of nine honor guards dressed in green military uniforms stood at attention in the middle of the large courtyard, having just completed a formation ceremony. Carrying their ceremonial flags and rifles, they marched in line to the east under the flashes of the tourists' cameras.

"In ancient Chinese theory, each of the five elements—wood, water, fire, earth, metal—had a color associated with it. Fire is represented by the color red. As you can see, it is the predominant color used on most every building and on the city walls, but not only does it represent fire and strength, it also symbolizes prosperity and happiness.

"Yellow represents earth; the imperial robes were golden yellow with a dragon on them to distinguish the emperor from man and designate him as the Son of Heaven. No one else was permitted to use or wear yellow.

"As you have also seen, China loves its dragons. There are dragons everywhere: in the artwork, in carpets and clothing, in the pavement and upon the rooftops. It is taboo to disfigure a depiction of a dragon in the same way it is taboo to burn the American flag, or desecrate the holy cross.

"In yin and yang terminology, a dragon is yang, male, and complements a yin, female, the Chinese phoenix. They balance each other. Alone they can wreak havoc; together, they bring balance and harmony."

After visiting The Hall of Supreme Harmony, where they felt an aura of solemnity and mystery and the spiritual presence of emperors long dead, Jenna led KC and Annie through several more opulent though smaller halls and palaces and finally ushered them through the imperial gardens, a labyrinth of old trees, pavilions, and flowers. "This is the last section of the Forbidden City before the north gate."

The garden was enormous, more akin to a park, and was the private enclave of the imperial family. Ancient maples, pine, and bamboo towered up into the skies with branches and leaves shading the walkways and structures.

Jenna directed them out through a gate into the eastern section, where they found themselves in a maze of tightly packed buildings. Like most others within the palace confines, the several dozen structures were red, all with similar architecture, making many indistinguishable from the next. There were long alleys and few tourists, though an occasional green-suited honor guard would pass by them, rushing through.

They emerged back into the enormous Court of the Imperial Palace and headed west. "In all of these buildings around us, in the various sections, are treasures the world could never imagine, from artifacts and paintings to jewels, gold, and treasure. Billions and billions of dollars' worth of Chinese history, the value exceeding a thieves' heaven."

"While this is all fascinating," Annie said in a mocking tone, "we really need to get to the lower level."

Jenna grew pensive as she led them across the vast courtyard before finally speaking. "You realize how many rules I'm breaking by taking you below?"

"But you understand why we must?" Annie asked.

"No, actually."

"We need to verify the contents of a single box from World War II."

"Sixty-five years after the fact?"

"The time that has lapsed is not what should worry you," Annie said.

"No?" Jenna prodded.

"You should be far more worried about how many people could die if what we suspect is in that case is there and gets out."

CHAPTER 18
MACAU

At 10:00 a.m. Michael sat in the safe house, on the other side of Macau, the plans of the Venetian laid out before him.

The roll of plans was more than a hundred pages thick, but he was focused on the structural and mechanical plans of the sublevels, all of which verified his earlier assessment of the difficulty of the heist.

Michael looked up at Jon, who lay on the couch, dozing intermittently. "I need to know about the box we are stealing."

"It's eighteen inches square, gun-metal gray."

"What's in it?"

"The diary of an admiral."

Michael stared at him, doubting his words.

"A man by the name of Marconi was selling it to a man named Xiao, the head of the Snake Triad. A very powerful and dangerous man. He attempted to steal it from Marconi, along with a red puzzle box, but the Italian had already hidden the book in a box in the depths of the Venetian."

"What would the head of a Triad want with this book?"

"There are secrets within the book."

"What kind of secrets?"

Jon ignored the question. "Xiao threatened to start a guerilla war against his enemies, and one of those enemies is the U.S. military."

"A street gang taking on the strongest military in the world?"

"This Triad is far from a street gang, and Xiao is far more dangerous than you realize. He is a terrorist; he has a network of not only street thugs, but accountants, lawyers, assassins. It is rumored that he has personally killed hundreds, yet no one has ever tied him to any crime. He is known for beheading his victims, priding himself on being an expert with a sword. He is about sending a message, about shocking people, about striking at his enemies' weaknesses.

"He was thought to have been killed by Colonel Lucas in the sea off the coast of Italy."

As Jon continued talking, Michael realized he knew Xiao—he'd seen him on the boat, the one with the ponytail, the one who had killed Marconi and his family, beheading them as Jon described.

"But Lucas believed he escaped and is about to unleash something."

"What?"

"I don't know what it is, but Lucas said the attack can be stopped if we can get hold of this diary."

"What's in the diary?" Michael pressed him.

"You asked me about the box and what it contains. I told you, that's enough."

Michael glared at Jon.

"If I was to tell you, you wouldn't believe me in a million years."

CHAPTER 19
BEIJING

The building was nondescript, no different from the other red ancillary buildings on the western side of the Forbidden City grounds. To KC's surprise, there was a parking lot nearby, shielded from the public areas, like a blasphemous intrusion of the modern world.

When Jenna opened the carved red double-wide door KC realized the structure was truly a façade, an ancient mask concealing the twenty-first century: a brightly lit lobby, an intercom on the wall, a freight elevator, its closed doors made of brushed aluminum, and a stairwell door.

The underground warehouse, three stories below ground, was vast, with more than six hundred thousand artifacts contained in the state-of-the-art facility. As ancient as the world was above, down below it was cutting-edge, modern, and ahead of its time. There were fire systems using halon instead of water so as not to damage the rich historic pieces; an environmental control system adjusted not only the temperature but the humidity in each storage room in accordance with the curator-determined ideal air setting to preserve the various pieces of art; the security system went far beyond cameras, monitors, and door alarms. The floor was embedded with a pressure-sensitive mesh to alert security of anyone's presence, day or night. It was coupled with an ID tracking card worn by museum personnel that would identify each individual and his function. The doors were magna-sealed and double-bolted, providing a fail-safe in the event of either system's being compromised.

The cameras were infrared-enabled, able to record in the dark, the logic being that intruders preferred the cover of darkness as opposed to smiling for the lens.

Forgoing the elevators, Jenna led them down three flights of stairs. At the base they were met by two large unmarked steel doors with no handles or visible hinges. Jenna pointed to the one on the left.

"The administrators recently moved their security headquarters to this underground bunker. It centralizes command, provides them with a cutting-edge police-style station. Plus, it keeps the measures of the new world from impinging on the old, allowing the illusion of history to be maintained above."

"Beijing police?" KC asked.

"No and yes; privatized but with all of the authority of the authorities. Armed and trained, most are former police; the pay is better and, even more appealing, the risk is minimal if not nonexistent."

Jenna turned to the door on the right. She waved a small white credit-card-sized card over the reader, and the sound of the lock echoed as it pulled back. Seconds later the door swung open.

The three women entered and walked into a small lobby. The black-and-white photos of The Hall of Supreme Harmony hanging on the wall above two couches, the fresh flowers on a side table, the art magazines in a rack made the space look like a doctor's office waiting room.

Without a word, Jenna waved her security card on the reader next to the only other door and they entered a large, antiseptic white corridor. Other hallways lined with doors ran off the main artery, extending hundreds of feet.

"Administrative offices," Jenna said as she pointed to the first door on the left. Continuing to walk, she pointed to a succession of doors on the right. "Environmental control, server room, cafeteria. Mechanical—"

Annie shook her head, uninterested, uncomfortably halting Jenna midsentence.

"How long did it take to build this?" KC said, trying to keep Jenna talking.

"Five years. There was a great deal of fear when this project was still in its early stages that the foundation would be compromised and the buildings above would be damaged. People forgot about the huge undertaking over forty years ago." Jenna walked briskly as she talked, KC and Annie listening as they kept pace.

"What was that?"

"At the height of the Cold War, when the Chinese feared nuclear war with the USSR, an enormous project commenced. Tunnels, shops, storage facilities, a literal underground city was built beneath Beijing. It was vast, employing thousands of workers. It was China's greatest undertaking since the Great Wall. There were fallout shelters, medical facilities, entire sections to accommodate the central government; living accommodations, roadways that are said to run for thirty miles into the mountains, an escape route for VIPs in the event of nuclear holocaust."

"Can you access it from down here?" Annie's interest perked up.

"No, there are multiple entrances around Beijing but most of them have been sealed. It's a home to rats and the indigent now. Dark and flooded in many areas. Though I have my suspicions."

"About?" KC asked.

"In the rear northeast section within a maze of buildings, there is Fengxian Hall, where they enshrined forebears; it is sealed, off-limits to even museum personnel. In my research I came across multiple references to a tunnel out of the city, constructed during the Ming Dynasty, an escape route constructed in the event the palace fell.

"In 1644, Manchu troops took over Beijing. The Forbidden City with its enormous walls and deep moat acted not only as a fortress protecting the emperor and his family but as a prison—with enemy forces on the far side of the water, awaiting his departure on all sides and all bridges. There was no escape.

"On the eve of its downfall, the emperor, Chongzhen, held a feast, gathering everyone of the imperial household aside from his sons." Jenna turned left down a deep corridor, continuing to speak as they walked. "With his sword, he killed them all except his second daughter, Princess Chang Ping, who survived though her arm was severed. It was said that Chongzhen fled to Jingshan Hill and hanged himself on a tree. But rumors persisted that the man found at the end of the noose was a servant dressed in imperial robes, his neck already broken before he was strung up on a thick branch. The body buried in Siling, in the Ming Dynasty Tombs, is that of an impostor. The real Emperor Chongzhen was smuggled out of the Forbidden City through an underground tunnel by his loyal advisors in the hope of his one day returning in triumph.

"One year later, when the Qing Dynasty took hold after the one-year Shun Dynasty had fallen, a wealthy man matching the description of Chongzhen tried to buy himself an army, only to be killed by bandits.

"I believe the story to be true." Jenna paused. "I know that the tunnel out of the Forbidden City exists."

"How do you know?" KC asked.

Jenna looked at KC, ignoring her question as she continued. "And it was the emperor's means of escape. I venture it was connected to the vast network of tunnels and bunkers dug as fallout shelters in the sixties. But I'm quite sure it has since been sealed." Jenna stopped at a door near the end of the hall, which was marked with a Chinese symbol that KC didn't understand.

"Why?" KC asked.

"No robberies," Jenna said matter-of-factly, "no workers or homeless wandering in. If the tunnel was accessible, we would have seen some kind of evidence of it."

Jenna ran her tag over the doorway and it opened with a hiss, the negative pressure released.

The room was nearly one hundred feet deep and

wide, partitioned by metal shelves that held various cases, boxes, and trays. In the far corner of the room were two men in white lab coats. They sat at a table, bright lights above their heads shining on an old painting, which they examined intently to the point of not even acknowledging Jenna's entrance.

Looking about, KC noted there were no cameras in the room. Annie's eyes searched the space for security devices.

"What are you looking for?" Jenna said to Annie.

"No security measures in here," Annie said. "Not very smart."

"No need," Jenna said as she began searching for the crate. "The cameras in the hallway will catch you as will the hallway floors."

"What? Do they rise up and suck you into the tile?" KC joked.

Jenna smiled. "No, but aside from the sensors in the floor, there is a security net that runs ten thousand volts through your body when activated, kind of like a never-ending stun gun. Won't kill you but it will take you down and make you squirm."

KC smiled. "Great. Should have worn rubber-soled shoes."

"It won't help," Jenna said. "Don't worry. It's only activated at night or when there is a security breach."

"So I guess nobody works late," KC said. "That must be nice."

"No." Jenna held up her white security card and pointed to a large red sign in bold Chinese lettering.

"Warning," Annie translated as she read. "Check

your pockets; did you leave it behind? All personnel, be sure to keep your key card with you at all times. Remember: RED LIGHT STOP, GREEN LIGHT GO."

Jenna looked at Annie, surprised at her grasp of Chinese.

"If you get stuck in here after closing hours, this card disables the system by each successive corridor you're in so you don't get tased." Jenna looked at KC. "It's not easy to find good Chinese historians."

KC and Annie looked at her, unsure if she was serious.

Jenna nodded. "Let me find that crate."

Annie handed Jenna a piece of paper with a number on it. She examined it, tucked it in her pocket, and headed into the rows of storage shelves.

As Jenna disappeared, Annie leaned into KC's ear. "When she returns with the box, I say we chew and screw, grab what we came for and go."

"We wouldn't get fifty feet before we're fried on the electric carpet."

Jenna returned carrying a large wooden crate. It was three feet by three feet, the stenciled markings on the side in Chinese, Japanese, and English: 9296273. She laid it on a work bench, opened a drawer, and pulled out a screwdriver.

"Most of these older boxes have never been placed on display," Jenna said as she jammed the screwdriver into the box lid and pried it upward, the old rusted nails squealing in protest as the top came free. "The curator wanted the original box left intact, because he believes the markings are a reminder to all that stealing from the Chinese is not possible, and that those who do so will inevitably fail and experience swift justice."

Jenna put on a pair of white gloves and peered into the box. There were six items in the wooden crate. She took each one out, laying it upon the work bench. A jade Buddha; an hourglass, its sands once again flowing as it was placed on the table; a whale tooth etched with a Chinese poem and a pouncing tiger; a tarnished brass bracelet; a porcelain crane; and a red lacquer box intricately carved with images on every side. She picked each one up, examining them as if she was holding history in her hand.

"It's as if you can feel the centuries; these were crafted nearly six hundred years ago." Jenna was in her element, inspecting the intricacy of each piece. Her strong focus seemed to transport her to another time. "The sand of this hourglass, from a beach six centuries ago. Imagine that beach . . ."

Jenna finally picked up the small red box, rolling it about in her hand. "Interesting."

"What?" Annie asked.

Jenna handed KC and Annie each a pair of gloves; they quickly put them on. She passed KC the small box. "What do you see?"

KC looked closely; the detail on the box was intricate, nearly photographic. A tall man, broad, with piercing eyes, dressed in elegant robes, stood upon the deck of a Chinese junk. On the other side was a fleet of Chinese ships, each dwarfed by an enormous six-masted junk in front, the black etching of equal detail and craftsmanship. KC finally looked up. "It's beautiful."

"Open it," Jenna said with a smile.

KC turned the box around, looking for a hasp or

lock. There was no hinge, no visible door or lid. She looked at Jenna, confused.

"It's a puzzle box." Jenna took the box and passed it to Annie, who ran her fingers along the corners and sides. "Do you know what's inside?"

"No idea," Annie lied.

Jenna pulled over a large book, thumbing through the pages, running her fingers down the Chinese numbers until . . . "Interesting."

"What?" Annie asked.

"It doesn't say what the box contains." Jenna took the box from Annie, sat at the bench, and pulled over the mounted magnifying light, viewing the red case through the magnifier. "Eight seams. These boxes were and are quite common. Shouldn't take long to open."

"How long?" Annie asked.

"A few hours unless you know someone who knows the trick."

Annie and KC exchanged a glance.

"That's odd," Jenna said.

"What?" Annie asked

"That's Zheng He," Jenna said, pointing to the engraved image of the man on the small case. She looked again at the book. "There's no reference to him in the catalogue."

Jenna grew excited as she looked closer at the intricate box. KC became caught up in her interest and looked over her shoulder.

"I should really alert the curator when he returns on Monday; this is a significant piece."

Annie took a step back, looked about the room, at

the closed door, at the lack of cameras, at the three Chinese men equally absorbed in their own piece of art on the far side of the room. She took a deep breath, reached into her long black coat, and drew out a pistol, her arm falling to her side as she looked at the three men. Annie turned to Jenna, who was still absorbed in the small red box, and raised the gun to the back of her head.

Her eyes darted briefly to the men at the table on the far side of the room, who were equally oblivious to her actions. Her finger wrapped the trigger, she took another breath, and—

KC snatched the gun from her hand.

Jenna jumped in her seat, nearly dropping the box; startled at the commotion, she spun around. "What's the matter?"

KC shook her head as she buried the gun within her coat. "Nothing, sorry."

Annie couldn't disguise her anger.

Jenna stared at her, suspicious. Finally, "You're annoyed."

"It's that obvious?" Annie said as she looked at KC. "You have no idea."

Jenna looked back at the crate. "What you were looking for wasn't in there, was it? Perhaps in one of the other cases." Jenna pointed to the hundreds of crates on the shelves.

"No," Annie said. "This is the right case."

"Do you mind if I inquire what you were hoping to find?" Jenna asked.

"No, you may not," Annie said.

"Of course." KC glared at Annie. "We were just making sure that certain U.S. property wasn't mixed in with the crate. A number of World War II files concerning war criminals."

"After sixty-five years?"

"The government's a little upside down and behind," KC said with a smile. She hated how she could lie so easily.

"Well." Jenna placed the items back in the crate. She picked up the red box last. "I'm sorry . . ."

"It's okay," KC said. "We just need to verify that mistakes weren't made. Thank you, though."

Jenna placed the red box in the crate, pulled a hammer from the drawer, put the lid in place, and banged the nails back in.

CHAPTER 20

1950

Jacob and Isaac Lucas were born January 3, 1950, to Admiral Howard and Lily Lucas at Naval Base San Diego, what some affectionately called 32 Street Naval Station, home to the Pacific Fleet. The boys came into the world a month early and several pounds underweight. It being the 1950s, the prognosis wasn't good, and neither child was expected to live. Placed in separate incubators, the three-pound boys were barely recognizable as human beneath all of the tubes, wires, and gauze.

Both were near death, neither expected to make it through the night. Howard and Lily were at their side, each laying hands upon the boys, as their frailness and need for oxygen prevented them from being held. The grieving parents bade them good-bye, left the ICU, and went to the lounge to wait for the inevitable.

Brittany Colin was the nurse on duty for the neonatal ICU. Her only charges were the boys, and she, too, sat in wait for God's hand to take them away. Seeing them alone, never to know the closeness of another human being, never to know what it was like to be held, broke her heart. They had lived for nine months together in their mother's womb, growing side by side, only to leave the comforting warmth to arrive sickly in a cold world. She couldn't imagine the confusion and loneliness the two brothers felt. Coming into the world early, only to know pain, never to know what it was like to laugh, to feed at their mother's breast, to jump and play, to feel the warmth of love.

With their end near, Brittany had a thought and immediately acted upon it. She looked down the hall, but no one was around: The doctor on call was sleeping in an upstairs office, the duty nurse at the desk was doing a crossword puzzle. In their short little lives, she would at least give them the feeling of knowing each other, of knowing what it was like to lie beside family, to feel the unconditional love of a brother's touch.

Arranging the tubes and wires in such a way as not to impede their function, Brittany moved Isaac into Jacob's incubator. She laid them face-to-face, their small legs touching, each feeling the small amount of warmth flowing from the other, both knowing what it was like to be in the presence of another human being, of the warmth of family.

Brittany climbed back into her chair and finally drifted off to sleep, fearing the fateful sound of the monitor alarm, of the crashing hearts of the infants when death came calling. But by seven that morning, there had been no alarm, no death. Looking back in the incubator, she saw both boys alive, their skin pigment improved, warm, red, and alive.

They had cheated death, as small and frail as they

were. With no one believing in them, no one giving them a chance, they were saved by each other.

WHEN THE BOYS were nine months old, well on their way to toddlerhood, their father was transferred back to Japan, where he continued to be in charge of repatriating the looted wares of China. Though the war had ended with the Allies victorious, the unwinding of the war effort continued for seven years. They mapped each of the sunken vessels of the war, both U.S. and Japanese. War crime trials lasted forever, and there were mysteries to be solved: Planes had gone missing and ships had sunk with their final resting places unknown. Families deserved closure and members of his office would see to that. Then there were the opportunists, the war profiteers who pillaged and plundered homes, museums, banks. Priceless artifacts had gone missing, huge stores of gold were nowhere to be found. And Howard Lucas was in charge of finding it, returning it, and closing it all out.

While the boys had started their lives so close to death, they had quickly recovered and caught up with their peers. Inseparable, they were twins in every way, not just in appearance but in manner and mind, except for one difference: Isaac was closer to his father while Jacob was closer to his mother. It was almost as if they bore the respective genes of each parent. As in most families, they loved their parents and their parents loved them in return, but there was a special connection, a certain subtle favoritism and closeness that was evident.

When the boys were three, their father was stationed

back to San Diego, and upon arrival, immersed his boys in everything American. He took them to baseball games, fed them hamburgers and hot dogs. He took them to the movies to see *Fantasia, Pinocchio, A Christmas Carol,* and the wellspring of 1950s cinema. And he introduced them to sailing.

The boat was only thirty-nine feet, but to the boys it was a grand yacht. They were Captain Ahab, they were Blackbeard, they were Columbus seeing the New World for the first time as they cut across the blue waters off San Diego. They slept on the boat on too many occasions to remember, their father regaling them with stories of pirates, of distant lands, of a far-off island he called Penglai, not on any map—a place filled with treasure, where life was simple, where magic existed and no one ever died; where the secret of life and death was forever hidden. Their father told them of the journeys of Jason and the Argonauts, Sinbad, and Odysseus, filling their minds with wonderment and adventure.

He taught them to man the jib, hoist the sail, guide the ship by the stars like the heroes from the stories of old. He taught them knots, currents, the tides, and the seasons; he taught them how to smell the air, feel the wind, and most important, to taste life.

Unlike their father, their mother, Lily, hated the sea and everything to do with it. She couldn't swim and had no desire to learn. Born in Hong Kong, raised in Macau, she grew up with her feet planted firmly in the ground. Of Han Chinese descent, she had a quiet beauty, dark eyes filled with emotion, black silklike hair that cascaded down her back, an ever-present jade and ivory comb tucked on the right side of her head. She was a woman who spoke only of her life since meeting Howard, as if the past had never occurred—though sadly, it had.

She had run away from home at the age of seventeen. Her parents had died, gunned down on the streets of Macau. Her older brother begged her to stay with him, promising he would provide for her, watch out for her, make sure she got an education, but she couldn't reconcile herself with his employment. He was rumored to be a strong arm in a local Triad. Her brother tried to convince her that he was merely embracing their heritage, following in the footsteps of their father, a man she had always thought of as a simple, peaceful merchant. But the newspapers, writing of his death, told her of a stranger, a violent man who controlled the streets, a man who was the antithesis of who she'd thought her father was. She boiled with anger for having been shielded from the truth, and was enraged that her mother had been swept into death at her husband's side.

Ashamed at her naïveté, of what her father had wrought, of the blood that flowed in her veins, she packed up in the middle of the night and left, running as fast as she could, looking for a new life, a new world in Hong Kong. She changed her name, created a new past of being orphaned in the war. She worked as a waitress, a maid, anything she could find that would provide her with enough money to afford the single room she rented in the darkest district of the giant city. Her beauty finally helped secure her the position of hostess at the Hong Kong Hilton, where she was the face all would see upon arrival.

It was there that she met Admiral Howard Lucas, fifteen years her senior, an officer in the United States Navy. A man of goodness, of strong moral fiber, who loved his country, defended his people, who would give his life for those in his command. He was the man she had thought her father had been until that fateful day when she'd learned the hard truths. He was the light to her father's darkness, the calm to her father's storm. He was the man who would bring balance to her life.

Despite his age, he swept her off her feet with promises of a new world and taking her back to America. She was enamored of him, enthralled with his power and dignity, with his black Irish looks—deep-blue eyes, jet-black hair—his broad shoulders and oversized charisma. She quickly fell in love. With nothing for her in China anymore, she left with him, marrying him, ever so happy in his arms, comfort, and safety.

IT WAS ON a Friday evening—their eight-year-old twins asleep in their beds—that Howard had asked for her help, something that hadn't been asked of her in all of her life, not by her father, her brother, not even by Howard up until now. He brought her into his study and closed the door, seemingly afraid he was being spied on. The rows of books and documents on the bookshelf were divided into sections, one for each location that Howard had traveled to on his sailing excursions, from the time when he was young upon his father's boat through the war, to most recently on his own boat; each section had materials on the destination as well as the accompanying sea charts of its location. It was a trophy case of his travels.

From the lowermost shelf he pulled out a lockbox, inserted a key, and opened it upon his desk. From within he pulled a small black lacquered box about the size of a clay brick, one side engraved with a fearsome dragon, wisps of smoke pouring from his nostrils as it battled a tiger whose bared fangs were poised to strike, while the other sides were covered in mythical creatures. Lily examined it closely. There were no seams or hinges; there was a heft to it, giving the impression of its being solid. It appeared to be an ornamental talisman from a forgotten age kept in households to ward off spirits.

Lily placed it on the desk as Howard reached back into the box and withdrew a large velvet bag, the red material worn and tattered with age. He smiled at her as he opened it and pulled out a book, placing it before Lily as if he were giving her the gift of his soul.

It was written in Chinese, elegant and old. She looked upon it with excitement, for she instantly knew what it was: It had been spoken of when she was a child, as part of China's great history, but the lines between reality and myth were always blurred in the minds of children. She did not ask Howard how he came to possess it, as she was overwhelmed with curiosity about what the book contained.

Over the coming year, when time would allow, they would open the box as if in ceremony, remove the velvet bag, and lay the book before them; they would set the wooden black talisman on the table for good luck, and become lost in history. They would sit together as Lily would painstakingly translate the ancient text, helping Howard to write it out, explaining in detail the meaning behind the words. When they finished for the evening, he would once again wrap up the book, place it along with the talisman back in the box, and put it on the shelf.

Fourteen months later, they were halfway through, the interruptions of his work and travels slowing their progress. It was Lily's favorite time with Howard; she was helping him, she had purpose, and they were together. It was in those moments she felt most complete, and she yearned for them, wishing it could be every night. But suddenly it all changed.

She was in the midst of translating a section, Howard jotting down notes beside the literal translation, when she suddenly stopped and slammed the book closed. Howard was startled by the abruptness of her action and as he looked at her he could see the fear in her eyes. Without a word, she put the book back in the bag, picked up the black talisman, placed them in the box, and closed it. Howard gently asked her what was wrong, but she just shook her head and went to bed.

A week later, Howard asked her if they could resume the project and Lily simply said no. He implored her to explain why, but she merely said she could never read that book again.

As time rolled on, Howard would ask her about it again, and she simply wouldn't respond. He explained that he needed to know what was in the book, but she refused to speak of it anymore.

A month later, when the boys were asleep in their room, he struck her, hard across the mouth, knocking her to the floor. It was after a long dinner with officers and wives from the base; she had prepared a traditional

Chinese meal in their San Diego home while her husband had provided traditional American whiskey. Everyone had left with smiles and laughter, she was cleaning the kitchen, and turned to Howard. She merely asked if she could go to school. He had screamed at her. How dare she ask such a thing of him when she denied him help, when she wouldn't tell him what the book said?

She had never seen that side of him. It was as if a monster had crawled out of the depths of his soul and possessed him. His drunkenness brought out a dark side, one that was violent and out of control, one that he had hidden from her and the Navy much in the way that she had hidden from him her past as well as the things within the Chinese text of the book that scared her.

But he was instantly remorseful, shamed by what he had done; he begged her for forgiveness, something that had never been asked of her before. And she saw this great warrior reduced to just a man who feared losing his wife for his actions.

He didn't raise a hand to her again . . . for another month. This time it was worse: He blackened her eye, left heavy bruises on her cheek. She didn't leave the house for a week. She had nowhere to go, no one to call or run to. She was a foreigner in 1950s America, married to a war hero. No one would believe, let alone listen to, the accusations of a Chinese woman.

And again, he begged for forgiveness, swearing he would never drink again. He loved her and couldn't live without her. He bought her things: a new necklace, a dress. He would pay for her schooling if she still wanted it.

One Sunday afternoon, the boys, being boys, got into a fistfight over who could run the fastest. Lily scolded them as she had done in the past for so many of their fights, knowing that within minutes the boys would be best friends again and the fight would be nothing but a distant memory. It was what boys did. But Howard had seen the incident from the window and came charging out. He had never seen them strike each other.

Though the matter was over, though Lily had already addressed it, he grabbed Jacob by the arm, shaking him, yelling at him while not once turning his anger on Isaac. Lily could see the fear in her son as he trembled in his father's grasp. And while the moment passed, she began to understand to whom Howard would direct his anger if she ever left.

One month later, he broke her jaw.

By now the boys were more than nine years old. And she began to fear that he would soon turn his drunken rage on them. She still feared the police, and finally succumbed to the idea that there was only one place to run to.

She loved Howard more than life, but feared him even more. It was the hardest decision of her life.

IN THE MIDDLE of the night, Jacob was awoken from his sleep by his mother. Fearing trouble, Jacob began to tremble, but Lily took his hand and pulled him from the bedroom. She told him everything was all right, they just needed to go out for a bit. But the next thing Jacob knew he was on a plane. His mother kept insisting it would all be all right, that they just needed to go away for a bit. They landed at the crack of dawn in a far-off city, only to be put in a car, then on a boat, to finally arrive in a run-down city. They had only the clothes on their backs and the metal lockbox that his mother carried in a shopping bag that she never put down for the duration of the eighteen-hour trip.

They arrived at the home of his mother's brother, a tall man with long, dark hair and a frightful scar on the side of his neck. He wore a black fedora and his fingers were adorned in chunky gold rings. Jacob had never seen anyone like him except in some horror movie. His name was Kwon, and though he scared him, Kwon spoke to him in English, spoke to him like a man, like he belonged in his world.

Jacob asked his mother when they would be going home and he would see Isaac and his dad. She told him soon, but soon never came. The days dragged on into weeks. Jacob missed his brother, his country, as he wondered about the strange world he was now in. He didn't understand the language, the people, or the customs, though his mother seemed perfectly at home.

She had assimilated back into Chinese society, shunning America and everything to do with his father. She enrolled Jacob in school, spoke only Chinese in their home, and insisted that Jacob do the same.

HOWARD AWOKE THE morning after Lily snuck away to find a small box and a note beside the bed.

Howard,

I can no longer live in fear. I'm taking Jacob but I'm leaving you Isaac. We both know he is your favorite. Though I fear for him, I know you will not touch him for you would not hurt your favorite son. And if you do, I will come back for him, taking him away, as I took away Jacob, to a place you will never find any of us.

Howard opened the box and looked at the jade and ivory item within.

Please give Isaac my comb, it is all I have to leave him. It was my mother's, all I had of her when she left me for heaven. Tell him I love him, that he will always be in my heart, and that he makes me proud.

I am truly sorry about the book, about not completing the translation. I know it is the root of your anger with me, the frustration that culminates in your drinking, but what I read within those pages, what that talisman contains, should be forgotten to history.

Lily

Howard returned to Hong Kong, searching high and low. He went back to the Hilton, hired a detective, but no one had ever heard of Lily. He implored his military contacts to reach out, but all inquiries came back empty. There was no doubt she had returned to her old existence.

Howard thought that when they had met, he was saving Lily, providing her with a life in America, a world so much better than China, so much more sophisticated, so much more intelligent than the old world she had come from. She had never voiced her concern, never spoken of her displeasure with her new life, and most important, had never spoken of her past. It was as if she had rejected everything to do with her upbringing. And having kept her past a secret from him, she'd found the perfect place to hide.

Howard returned to the United States a broken and hollow man. He poured all of his efforts into Isaac, ensuring he attended the finest schools and participated in sports, taking him to West Point the June after high school graduation. They were as close as any father and son could be.

And though both of them continued to wonder where Jacob and Lily might be, neither of them spoke of it. It was as if half of their family no longer existed, as if they had fallen off the face of the earth.

CHAPTER 21
BEIJING

"I'll get the access card from her," Annie told KC as they walked back into the hotel.

"Not a chance." KC stopped in her tracks. She knew Annie wouldn't hesitate to hurt her, or even silence her. "Let me get it."

"How do I know you're not going to try something foolish?"

"Seriously? Where the hell am I going to go?" KC said. "Do you think I'd play with Michael's life like that?"

THE HOTEL RESTAURANT was half-empty. It was just after one in the afternoon. KC and Jenna were halfway through lunch; though it was only midday, KC felt like it was midnight. She had had a headache all day and the pain seemed to be creeping into her joints. She had taken two Tylenols when she awoke that morning and two more fifteen minutes earlier, but they weren't helping . . . and probably wouldn't until she knew Michael was safe.

Jenna had combed her hair and put on a J.Crew dress, trying hard to keep up with KC's appearance. They talked of life, China, weather, the Imperial Palaces, and made general small talk until dessert arrived.

"Can I ask you a question?"

"Of course," Jenna said.

"How do you know those tunnels beneath the Forbidden City exist?"

"Because . . ." A hint of mischief filled Jenna's eyes.

"You went down there," KC said with a smile, "didn't you?"

"Yeah." Jenna nodded, and finally gave a guilty smile. "I heard about them. No one would confirm it. I'm a curious woman, I want answers, I want to unlock history, so that's what I did; I've written a thesis on it, but I have to be careful how I put it out there. Most of the museum staff is male, and they are very dismissive of women, particularly American women."

"What were the tunnels like?"

"Not great. They're flooded, but once you get past the water they join up with the Beijing tunnels." Jenna paused. "Intriguing, right?"

KC smiled as their coffee arrived, remaining silent, as if she was building up to something.

"Did you ever make a mistake?" KC asked.

"Every day," Jenna said with a smile.

"I mean the type that blows up your life and throws everything good about it out the window."

"I got married when I was eighteen," Jenna said. "High school love, you know, the one that no one can talk you out of. Tim and I were freshmen at Berkeley, I was a dual major, Chinese and art history. Tim was philosophy and world politics. We were both filled with anger and angst; we had all the answers. March on Washington, the UN—decry capitalism, the military, hell, half the time we didn't even know what we were marching for, but we both had this rage in us and wanted to change the world, make it better. One night, I'm studying and I have this epiphany: Our parents paid for our college and it occurred to me I was protesting the system that they succeeded in, that gave them the money to send me to school. I was railing against the means that gave me the power to protest. Confusing, right?"

KC nodded and smiled. "On so many levels."

"Well, Tim didn't see my point. I told him I was thinking about getting focused, spending a semester here in Beijing to get closer to what I loved. He couldn't understand; he said I was his wife, how could I do that to him, leave him? I told him I wasn't leaving him, that I loved him, that it was just for a semester. We had a terrible fight over it, but I knew somehow we'd figure it out.

"He was killed two days later in a car accident; he was just short of DWI. I couldn't help thinking he got drunk trying to come to terms with my leaving for six months."

KC stared at her.

"So, yeah. I think I blew up my life."

Seeing the pain in Jenna's eyes, KC let the moment hang.

"Would you change what you did?" KC whispered. "What you said?"

"To get Tim back, I would do anything." There were

tears in Jenna's eyes. "I love what I do, but not a day goes by without my regretting that I'm here alone."

"I'm sorry," KC said, then paused. "There's a man I love, his name is Michael."

Jenna smiled. "Are you married?"

KC shook her head and held up her naked ring finger.

"You don't need a ring around your finger to be married." Jenna smiled. "Our hearts tell us we are committed to each other, not bands of gold. Too often we define our lives by ceremonies and deny the reality of the situation."

KC nodded, knowing Jenna's words were true.

"I'm sorry if I overstepped my bounds, if I said—"

KC stopped her. "No, it's not you."

Jenna tilted her head in sympathy, urging her to continue.

"The woman I'm with—"

"Annie?"

"The people she works for—"

"I thought she works for the U.S. military."

"She does. A rogue section, I believe. They have Michael."

"I don't understand."

"If I don't do what she wants, they'll kill him, and she will kill me."

Jenna looked scared and nervous. She gazed around the restaurant as if people were watching her. "You should go to the embassy—"

"Can't," KC said quickly.

"Police?"

KC shook her head.

"Why you?" Jenna said.

KC explained what had happened; she told her everything short of what she was planning to do tonight.

"Two days ago, I blew up my life. I walked away from everything, the man I loved, the friends and the world I had grown fond of. I can't help thinking all this wouldn't have happened if I had just stopped and looked around, if I had thought about him instead of myself. He's the man I love; I would do anything to save him."

"Why are you telling me this?" Jenna's voice was laced with fear.

"Relax," KC said. "No harm will come to you. The focus is on me."

"You're telling me for a reason, KC."

KC picked up her napkin and wiped her mouth, and as she laid the napkin back in her lap, she saw the drop of blood. She had always been healthy and ascribed it to the incredible stress she was under.

"Are you okay?" Jenna asked, seeing the concern on KC's face.

"I'm fine," KC said. She took a breath and whispered, "I need your security card."

"Why?"

"You can just say that you lost it."

"I don't understand," Jenna said.

"They have the man I love. I have to make this right."

Jenna sat there, staring at KC, thinking, the moment dragging on until . . .

She reached into her bag, pulled out the card, and

handed it to KC. "Do you want me to call the embassy?"

"No. All they'll do is arrest me, and Michael will die."

"I can't stand that woman," Jenna said. "I didn't like her from the moment she hired me."

KC smiled. "You and I have a lot in common."

"Are you going to be all right?" Jenna was regaining her composure.

"We'll see." KC nodded.

"That's why you wanted to know about the tunnel?"

KC nodded. "Yeah."

"Well," Jenna said, leaning closer. "There is something you should know about those tunnels. . . ."

CHAPTER 22
MACAU

Michael had a plan. He sat at the work bench in the safe house in the heart of Macau, alone with his thoughts, while Jon headed back to the Venetian.

As much as Michael didn't want to include Jon in his planning, he knew he needed him not only to gain access to the depths of the Venetian, but to help him understand the mind-set of the guards and the security personnel, to offer cultural details, to procure supplies, and to translate the Chinese language.

Michael had sent him out at dawn with a shopping list: Many of the items were common, some were difficult to procure, and several near impossible to obtain. But six hours later, Jon had returned with everything on Michael's list.

In the small kitchen of the apartment, two large pots were at a boil, a makeshift ventilation hood above them drawing the noxious fumes through a tube out the window. The mixture of mothballs, sugar, and hydrogen peroxide was already almost a paste. The electronic detonators lay in wait on the counter.

Alone in the apartment, Michael took inventory of the weapons on-site: a small arsenal, enough to equip a strike force with not only pistols and submachine guns, but explosives, communication devices, and body armor.

He made quick work of the lock on the filing cabinet. Michael was more than shocked at the various clandestine Asian operations conducted by Colonel Lucas and his various teams over the years, operations on allies and enemies alike. He examined the redacted dossier on Jon Lei. He was a subcontractor from the Tridiem Group, but beyond his military service there was nothing but blacked-out history—his birthday, his relationships, everything hidden from Michael's prying eyes.

Michael looked at an operation file dated three days ago. It contained a vague outline on the procurement of the box in vault number 16; it showed a time frame and bios on him and KC, their talents, and recent jobs. No one outside of his close inner circle of Simon, Busch, and KC was aware of his recent activities, or so he'd thought. With an unsettled feeling in his gut, he closed the file, and laid it on the workbench.

He picked up one of the Venetian's gambling tokens and examined it. Having seen the sublevels, having walked the areas he needed to access, he was more equipped to identify vulnerabilities. Michael realized that the one thing that could roam freely within the casino was its most precious item: the token, the elegant house money that was a conduit to capturing the contents of people's pockets, their credits cards and their wealth. The Venetian's emphasis on protecting the token and its fear of the token's vulnerability were the beginning of a plan.

Before him sat circular tokens of each denomination: $5, $10, $25, $100, $500, $1,000, and $10,000. The intricate design of the larger denominations—the holograms and artwork—could be replicated, but not in the time frame Michael had to work with and not on the scale he would require. But that was not his plan. He had delicately cut each token open with a small electric handsaw and extracted the RFID chips, the heart of the token's security.

Michael took a chip and laid it under the mounted magnifier, enhancing the image tenfold. The wafer-thin RFID microchip was manufactured by TSI, a company he was familiar with; it looked like a piece of copper foil no larger than a U.S. dime. There were two parts to the device: a programmed, integrated circuit for storing and processing information, modulating and demodulating a radio-frequency signal, and the antenna, which wrapped around the chip like a tightly wound maze, for receiving and transmitting the signal. This particular microchip was an active RFID tag, with a microbattery that allowed the chip to transmit signals once it was placed into service and activated by the Venetian's security system.

While Carl, the security manager, had spoken of the token, he did not realize that, as with every security system, there were vulnerabilities, safeguards, and back doors.

While Michael was an expert in security and his company had the reputation of being a leader in preventing penetration, much of his work had shifted from the mechanical world of locks and safes to computer-assisted safeguards. He had designed all manner of firewalls, encryption, and ID cloaking for his clients to supplement the alarm systems hardwired into bricks and mortar. He understood the simplicity of the RFID chip before him as if he had designed it himself. While Rene Clauge, the young MIT grad, might have pounded his chest in pride at his innovation, Michael spoke the language and knew that the former MIT student had simply enhanced a safeguard similar to the one used in the retail industry to prevent the theft of ladies' dresses, electronics, and sneakers.

Michael fired up the computer, affixed several small wires to the chip in front of him, started the diagnostics, and began to backward-engineer the chip.

In a similar fashion he figured out how to penetrate the sublevels of the Venetian—for just as with the RFID chip, the more sophisticated the security system, the more room it contained for error and vulnerability.

Michael looked back at the operation file on the desk, picked it up, and reread it. In the dossier on him and KC and their illicit backgrounds, the identification of who supplied the info had been redacted. Michael trusted Simon and Busch with his life, as did KC. He couldn't imagine who would sell them out, but someone had.

Michael glanced at the security monitor and saw Jon returning, no doubt to seek an update, to emphasize their deadline, to hear the plan.

Michael returned the operation file to the filing cabinet and locked the cabinet. Even though Jon had a bull's-eye on Michael and was itching to take his life, Michael would include Jon in his planning. But that didn't mean he'd include him in his endgame.

Because Michael had every intention of spending the rest of his life with KC.

Michael had a plan.

THE LEARJET FLEW in over the China Sea, swooped down over the Pearl River Delta, and touched down at Macau International Airport, taxiing to the private terminal.

The two men exited the jet with their luggage over their shoulders; dressed in khakis and sport coats, they looked like they were heading to the golf course instead of the casino.

Sergeant Ken Reiner was large, intimidating, with a hard jaw and a heavy brow. He was known for his toughness both in and out of the ring and had escorted many full-bird colonels and generals abroad not only because of his intelligence and ability to get things done, but because of the sheer brute force he projected. Reiner was a last-minute addition to the team; General Garland had called him personally, apologizing for pulling him from his family after only one day back from a month in Germany.

The general was concerned for Colonel Lucas's well-being. Lucas had lost several members of his team in a botched operation off the coast of Italy only days earlier, and had yet to stop since. He had been to New York, Los Angeles, and now China all in a matter of days, assembling a team outside the military, a group of for-hires composed of former spec-ops and private contractors, their identities being held close to the chest for fear of a breach of security in light of the Italian debacle.

Lucas was known as a tough commander but he looked out for his team as if they were his family, putting his own life on the line too many times to count in order to save a man in trouble. He was equally ruthless in carrying out his assignments, known for crossing the line on several occasions, breaking rules and laws to get a job done. Some said it was why he had yet to make general after so much time in the military, but truth be told, Lucas preferred the field over the desk and politics.

Reiner read the eyes-only file. Lucas had been after a man named Xiao for several years on suspicion of terrorist activity, supplying arms to enemies of the state, and, most recently, a direct threat against military personnel. Lucas's intel had uncovered that Xiao was close to possessing a weapon that he was looking to sell and would be publicly demonstrating it before the week was out. Lucas's team had failed to intercept the unidentified weapon, and now Lucas was in an all-out race to find it before others did.

While the file stated that Xiao had been left for dead on a scuttled yacht in the Tyrrhenian Sea, there was mention of a suspicion that he had survived and was far closer to obtaining the lockbox with the weapon than Lucas was.

They were up against a hard clock, a drop-dead time only three days away. It was Reiner's express directive to assist the colonel and keep him safe, for it was feared that Xiao's ultimate target was not a military base or a U.S. installation or facility, but Lucas himself.

CHAPTER 23

1960

Lily and young Jacob moved into her brother's house in a small, affluent section of Macau. The house was large by Macau standards and afforded Lily and her ten-year-old son their own rooms in a small wing of the Mediterranean-style house.

While Lily had rejected her heritage, her family legacy, she couldn't help the familial bond she had with her brother, Kwon. Despite knowing what he had become, how dangerous he was, he was only dangerous to others and would protect her and Jacob with his life.

There was no disguising her bruises and injuries, so Lily had no choice: She told her brother what had happened between her and Howard, told him of the alcohol-induced violence, the way he treated her as inferior, how she feared leaving Isaac behind. But she was very careful not to tell him of the box she carried and what it contained, for as much as she loved her brother she feared what he would do if it came into his possession.

Kwon became enraged at the sight of her, that someone would do this to his sister. Lily had to do everything she could to stop him from sending people after Howard to seek retribution. He was Jacob's father, Isaac's father.

She couldn't bear what the death of a parent would do to them. She made Kwon swear that for as long as he lived no harm would ever come to Howard Lucas.

Kwon was unmarried, his focus always on business, though he longed for a son—someone he could trust, someone who could assume his mantle when the time came. He grew close to Jacob, but Lily insisted that Jacob be shielded from Kwon's world, from the violence and darkness of it all. And Kwon agreed; he loved and respected his younger sister and would do nothing to offend her as long as she lived.

One evening Lily went for a walk. She passed St. Christopher's Church and the Rao Buddhist Temple, glad to be in a world she understood, among people she felt comfortable with. Despite what her father had been and her brother had become, this was the world she knew and where she felt at home.

And it was on those streets as she walked back to her brother's house that she was killed. No one saw the assailant, no description was given. She was merely found dead in the street in a pool of her own blood, a single bullet through her head. There was skin beneath her nails; she had struggled against her attacker only to die in the end.

Her brother raged against the world at his sister's death. He ordered the assassin found, a bounty placed on the head of her killer. There were whispers on the street of retribution, of revenge not against Kwon for his past deeds but against Lily. Word of an American talking to her in a café, arguing with her, demanding the return of something she had stolen, but beyond the man's young appearance, his tattered green military shirt and blue jeans, no one knew anything else.

Kwon searched her room, trying to glean why someone would kill Lily, why someone would go after the innocent sister of the head of a Triad, knowing it was a death sentence. It didn't take him long to find the lockbox with Howard Lucas's name on it. He broke off the lock and found the book, marveling at its antiquity, thumbing through its pages. He drew out a black lacquered piece of wood, an antique whose images would frighten some, but certainly not a man who possessed more fearsome tattoos on his body. But being prudent, he sealed it back up, putting it back in the box and tucking it under the bed.

Kwon broke the news to Jacob, holding him as he wept. Jacob had loved and worshipped his mother, and when he finally looked up from his grief, he told Kwon that he had to tell his brother and his father of her death.

And in that moment, Kwon made the decision that would shape the boy's life, his entire world. He had wanted a son and loved Jacob dearly as his own. He couldn't bear sending him back to the U.S., back to his father, a man who filled him with such anger. For Lily's husband had struck her, beaten her on numerous occasions, and had never reached out to his own son, never made any attempt to contact him.

It was the last place Kwon would let Jacob go. So in order to erase the longing Kwon knew would arise, he told him a story. He told him of his mother's death, how it was at the hands of the American military, at the hands of his father, who had sent an assassin for hire to steal a box from his mother. It was an action of jealousy and hate of all things Chinese.

Kwon took the devastated boy as his own, a child who had lost both his mother and his father on that night. He thought of killing the man, Lily's husband, but he had made her a promise. More important, having Howard alive could prove to Kwon's advantage.

And in his dark ways, in much the way he manipulated his own people, he further shaped Jacob's thoughts and opinions. Slowly, Jacob began to embrace his uncle, embrace China, Macau, and Hong Kong. He learned the ways of the street and the world from his uncle's perspective, finally developing a thirst for it, a need to cast away his father's lineage and embrace his mother's heritage, his Chinese half.

Kwon taught him how to fight, a combination of styles more suited to the streets than some dance or movie. He taught him the various styles of wushu, what Americans called kung fu; he showed him how different situations required different methods. He taught him the *dao*—the Chinese sword. He taught him of its beauty and how it should be handled and revered. He taught him the *gun* (staff), the *qian* (spear), and the *jian* (two-sided broadsword). These were elegant weapons from a forgotten age, which most considered inferior to a gun, but Kwon thought of them as honorable and equally deadly.

Kwon had kept Lily's box, never revealing its contents or existence to Jacob, thinking it cursed, thinking that it was followed by death. He had skimmed the book, understanding its value, but not comprehending its true historic worth. He sold it to a friend, his attorney and business associate who had helped to make much of Kwon's business legitimate, assisting in laundering money, keeping his name apart from his true underworld dealings. The man was as violent and deadly as Kwon but hid his dealings behind titles, degrees, and pinstripe suits. The Italian was a collector as opposed to an investor who would seek to sell the book at a profit; he had a passion for antique weapons, swords, guns— items that dated to the feudal ages.

In the year of Jacob's sixteenth birthday, in Kwon's eyes Jacob became a man. On his way home from school— Kwon insisted upon not only high school, but college— Jacob was attacked. It was a young gang, four of them, like a pack of dogs, their strength in their numbers. They leaped upon Jacob, knocking him to the ground, kicking him in the gut, the face. They ripped the school bag from his shoulder, the shoes from his feet, the shirt from his back, all the while taunting him as *gwailo,* a foreign devil.

While Jacob had been trained in wushu, had mastered sparring and street fighting, it was always within the confines of a gym, under the tutelage of teachers, never in the outside world, where his life was on the line, where there was no second chance, where there was no do-over.

As he lay in a ball, burying his face in his knees, Jacob was gripped in fear and shame. All that he had been taught was useless, the arrogance for thinking himself immortal, indestructible, was a façade of wrongful pride.

And as the thought of death filled him, he thought of his mother, dying on the streets in the same manner, unable to defend herself against the assassin, against the man his father had sent. And as the rage filled him, it wiped away his cowardice. An awakening took place within him, as if his true self had lain dormant all of these years. He buried the pain deep inside him, the fear left him, and instinct finally took over.

With unexpected power, Jacob kicked outward, swept out the feet of the largest boy, the aggressive alpha, knocking him to the ground. And as he jumped to his bare feet, the three others dove upon him, but this time it was different. Jacob spun about in a whirl of kicks and jabs, his movements turning his aggressors' momentum upon themselves.

His blows were direct and harsh, shattering jaws, breaking noses and arms—something the three underlings had never experienced.

The alpha leaped to his feet, knife in hand. Jacob saw anger and fear in the teen's eyes, a wanton lust to kill. But Jacob didn't turn and run. He centered himself, his mind free of thought, allowing his body to react.

As the older teen lunged at him, Jacob blocked his attack, snapping his attacker's wrist as he snatched away the blade. And in a series of lightning-quick moves, Jacob turned the knife on his assailant. He slashed him about the body, legs, and arms, neck and face, shallow strokes neither deadly nor debilitating, though horrific in appearance. Blood flew about in a mist as Jacob handled the weapon like a master. The three others, broken and helpless, looked on in horror as their friend was disfigured before them.

As the teen fell to the ground, beaten, bloodied, and humiliated, Jacob stood over him, his heart swelling with pride, a newfound ego resulting from the power he realized he possessed. He could take life from others, like a child crushing a bug.

In that moment, looking down at what was now his victim, he thought of his mother lying dead in the street at the hands of someone like the teen before him. He thought of his father and what he had done to him: killing his mother, robbing him of everything. It at once emptied his heart of feeling, leaving him hollow inside, while filling him with unbridled rage.

And with those feelings coursing through him, he leaned down and slashed the teen's throat as if the boy were his mother's killer, or his father. He would not give this street thug the opportunity for retribution; he would not let him attack another innocent.

Jacob turned and walked to the other teens, who lay there in horror at their friend's death. He took back his shoes, his bag, and his shirt. He finally leaned down and whispered in perfect Mandarin, "Speak of this to anyone and I will hunt each of you down. While your friend's death was quick, yours will not be."

JACOB CAME OF age. He told Kwon what had happened and the matter was swept away. No mention in the paper, no police investigation, just rumors in hushed tones of a new member of the Snake Triad.

And with Jacob's first kill, Kwon renamed him. He was not a *gwailo*; his Anglo-Saxon name of Jacob Lucas would be cast aside. Kwon explained that he must embrace his culture, embrace who he truly was. He called him Xiao Yan Wang, a name that combined the words for a mythical demon of the mountains and the Chinese god of death.

CHAPTER 24
BEIJING

KC entered the hotel suite and saw a cache of weapons spread out on the large four-poster bed. Two Galil sniper rifles, three Glock 9mms, four radio earpieces with subvocal mics. There were also two black outfits, dark stocking caps, a mousy-brown wig, several ropes, grappling hooks, and two sheathed knives.

Annie picked up a pistol and threw it to KC, who caught it but immediately dropped it on the bed.

"Skittish, are we?"

"No guns," KC said.

"No guns . . . ? Really? How long do you think we'll survive in there without guns?"

"I will not carry a gun."

Annie stared at her a moment, then changed direction. "How was lunch?"

KC held up Jenna's security card.

"Nice." Annie smiled. "Maybe you won't need a gun."

KC took a seat at the small dining table in the corner and laid out a large map marked up with red ink: multiple points of entry, multiple points of exit. "We can't enter from the western wall, too much traffic and too many buildings with windows that look out on it. The entrance two hundred yards north of the southeast corner has the most shadow coverage. But we are going to need a diversion."

"What kind and where?"

"Something that's going to hold people's attention for at least a minute on the streets opposite the southeast corner. That section of the wall may be shadowed, but it won't make us invisible. We need to pull people's eyes away from us or we won't even get over the wall."

"What do you have in mind?"

"That's your department, but you better make it big and far from boring."

"The one thing I've never been is boring."

KC stared at the map, committing it to memory so she would know every corner, every door as if it were her own home. She finally looked up to see Annie staring at her.

"What?" KC said abruptly.

Annie pointed at her nose.

KC reached up and touched her nose, drawing her finger away to find several drops of blood. "What the hell?"

KC went into the bathroom, grabbed a tissue, and blotted her nose. She looked in the mirror, studying her face as if that would somehow reveal the cause of her bloody nose. She shook her head and went back to the table.

"You okay?" Annie said.

"Fine." KC turned back to the map, running her finger along the red route she had sketched out. "This way keeps us in the shadows—"

"And if a guard spots us?"

"Not if we spot him first. We go in staggered; you lie on a roof, confirming a clear route. I move and then I spot for you."

"And you still didn't answer my question. What if a guard spots us, the whole thing is done?"

KC didn't answer.

"There is going to be blood whether you like it or not."

KC had never hurt anyone except in self-defense.

"If it makes you feel any better, the blood will be on my hands," Annie said. "Not yours."

KC looked at the bloodied tissue in her hand; she knew Annie's words were far from the truth.

COLONEL LUCAS AND Sergeant Reiner checked into their suites at the Venetian. Reiner made a quick sweep of the colonel's room, ensuring there were no bugs or other devices.

Lucas flipped open his cell phone and dialed.

"You made it?" Jon asked in answer.

"Where are you?"

"Just picking up some supplies, I'm in downtown Macau."

"A Sergeant Reiner has joined us; I need you to give him a full briefing on where we are."

"I'll be back within two hours."

"Good, you can brief me on our progress then, unless we are off schedule, in which case you'd better tell me now."

"We're good on this end," Jon said as he hung up the phone.

"We'll meet with Jon Lei in two hours," Lucas said to Reiner. "We'll eat then. But first . . ." Lucas handed him a memory stick. "You need to read this, know what and who we are dealing with. I will expect you to be an expert on this material by this evening."

"Yes, sir," Reiner said.

"And seeing you're here as my assistant, you can assist me by saving me a trip to our safe house on the other side of town to pick up a file."

"Of course," Reiner said as he nodded. "May I ask you something?"

"Go ahead," Lucas said as he threw his bag on the bed and unpacked in military fashion, moving his clothes into the drawers of the vacant dresser.

"Xiao . . ."

"Yes?"

"Is he alive?"

"Do you mean did I kill him on that boat?"

"Yes."

Lucas finished putting his things away, closed the drawer, and turned to Reiner.

"I left him to suffer and die. As unbecoming as that sounds coming from the lips of an officer, I didn't think this man deserved the easy death of a bullet. He has walked this earth for decades above the law, killing, torturing as he sees fit.

"I came across him once, unaware of who he was. He killed a man before my eyes without emotion, without remorse . . ." Lucas became lost in thought.

"Sir, do you believe he is here in Macau?"

"Yes, I do. And yes, he is going to try to kill me. He is

going to want me to suffer in the same way I made him suffer. He'll try to kidnap me, ensnare me in some trap, poison me . . . But it won't be on the grounds of the Venetian. He won't cross that line."

"How do you know that?"

"Because he's going to want to send a message with my death. The security team at the Venetian are experts at covering up crimes that occur here; it wouldn't even hit the papers. He'll try to grab me outside, on the street, between here and the airport."

"That doesn't mean we let our guard down," Reiner said.

"Don't forget, we have a large advantage."

"What's that?"

"He has no idea I'm even in the country. But, Sergeant, if you see him, don't make the same mistake I did. You shoot that man on sight."

CHAPTER 25

1974

Highly intelligent, educated, yet possessing the feral quality of a dog from the street, Xiao rose through the ranks of the Snake Triad, through promotion and death. While his uncle was its leader, Kwon did not deal in favoritism, as decisions based on the heart were the first step to losing control. Nonetheless, Xiao had achieved a level of discipline, skill, and ruthlessness that Kwon couldn't have predicted or planned, rising to his second in command in a matter of years.

Xiao attended university in Hong Kong, studying warfare, international relations, accounting, and statistical analysis. He was what his uncle called the "new breed." The cultural revolution of the sixties and seventies was sweeping the world, and Xiao would help his uncle usher in the new age. But it would be an age that his uncle would never see.

Kwon had arrived home late, gripping the custom wood steering wheel in his ring-encased fingers. He loved to drive his '64 Corvette hardtop; it was his favorite, and he had no taste for those who thought themselves worthy of being chauffeured about.

He pulled up to his home in the Ju Wong district

after concluding a meeting in which his operation had successfully taken over a territory formally held by his rival. It had been a bitter dispute but had been resolved in a face-to-face meeting without bloodshed, at which both sides agreed that Kwon was the rising force better equipped and more worthy of controlling the drug trade.

As Kwon pulled into his driveway, the bomb tore the silver sports car apart, shredding the fabric of the night, the fireball rolling up into the sky. The heat of the blast ignited the wooden benches on his lawn, melting the plastic façade of the small pagoda in his yard. As the smoke cleared, as the neighbors came running, everyone saw that there was nothing left of the vehicle, nothing left of Kwon but the charred remains of his favorite hat and the blackened rings from his left hand.

TAO WAS THE leader of the Tiger Triad, a man of sixty who was equally adept at cards and death, a man who controlled the old casinos and drug trade, who dressed in Western clothes yet insisted on wearing his prized sword at his side like some forgotten warrior. His gang was the chief rival of Kwon's Snake Triad, and while his power was waning, he was happy to send a message that he was not weak. Kwon had thought his new modern style of negotiations—business meetings at which statistics and margins took the place of muscle—was the future, but Tao knew the way to success was always through the past.

Xiao entered the run-down casino through the rear door. While the small main floor had its share of one-armed bandits, mahjong, and card tables, it was on the upper floors in the private rooms where the legend of Macau's gambling had been created over the last hundred years. While tourists came from Hong Kong to gamble the night away, getting drunk and boarding the ferry back, it was the private clients, those with money to burn, who filled the private rooms and stayed for days on end.

Two guards flanked a small concierge desk, their large shoulders stretching their pin-striped suits.

Xiao stepped through the door, his raised pistol exploding bullets, shattering the two hulking doormen's heads before either man could react. Before the bodies had hit the floor, he disappeared into the fire stairs.

Tao's men raced down the stairs, but by the time they saw Xiao, bullets had already careened their way, killing them on the spot. Xiao exploded out the third-floor door, ducking as he entered the hallway, his position surprising the two men who flanked the door at the end of the hall. But their surprise was short-lived as a hail of bullets took them both out.

Xiao kicked in the door to find four men playing cards in a smoke-filled room, stacks of chips piled before each of them as they each sipped a glass of wine. Without hesitation, Xiao raised his pistol and shot them all dead except for the man with the most chips. He was dark-skinned, a hint of Portuguese in his Chinese eyes. He smoked a thin hand-rolled cigarette while barely paying mind to the dead bodies that now sat around him.

"Xiao, the *gwailo* that now heads his uncle's Triad. Are you here to thank me for your promotion?"

Xiao walked up to the man, assessing him as he approached.

And Tao stood. Not a large man but exceedingly well built for a man of sixty. He was dressed in loose-fitting pants and a tweed sport jacket; at his side was a *dao,* a sword encased in a highly polished black sheath.

Xiao glared at the man and smiled. There were eight bodies left in his wake; this would be one more and most certainly not his last. He aimed his gun at the old man's face.

Three guards burst through the door, but Tao raised his hand, staying their actions. "Perhaps you are wiser than your uncle. Being of mixed blood, you walk in two worlds. But you must realize that there must be a balance in life, embracing the old and the new as one circle, the yin and yang. Your uncle wanted it all, wanted to forget who I was, what I represented. We can forge an alliance, create a Triad that would allow us to coexist."

Xiao walked into Tao's space, up in his face. The three guards, despite their orders, moved in on Xiao, encircling him just feet away. But Tao was not a man who played games or let others dictate his fate. He reached into his jacket and pulled out a 9mm pistol, aiming it at Xiao.

With his hand gripped tightly about his own pistol, aiming it at Tao, Xiao knew as soon as he pulled the trigger the three guards would fire.

"Perhaps we can sit and discuss—"

But there would be no discussion, no witty repartee.

With lightning speed, Xiao snapped out his left hand, ripping the sword from Tao's side, and in a fluid motion, before the three men could pull their triggers, he spun about, the blade humming through the air, slicing them each across the belly, spilling their insides, their hands grasping their stomachs vainly trying to hold on to their lives.

Tao focused, his finger wrapping around the trigger, but Xiao's motion had already spun him 360 degrees, and with the blade continuing its arc of death, he angled the *dao* and sliced Tao's wrist, severing muscle and tendon, the gun now clutched in the useless grasp of his dangling hand.

The following morning, a wooden box arrived at the *Macau Daily*, addressed to the editor-in-chief. As it was unmarked, the bomb squad was called in; their sniffing dogs indicated there was no explosive but reacted nonetheless. The box was finally opened, and to everyone's horror, Tao's head was drawn from the box—an announcement that there was a new leader of the Tiger Triad.

CHAPTER 26
MACAU, PRESENT DAY

The lower level of the underground facility was dark, windowless, and in the center of Macau. The basement level was simple: a large open room with couches and a TV; a small office; a bedroom; and a ten-by-ten empty room with a single chair and nothing else but a bare lightbulb on the ceiling and a drain in the center of the floor.

Three men stood before a desk in the office, dressed in dark clothes, their arms and necks covered with tattoos, listening intently to the man before them. It was the first time they had ever seen the man—they had always answered to lower members of the Triad—and they had actually thought of him as a ghost, as some legendary being who could rip the heart out of his enemies with a whispered thought.

Their assignment was simple. They had spent the last year on debt collections but had been chosen to carry out this one task. Each of them knew that when he succeeded it would afford him a greater honor within the triad.

"It is understood, you are not to kill him," Xiao spoke quickly in Chinese. "You are to bring him to me. If he dies in your hands you will suffer the fate that I have waiting for him."

Xiao stood before them, his shirt on the desk beside him. He was tattooed with a large demonlike beast, the centerpiece of a horrific tapestry that wrapped his torso. He wound fresh gauze around his muscled stomach, re-dressing a large burn, the fresh scar tissue seeming to melt his skin, corrupting the tattoo into an even more frightening scene.

He turned back to his men, his point made, and dis-missed them with a nod of his head.

Xiao was considered the most powerful man in Macau, his business interests stretching from gambling, prostitution, and immigrant trafficking to kidnapping, drugs, and credit-card fraud; from software piracy, por-nography, and counterfeiting to politics, finance, and real estate. He owned the building he was currently in along with thirty others throughout the city. His illegal operation had no seat of operation but rather floated through a random series of locations depending on the day of the month, much like the emperors of old who never slept in the same bed in the palace so as to keep their enemies guessing.

While his criminal dealings were spoken of in hushed tones, there was never any direct evidence of his involve-ment; prosecutors, law enforcement, and Interpol had fruitlessly tried to connect him to any of a multitude of il-licit enterprises but had failed. To some he was a legitimate businessman who supported the community, to politicians he was a man who could ensure an election, while to others he was the all-powerful leader of the Snake Triad.

The Chinese Triads grew out of the ancient secret societies, the religious groups and public agitators, who had rebelled against the Emperor. The Triads had a strange history, having fought against the Japanese in World War II, then helped Chiang Kai-shek in his war against the Communists, and even assisted the U.S. Army during the Vietnam War.

Triad stood for the sacred symbol of ancient secret societies—a triangle enclosing a modification of the Chinese character known as *hung,* symbolizing the union of heaven, earth, and man. New recruits partook of various rituals and ceremonies to gain an understanding of duty, honor, and responsibility. They took an oath of loyalty that locked them into the Triad for life. They could retire, but their services could be requested for everything from transporting fugitives, to dealing with drug matters, to assassination.

The various Triads throughout Macau and Hong Kong were separate, autonomous societies, and much like traditional Mafia families, historically exclusive to the Chinese. The larger Triads, the Black Dragon, the White Spirit, and the Lotus Triad, were all dwarfed by Xiao's Snake Triad, which was truly a criminal operation with no equal. Unlike the Triads of old, Xiao had consolidated power and successfully projected it outward, dealing with the capitalists and the communists, with criminal organizations of various faiths, creeds, and colors.

But with all of his power, all of his strength and reach, his goal had become simple and focused.

He turned and picked up the black lacquered talisman, the small antique wooden box engraved with a fearsome dragon entwined with a tiger in a battle to the death, the image a frozen moment with the final victor left to supposition. The box had rested on a shelf in his study at home for years, a sentimental heirloom that had belonged to his mother.

It had been in a metal lockbox with his father's name on it, hidden away in his uncle's house, which had become his house after his uncle's death. He had found the lockbox after his uncle's assassination, recalling it to be the lone possession his mother carried to Macau when they fled the United States so many years ago.

For years he had looked upon the black lacquered box and thought of his mother, feeling anger and a deep sense of loss. His mother thought the box was a cursed piece of artwork, never suspecting it was a puzzle box, never understanding what it held.

It was five months ago when he learned the box's truth, when he pressed the eye of the dragon and performed a succession of intricate moves, the top panel of the box popped open, and he found the black porcelain vial.

The small container held so much death; it was as if someone had dipped it in hell, scooping up a darkness that would steal the soul. It had sat within the black puzzle box for all these years, hidden away by his mother, who feared its power—never imagining that it would be her son who would unlock its mystery, unleashing it upon the world.

CHAPTER 27

1975

Xiao stepped off the plane in San Diego. Though he was untouchable in Macau and Hong Kong, he was listed on Interpol's Most Wanted list, which could make travel difficult. But since he was half-Caucasian, he could easily assume multiple nationalities depending on his mode of dress and hairstyle. And having been raised in the U.S. for the first ten years of his life, he spoke English without accent, which was far more helpful than a disguise, for everyone looking for Xiao was looking for a Chinese national, a man who spoke with a heavy accent and who had unmistakable Chinese features. No one ever suspected his heritage, his *gwailo* father.

He arrived at his old home, and except for the white paint job, it was exactly as he remembered it. He entered the unlocked house without knocking and walked about, memories pouring forth: times of innocence, when death was just something others spoke about. The furnishings had not been changed—the same dining room table, the living room couches—it had all been in his dreams for these past years but now it was alive once again.

But there was one difference: The pictures of his

mother that had sat on the table in the foyer were gone, his parents' wedding album from the coffee table in the living room was missing. It was as if she had never lived there, never existed.

Xiao walked into his father's study. On the shelves were pictures of his brother, Isaac, playing baseball, football, and basketball; there was a prom picture with an average-looking brunette. It was a chronological series so quintessentially American, so different from his own upbringing.

And for a moment, he felt regret, a longing for his brother, from whom he'd been torn so many years ago. Seeing the images of Isaac's life was like looking at a dream of himself, seeing the world that might have been.

There were nights when he would awaken, covered in sweat, longing for comfort from his dead mother. And he would think of his brother, the one person he thought he could trust, for despite being torn apart, being raised on opposite sides of the planet, they were still brothers, joined in birth, forever linked. He wondered if Isaac had felt the same pain at being torn apart, curious if he'd wondered where his brother had gone, if he knew what their father had done, if he'd ever suspected that their father had had their mother killed.

He had thought of Isaac often but never sought him out, never looking to open up his past until now. And despite his hatred of their father, and his intention to kill him, he wished he could see Isaac again. But he knew that once he followed through on his plans, it would remove the possibility of that ever happening, for his brother would never understand.

In that moment, Xiao thought of himself as Jacob, he thought of himself and his brother and the truth that they could reunite, reestablish what had been lost. For the briefest of seconds, he felt regret at coming here, for considering patricide, for thinking of killing his own flesh and blood. Maybe his uncle was wrong, maybe it was not his father who had killed their mother. Maybe . . .

And then his eyes fell on the last shelf of pictures, and what he saw sent a shudder through him. There was a picture of his brother at graduation in his dress uniform. He had followed in the steps of their father, becoming a soldier, a man of war. Isaac had become their father.

And Jacob was washed away; Xiao stood there, filling with anger, not just at his father now, but at his brother. For he was embracing the world of the man who had killed his mother.

Mounted above the fireplace was his brother's sword, nothing like what was created in the Orient. There was no folding of the metal thousands of times as in a Japanese katana, no care to detail as in a Chinese *dao*. This was a mass-produced weapon of military symbolism whose bearer would never understand how to wield it except in a parade, at a funeral, at some ceremony.

He looked at the shelves he remembered from his youth, floor to ceiling, five feet wide, containing books, charts, and files. These documents pertained to the places his father had visited, had sailed to on his own. Some fathers collected gold trophies, others diplomas, still others bottles of beer; his father collected charts and books to commemorate the places he had sailed as if they were badges of honor. He had ignored the names when he was a child, not understanding or caring about the significance of a man's piloting his own craft to such places. Now he read them all: Bermuda, Easter Island, the Azores, Tahiti, and the Seychelles. But it was the last shelf at the bottom that gave him pause. Unlike the other shelves, this one was empty except for a single handwritten label.

It was his favorite story, like something from a Robert Louis Stevenson novel, a story of treasure and magic, of life and death. His father had spoken of the island as if it were a fairy tale. He looked once again at the name on the label, mixed in with the other labels bearing names of islands in the world, as if it was real. And it struck him to his core. The label read *Penglai*.

"Isaac?" the voice called from the doorway.

Xiao didn't turn around, still staring at the bookshelf in the den.

"How did you beat me home?" Xiao's father's voice was as deep and strong as he remembered, though there was an unsteadiness to it, a whiskey growl, a sign of age.

Xiao slowly turned and stared at his father.

Howard smiled as he threw his sweater on the couch and finally turned to look at the man he thought was Isaac. But his smile was washed away by confusion. His eyes struggled to refocus as he stared at his son. It was like an illusion, a picture that was slowly coming into focus. And the realization hit him.

"Jacob?" Howard slowly said.

Xiao stared at his father. He centered himself, trying to maintain calm. He had thought of this moment for years. His dreams and fantasies of what he would do to the man who had killed his mother had evolved with time, from the anger-filled messiness of a child to the methodical acts of an adult who had grown adept at meting out death. Xiao studied his face, the hard jawline and strong nose that was reflected in himself. This was someone he had loved, had worshipped, someone who had shaped the first ten years of his life.

But his most formative years, the last fifteen as he grew into a man, as he fell under the influence of Kwon, of China and Macau, were far more powerful and wiped the memories of those emotions away. And throughout it all, the anger of being torn from his childhood, the horror of the nightmares of his mother's brutal murder in the streets, the bottled-up rage he could barely contain was trained in one singular direction.

"My God." Howard stood there in shock, his face a fountain of emotions; his knees finally buckled and he sat on the couch. He slowly smiled as his mind spun. "Look at you."

Xiao listened, shocked by the tone of his father's voice; there was a sense of pride there. For all this time, he had thought of his father as hating him as much as he hated his mother.

"Why did you do it?"

"Do what?" his father asked, but Xiao could see he understood.

Xiao slowly walked to his father, standing above

him, and violently lashed out, striking him in the side of the head.

"You killed my mother."

Howard threw up his arms, hoping to ward off the next strike, utterly shocked by the attack.

"You can't deny it." Xiao grabbed his father by the arm, yanking him off the couch and thrusting him into the hardback desk chair. He spun him about, pulled zip ties from his pocket, and tied him tightly into the chair. "She loved you."

"And I loved her."

Xiao drew back his fist and hit his father square in the nose, shattering it, blood exploding out, pouring down onto his white golf shirt.

"No. No man kills that which he loves. Unless . . ." he said slowly, a sadness in his voice. "He loves himself more."

Howard hung his head in shame. "I will burn in hell for what I did."

"Dad?" Xiao heard the sound of his own voice call out from the hall, yet it wasn't him.

Xiao looked at his father. "Make a sound and I'll kill him."

Xiao stepped into the hall to see Isaac standing there.

The moment hung in the air as Isaac realized who the other man was. The two brothers stared at each other, a world of emotions pouring forth.

Isaac was nearly a carbon copy of his brother except for his shorter hair and more muscular body. Otherwise when the brothers looked at each other, it was like looking in the mirror.

Isaac stepped forward to hug his brother, but Xiao

just stood there, his body language cold and dead. Isaac halted himself and smiled.

"My God, I never thought I'd see you again."

Xiao remained silent.

"Where have you been?"

Xiao finally spoke. "China."

"For all these years?"

Xiao nodded.

"We assumed . . ."

"That I was dead?"

"Yes . . . no. I just thought after all this time, I'd never see you again. And our mom?"

Xiao shook his head.

Isaac's face swirled with grief.

"Why don't you come in?" Xiao said, pointing toward the study.

And as they stepped into the den, Isaac saw his father beaten and bleeding, trussed to the chair, and immediately spun about. "What's going on?" Isaac said, his voice filled with confusion.

"*Dad*"—Xiao paused—"is going to tell you what happened to Mom."

Isaac looked at him, confused, as Xiao now pointed a gun at him, urging him to sit, drawing more zip ties from his pocket.

A fire grew in Isaac's eyes, one that Xiao was more than familiar with. He understood the anger in his brother, the frustration he was feeling, for despite their years apart, they were still one.

Isaac finally sat. Xiao kept the gun on him as he tied his brother's wrists to the arms of the chair.

"Why are you doing this?" Isaac said, struggling against his binds. "Where did you go?"

"Our mother took me away. She feared for her own life, for my life."

"I don't understand what you're doing . . ." Isaac looked at Howard. "Dad, are you all right?"

Howard nodded as he took a breath.

"You don't know what it is like to have your world turned upside down," Xiao said. "To lay awake at night wondering—"

"If your brother is alive?" Isaac said. "If your mother is alive? Why she abandoned you? Yes, I do. So fuck you."

"He killed our mother," Xiao said. "He sent a soldier in the night to—"

"No," Isaac said quickly, denying the impossible, looking at his father.

"I would never kill your mother," Howard said as he looked into Isaac's eyes.

"You lie," Xiao snapped.

Howard stared at Isaac. "I drank, I struck your mother—I don't deny that—but I loved her and could never kill her."

"No, you would have someone else kill her, distance yourself from blame."

"You think I would kill the woman I love? The mother of my two sons?"

Xiao and Isaac stared at their father, who looked up, his gaze alternating between them.

"What I had done—and your mother knew—I could be court-martialed for, thrown in prison, disgraced." He paused, his voice growing angry. "Admirals don't get court-martialed."

"What did you do?" Isaac whispered.

Howard took a moment to gather himself. Then he finally spoke.

"After V-J Day, I was in charge of repatriating the spoils of war, getting them back to their homeland, their place of origin. The Japanese, much like the Germans, raided museums, homes, banks, stealing everything they could: gold, artwork, pieces worth millions thought lost to the devastation of war. We're talking billions of things thought destroyed that would never be seen again. As ugly as war is, beyond the killing, this is the ugliest: You're not only stealing their history, you're stealing their sense of self. I think the possession of others' belongings stolen in times of war, through pillaging and death, is a horrific rape of their soul.

"And when war is over, when it comes time for the victor to be honorable and return these precious items, it's all too easy to slip them in a drawer, to say they were never found, to fold them into a museum's collection or, worse, into our own coffers. The temptation to many to dip their finger in the pot, to take just one object, justifying that it would never be missed, is something that lies in all men, for we are all fallible. It was why we must rise above and do the right thing. And it fell to me to be sure America did the right thing.

"During the war, in June of '43, I had hopped a transport from Australia back to our base on Guadalcanal. The plane was a Douglas C-47. We hit a storm, lost both engines, and had to ditch it in the sea. The pilot died on impact; the two other passengers, two young army sergeants, were badly injured. I managed to get us into an inflatable raft. By the time we washed up on the shore of an island, they were both dead.

"I knew the storm had thrown us way off course, far from the shipping lanes. I feared my stay would be forever. But God provides: There was fresh water, plentiful fish, and fruit. I crafted a shelter out of palm fronds and fallen trees and waited. Two days in, I knew no one was coming. There was a war going on; no man could be spared to look for a plane of four. I knew we were already listed as killed in action. I couldn't help thinking of myself as Robinson Crusoe.

"I set out one day to circle the island, to learn its size. It took me four days to circumnavigate it; the island was larger than I'd thought. But I found no sign of man, of any other inhabitant. The island was a dormant volcano somewhere within what is known as the ring of fire, which emerges from the Pacific plate. The mountainous center of the island climbed at least two thousand feet, but to truly see its size I had two choices: make my way through the rain forest, a thick jungle that was devoid of paths to follow and filled with who knew what predators, or venture up the central river that emptied into the sea. In my third week, I crafted a small raft out of fallen trees and ventured up the river into the heart of the island. The river was deep and wide, formed in a volcanic fissure; the banks were thick and lush with greenery that climbed into a canopy above that blotted out the sky. I felt like I was in a Joseph Conrad novel as I traveled upriver into the heart of darkness.

"And what I found at the river's end was beyond my imagination: a vast temple hundreds of years old. It sat one hundred yards in from the edge of a freshwater cove, a port like one might find in an old fishing village from the past.

"There were ships in a dock, ghost ships, six of them, of different vintage, as if a museum of boats showing their progression through time. There was a Chinese junk, its sails furled—the ship was enormous, larger than any junk I had seen—a Spanish galleon with a large forecastle and nearly intact sails, like something out of a Patrick O'Brian novel; a paddlewheel steamer; a merchant ship from the thirties; a Japanese war boat that I knew had been rumored lost at sea; and a sloop.

"I inspected each of the ships. They were fully operational, even the tall ships, all protected in the cove from weather; it was as if they had been frozen in time. The only odd thing was the compasses: None of them held true north, their needles spinning, in constant flux.

"There was no sign of life either on the ships or in the compound. I approached the temple, which was enormous; it had sloped roofs of Asian design, large columns and stacked timber walls. The exterior was sun-faded red, and on the corners of the structure were highly detailed carvings of dragons and tigers locked in battle. It was as if the building had been scooped out of the mountains of China and dropped in this thick rain forest.

"Around the building, the vegetation was held at bay as if someone had been tending the place, but there were no footprints, no sign of movement but the natural world."

"What does this have to do with my mother?" Xiao interrupted, growing impatient.

Howard took a breath. "Everything."

The two sons stared at their father waiting for him to continue.

"I climbed the smooth white stairs to the main entrance, pulled open the large doors, and it was like stepping back in time. An overwhelming feeling filled me, as if I were desecrating the firmament of heaven. Peering in, I could see a vast entrance foyer with a wide hall running off in all directions. But there was something haunting about it—I did not enter.

"I closed the doors and walked around the side, and that's when I found everyone. The graves numbered in the hundreds, all with makeshift markers that were weathered and faded by the sun and elements. They were grouped, and as I looked upon them I understood why. The first grouping contained thirty markers, Chinese; I had no comprehension of the writing. The second was Spanish from the 1760s, a crew of twenty-six, all having died within days of one another; there was a Dutch section with thirty-two graves, all dead in the month of March 1888.

"It felt like I had stepped into a nightmare. I wasn't sure if it was plague, some tropical virus, or if someone had been overtaken by madness and killed everyone else. But a question occurred to me: Who had buried them when they finally passed?

"The warning was more than clear, illustrated by the

grave markers, by the uninhabited island, by the feeling that was permeating my very being. I needed to get off the island.

"Nighttime came quickly. I didn't chance heading back downriver in the dark. I stayed in the forward cabin of the sloop.

"And then in the morning, I saw them—footprints, several sets, different sizes, a trail that started at the door of the building and ended at the water line. It appeared that there were at least six different individuals, but they were gone now, as if ghosts in the night.

"I had no intention of looking for them.

"The small sloop was beautiful, her rigging was intact; she was seaworthy and would be my way home. I gathered food, fish, fruit, and water to last me a month, and set sail. I quickly headed downriver and made it to sea within a half-hour. The waters were incredibly rough and it took me several hours to find an opening in the surrounding reef to get clear of the island.

"Not one hour out, I hit storm-filled seas, twenty-foot waves from crest to trough. Night fell quickly and I had no heading; my compass was useless, compromised and in constant flux. The storm clouds obscured the stars in the night sky, and come sunrise, the day was black and rain-filled. I was alone at sea, fearful for my life, thinking the tempest would never end.

"It was on the fifth day that the waters calmed, that the skies cleared.

"I made shore on a small island in the Philippines and got word to my command, rejoining them within days. I told no one of what I had found, telling my commanding officers that the island was small, the sloop had been shipwrecked. We learned it belonged to a professor who disappeared in the thirties, a historian who had no family. After the war, I kept the boat, since it had saved me. I rechristened the sloop the *Calypso*, the boat that you know so well. I sailed it while on leave to all the places I dreamed of. Though I tried to find that island again, I couldn't. It was on no map, I had no compass heading, no read on the stars; it was lost to my imagination.

"For years I kept it a secret until I finally told your mother. She sat there in disbelief before asking me a series of pointed questions about the Chinese junk, about the templelike structure, finally saying she knew where I was: Penglai, an island some spoke of as myth, others as fact. Some say it holds the key to life, riches, magic, while others say it holds nothing but death.

"She told me of a great Chinese explorer, Admiral Zheng He, of his travels and the rumored discovery of the same island. We had a laugh, a few what-if conversations, and forgot about it.

"A year later, while cataloguing artifacts to be returned to China, I found a reference to a book among a stolen cache of artifacts in the belly of a ship in Japan, the diary of the Chinese admiral Zheng He. The Japanese had taken it during the war along with countless other objects, with no idea what it was.

"I went alone into the belly of the ship. I located the book. It was stored in a box within a tattered velvet pouch along with various artifacts: a small red satchel filled with diamonds, some brass trinkets, and two engraved pieces of wood, one black, one red, beautiful, polished artifacts with fantastic dragons and tigers upon them. They were possessions of Zheng He scheduled to be returned to the Forbidden City in a week's time.

"For nights I lay awake, curiosity burning inside me. I could have the answers to the questions that had haunted my dreams since the day I escaped that island. I could return there to find the answers that vexed not only me but so many others. I knew that at the end of the week, the answers would disappear into the Forbidden City, slipping through my fingers forever.

"As the days went on, the clock ticking down, I became more and more obsessed. It was my only thought and it obscured my logic; it obscured my morals and judgment. There was nothing I loved more than the Navy, my command, my station in life, and I knew I was risking it all with one single act. But I convinced myself that no one would ever know, that I could control the situation.

"I returned to the belly of the Japanese ship with a small crate labeled *Top Secret*. I picked up the velvet pouch and removed the book, holding it in my hands. It was bound in thick leather and was exquisite, a work of art in and of itself. I placed it in the wooden crate. But before closing up the case, I took the small black engraved artifact; the engravings fascinated me. I had never seen anything so detailed, so intriguing. And I took the diamonds. It was impulsive; they were a means to funding a better life than my naval pay could provide, a way to give your mother things that were out of our reach, a means to affording a life at sea. I hadn't planned it, hadn't thought about it once. I just did it.

"I sealed up the case and left the ship. No one questioned me, no one would dare ask an admiral what was in the top-secret case he was carrying.

"I was not infallible. I had every intention of returning the book once I unlocked its secrets. But it was written in Chinese, a language I had no prayer of ever learning; it might as well have been locked away in the bowels of Fort Knox.

"And so I revealed what I had done to your mother—not the diamonds, just the book and the artifact. I explained that I would return them, I just needed to know what the book said, if it had the answers I was seeking. She did not hold me in judgment, but helped me to begin the translation.

"I hid the diamonds in my study and over the coming months and year, after you two had gone to bed, your mother would help me translate the book. It contained a detailed account of Zheng He's seven voyages, a catalogue of what he had found. There were cryptic notations of wealth, of cures to disease and death. But halfway through, she stopped. She said she would go no further. There were things on that island, she said. She wouldn't say what, but I could see the fear in her eyes; it was as if she'd stood next to me on that island staring at the graves.

"I begged her. You don't understand what it's like to have all of the answers to your questions in a book before you but not be able to read it, to understand what was within. It was taunting me, my mind exploding with a need for answers. I couldn't take the book anywhere else for fear of being found out. She was my only means, she was in control, a rare position for a woman in the fifties or even now, fifteen years later. Your mother and I fought and we fought often. I wasn't used to not being in control; I was the man, she was from a culture where women were inferior.

"I knew there was a map in the book, but I had no way to understand it. It didn't match any known charts, and its headings pointed to empty seas. And now, every time I looked at the book, I was filled with fear, always concerned that I would be found out, that I would somehow be caught with not only the book and artifact but the diamonds. It was a mistake that haunted me; I felt such guilt for violating my mandate, my own ethics. I had risked my career and yet I had no answers to my questions about the island. So I began to drink to deaden those feelings."

Howard paused, his eyes closed. He was speaking as if he were in confession, as if he was arriving at the truth that he had concealed for so long.

"Drinking awakened the dark side of my soul, something I couldn't control: My emotions, my fists were not my own. I would awaken in the morning after a bender to find your mother bruised, her eyes red from tears. My shame knew no end, worsened by the fact that she acted as if nothing had happened. As the weeks and months went on, she threatened to leave me. Her resolve growing with time, she said she would contact the Navy and tell them everything, about the island, about the diamonds she had found in my study. Something she knew would destroy me and my career. I thought it was just a threat.

"After I hit her the last time, she disappeared with you"—Howard looked at Xiao—"and she took the book and the black engraved artifact. She left me a letter telling me to never look for either of you or she would end my career with a single phone call.

"I couldn't allow that. I would be court-martialed, thrown in prison." Tears welled in Howard's eyes.

Isaac and Xiao stared at him in shock.

"I never meant for her to die. I just wanted the book back. I sent a special-ops officer just back from Vietnam to find her. He wasn't supposed to harm her, just get her to turn over the book. She fought back . . ."

Isaac stared at his father, a world of emotions pouring over his face. Xiao smiled, having won, having had his suspicions confirmed. Smiling, as it made what he intended to do even easier.

"What is in the book?" Xiao asked.

"The way back to Penglai. It detailed what was in the temple, things I could never have imagined."

Isaac and Xiao hung on his every word.

"Tell me where the book is." Howard looked at Xiao. "Stop this nonsense and let's find the island together."

"You killed her, you expect me to just forget that?"

"Please know, I loved her—"

Xiao glared at his father, halting his words.

"Then at least let your brother go," Howard said. "He has nothing to do with this."

Xiao looked at Isaac but he was staring off into the distance in shock.

"Bottom left-hand drawer," Howard said. "There's a naval reg book."

Xiao opened the drawer and found the book, pulling it out. He looked at his father, at his brother, and finally opened it to reveal a false interior. He reached in and pulled out a small satchel; he spilled the diamonds into his hand.

"Take them, let us go."

"You think diamonds will erase the pain?" Xiao said as he laid them on the desk.

"Jacob," Howard said. "Please know, I never stopped loving you."

Xiao looked at the man he had once known, whom he had once loved. He reached up above the mantel and drew down the dull-bladed sword, a crude weapon whose only purpose was for show.

"Jacob," Isaac finally spoke. "Don't do it. It won't bring her back."

"But she will see that she is avenged."

"Please, don't do this . . ." Isaac pled.

"You say you love me, though not once did you seek me out," Xiao said to his father. "I will see the truth in your eyes as you die."

"If you do it," Isaac said, "I will hunt you down . . ."

Xiao looked back at Isaac, tied to the chair, his face filled with a rising anger, then turned back to his father, staring into his eyes.

And without another word, he drove the sword into his father's belly, watching as the pain rose in his face, as the life seeped from his eyes.

"No!" Isaac screamed, his cry filled with anguish and rage as he struggled against his binds.

Xiao spun about quickly, withdrawing the blade

from his father with a sickening slurp, the blade humming at his brother but halting its advance at the edge of his throat, silencing him.

There was no fear in Isaac's eyes, only anger, only revulsion. They glared at each other, all of the love they had had for each other, all of the experiences of their childhood, the bond that was supposed to be eternal, severed, washed away in a sea of mutual hate.

With his free hand, Xiao snatched the diamonds off the desk, threw the sword to the floor, and disappeared out the door.

CHAPTER 28
MACAU

Michael, Busch, and Jon walked through the ornate lobby of the Venetian. They had spent the last hour getting a feel for the layout, walking the casinos, trying their hands at fan-tan, poker, craps, the slot machines, with only Busch winning. In fact, he was up four thousand dollars in a short period of time, seeming to have a sixth sense when it came to playing the odds.

"Nothing like a good old 'abusement' park to lift your spirits." Busch couldn't help smiling.

"Or suck you dry," Michael said as he watched the different expressions on the faces of the people checking in as opposed to those checking out. "So many people arrive thinking they're going to win but walk out with holes in their pockets."

"But the trick is that they had fun while losing," Jon said. "That's the magic of a good casino. They fleece you but you always come back for more. The casinos that fail are the ones that take your money and kick you to the street with a bad taste in your mouth."

"That's not all that puts a bad taste in my mouth," Busch said as he looked at Jon, his words sharp and challenging.

"Are we on schedule?" Jon asked, ignoring Busch.

"Where's your colonel?" Michael asked.

"In the room next to yours. He arrived a few hours ago. Do you want to see him?"

"I want assurance that KC is unharmed and will be freed when we are done."

"Fair enough," Jon said. "I'll see what I can do."

"If you want this done tonight," Michael said, "there are still obstacles."

"Is it the safe?" Jon asked.

"I'll get into the safe," Michael said. "But I can't get past the guard on Sublevel Six."

"What about the security, the cameras?" Jon asked.

"What can you do about the guard on Sub-Six?"

"I will deal with that," Jon said.

"How?"

"Not to worry, I will own that man before we go in."

"What do you mean 'we'?"

"I told you, I'm going with you."

Michael stared at Jon. He knew he would need his help, but up to this point he had thought it would be limited to supplies, logistics, and reconnaissance. While he had had Busch with him in the past, Simon, even KC when he was pulling a job, he had never worked in the presence of someone he considered an enemy, a man who would gladly kill him upon the job's completion.

"You know you need me," Jon said. "You may be brilliant at getting past security, compromising safes, ripping people off, but I'm the one you need to deal with the Chinese factor."

"If you leave a trail of bodies . . ." Busch glared at Jon.

"Who said anything about bodies? I told you I will deal with getting you past the guard; I didn't say I was going to kill him," Jon said. "My question is, how are we going to get out of not only the lower level but the building with the box?"

"How confident are you of getting inside help like Carl?"

"Just tell me what you need."

Michael handed him a sheet of paper. "If you can do that, then you will have your precious box. We're heading back across town; call me when it's arranged."

CHAPTER 29
MACAU, ONE MONTH AGO

It was by pure happenstance combined with an over-indulgence in scotch that Xiao learned where the book his mother stole from his father was hidden. He had spent years searching for it, knowing of its existence; he knew he wasn't chasing fairy tales. And as his quest broadened, he learned more and more about what it was thought to contain, all of which made him double his efforts.

He had been sitting in a private gambling room at the Venetian dressed in his favorite Armani suit, his long black hair pulled back in a ponytail. Marconi sat across from him; the older man had the deal as he spoke fondly about his relationship with Xiao's uncle Kwon, regaling Xiao with stories of his uncle's fearsome temper, his sense of humor, his love for his sister Lily. Marconi's two trusted associates sat in silence as if their sole purpose in life was to pour money into the pot, which was only being won by Xiao or Marconi.

It was when Marconi was up nearly one million dollars and on his sixth scotch that his lips loosened a little too much and he spoke about the book, the diary that he had purchased from Kwon, the elegant Zheng He diary.

Xiao smiled and listened to the old man, shrouding

his emotions as he absorbed what Marconi said. Marconi had had the book translated in its entirety, laughing as he spoke of having the translator killed upon completion. He spoke of what the book said, where the book led, and what it revealed, and he spoke of a small black puzzle box that held death, death in its worst form, a death that could sweep away an enemy's family with only a few drops . . .

The two men retired to Marconi's private suite on the twenty-sixth floor of the Venetian to negotiate Xiao's purchase of Zheng He's diary. As one of the casino's biggest clients, Marconi had not only a private suite but his own vault in the lowermost level, which was considered one of the most secure places in the world. As food and drink were laid out before them, Marconi dismissed his butler and the two men began discussions.

Xiao was willing to buy the diary back from Marconi at triple his original outlay. But Marconi didn't want to sell, explaining he had not bought it as an investment.

When Xiao offered ten times, Marconi became interested. He would sell it in a month's time. Xiao would have to come to his seaside castle in Italy as his guest and they would conclude the transaction.

But Xiao had had no intention of paying for something that was rightfully his. His attempt to steal Zheng He's diary had failed and Isaac had nearly killed him on the waters of the Tyrrhenian Sea.

But now, as night was falling over Macau, Xiao would beat his brother to it and finally unlock the mysteries the book contained, the mysteries his mother had so feared.

CHAPTER 30

"Good evening," the tall woman with a polished English accent said into the house phone of the Venetian. "Suite 3402, please."

As the line began to ring, she smiled. She couldn't bring herself to ask for Warren Grossberg, couldn't imagine lying in bed in the moments after passion with a man named Warren, as if it were the name of the over-weight neighbor from her childhood in London. Look-ing around the casino, she wondered how many people were actually registered under their own names and how often the desk clerk had to stifle a laugh at the creative aliases that were thrown about.

With no answer on the other end of the line, she left a brief, innocuous message and hung up.

Brushing her hand through her thick red hair, Pam-ela Weiss adjusted the jade and ivory comb that "Warren Grossberg" had given her, picked up her small travel bag, and headed for McSorley's Old Ale House. Except for the three bags of nuts and two glasses of wine on the plane, she hadn't eaten since last night. So many asked her how she stayed in such great shape at forty-five, and while she was able to squeeze in yoga and running a few times a week, her real secret was never having time to eat: always in meetings, traveling for business, forgoing food for stress or just one more phone call. She was as much a workaholic as "Warren" was.

He had given her the name and his room number in case of emergency, with strict instruction to use the alias. She was supposed to be in Tokyo for the next week on assignment but wanted to surprise him with an early-evening visit. She needed to see him as much as she knew he needed to see her. Just a few hours and then the warmth of each other's embrace while they slept.

As HE HIT the Cotai strip, Sergeant Reiner was thankful to be free of the colonel for the next hour. Assigned at the last minute as his attaché, Reiner obeyed the directive from the Pentagon without question, as he had always followed orders.

The colonel, while not verbalizing it, was not happy about the assignment, preferring to select his team himself, but the upper brass was growing concerned about the colonel's safety and ordered him to bring along an attaché—reminding him of his station within the military, and that others should be handling the mundane tasks so he could maintain focus on the current assignment. Despite Lucas's displeasure, they had made a connection; Lucas realized the danger he was in and accepted Reiner on their team.

Reiner was apprehensive about leaving the colonel alone at the hotel, but the man had insisted. The colonel wanted a specific file from the safe house, and if the upper brass insisted Lucas had an errand boy, he would put that errand boy to work, allowing himself to check in and get up to speed with the rest of his team. If there was an issue, he already had a man in the hotel whom he could turn to.

Reiner had never been to Macau and refused to look the part of a tourist. He had memorized four separate routes to his destination, as the last thing he wanted to do was carry around a trifold map like some lost puppy. Dressed in a blue sport coat, his hair cut one level above bald, he rejoiced in the twenty-minute walk over the bridge and into downtown Macau. He hated long plane rides, and while the military jet they had flown over on was well appointed, there was no amenity that would help one forgo jet lag and fatigue.

While the bright lights and heavy security on the Cotai strip projected a sense of safety, that soon evaporated as he walked several blocks into the run-down section of old Macau. He was surprised to find it looking more European than Eastern with its stuccoed buildings, torn and soiled awnings over the windows, cobblestone streets, and alleys. The humid air, trapped within narrow streets bordered by run-down structures, was thick with the alternating smells of urine, sweet meat, and rotting garbage.

This was the area never spoken of in the brochures, never mentioned in the marketing materials that attracted people to this new gambling mecca. Much as with Paris, New York, and London, the seamier sides of town were never mentioned, always shunned, and spoken of as something from the past.

The sidewalks were packed, people moving with

purpose, quickly hurrying away from or to a safer destination. He saw the gang lookouts on corners, the low men on the totem poles who kept an eye on all activity, feeling their stares at his back as the lone American walked quickly through their territory. He felt a tinge of claustrophobia, something that always rose up when he was in a foreign land with people of different customs and appearances. He always said that he was open-minded, far from prejudiced, but he couldn't help feeling far more comfortable around his own kind.

He was surprised at the location of the safe house, as the area didn't seem safe at all, though he understood it would draw little attention with everything else going on in the vicinity.

Reiner had known fear, every soldier had; he knew it in Iraq and Afghanistan, but it was his mastery of his fear, of keeping his mind focused, that allowed him success on the battlefield. He had never thought of Macau as a battlefield, but as the streets grew darker and more run-down, he sensed that it was just as dangerous as any area of conflict he had been stationed in.

He felt the weight of the .45 in his shoulder holster, taking comfort in its familiarity. He was near marksman status with it, but outside of war, he hadn't fired it except in the range, usually allowing his fists to settle any confrontation.

He found the nondescript brothel, entered, nodded to the madam, and headed up the stairs. He had never been in a house of ill repute, having been raised a strict Catholic. With a singular focus on his beautiful dance-coach wife at home, his thoughts never ran to having to

pay for sex. And though he wasn't there for carnal pleasure, he felt the guilt fill him nonetheless, like a child
who sneaks a peek in a girly magazine at the corner shop
and gets caught by his mother. He wouldn't be mentioning this part of his trip to his wife.

He went to the door at the far end of the hall, inserted the special key that the colonel said would override the thumbprint, punched in the code, and entered.

His hand shot to the pistol inside his jacket when he
saw the man with the head of thick brown hair sitting at
the large table, reviewing schematics, furiously making
notes, and completely ignoring him. Beside him was a
large man, six feet four, blond hair, engrossed in a novel.

With his nerves still on high alert, he hadn't expected to find anyone there; realizing his mistake, he left
the gun in its holster.

"Sorry," Reiner said. "You startled me."

The two men looked up and nodded.

"Sergeant Reiner," Reiner said in introduction, glad
to see a non-Chinese face.

"Michael," the note-taking man said in response,
barely looking up from his work.

"Paul," the other said as he looked up from his book.
He was large, his eyes wary as they assessed him before
falling back to the page.

"Just need to grab something." Reiner quickly went
to the filing cabinet, retrieved the thick folder labeled
Xiao—Level-5 Clearance—Eyes Only. He quickly looked
through the dossier; it was thick with details on Xiao's
criminal past, on his rise to the head of the Tiger Triad,
on its links to terrorism. It detailed his financial hold-

ings, his drug distribution activity, his terrorist contacts abroad.

Reiner looked back at Michael. He was constructing something out of metal, something intricate, with electronic components that fed out to a mechanical armpiece. Beside it was a Venetian room key and a host of small computer chips.

He had no idea what it was and knew better than to ask. Tucking the file in a large envelope, he picked up the *South China Morning Post,* wrapped it around the envelope, and stuck it under his arm.

"Nice to meet you," Reiner said as he stuck the small key in the security box and thumbed the numbers.

"You, too," Michael said without looking up.

Reiner exited the building and turned left, taking a different route back to the hotel, his military training well-etched in his mind.

He moved quickly through the crowds. It was only six blocks to the bridge to the Cotai strip. He thought the place gaudy, and a slap in the face to the decay he walked through now, but with the file under his arm and his uneasiness in the unfamiliar world, he was looking forward to getting back, settling into his room with some room service, and collapsing from exhaustion.

And then he saw him, just up the sidewalk, standing at the corner facing him, his eyes hidden behind black sunglasses. Reiner didn't need to look anywhere else to know he was staring at him. Without further thought, Reiner crossed the busy street, cars honking, drivers leaning out their windows, cursing him in Chinese.

Stepping onto the adjacent sidewalk, he saw the sec-

ond man . . . and the third. They were in front and behind him. The first sprinted through the traffic to join
his companions. The three were dressed head to toe in
black, their shirt pockets decorated with a flowing gold
design, 949, shaped like a snake. Their slicked-back black
hair coupled with their clothes and sunglasses gave the
three the appearance of brothers, though the disparity in
their skin tone and height indicated otherwise. Each was
thin, sinewy, projecting an aura of violence, of a wild animal coiled and ready to strike.

In his peripheral vision, Reiner could see people
hurrying by, rushing to get away from what they all
sensed.

And before he could think another thought, the first
man struck, his leg sweeping up, striking Reiner in the
ribs. Reiner quickly shook off the blow and drew back
his fist, but with his focus on the lead man, the other two
moved in with a flurry of punches and kicks, a coordinated attack from opposite sides. Before Reiner knew it,
they had snatched his gun from his shoulder holster,
tossing it aside, and the newspaper-encased file fell to the
sidewalk.

Reiner was strong and muscled, his body absorbing
the blows as he fought back, his iron fist connecting with
the first man's jaw. But when Reiner's arms struck a blow
or moved to block a fist, another attack from the second
or third man would hit him on the blind side. His focus
was pulled in all directions as he desperately tried to defend himself; each blow from the gang members was well
placed, not deadly but debilitating, each one crushing a
piece of his life, like a death by a thousand wounds.

And through it all, people continued to rush by, no one wanting to get involved in defending a foreigner, risking their lives for an American. There were no cops, no shouting and screaming for someone to do something. Everyone moved on, thankful not to be the victim.

Reiner quickly tired, yet the three continued, increasing their attacks, their kicks, cracking ribs, shattering his jaw, his blood flowing freely. Though his attackers were far smaller, they were more than winning; they were slowly killing him.

His vision blurring, he glimpsed the newspaper, the file protruding from its folds on the ground no doubt their goal. He needed to keep it out of the open; he had to get it back to the colonel. But as he reached for it, his body beyond the point of exhaustion, he finally collapsed.

And his feeling of claustrophobia rose up, enveloping him, squeezing his lungs, squeezing his mind. Pain covered his body, broken bones burned with agony as the three lifted him up and dragged him into a nearby alley.

A stench filled his nostrils, but he wasn't sure if it was the alley or his body as it edged near death. He was dragged down a long set of concrete stairs into a room with nothing but a single chair, which was cast aside as he was thrown to the floor. The lead man tore through his pockets, emptying them, tossing everything aside but his room key and wallet.

The door was closed, and as he glanced up, he saw a man emerge from the shadows, his face obscured.

The lead gang member handed the newspaper-encased file to a shirtless, heavily tattooed man, a fresh bandage on his stomach. Though Reiner couldn't see his face, he had no doubt who it was. Xiao opened the file, examining pages, turning them, nodding his head, finally closing it. The gang member then passed over Reiner's wallet and key card.

Struggling to remain conscious, Reiner felt his thoughts drift to his wife, her warm smile, her dark eyes. She had been so relieved when he had left combat for good, thankful that her husband was finally out of harm's way, that she would never be visited by an Army captain with an American flag delivering news she couldn't bear to hear.

Reiner lay there broken and bloody. He had survived two wars, countless battles, two bullet wounds, and countless bouts in the ring. His mother ascribed it to prayer, his wife to skill, but he always ascribed it to luck—which finally seemed to have run its course.

Reiner looked up at the weapon in this new man's hand. He had prepared himself for death since his first deployment years ago; he had gone to confession weekly without fail, always ensuring his soul was pure, that no sin would bar him from the afterlife. He imagined death by bullet, roadside bomb, an IED, or a land mine, but in all his military life he'd never thought he would die this way. His eyes were fixed on the razor edge of the sword as it cleaved the foul air in a shimmering blur.

And as the blade pierced his skin, slicing through his neck, there was the sensation of fire, the feeling of drowning, the loss of all hope before the world turned to darkness.

CHAPTER 31

"Only one message," the young concierge said as she handed Colonel Lucas a sealed envelope.

"Thank you," Lucas said with a nod. Dressed in khakis, a dark oxford, and a sport coat, he looked every bit the businessman trying for casual. He had made a quick sweep of the casino floor, his eyes focused on the rear service-area door. His goal, his prize, was so close, one hundred feet below where he stood.

He finally turned around to read the letter in private.

> *Starving, gone to grab a quick bite, back by ten. It's been so long, I've missed you! In case you forget, I'm the redhead with the beautiful jade and ivory comb in her hair.*
>
> *Love, Pam*

Lucas smiled as he tucked the letter in his pocket. "Isaac?"

Lucas turned to see Jon approaching. The younger man knew better than to address him with a title that would draw attention.

"How's our friend making out?" Lucas asked.

"He's pissed but scared for his girlfriend."

"To the point of distraction?"

"No. He seems professional, focused. And I think he's got a plan coming together."

Lucas nodded. "I'm heading to my room for dinner. Join me."

"Can't. I've got some things to arrange. I'll stop by when I'm done to give you a full debriefing."

BUSCH SAT IN the back of McSorley's Old Ale House; it had always been one of his favorite bars. Situated on Seventh Street in the East Village in New York City, it was one of those places where you could just smell the history. At more than 150 years old, it had served celebrities and thieves, sports stars and politicians: Lincoln drank there, Mickey Mantle, John Lennon, Teddy Roosevelt. Their motto for 120 years was Good Ale, Raw Onions, No Ladies . . . until 1970, when they were forced by the courts to allow women, though management ensured that the only bathrooms were for men.

Of course, the McSorley's that Busch sat in now was in the Venetian. Much like many of the restaurants and shops in the enormous facility, it was as if management had stolen the ambiance, menu, and design from Manhattan and dropped it in this Chinese city.

But to Busch, it didn't matter; it was a taste of home. A plate of buffalo wings, a hamburger smothered in Texas chili, a bucket of fries and a tall mug of lager would help to soothe a yearning for home let alone his craving for normal food.

Busch was hungry as usual, and Michael had insisted he eat without him as he was dealing with some logistics and wasn't hungry at all. Of course, Busch would order him the same dinner he was having, to go. He knew his friend would be hungry and would make sure he ate. And besides, he knew he himself would be hungry again later anyway.

A tall red-haired woman entered the restaurant; she was elegant, turning heads as she made her way across the room. The blond hostess greeted her and escorted her to the table across from Busch. She turned Busch's way and smiled as she sat down and ordered a white wine.

"Here on business?"

"How did you know?" Busch said.

"Business travelers, when not entertaining a client or the boss, usually eat alone."

"Actually, I'm with friends, kind of a business-pleasure trip," Busch said, a hint of nerves in his voice. "And you?"

"I'm meeting my boyfriend later, but I'm starving; I can't wait for him."

"I'm always starving. My wife, Jeannie, says I'm eating for two."

"Do you mind if I join you?" The woman stood up and offered her hand. "Pamela Weiss."

"Paul Busch," Busch said as he stood, smiled, and shook her hand.

"I wouldn't normally invite myself," Pamela said as she sat, "but you brought up your wife, which says so much about a man, and I hate eating alone."

Busch continued to smile. He loved Jeannie, and stepping out on her had never crossed his mind, though he always enjoyed the ego boost when a woman offered him attention. He had made a new friend, a female friend, and he was up eighteen thousand dollars and feeling pretty proud of himself. Luck was on his side, which made him feel good about their chances later on.

CHAPTER 32

Michael and Busch rode up the elevator to their rooms in the Venetian; each carried a large duffel over his shoulders, looking as if they were just arriving for their stay. They entered Michael's suite and dumped the bags on the bed. Michael looked at his watch; it was just after 10:00.

Busch reached into his duffel and pulled out four coils of climbing rope, three climbing harnesses, carabiner clips, and descenders; three knives; and three Lycra jumpsuits.

Michael opened his bag and removed a reed-thin flexible tube, a small diamond-tipped drill, and several black electronic boxes. Then he pulled out an oversized briefcase, a book-sized metal box with a long, protruding wire, and two Venetian key cards.

"Before we do this, I need the answers to a few questions."

"Such as?" Busch said as he grouped the equipment together.

"Where the hell did Lucas get such detailed information on KC and me?"

"I don't know, Interpol—"

"Bullshit, I'm not ever on their radar, neither is KC. Lucas has too much intimate knowledge. He knew about jobs I committed that the places I hit didn't even know had happened. He knew about the Vatican, the Kremlin, Topkapi Palace. He knew KC's gigs as if he were there."

"Well, who knows so much about you guys?"

"Just KC, Simon, and you."

Busch nodded, thinking. "I've got to admit, I'd sell you out, but not to the government. I mean, please, they're known as the lowest bidder." Busch smiled. "It's not Simon, and it sure as shit isn't KC."

"Exactly. So if we somehow squeeze out of this, what's stopping that info from getting out? I've got to get my hands on the source and shut it down. Not so much for me, but for KC."

"Okay." Busch nodded. "But that's a barrel of fun for some other day; right now we need to stay focused on getting KC back. And since I know you, and I'm not telling you to tell me how, tell me you've got a plan to screw this guy over, to bury his and his comrade's asses and still get the girl."

Michael smiled.

"That's all I needed to see," Busch said, and laughed.

Michael checked his gear, flipping on the small black box to see its display illuminate with altitude and positioning readouts. He flipped it off, laid it on his bed, and grabbed one of the key cards.

"What's that?"

"It's my God key."

Busch's expression said he didn't understand.

"I hacked their security, encoded this to let me

pretty much go wherever God can go, at least with re-spect to the rooms."

"Awesome, so where're we going?"

"We're going to see KC."

MICHAEL SLIPPED THE dummy key card in the door and the latch released.

He and Busch walked in to find Lucas sitting in his suite, a food cart off to the side, eating a steak as he read through a file.

"Michael," Lucas said, unfazed by his illegal en-trance. "Have you come to tell me about your plan?" Lucas put down his fork, closed the file, and stared at Busch, assessing his large size.

"Where's KC?" Michael asked.

Lucas stared at Michael.

"I want to talk to her, and I want to talk to her now."

"Well, if you thought you'd find her in here, you're mistaken." Lucas rose from his chair and approached them.

"I want to know that she's alive and unharmed."

"Not happening," Lucas said.

"Oh, it most certainly is," Michael said. "You with the power of your government, the power of guns for hire, and the underworld—make it happen."

"That's impossible."

"Really? It seems you had no problem getting a video of her in the airport in New York. Get the video feed. You built a file on us like you read our minds, so—"

Busch's arm shot out, grabbing Lucas by the throat and slamming him into the wall, pinning him there.

"I want answers," Michael said as he walked to within inches of Lucas's face.

Lucas looked between the two men, unfazed by Busch's attack as he was pressed against the wall.

"Who gave you the files on KC and me?" Michael continued.

"Safe to say, you came highly recommended," Lucas said as he kept his arms at his side, offering no resistance, making no attempt to escape.

"I want to know."

"That's classified."

"Bullshit," Busch yelled, his large hand trembling around Lucas's neck. "You know way too much."

"Mr. Busch, I know far more than you realize." Lucas paused. "How is your wife, Jeannie? Your two kids?"

Busch's eyes filled with rage as they bored into Lucas.

"I'd answer his question," Busch said as he squeezed the colonel's throat. "Or it's going to get real hard to swallow."

The door flew open, Jon rolling into the room, his gun drawn. He quickly leaped the ten feet between them and thrust the muzzle into the back of Busch's head.

"Let him go," Jon whispered to Busch. "I'm only going to tell you once."

Busch's eyes remained locked with Lucas's, his hand squeezing, Lucas turning red.

Michael laid his hand upon his friend's shoulder. "Let him go."

Busch reluctantly released him.

Lucas rubbed his neck, flexing his jaw. Jon didn't remove the gun.

"You were never part of this equation," Jon said. "I should shoot you now—"

"Shoot him and all deals are off," Michael said.

"Really, all deals are off?" Lucas said raspily. "Would you trade the life of the woman you love for your best friend?"

"Excuse me?" Michael spun about.

"If you had to choose between the two, who would you save? Answer me," Lucas said softly.

Busch turned to Michael, the gun at the back of his head. "It's okay."

The moment dragged on.

Lucas exploded, "Answer me!"

"Kill me," Michael said as he slowly reached out, grabbed the barrel of Jon's gun and pulled it from Busch's head toward himself.

Lucas stared at Michael, assessing him, then turned to Jon and nodded. Jon lowered his gun. Lucas went to his bed and dug through his bag; he pulled out an iPad and file and laid them on a table before Michael.

"You're an interesting man: brave, honorable, like a true soldier," Lucas said as he continued to rub his neck. "So I'm going to give you a choice."

Lucas pushed the iPad toward Michael. "You can have a little video chat with your girlfriend or"—Lucas put his hand upon the file, his eyes darting between Busch and Michael—"I'll tell you which of your friends revealed everything about the two of you."

Michael looked at Lucas.

"I want you to understand that no matter how smart you think you are," Lucas said, "how far ahead of me you have planned, I control the situation, I control KC . . . and I control you." Lucas looked at the iPad and file. "You've got five seconds to decide, then you get nothing."

MICHAEL HELD THE iPad in his hand, the green light of the camera lit but the screen still black. He sat alone in his room. Busch, Lucas, and Jon had gone to Busch's suite to allow Michael some privacy.

KC's face suddenly filled the screen. The image was dark, the room nondescript. Her eyes were red with exhaustion.

"Michael!" KC said. "Thank God."

"KC, are you all right?" Michael asked.

"I'm fine," she said as she wiped her long blond hair from her face. "What about you?"

"Don't worry about me."

Michael stared at her, her image as clear as if she were right in front of him. He looked at her as if seeing her for the first time: her green eyes, her blond hair, her perfect lips. But as he looked closer he noticed her coloring was off, her face pale and worn. Then his eyes fell on the red stain on her white collar. And his anger rose . . .

"Is that blood on your shirt? So help me God—"

"Relax, I had a bloody nose."

"You don't get bloody noses." Michael's heart began to beat. "How do you feel?"

"Heartbroken," KC said quietly.

"Physically?"

"Tired. It's not like I've been getting much sleep. Don't worry about that."

But Michael was worried. In all the time he had known KC she never had even a runny nose and an instinctual fear grew within him.

"Where are they holding you?" KC asked.

"Macau. Do you have any idea where you are?"

"Beijing—"

"Beijing? What are you doing there?"

"They're making me steal an artifact from the Forbidden City; they said they will kill you if I don't."

"Mmmm, sounds familiar."

"You, too?"

"Yeah," Michael said. "Can you get away?"

"Can you?"

"Paul's here," Michael said, diverting her attention.

"How come you get to bring help?" KC smiled. "Tell him I said hi. You should see my help."

"You mean Annie?"

"You know her?" KC said with surprise. "She wouldn't be a former girlfriend or anything, would she?"

"Be careful," Michael said, brushing off her comment. "I watched her kill a man in cold blood."

"Yeah," KC said. "Me, too. Don't worry, though, she underestimates me."

"I made that mistake once." Michael smiled.

"And look at where that got you."

Michael was doing everything he could not to break. Seeing KC as if she were right in front of him filled him with a welter of emotions. Relief that she was alive, but a confirmation of his fear knowing she was with Annie, knowing that Annie would kill her once she was done with her.

"Listen to me. If you get that artifact, whatever it

may be, you hold on to it, that's your leverage. Once you give that up, they no longer have a need for you."

KC nodded. "And you?"

"It's me." Michael smiled. "Don't worry about me."

The moment dragged on, both searching for the right thing to say.

"I'm so sorry," KC said.

"Hey, not now."

"If something happens, I need you to know—"

"I love you," Michael said softly. "Always know that."

"If I didn't leave—"

"If I didn't go to Italy . . ." Michael stopped her and looked deep into her eyes. "This is all my fault."

"No . . ." KC smiled. "We're just paying the price for helping a friend. These people . . . they are the ones at fault, not you."

"Were you really running away?" Michael asked. "Were you really going to stay in England?"

"Were you going to come and get me?" KC said. "I was kind of looking forward to the chase."

Michael smiled as if there were no problems, as if death wasn't hanging over their heads.

And then Michael saw it, a slight trickle of blood on her left nostril. "What if we both cut and run?" KC asked, unaware of the blood.

"No." Michael shook his head, trying to stay focused. "You can't take that risk. Annie might be underestimating you, but don't you dare underestimate her. KC, I can't lose you. I will not go through that again."

"Michael—"

"You listen to me, you get that artifact, hold on to it,

and you stay alive, no matter what," Michael said. "Because I'm coming to get you."

LUCAS AND JON walked back down the hallway, the iPad tucked under Jon's arm. They had left Michael to ponder KC. Lucas had always intended for Michael to see her, to talk to her; it would help to keep him focused.

Returning to his room, Lucas opened the door and saw a large gift-wrapped package on the center table by the window.

"What's that?" Lucas said.

Jon halted Lucas by the door as he walked to and inspected the package. He ran his hands over it, sniffed it, looked beneath the table.

"Nobody knows I'm here," Lucas said.

"That's not true," Jon said, looking up at Lucas. "Is it?"

"My girlfriend's arrival was unexpected," Lucas continued, staring at the blue gift-wrapped box from across the room. "How did you know?"

"We have a hack into the phone line on all of our rooms, including yours; it's security protocol. She called you earlier, left you a note." Jon paused, seeing Lucas's annoyance at the invasion of his privacy. "Though it is good to see you have a girlfriend."

Lucas nodded, his focus still on the package.

"You think it's from her?" Lucas said.

"You would know better than I would."

Lucas approached the box, studying it.

"While it may help as your cover," Jon said, "her being here is a mistake."

"I'll talk to her; she'll be gone before anything happens. Anything else you want to criticize me on?"

"No, sir," Jon said.

Lucas turned his attention back to the box.

"I doubt it's a bomb," Jon said. "That's not the style in Macau, of the Triads, and certainly not of Xiao."

"You're paid to find that out," Lucas said in a commanding voice.

Jon looked at the box, laid his ear to it, listening. And then the smell caught him: earthy, familiar. He tore off the paper to reveal an elegant Tiffany-style box, taped along its seams. He pulled out his knife and ran it through the taped edge, opening the box, staring in at its contents.

He held his breath as he turned around, circling the box, his eyes fixed on the item within.

He finally looked up at Lucas, the moment hanging in the air, then reached in and pulled out Ken Reiner's head.

Holding it up, Jon examined the base of Reiner's severed head; the skin's edge was smooth, as if the execution had been surgically performed.

"We know this was not done by a scalpel, so the blade was either a *jian* or a katana, the edge near perfect. Reiner never felt a thing."

"Shit," Lucas said.

"Xiao's here," Jon said without emotion. "We need to move you and we need to move you now."

Without another word, they left the suite and went to Jon's room. "No phones, room, cell, or otherwise," Jon said. "We need to move you to a different floor."

"Do me a favor, then: Find Pamela Weiss. She was to meet me at my room after dinner."

Jon pulled out his pistol and handed it to Lucas. "Keep it with you. If anyone comes in and you don't know them, shoot; if in doubt, shoot anyway." Jon nodded as he headed out the door. "I'm going to arrange for some protection."

"I'll be fine."

"Your bodyguard would disagree."

As Jon left the suite, Lucas locked the door behind him and ran his hand across his face. He stepped into the bathroom and ran water in the sink. Wetting a washcloth, he wiped his brow, his cheeks, the back of his neck, and finally looked in the mirror . . .

And saw the small trickle of blood running from his nose.

PAM BOARDED THE elevator and hit the button for the thirty-fourth floor. It had been nearly three weeks since she'd last seen Isaac. He'd disappeared on some assignment and had to run back to the U.S. to handle some additional military business.

She missed him. She missed his warmth, being held in his arms. Isaac was a serious man not known for smiles or laughter. But when they were alone, when the world was quiet, she had a way of drawing out a smile, making him lose himself for hours on end, awakening in him a momentary joy where he could seek solace from his life. She recognized the deep pain he held; he had told her of his life, of his mother and what his father had done. And he had told her of his brother, of how he had killed their father in front of him.

She couldn't deny her attraction to a man in uniform.

It was so cliché, but when that uniform represented a colonel in the U.S. Army, when it was respected the world over, it created an allure that she couldn't deny. It represented strength and power, command and confidence, all the traits a woman seeks in a man. It was a level of success achieved through hard work and dedication, a recognition of achievement by an assessment of character. The façade of so many men, in law, in business, captains of industry dressed for success in designer suits, was but that, a façade. Their station in life hadn't been achieved by putting their life on the line for their principles and ideals, for their country and others. It had been arrived at through self-promotion, personal greed, without care for others.

Isaac's and Pam's relationship was eight years in the making. Neither of them sought the false commitment of a wedding ring or felt they needed to make vows before God in order to love each other. They knew how they felt and were comfortable with that, trusting in each other through their deeds and actions. She would surprise him with unannounced visits; he would send her just-because gifts like the jade and ivory comb that had been his mother's, gifts from the heart as opposed to some last-minute online purchase.

As with Isaac, the world was Pam's office. Working for Nascent Global, she was in charge of compliance, so her work could take her to Europe, Asia, the Americas. She had accumulated a rather substantial portfolio not just from her generous salary and bonuses, but through the shrewd investment of her inheritance. She had lavish apartments in Tokyo, Hong Kong, New York, London, Paris, and L.A., each with a full complement of designer clothes, shoes, and accessories, which allowed her to travel light yet maintain appearances. She was a woman of the world, and the only time she ever felt roots was when she was with Isaac.

They had made a pact that when Isaac had completed his current assignment they would each plan for their retirement in a year's time. Isaac had assured her that once he completed his current dealings he would be able to put the darkness behind him.

The elevator rose toward the thirty-fourth floor. Pam's heart began to race as if she were a teenager anticipating her first dance.

When the doors opened, she reached down and picked up her small bag, and as she stood she saw him. Everything she had heard, everything Isaac had said, was in the eyes of the man before her. Dressed head-to-toe in black, he looked as if the man she loved had been possessed. She knew they were twins, but to her, they couldn't be more different. He was truly evil personified.

She didn't scream, didn't feel fear. The only emotion that rose in her was anger, for this was the man who had clouded Isaac's heart, who consumed him, who was responsible for all the pain in his life.

As he snatched her from the elevator, covering her mouth with his black leather glove, he whispered in her ear. "So nice to meet you, Pamela."

And as he dragged her down the hall into a vacant suite, his powerful arms lifting her in the air, she feared for Isaac, for she knew she was now a pawn in the escalating battle between the two brothers.

CHAPTER 33
THE FORBIDDEN CITY

The rain was heavy, falling in large drops whipped by intermittent winds into spinning sheets that danced along the vast outer courtyard of the Forbidden City. KC was already soaked through; the black hat that covered her long blond hair was plastered to her head.

She was thankful for the rainstorm, as it limited not only vision but hearing. It would impede the guards' overall awareness, offering KC a slight advantage if she was spotted. Second, the rain reduced the guards' diligence; she knew their focus would be dulled by the fact that criminals were rarely active in bad weather.

They had entered from the east near the Gate of Eastern Glory. Slipping under the bridge span, crawling along its undercarriage over the moat, they arose on the far side.

It was the area of deepest shadow, out of the line of sight of any roadway or distant building. The enormous turreted guard tower to their south posed no threat, unmanned since the days of the emperors; there was no need for guards in the high structure, as no one would be attacking a museum.

KC removed the coil of rope from her shoulder,

reached into her satchel, pulled out the grappling hook, and affixed it to the end. She and Annie quickly scanned the area, and without delay, KC swung the rope around and tossed the hook to the top of the wall thirty feet above them.

As the carbon-composite device sailed over the parapet, the four arms sprang out and caught hold within the merlons, the slotted section of the battlements.

KC pulled tight on the rope, testing its hold, and immediately began her climb, her body angled to allow her feet traction as she pulled herself up hand over hand. The smooth outer surface was far different from the rock faces she was accustomed to climbing, with their uneven texture that made for such good footholds. She crested the top in less than ten seconds, flipping over the parapet and lying flat. Five seconds later, Annie was by her side, pulling the rope up, coiling it, and throwing it over her shoulder.

Staying low, they ran along the twenty-foot-wide battlement for seventy-five yards, tied off the rope on a merlon, and rappelled down into the royal stable area.

They had prepped back at the hotel. Annie had taken a rifle and two pistols; she oiled them, checked them. She affixed a weapon light, a small bright flashlight underneath the barrel of the rifle so she could see what she was shooting at. She handed KC one of the pistols, but she refused. KC hated guns and was not about to kill someone either on purpose or by accident. They had packed it all up and headed out to the palace, getting dropped off in a nearby neighborhood before approaching the bridge.

Once in the stable area, they split up.

KC hugged the wall of a small storage building, looking out over the vast open space before her. In the dark shadows of night, the buildings along the perimeter of the wide-open space took on the appearance of a mystical dream; fading in and out of vision with the driving rain, their red walls appearing to bleed as water cascaded down the façades. The sound of the droplets against the ground and the yellow-tiled roofs, strung together, sounding like the rasping breath of a dying animal.

There were eight guards on patrol—two pairs, four solo—moving about in prescribed patterns, checking doors and entrance gates, following routines as they had done for months and years without incident. Dressed in green and black with sharp-brimmed hats, they carried no umbrellas against the elements and were drenched from the moment they started their late-night shifts.

KC peered upward to see Annie lying prone upon the roof of the silk museum, the rifle tucked beneath her. It bothered her: Women were supposed to be the givers of life, not the assassins, the takers. And Annie seemed to love her job.

KC readied herself; she purged her mind of fear and worry . . .

"Okay," Annie said through her earpiece. "Go."

And KC took off across the courtyard of the Imperial Palace, in the shadow of the Imperial Gate. It was more than six hundred yards: ninety seconds of being a target. She had never run harder in her life. Her long legs, pumping, barely touched the wet ground as she sprinted not only for her life but for Michael's. And as fast as she was going, she felt as if she were running through mud, as if some force were reaching out to slow her. But the shadow of the Porcelain building was up ahead, and once that blanket of darkness was about her, her chance of survival would go up tenfold. The heavy rain pelted her face; it felt like needles. It ran up her nose, into her mouth and eyes, playing havoc with her senses. She kept her head down while trying to maintain awareness of any guard presence around her.

Hitting the umbrella of shadow from the Imperial Gate, she didn't let up until she reached the safety of the side of the Porcelain building. She pulled up, hugging the wall, her eyes darting left to right, looking for a pursuer, her ears attuned for movement above the din of rain, for voices, for anything, hoping it wasn't masked by the weather.

"Clear," KC finally whispered. She turned back and watched Annie slide to the ground, watched as Annie ran the long distance through the shadows on the far side of the courtyard and disappeared behind the Shan building, only to see her alight upon its roof seconds later. The glint of her scope caught KC's eyes as she scanned the area.

"Okay." Annie's voice filled her earpiece. "Hold. You've got two guards on your three o'clock, walking between the two buildings."

KC hated military-speak. She looked right and crouched low, her body blending with the shadows of the steps and rail of the Porcelain building. Her heart was racing; despite the cover of night and shadow, the cloak of rain around her, she felt as if she were under a brightly lit microscope.

Twenty feet away, the two guards passed her by, unaware of her presence. It was five seconds. And then . . .

"Go," Annie whispered.

KC exploded from her crouch into a full sprint in the driving rain toward the Imperial Workshop. Ten strides in, she saw the shadow as she passed the Fanlue building, and at once knew she was in trouble. In her peripheral vision she saw the man break into a run.

She ran harder than she ever had, her heart pounding, her fear rising as the splashing footfalls behind her seemed to close in. She could hear the quick staccato breath of her pursuer. And then she could feel the clawing of his hand, his fingertips grazing her, trying to reach her, to bring her down. And she knew he would, at any moment . . .

Thwap. And the patter of the man's feet ceased as if his legs had been stolen out from underneath him. She felt a warm splatter hit the back of her neck, instantly knowing what it was. The sudden silence as his body went airborne ended with a crunch as he tumbled to the ground.

KC didn't look back as she continued to run—

"Stop," Annie said through her earpiece.

KC pulled up.

"You've got to get the body out of the open, hide it."

KC ran back to the guard, to find him in a twisted pile on the ground. The right side of his head missing. She refused to reach back and wipe what she knew was his blood off her neck and back. She grabbed him by the feet and dragged him into the shadow of the Tao building.

She pulled the zip gun from her pocket, stuck it in the door, and pulled the trigger. The thin tip vibrated, slipping the pins, and within seconds the lock released and she opened the door. She grabbed the guard by the feet and couldn't help noticing the shine on his shoes, the perfect double-knot laces. He was a meticulous man, proud of his appearance. She immediately felt shame at his death. He was just a guard, someone who was protecting his culture, someone who dealt with pickpockets and rowdy tourists, never expecting to die in the line of work as a museum guard. As she dragged his body into the supply shed, she could see the ring on his finger and cursed Annie. She cursed her for what she was doing, for how easily she had killed this innocent man.

"Close the door," Annie said. "Quickly."

KC could hear the sound of footsteps splashing on the soaked ground. She reached out and gently closed the door; holding the handle until the door was silently shut, she slowly released the knob, allowing it to latch. She ducked below the window and attuned her hearing. She could hear the guard just outside as he slowly walked by, could hear the way the sound of the falling rain changed with his moving presence. He passed the window, passed the door, the sounds of his footfalls finally fading as he continued.

She breathed a sigh of relief.

"All right," KC whispered into her mike. "Are we clear?"

But there was no response.

"Annie?"

Again there was nothing.

And the sound of footsteps returned, coming closer.

"Annie? Is he coming back?"

The footsteps stopped before the door, the handle slowly turned, and the door opened.

A Chinese security guard stood there. KC's breath caught in her throat until she saw his arms were held out. Annie stood behind him, drenched, her black hair plastered to her face, her rifle slung over her back as she jammed her pistol against the base of the guard's skull. She shoved him into the dark room and looked at the body on the floor, inspecting her handiwork.

"Are you proud of that?" KC snarled. "Did you have to kill him? You weren't aiming to wound, you took the kill shot without hesitation."

"And saved your life," Annie said. She turned and yelled at the Chinese guard in her grasp, "*Xia guì!*"

The guard knelt before her, interlacing his fingers upon his head. She placed the gun to the side of his head and—

"No," KC shouted at her, grabbing the barrel of the gun.

"What do you think, this is a game?"

"You can't kill this man," KC said as she looked at the wedding band on the man's finger.

"We've—no. *You've* got one shot at this, so don't be preaching to me. What I do is for the greater good, for my country, for the colonel. What about you? You're nothing but a thief, stealing from others, from the innocent."

KC didn't answer; she knew that wasn't the case. She resented Annie's self-righteous words. It was one thing to justify stealing to survive; it was another to take a man's life when you could have merely shot him in the leg.

Annie looked down at the guard and finally smashed her gun against his head, knocking him to the ground. She reached into her bag, withdrew some zip ties, trussed his wrists and ankles, and mumbled, "This is such a bad idea."

KC ignored her as she reached into her satchel and pulled out a long-haired brown wig. She removed her wet hat, pulled up her hair, and put on the wig, tucking her errant blond strands in. It was a red herring but it would do.

Annie crouched and took the unconscious guard's radio. "At least I'll know when the shit hits the fan."

She turned to the dead guard, removed his radio and crushed it under her boot, then tore the blood-covered tie from his neck and stuffed it in the unconscious guard's mouth. "Timetable was just cut in half. They'll be looking for these guys when they don't check in."

"Know this," Annie continued. "I let that man live against my better judgment. If you don't want anyone else to die, you pull this job off as planned."

KC didn't answer as they slipped out the door. They looked left and right, north and south. Annie broke into a run and dove into the shadows fifty yards up the way. Seconds later she was atop the roof, rifle tucked to her shoulder.

"Go," Annie said through KC's earpiece.

And KC exploded out into the pouring rain.

CHAPTER 34
THE VENETIAN

While activity had died down at 2:00 a.m. within the walls of the Venetian, compared to most places in this world, it seemed like New Year's Eve. Tables were still three-quarters full, more than two thousand slot machines were singing, and the bars and restaurants were still serving. These were the diehards, the ones who took the gambling more seriously, the ones who didn't arrive at the Venetian for the shows, concerts, and food.

The staff was alert with smiles and nods of accommodation as if it were ten in the morning: waitresses with drinks, croupiers with their welcoming patter, wandering concierges observing and anticipating the needs of their patrons. New carts of chips were wheeled out every twenty minutes, ensuring the flow of money never ceased.

Carl greeted Jon and led him, Michael, and Busch past the guards into the staging area he had brought them to earlier. It was Carl's last night, his last task. He had already cleared his accounts, packed, and would be boarding his flight to the Philippines at 6:00 a.m. with the hundred-thousand-euro payment already wired to his account.

The three were dressed in suits, pin-striped, high-end. Each carried a briefcase and a computer shoulder bag, looking as if they were preparing for a Wall Street battle or courtroom war. Around their necks were laminated IDs on black lanyards that precleared them past the guards and allowed them access to the Sublevel Two clerical offices.

There was nothing of value there. It was where the least-exciting aspects of casino life occurred, where the administration, HR, and business accounting functions took place. There were midlevel executive offices with fish tanks instead of windows, a large corral of cubicles for support staff, along with several conference rooms used for discretionary meetings when executives didn't want to be seen in the more elaborate facilities on the third floor.

As they stepped into the elevator cab, Michael looked about the space, its large size and rich appointments. He nodded to the guard with the highly conspicuous gun on his belt; the six-foot-three man didn't return the gesture, maintaining his focus. He reached forward, hitting the button for 2, their trip prearranged by Carl, and the cab started its descent. Busch looked at Michael, with that "point of no return" cocked-head glance. But in his own mind, Michael had reached that moment when he'd learned they had KC.

As the four exited the elevator, Michael nodded again to the large guard, but the man just stared ahead as the doors closed.

They stepped into the middle of a well-appointed long hallway. The decor matched that of the hotel above.

There were offices with open doors, all dark for the night. The fragrance from fresh flowers filled the air. Two cameras faced the elevators, with additional ones at either end of the far halls.

The three followed Carl to a conference room that was adjacent to the elevator bank. A large mahogany table surrounded by eighteen chairs was in the center, an oversized flat-panel TV on one wall, and a small bar on the far wall. Bottles of American scotch, Russian vodka, French wine, and Chinese huangjiu and baijiu, with appropriate crystal glasses, covered the mahogany counter. A humidor with a selection of Cuban cigars lay adjacent to a tiger-etched silver cigarette lighter and books of Venetian matches.

There were modems, speakerphones, and various outlets scattered about the space that provided the communication one would need to conduct a business meeting.

Busch opened the humidor and removed a cigar.

"Put that back," Michael said.

"They're for smoking."

"Not for you."

"Right, Mom, whatever you say."

Busch reached into the humidor, took three more, and tucked them in his pocket.

Michael had laid out his plan, explaining the precise timing, the no-room-for-failure approach. He detailed how he would overcome various security hurdles, but there were certain things he could not overcome due to their timetable. And that was where he was forced to rely on Jon, someone who could influence personnel, buy loyalty. Jon had told him he would take care of that and that Michael was not to worry. But Michael worried. He hated relying on others. And he didn't trust Jon.

Jon had procured Michael's supplies. Nothing was missing, and in many cases he had gotten duplicates, something Michael would have done if he had been doing the shopping himself. Michael had to remind himself that Jon was military-trained, efficient, focused, with a nothing-is-impossible approach. An approach Michael knew he and Paul would have to extricate themselves from if they were to survive to save KC.

Carl spoke in quick, hushed tones to Jon, all in Chinese, and quickly left.

Jon's briefcase was large, accordioned, designed for accountants transporting a large amount of work. He laid it upon the table and opened the top to reveal the edges of papers and files that stretched the case to nearly twelve inches in width. He reached in and lifted off what was a false top; the papers and files protruded from a false sleeve that concealed three pairs of sneakers, two guns, and three coils of rope.

Jon and Busch stripped off their suits, revealing tight-fitting jumpsuits, slipped on the sneakers, and slapped digital watches on their wrists.

Michael removed the false top from his briefcase and withdrew a satchel, shaking it out. He gathered a variety of handmade precision tools from the case and slipped them into the satchel.

He grabbed the book-sized black box from his briefcase and walked out into the hall, past the elevator hall camera, out of its line of sight. He uncoiled a black plug, plugged it into a nearby outlet, and affixed the box to the wall. It took fifteen minutes for the power soak to charge.

The power supply for the security camera system was supplied through two trunks that fed in from two separate locations and circuits. If one was to go down, the redundant backup would kick in without interruption. The camera feeds were hardwired through two-inch steel conduit buried within the slab-and-concrete walls, while the computer network on Sublevel Three that it was all fed into lay comfortably ensconced in the center of the security station.

The system's mainframe, the computer that recorded and distributed the hundreds of feeds, was protected against power surges and spikes with electrical filters, but through Michael's experience, he knew of a single weakness. He had become aware of the fault through an installation he had done for a man by the name of Shamus Hennicot back in New York two years earlier.

A massive surge through the video feed, a line that carried a low-voltage current, would enter the video mainframe directly, a route that had no need for a voltage filter as the line was outside the power feed. And the computer's internal surge protection would activate, temporarily shutting down the system to protect all the data on the mainframe.

All cameras would go down, all monitor feeds would cease. The entire system would have to reboot before eyes were restored.

With a security failure, as was protocol, all activity on all sublevels would halt until the system was back up: The two elevators that accessed the lower levels would be re-called to the main floor, the fire stairs locked tight. If there was a fire, if someone died, the cost of the settlement would be but a fraction of the cost of their exposure to theft.

Michael pushed a small button on the box and two metal spikes protruded. He lined them up over the ex-posed video wire and drove them in.

Like a tsunami, the massive power surged through the video line and to the main computer, and, while they were not in the security room to verify their success, Mi-chael knew the mainframe was instantly shutting down as he heard both elevators power up and rise past their floor, heard the heavy thud of the deadbolts in the doors to the stairwells.

They had five minutes.

CARMINE RIOS WAS fourth-generation Portuguese, his family having come to Macau when it was a colony of the once-great Portuguese empire, back when they still influenced the world.

He had the command for the night. A night most would call boring, filled with overseeing a team that needed no monitoring: They were focused, hardworking, and without complaint. He stood upon the dais, oversee-ing the night staff of eighty-six, whose attention was fo-cused upon 481 monitors.

And they all went dark. The central alarm sounded; it wasn't loud, though its high screech pierced their ears. Not a single member of the team moved, their eyes still upon the monitors, awaiting the images' return.

As if by instinct, Rios fingered information into the computer tablet in his hands. The mainframe was still active, as was voice communication. A spike had somehow hit the video system's server.

Upon hearing the alarm, the floor captains on Sublevels Four, Five, and Six each picked up the phone, calling central command, reporting nothing unusual, nothing out of order. The main floor was operating normally and would continue operation as if nothing were wrong, though all activity in the rear staging area would stand down until the all-clear was rendered. Nothing was out of the ordinary on the subfloors; all were told to stand by while the situation was corrected.

Within twenty seconds, the lead tech confirmed to Carmine that the video mainframe had been shut down and that it was already rebooting and would take five minutes.

Though each floor had been confirmed secure, though each floor had security protocols in place for such an instance as this, though each was armed and trained in the event of an incident, Carmine picked up his radio and called the head of floor security. His gut was gnawing at him. He'd send a few personnel to make a sweep, the personnel who were trained for situations like this, who were hired out of the military, out of SWAT units, for their expertise in these types of matters. They had the nickname Shuāng O, a fitting term that meant double O as in 007. Though they were encouraged to wound, to keep a criminal alive so he or she could be questioned, they would not be held accountable in the event that they killed someone perpetrating a theft in the Venetian.

BUSCH PRIED APART the elevator doors. He reached into the shaft, affixed the three kernmantle ropes to the service ladder that ran the length of the shaft, and let them uncoil into darkness. He checked each line and passed one back to Michael and Jon, who stood behind him. He craned his neck, looking up at the two elevators above, both called home—as in the event of a fire, returning to the main ground floor—when the cameras went out. He glimpsed the red LEDs on a shaft security camera, glad it was dark. He affixed the clip to his line, said a quick prayer to himself, and without a word . . .

Busch leaped out into space.

CHAPTER 35
THE FORBIDDEN CITY

KC slipped over the wall and landed in a crouch within the shadow of trees. She wiped the wet brown hair out of her face, reached into her pocket, and pulled out the glasses, slipping them on. Up close there was not a chance she would pass for Jenna, but soaking wet, the brown hair of the wig dripping, matted to her face, all filtered through a video camera onto a monitor, it was good enough.

One of the biggest ironies that KC found was that when a woman was not where she should be, when she was walking in a restricted area, a dark street, people immediately assumed she was lost; when a man did the same thing people assumed he was causing trouble. This was a fact that had saved her on more than a few occasions. Right now, with a dull video image, reinforced by the security card, she hoped it would be enough.

KC pulled open the red door and stepped into the small elevator vestibule, the lights at half-power for the night. She moved immediately for the stairs, trailing water behind her as she ran down the three flights. KC pulled out the white ID card, the moment of truth before her as she entered the utilitarian two-door landing.

She swiped it over the reader on the door on the right.

There was no pregnant pause, no drama as the door clicked and opened. She walked through the small waiting room, swiped the card again, and opened the door to the white corridor, the bright lights, the white walls straining her eyes. As she stepped forward, it felt as if time fell to a crawl as her left foot moved toward the white floor; despite the white card's opening the door, she feared its failure in disabling the floor security, awaiting the disabling jolt of electricity that would cripple her, that would not only stop her in her tracks but stop her from ever seeing Michael again.

But as she looked down the corridor, she noticed a red light in the center of the ceiling suddenly turn green, and she understood; it was safe to walk on the floor. She looked straight ahead, fighting the urge to look up at the cameras, and walked purposefully down the long corridor. Thirty seconds gone. She didn't need to look at her watch; it was as if she could see the march of time behind her own eyes. She arrived at the destination hall, and as she turned toward it, she once again glimpsed the red light that upon approach had turned green as she made a left down the hall. As she walked, she looked behind her to see the main corridor's ceiling light wink from green back to red and wondered if the current flowing through the floor was enough to kill someone.

She soon arrived at the door to the workshop and storage room. She pulled out the card and swiped it over the reader, the door hissing open before her. She stepped into the room and found it fully lit. To her surprise, the three men sat at the far work table absorbed in the same painting as they'd been earlier in the day. But this time they turned to her.

"*Nihao,*" one of the men said.

KC nodded in recognition, hoping he would turn back to his work, hoping the illusion would hold, but as good as the disguise might have been, there was no concealing the disparity in height between her and Jenna. KC turned down the short aisle of shelves, looking up and down until she spotted the wooden crate 9296273. Pulling it down, she carried it back and laid it on the workbench. She opened the drawer and pulled out the same screwdriver that Jenna had used. Jamming it in the lid, she pried it off and laid it on the table beside her. She reached in and grabbed the red lacquered box.

And a hand fell upon her shoulder. KC spun around.

"*Nǐ shì shuí?*" the tall man asked, the confusion in his dark eyes turning to anger. His hand reached up and tore the wig from KC's head, her blond hair spilling down onto her wet black jacket. The two other men approached

"*Nǐ zài zhèlǐ zuò shénme?*" the man shouted in KC's face as she fought to mask her fear.

The older of the two men looked at the open crate and picked up the phone.

"*Diàoyòng ǐnquán,*" the tall man in front of KC said. He grabbed her by the arm, jammed his hand in her pocket, tore out the white security card, and said in very rough English, "Call security."

ANNIE LAY UPON the roof, her eyes on her watch, three minutes gone, no word. And the walkie-talkie at her side squawked. "Yi? Where are you?" the man said in Chinese, his voice tired and upset.

"Cafeteria, you want some coffee?"

"Please take a swing by room 4864. One of the egg-head historians is having trouble with a woman. Yeah, and bring me back a soda."

Annie threw the rifle over her shoulder, tucked the walkie-talkie in her pocket, and leaped down from the roof. She was sprinting down the alley when up ahead she caught sight of the guard she had tied up, the one KC wouldn't let her kill, running for the art and security house.

The guard ran through the pouring rain. With his radio gone, Annie knew he was running to alert the world of their presence. KC was caught and a single guard was going to investigate. A single guard Annie could handle, but if this running man was to alert his superiors to what was happening . . .

Annie pushed herself, pumping her legs harder than ever before. She pulled her pistol from her shoulder holster. Though she was thankful it was equipped with a silencer, it didn't matter; she knew she couldn't make the shot on the run, and couldn't risk slowing for fear the man would get away. But once they got to the building, once he slowed to go inside . . .

The man cut through an alley door and Annie briefly lost him, but she rounded the corner to see him slip through the double-wide door into the art and security building.

Annie tore the rifle from her back and ditched it behind the stand of trees, racing for the red door that the man had disappeared through. Raising her pistol, she ripped the door open to see the last crack of light escaping from the closing elevator doors, the elevator pulling the guard down and away from her.

Annie raced down the stairs, holding tight to the pistol in her hand as she ran. In less than fifteen seconds, she arrived at the bottom landing. She tore open the door just as the elevator arrived with a ping. She faced the door, squared herself, and raised the gun, two-handing the grip. And as the doors parted she fired, the silencer reducing the crack of the bullet to a muffled spit. The bullet caught the guard just above his left eye, spraying the rear of the elevator wall with an explosion of blood. Without pause, she leaped into the large cab, knelt over the crumpled body, and took his white security card.

She pulled four climbing cam-nuts from her pocket and turned to the handleless security office door, inserting them in the door seams: two on the left, two on the right. Turning the outer clip, she released the self-expanding devices; inserted in rock fissures, their grip could hold three thousand pounds. But in this case, the outward pressure wedged the door, and as anyone on the inside tried to open it, it would only make the grip that much tighter, sealing it from opening, locking whoever was inside within the command station.

Annie waved the guard's white card over the reader on the storage-facility door and charged down the hall, never noticing the green light above her head. Running as fast as she could, she turned left down the hall and soon reached her destination.

She waved the card over the reader and ripped open the door, her gun hand raised, her finger wrapping around the trigger. Reacting as she saw the guard named Yi spin around, reaching for his sidearm, she shot him in the throat, throwing him back in a heap on the floor.

She turned the gun on the first of the three white-coated men, but before she could pull the trigger, KC knocked her arm up in the air.

"No! Enough death," KC yelled.

"They will follow us and kill us," Annie snapped. "Do you not grasp the world you play in?"

KC walked over to the tall man who had taken her card and snatched it out of his hand, tucking it in her pocket.

"They are intellectuals, not soldiers, not killers," KC said as she walked to each of the three museum workers and took their security cards. She finally turned back to Annie. "Give me the card."

"What card?"

"The one you used to get down here. You killed someone for it. Was it a guard?"

Annie reluctantly held it up.

"So when they find his body without his security card, they'll track you, they'll know where you are."

KC took the card.

"*Shǒujī?*" Annie yelled at the tall man, jamming her gun in his face. He pulled out his cell phone and handed it to her. She stared at the other two men, who quickly handed over theirs. She dropped the phones to the floor and stomped them into pieces.

KC ripped the handset on the desk phone out of the base, quickly following suit on the phone on the far desk.

Then she took Annie's security card, along with the dead guard's and those of the three museum workers, and laid them on the workbench. She reached into the drawer, drew out a pair of large scissors, and cut the first card in half to reveal a small circuit board. She quickly cut the other three and tossed them in the garbage.

She grabbed the red lacquered box off the table and tucked it in the bag at her side, then looked up at Annie. "We've got to go."

"We can't let them follow us." Annie waved her gun at the three men.

KC pointed at the sign on the door. "Don't worry, they won't unless they're itching to get a shock." KC pointed a finger at Annie. "You better keep up with me or you'll be tasting that electricity."

KC yanked open the door, checked the hall, and they took off.

As the door closed, the tallest museum worker ran to his desk, reached into the drawer, pulled out a 9mm pistol, and checked the clip. He reached back into the drawer and pulled out a second gun, tossing it to the older man.

ANNIE AND KC were running side by side, charging down the hall, when they heard the door open behind them and saw the two men in white coats come charging out, guns in hand, screaming.

"How the hell are they following us? I thought this floor—"

"It's disabled by my card, they're riding our clearance. Move it. If we can get down the corridor far enough before they leave the hall—"

Annie understood and ran harder. KC looked ahead; she could see the red light in the corridor ceiling and prayed there was no delay in the switchover before their feet turned the corner.

Behind them the taller man was much faster; he was gaining while the shorter, older man was already heaving, falling back.

"Go!" KC shouted as they turned down the corridor, running for their lives. Chancing a glimpse over her shoulder, KC could see only the tall man round the corner.

She couldn't see the green light in the hall ceiling they just left turn red; she didn't need to.

As the older man watched the woman round the corner, his colleague right behind them, he regretted being ruled by his emotions, regretted thinking he was somehow invincible and could catch the thieves. He knew what was coming. If he could only push himself just a bit harder, if he could leap before the current surged, before the light turned red . . .

But then, without warning, as his racing right foot touched the floor, it exploded in a hail of sparks, and lightning from the floor coiled up his leg, enfolding his body. His muscles seized, spasming with the flow of current as it took over his nervous system, dragging his body to the floor, where he convulsed, his bladder releasing, his jaw snapping closed on his tongue. And by the time the current finally ceased, he had already blacked out.

KC AND ANNIE ran for their lives down the central corridor, the tall man five paces back, gun in hand.

And he fired the gun, the bullet hitting the wall to KC's right, the man's aim erratic with his pumping arms.

KC reached into her pocket, drawing out the security card. There was nowhere to turn, no more hallways to duck into.

The man slowed his pace, raising both hands, gripping the gun, and began firing. The bullets skidded off the floor, off the wall. He kept firing, and the women knew it wouldn't be long before his erratic aim got lucky.

The door to the vestibule was just ahead.

They wouldn't make it. If they had one more second.

"Jump!" KC screamed.

As they both leaped in the air, KC snapped the card in two. She could see the green light above wink out, replaced with red.

The arcing sound of electricity sounded like a beast scratching the air, growling as it tore down its prey. The man in the white coat fell where he stood, his body shaking uncontrollably upon the floor. His gun hand slapped the floor with convulsions and the gun skittered away.

KC's and Annie's momentum threw them against the door; it burst open, both of them tumbling into the small vestibule.

The sound of fists hammering on metal diverted their attention from the thrill of their survival. With no time to recover, they rolled to their feet to see the chucks in the security office door seams nearly loosened by the thunderous pounding from the guards within.

They charged up the stairs, exploding out of the door into the pouring rain. Annie ran to the bushes and snagged her rifle.

But when she turned, she saw that KC was gone.

CHAPTER 36
THE VENETIAN

Busch zipped down the line into darkness, descending the hundred-foot elevator shaft at nearly twenty miles per hour, past the chaos and confusion in the security office on Sub-Three, past the money floor on Sub-Four, past the gambling chips on Sub-Five . . .

If his wife, Jeannie, had any idea of what he was doing she'd kill him before the guard they were about to confront had the chance.

Finally slowing his descent, he arrived on the lip of the Sub-Six landing. The elevator pit, a story below him, was dimly lit with an orange glow. Michael and Jon landed seconds later, checking their gear and unhooking from their lines. Busch released the door and the three entered the vestibule.

Twenty seconds gone.

BRAD DOREN was former British Special Forces—SAS. Having spent fourteen years in the service, he had seen enough of war that if his nephews ever considered such a career he'd shoot them himself and save both himself and their parents the anguish.

Stationed in Hong Kong for two years, the Englishman had fallen in love with the city. He had met his wife there and was raising his two daughters in a small apartment with spectacular views of Victoria Harbor. The one-hour commute across the water four nights a week was well worth the inconvenience; his pay was higher than he'd ever imagined, the three-day weekends were more than appealing, and the fact that he hadn't had to draw his gun once since he'd started eighteen months ago made this the best job of his life.

When the lockdown hit, he and Lao Che were directed to inspect the lower levels. He was more than happy to go, actually excited about getting out of the lounge where he sat around discussing his war efforts with the security team. He was like a rock star to them, as they all came out of various police forces in Asia and Europe. He was particularly fond of Lao, a former cop. The man had a quiet wisdom, knowing when to listen and never asking sycophantic questions about battle and death as the others did. The former Hong Kong SWAT sniper was bright, talented, and had leaped at the chance to earn a salary well above what he'd been looking at for the next ten years.

The two checked their guns and holstered them. With a special key, Brad opened the door of the sealed stairwell and headed in, the deadbolt auto-locking behind them. Though he had been told nothing was going on, deep down he hoped something was, that maybe he would get a chance to fire his gun again. It would give the staff something to talk about for the next month besides war.

* * *

JON WALKED INTO the vault room just as Rama Schavilia hung up the phone. The grotesque guard leaped from his chair, holding a gun, his finger tight around the trigger. But instead of shoving a gun in Schavilia's face, Jon shoved a picture. It was small, date-stamped an hour earlier, and far more effective than a gun. Schavilia stepped back, his foot now clear of the alarm button, laid the pistol on his desk, and put his hands in the air. They could have taken his wife, his father, or his brother and it wouldn't have mattered to him; he would have stepped on the alarm even if it meant their death. But his grandfather was different. He had lived a hard life, yet he'd always been there for Schavilia. He had helped him with school, when he was in trouble with the law, when he needed money. And he was the one who had straightened him out.

"Security is down for another four and a half minutes," Jon said in Chinese. "What we are here for no one will miss; its owner is dead. When the cameras come back up, give the all-clear, and once we leave the casino, we will release your grandfather and pay him twenty-five thousand dollars cash for his and your silence."

Schavilia said nothing. He pulled his chair away from the desk into the middle of the room, away from the foot switch, and sat.

MICHAEL REACHED INTO his bag and grabbed the long, thin gooseneck scope and a precision drill. He looked at vault 16. There was one vulnerable point: a thin plate over the tumbler mechanism. The schematic showed it was two inches thick, but Michael and those in the trade knew it was really only a sixteenth of an inch thick. It was an unspoken fail-safe, a means to accelerate the opening of the safe if it was ever a matter of life and death—which right now it surely was.

With the drill already spinning, he quickly drove it through the plate and slipped his scope in. He had crafted the 1mm fiberscope from fiber-optic cable, its pliable, threadlike construct slipped through thin flex tube making a device like a periscope that could bend, twist, and peer around corners. He had attached four hair-thin wires that protruded from the rear and were affixed to small dials that allowed him to control the flex scope like a puppet. He had also attached a lens that the fiber cable ran to. Like a doctor performing emergency surgery on a patient seconds from death, he rested his eye on the lens cup and looked through the fiber-optic lens. A small LED fed a glow through the device and illuminated the inner workings, which were polished and brand-new. Michael could see everything as if it were right in front of him. He twisted the gooseneck, dialing the contraption, looking, seeking . . . and found the central lock mechanics. A series of four metal wheels, each with notches and a single pin that aligned to a number on the exterior dial.

Reaching up, Michael spun the dial three revolutions, clearing the pins. He focused himself and turned the wheel to the right, watching as the dial turned and a pin finally fell into the seat of the second dial with a subtle click. He paid no attention to the numbers on the wheel in his hand; they didn't matter, and besides, he only had one shot at this. Back to the left he went, watching closely until the second pin fell into the seat of the third wheel; back to the right and with two more iterations the final pin fell. Michael reached up and gently turned the handle, and a loud click echoed in the room.

Busch stood staring at his watch; he had never seen the seconds tick by so quickly.

Michael pulled back the safe door, an interior light automatically illuminating the contents. What Michael saw was not what he had expected, and certainly not what would normally be found in a casino. The bright light revealed what could only be described as a collection of museum-quality artwork. There were paintings—Govier, Picasso, Renoir, Monet—stolen, missing from history and mankind. The walls were lined with statuary and sculptures.

The floor was clean, as if freshly painted, and sitting in the center of it, by itself, was a single box. It was eighteen inches square and high, gun-metal gray, marked with a single name on top: *Zheng He*. Michael quickly unhasped the single lock and peered inside.

"Let's go," Jon said, standing at the exit.

Out of everyone's line of sight, Michael pulled something from the box and tucked it into his pocket. He closed the box and handed it to Busch, who tucked it into the bag on his back.

And they were all on the move.

"Not a word and we'll release him in two hours," Jon shouted as they ran by Schavilia. "If you alert anyone before then, he will be dead by the end of your shift."

Busch held open the door as they re-entered the elevator shaft. He let the door close behind them and glanced at his watch.

Two and a half minutes gone.

They each grabbed a rope and began to climb.

BRAD AND LAO raced through Sublevel Four, Brad's command master key overriding the locks. Peter Huang, fifty years old and frail, wearing horn-rimmed glasses, met him in the hall and escorted them into the work area.

"Is this a drill or the real thing?" Peter asked.

"As far as I'm concerned, it's always real. Nothing out of the ordinary tonight?"

Peter shook his head as he pointed to his staff. "All on time, no complaints."

Everything was quiet; everyone was in place. The team of ten was busy running a series of machines that counted and bundled cash, every dollar logged into the system, which, unlike the video server, was running just fine. The bundles of cash were then dropped into a repository that auto-packed the cash and stored it in the holding vault beneath their feet until morning. On the far side of the room five accountants in short-sleeved white shirts were busily working the computer ledgers and spreadsheets, as lost in their work as their counterparts counting and bundling the cash. No one looked up or appeared aware of the severity of the camera outage all around them.

As Brad had suspected, nothing was out of the ordinary. Only a fool would think he could steal from the Venetian. "Thanks." He nodded to Peter and walked back to the vestibule.

He thought of heading straight down to Sub-Six, but unlike Sub-Three's cash and Sub-Four's chips, nothing was out in the open on that level; everything sat behind ten-foot steel safe doors. And no one short of God was getting those things open. He'd continue in sequence.

He slipped his key into the lock, opened the door, and he and Lao headed down to Sublevel Four.

ARRIVING AT SUBLEVEL Five, Michael stepped on the narrow lip of the landing and turned to Busch, who was trying to catch his breath from hoisting his large frame up the forty-foot climb. It was a deadly fall into darkness, and as Jon arrived, gaining purchase, Michael felt like a bird on a narrow branch that was about to snap.

Michael reached over, grasped the metal box on Busch's back, and pulled it from the bag. Busch re-adjusted his footing on the lip of the elevator landing and released the elevator door.

And as the door glided open, Jon snatched the gun from his waist and stepped inside.

Unlike Schavilia, who had been surprised to see him, Shi Shou Nu was expecting them and had vowed his compliance several hours earlier before his midnight shift had begun.

While it was every parent's Achilles' heel, Jon hated threatening children and knew he could never go through with the threat of death to a six-year-old girl. But the men who held her now in a basement in the Macau slums were different.

She had been taken from her bed at gunpoint just as

her father was leaving for his midnight shift. Jon's instructions were simple and to the point: compliance, she lives; noncompliance . . .

Shi was an in-house courier, part of the security personnel who shepherded gambling chips between Sublevel Four and the tables. His large cart would be loaded hourly with eighty boxes of chips, its contents verified at the door. He would wheel it into the secure vestibule and, by himself, free from interference, await the elevator. Following protocol, he would ride upstairs alone, where he would be met by an armed guard who, using the security wand, would verify the value on the cart before escorting Shi to his points of delivery.

Shi was alone in the security vestibule, dressed in his uniform of blue jacket and maroon pants. Since the security camera had gone out and the elevators had been locked down, he had been nervously awaiting not only the all-clear signal but Jon's arrival.

As soon as Jon came out of the elevator shaft, gun in hand, aimed high, he and Jon set to work, removing dark maroon cases from the center racks of the cart, creating a cavity. Busch handed Jon the metal case and he quickly slipped it into the hole while Jon passed the boxes of chips to Busch, who stuffed them in the satchel on his back.

Michael reached into his pouch, pulled out a small chip coated in adhesive and a small black box device with a built-in screen, and ran it over the maroon boxes in Busch's satchel. The screen instantly flashed the denomination of $1.5 million. He hit a small red button, disabling the RFID in every chip within, and watched the value drop to zero.

He punched "1.5 million" into the device's touch keypad, entered a code, and hit Send. He then passed the scanner over the tiny chip in his hand, watched the screen flash $1.5 million, and quickly slapped the single chip onto the metal case. As Michael touched the screen again, the keypad disappeared to be replaced by a four-quadrant screen with a small blinking red dot in the center. With a nod of his head, he tucked the device into his pocket.

Shi and Jon set several boxes in front of the metal case, completely obscuring it within the large cart, camouflaging it from the world.

Jon stared at Shi, an unspoken message passing between them. The three stepped back on the elevator lip and let the door close in front of them.

Michael glanced at his watch: three and a half minutes gone. He looked up the dark shaftway, a forty-foot climb. They needed to not only get back up to Sublevel Two but get the door open and return to the conference room before the cameras were back up.

Ignoring the rope, Michael grabbed hold of the service ladder and began to climb.

BRAD AND LAO entered Sublevel Five and found the area locked down. Brad slipped his special access key into his pocket, quickly spoke with the floor captain, inspected the area, and found nothing out of place. There was a chip courier in the holding vestibule, awaiting the elevator. Otherwise, all personnel were accounted for.

It occurred to Brad that he would find that to be

the case on each of the lower floors. If a robbery was in progress, the criminal would already be on his way out. The rebooting of the system would take five minutes, and anyone attempting to breach the security would have been in motion when the system went down.

The chance that a robbery was in progress was slim to none. But it was that slim chance that was giving him anxiety. If something was occurring and he missed it, he would be held accountable not only to the Venetian but to his own conscience. A good thief, a top thief, would be thinking out of the box, and that was what he should be doing. An exceptional thief would have already pulled the job and be hiding behind the momentary blindness of the security system.

Brad reversed direction and raced up the stairs.

They bypassed Sub-Three and went to Sublevel Two. The main floor above was filled with guards at the elevators and at the stairwells, both of which were locked. If someone had stolen something from the depths of the Venetian, Sublevel Two would be the perfect place to hide. No personnel around at three in the morning, no security to deal with.

He explained it all to Lao as they ran up the stairs and, using the access key, entered Sub-Two and found it vacant. The manifest said there were four people here, in conference room A.

Brad drew his gun, Lao following his lead, and approached the conference room.

"Thank God," Carl said as he emerged from the conference room, closing the door behind him. "We're trapped down here. No elevators, the stairwells are locked."

Brad stared at him a moment, finally letting down his guard. He recognized the man. He was a security liaison.

"Carl," the man said, introducing himself and offering his hand.

"Brad," he said in response, shaking his hand. "We should only be in lockdown a few more minutes. Cameras are down, the system is just rebooting. Only a precaution."

"You using that to fix the cameras?" Carl said with a half-smile as he pointed at Brad's gun.

"Better safe than sorry." Brad turned and headed back toward the stairwell. He glanced at his watch. "The system should be rebooting any minute now. Once the cameras are live, the elevators and doors will be back in operation."

"No problem." Carl thumbed his finger back at the conference room door. "These guys are so wrapped in discussion, they never realized they were stuck down here."

But as Brad passed the elevators, he looked to the right, up at the camera, and saw the small thin wire; he followed it from the camera down to the black box on the floor. Suddenly his mind was spinning.

"Carl," Brad said without turning his way. "Would you be so kind as to bring those men out here?"

Carl froze in his steps. He didn't answer.

Brad looked at Lao, who decided against holstering his gun and walked toward Carl. But he passed right by

him, reaching for the handle and opening the door to
the conference room.

Lao glanced back at Brad and shook his head.

MICHAEL, BUSCH, AND Jon climbed the service ladder
up through the shaftway, letting their ropes dangle
uselessly beside them as they raced upward. Michael was
in the lead, climbing as fast as he could, glancing at his
watch; they had a minute to get back into the conference
room before security once again regained their eyesight.
He tempered his emotions but couldn't help allowing
a tinge of satisfaction to slip in as he neared his goal.
And once he was in possession of what the colonel so
desperately needed, he would have his means of getting
KC back.

As he reached the lip, he released the elevator door
and climbed onto the floor, rising up only to stare into
the barrel of a pistol.

A second man trained his pistol on Jon, urging him
up and onto the floor. With his gun trained on Jon's
head, he took the pistol from Jon's side.

"How many are you?" the tall man said in an English accent. His voice was calm, as if this were common-
place.

"Two," Michael said, not looking back into the elevator shaft.

BUSCH REMAINED IN the shadows, listening to Michael's
words above. He held tight to the ladder, the weight of

the bag full of chips on his back straining him. Though his arms and legs were exhausted from the climb, his pain quickly disappeared as he heard Michael's captors.

He glanced up the dark shaftway. He could see the light wash coming through the doors thirty feet above him, the doors to the main section of the casino. The light was landing on the two immobile elevator cabs. He held tight to the ladder and focused on his watch, Michael's words ringing in his ears. Five minute to re-boot, and that five minutes was almost up. And when it was, the elevator would start moving.

Busch needed a plan and needed to formulate it in the next twenty seconds, for if he didn't, not only would Michael be captured, but he himself would be swiped off the ladder by the elevator as it went back into service.

"Sit down," Lao said in Chinese to Carl. "Against the wall."

He waved his gun at Michael to follow suit, and turned his gun on Jon, who stood with his hands against the wall.

Brad reached for the radio hanging from his side, but Jon spun out, his kick rising with a blinding snap, connecting with the radio, sending it careening into the wall, where it shattered. Brad's finger wrapped the trigger of his gun, but Jon snatched the barrel, twisting it over until it was wrenched out of the man's hand.

But the man was an equal match. He knocked the gun away from Jon, hurled it aside, and attacked Jon with his bare fists.

*   *   *

WITH THE MOMENTARY distraction, Michael jumped to his feet and moved toward Lao, but he responded by double-fisting his raised pistol in a classic marksman's stance, his eyes locked on Michael, and there was no question he was about to pull the trigger if Michael made one more move. But with his back to the open elevator shaft, with all of his focus on Michael, with Brad and Jon fighting in the hallway, he never saw the figure emerge from the shaft, never saw him approach from behind.

Busch snatched Lao's pistol, twisting the gun from his wrist while driving his right fist into the man's temple, sending him sprawling to the ground.

Lao rolled, but instead of rolling for a gun, he grabbed the radio on his belt, a weapon that would prove just as deadly to the three. Busch dove upon the man, grabbing the radio, throwing it aside and pouring his 230 pounds into a right cross that caught the man in the jaw, dazing him.

BRAD PUNCHED AND jabbed, but Jon blocked his attack, countering with a series of strikes, which were all deflected. All the while Jon was analyzing his style, his opponent's strengths and weaknesses, and he soon found Brad's biggest weakness. The man was overreliant on his size and strength. Jon quickly switched strategy and directed his kicks at the man's legs, moving in, falling back, and finally crushing the man's kneecap with a low roundhouse kick, sending him to the floor. As he fell, Jon leaped for his gun, grabbing it and turning it on the man.

"Get up," Jon barked. "Hands on your head."

Brad struggled to his feet, leaning against the wall for support.

"Clear his pockets," Jon ordered Michael.

Michael dug through his pockets, pulling out a wallet, a car key fob, and an odd-looking key.

"Please," Jon said. "Go stand in the elevator doorway."

With his hands on his head, Brad stumbled to the doorway, staring into the dark shaft.

Michael looked at his watch: five minutes gone. He glanced up at the camera; the red light was still out.

"We're out of time," Michael said.

Without hesitation, Jon shot Brad in the back, left side, heart-high. Brad arched back, but the force of the bullet drove him forward and he tumbled away into the dark shaft.

Jon quickly spun, turning the gun on Lao, who lay helpless upon the ground, and shot him in the heart. He quickly leaned down, picked him up, and tossed him into the darkened shaft. The sound of a buffeting wind could be heard as he fell into the abyss.

Jon reached up and released the elevator door, allowing it to close.

Busch glared at Jon, incensed at his ruthlessness. "You didn't have to kill them."

Jon ignored him.

"You son of a bitch—"

"You listen to me," Jon said with a chill in his voice. "I'll kill whoever I need to kill to get this job done, including you, your friends, your families—"

Busch's hand rocketed out, grabbing Jon around the neck.

"You threaten my friends, my family again, I'll kill you. I don't care what Hong Kong kung fu shit you know. I'll snap your neck like a twig."

Jon shoved his pistol up against Busch's heart.

"And I don't give a shit if you take me down in the process," Busch continued, unfazed by the gun, "I'll be happy knowing that you no longer walk this earth."

Michael again looked at his watch; thirty seconds past five minutes. He reached over and pulled down the power soak that he'd used to disable the cameras and stuck it in the satchel on his shoulder.

"We need to get back in the conference room . . . Now!"

CHAPTER 37
THE FORBIDDEN CITY

The storm intensified as KC ran across the six-hundred-foot expanse between the outer and inner courtyards of the Forbidden City, past the Gate of Heavenly Purity, her heart pounding, her lungs burning. She felt as if she were running through time, through a ghost world where the only sound was the driving rain across the pavement. The small building, with its incongruous Starbucks, was seventy-five yards away.

And the bullet skittered off the ground, the silencer spit of the gun's report lost in the sound of the pouring rain. Annie was behind her. KC didn't dare look back. It didn't matter where she was, KC was out in the open like an animal separated from the pack, with the predator smiling, knowing she had nowhere to turn.

The shots rang out anew. KC could hear the muffled sound of the gun now, could hear Annie's footfalls; she was gaining on her. KC was an excellent runner, both sprinter and distance, but she had never run for her life, never like this. Not only was her life riding on her escape, but so was Michael's.

KC cut left down the east alley; adjacent to the inner courtyard, it was a two-hundred-yard passage, formerly used by servants, now simply a favorite throughway of the staff. KC had thought the move would increase her chance of survival, but she realized too late she had run into a confined space, her chances of survival narrowing with her poor choice. The walls were twelve feet high, the only exit six hundred feet away. She ran as hard as she could, her legs wasted, her heart near exploding.

But up ahead, she saw her chance. The stone lion was three feet high, a paw resting upon the world. It sat adjacent to a small side entrance to the inner courtyard, upon a raised terrace entrance. The awning hung out over the alley, a waterfall of rain raging over its edge.

KC leaped upon the lion, her left foot landing on its shoulder, and launched herself up onto the overhang, her hands struggling, slipping along the slick tiles, finally catching hold; her legs swung upward, gaining purchase. Up on her feet, she reached up and grabbed the lip of the wall above. Pulling herself up, she broke into a sprint along the narrow wall, blocking from her mind that it was only two feet wide.

KC's heart pounded as she struggled to escape, her back on fire in anticipation of a bullet hitting her between her shoulder blades, imagining herself tumbling to her death to the alley below. Bullets shattered the wall beneath her, rapid-fired, Annie unloading her pistol in a hail of gunfire. But it suddenly stopped.

KC chanced a view over her shoulder to see Annie hauling herself up onto the awning, pulling herself atop the wall, but Annie stopped her pursuit there. Holding the rifle now, she straddled the wall, lying prone, tucking the scope to her eye.

KC knew Annie wouldn't miss. Till now it had been

nothing but a slim chance that Annie could shoot her on the fly. But now with KC running along the wall with no doorway to duck into, no hallway to turn down, Annie's shooting would be like target practice, her mark in her line of sight with no escape.

There was nowhere for KC to go. If she leaped back into the alley she would surely break a bone, sprain an ankle at least, and she would be at an even greater disadvantage, giving Annie the high ground. It would be like shooting fish in a barrel.

KC pushed herself as hard as she could, her lungs on fire, her legs heavy with fatigue. She didn't need to look back to know the shot was being lined up; she imagined it in her mind's eye, Annie adjusting the scope, her finger wrapping around the trigger.

And with the crack of the rifle, KC did the unexpected.

She launched herself across the alley, twelve feet above the ground, ten feet across.

She hit the other side, her body slamming into the wall as her hands caught the edge. She pulled herself over the wall, landing atop a roof, skidding down its sloped tiles to a small courtyard.

Without pause, she continued to run, finding a new, smaller alley to navigate, and slowed her pace. For as she turned the corner and saw the small red buildings before her, she knew where she was . . .

It was truly a maze, the dozens of closely grouped buildings with their red walls and similar design forming a labyrinth; she felt like Theseus escaping the labyrinth.

But while she had momentarily lost Annie, she realized she, too, was lost. There was a single building that held her salvation, but entering via the unorthodox route, she had no bearing as to her location, no line of sight to pinpoint her escape.

In daylight, the red buildings with their similar design were confusing, but now in the dark, the heavy rain falling, blotting out what little vision she had, she might as well have been blind.

She caught sight of a small light, blinking blue, coming from the other side of the courtyard. She raced toward it only to find herself in another small courtyard, nearly identical, the blue light flickering, just not where she stood now.

"Can you hear me, KC?" Annie's voice cried out through the rain.

It seemed to come from all around, the effect of the rain causing her voice to sound as if it was everywhere. KC ignored her, continuing her search, hoping Annie didn't see the blue light, didn't understand what it meant.

"You have no idea what you are doing," Annie called out again. "If you don't show yourself, if you don't turn over that box, you will die."

KC couldn't let Annie get hold of the box; it was all that was keeping her alive, it was all that would keep Michael alive.

She cut left, then right, the driving rain slapping her face, confusing her. She strained to see. There were so many small buildings on the northeast side, throwing her into confusion.

But then it was there: the small building behind Fengxian Hall, the blue flashing LED above the door. She quickly tore the LED down and crushed it beneath the heel of her shoe, disabling the light. She picked it up and tucked it in her satchel.

The lock on the door had been removed. KC turned the handle and entered, silently thanking Jenna for not only lighting the way but providing her with a means of escape.

The room was simple, carpeted, the walls covered in oil paintings of distant mountains. Annie had no idea which building she was in, but it wouldn't be long before she figured it out.

The bag Jenna had tucked away was on the right, in the corner; it was made of neoprene, waterproof, the tag still on it. Without delay, KC grabbed it and threw it over her shoulder.

She reached down and tore the carpet back to reveal a large drain. Made of thick black iron, it covered a four-foot circular hole.

Wrapping her fingers through the grate, KC leaned back, pulling with everything she had until the grate finally budged. She pulled it aside, dragging it over to the shadowed corner, leaning it against the wall. She drew down two of the oil paintings and leaned them against the grate, concealing it in the darkness.

While the space was dark, there were six wall sconces in the room. KC pulled the wool hat from her bag, ran to the nearest sconce, wrapped the bulb in the hat, and crushed it, the hat muffling the sound, protecting her hand. She followed suit with the other bulbs, ensuring darkness until the rays of dawn came through the window.

KC checked the bag on her shoulder, double-checked to be sure she had the red puzzle box, and stepped into the narrow hole, her feet finding purchase upon the rails of the ladder. But as she took her first step down, she stopped. She reached over and pulled the carpet back over the open hole, concealing it from the world and shrouding herself in total darkness.

She grabbed hold of the ladder and descended, each step echoing in the narrow vertical tunnel. She could feel the rust upon the rungs and hoped they would hold; Jenna had said the tunnel was out of commission, not on any maintenance schedule or repair list.

Thirty seconds in, she knew she had dropped at least three stories beneath the surface, probably four, the inky blackness warping time and distance within her mind. And then she heard the trickle of water coming from below.

She looked up, left, and right, but her eyes were wrapped in darkness. She stopped and quickly unzipped the neoprene bag at her side, reached in, and felt around. Her hand finally falling on what she hoped was there, she pulled it out and zipped the bag shut.

She flipped on the light, the startling brightness illuminating stone and brick walls thick with moisture seeping in from the rain above. She looked up and estimated she was at least fifty feet down. She shined the light down and it refracted off the smooth surface of water; the upper arch of a doorway was visible on the near side. It was a well whose design had allowed an emperor's escape more than five centuries earlier.

She continued climbing down, not stopping as she hit the water, immersing herself in the frigid well, shocking her lower half as her foot finally ran out of ladder and hit the bottom. The water level was just above her waist; she was thankful for the suggestion of the neoprene bag.

She stepped through the doorway and emerged into a flooded room built of stone, the walls, floor, and ceiling centuries old. The smell of decay and rot told her this was not a place for the living.

She continued walking through a long stretch that ramped up from the cold water, allowing her to emerge onto dry ground. Shining her light around, she found that the cavelike space was man-made, hewn from the earth, reinforced with stone, and forgotten to time. She could hear the skittering of rats in the shadows avoiding her flashlight as if it were flame. There were two passages running in either direction.

She unzipped her bag and pulled out a map, hand-drawn, rudimentary, but more than she could have asked for. A note was written along the bottom:

KC

I have marked a route on this chart that will bring you to the Beijing tunnels, but you should know that the Emperor's Passage is unstable, the earthen walls and ceilings subject to collapse. There are pockets of water and flooding is rampant. Please be aware that you will come upon several tunnels that were dug but abandoned when found to be encumbered by too much rock. Do not venture down these as you will become lost in a labyrinth of darkness.

I can't imagine what you're going through. My thoughts and prayers are with you. Please contact me when you have reached safety.

Jenna

CHAPTER 38
THE VENETIAN

Michael pulled out the electronic box and looked at the screen. The red dot was slightly off center; a series of numbers were scrolling down. Michael watched it and focused his hearing, listening to the elevator ride up by their floor. The numbers continued to scroll down until they hit zero. After a moment the dot moved further from center and stopped.

Michael quickly put his suit back on and transferred the small black box into the interior breast pocket of the suit.

Jon dressed in his suit, removed his sneakers, and tucked them into a drawer beneath the bar. He picked up his briefcase and, once more looking the part of a harried businessman, walked out into the hallway.

As Jon left the room, Michael whispered to Busch, "Watch the door."

Michael reached within his shirt and pulled out an envelope. He opened it and withdrew three sheets of paper covered in Chinese handwriting, which he laid out on the table, quickly smoothing them out. He pulled out his BlackBerry, hit the camera button, and took three quick pictures. He typed in an address and hit Send.

He grabbed the papers and envelope from the table, crumpled them, and threw them in the garbage. From the small bar, he picked up the vodka, poured it in, grabbed the silver cigarette lighter, flicked it, ignited a book of matches, and dropped them in, the can spitting out a ball of fire.

"What the hell is that?" Jon said as he came back into the room.

"Relax," Busch said, trying to block Jon's way.

"What was that?" Jon raced over to Michael and looked at the flaming ash in the can.

"Insurance."

"Bullshit, you tell me now."

"I'm covering our tracks," Michael said. "Your box is safe, I just watched it ride upstairs, and if we don't hurry, it's going to get out on the floor ahead of us."

Jon glared at Michael. "So help me—"

"I'd be happy to help you in more ways than you could imagine," Busch said as he stepped between Michael and Jon.

"Hey," Carl said as he poked his head in the doorway. "Elevator."

The three grabbed their bags and headed out the door.

And as they walked, Michael glanced down and saw he had no signal; his email hadn't gone out yet, nor would it until he had service again.

Busch leaned toward Michael's ear. "Insurance?"

"Not if we don't get topside and get a signal."

CHAPTER 39
THE FORBIDDEN CITY

As Annie saw KC make the jump over the alley, she made a quick decision. She threw the rifle over her shoulder, ran across the narrow wall, gaining speed, and jumped right, sailing over the ten-foot expanse, catching the wall on the far side. But as she lowered herself into a small stand of trees, she realized too late her mistake. She had dropped into the south side of the partitioned section, fifty yards from where KC had landed, each of them on opposite sides of the maze of buildings.

Annie ran through the alleyways, vainly trying to find KC, ducking into courtyards, seeking her out. She had narrowed her search to twenty-five buildings. She had seen where KC went over the wall, had seen the approximate area where the flashing blue light had glowed, something that was nowhere else in the city. She cursed herself for allowing her to escape. She realized KC had always intended to escape; she had planned it from the start.

Annie had been conflicted since they had met. She had seen in KC a kindred spirit, someone who lived outside the conventions of society, someone who might be able to understand the decisions she had made in life, the choices that had brought her to where she was. Society's expectations for women, which she had had thrust upon her, had always angered her. She was as smart, resourceful, and deadly as any man.

She was angry at herself for allowing KC to hold on to the red box, for being lulled into trusting her, into thinking that the threat to Michael's life would keep her in line.

But now, all things being equal, when she found KC she'd take back the small box and kill her.

In the eleventh courtyard she saw the small shard. It was by the door, no bigger than a quarter, but in a facility that was impeccably clean, in a restricted, untrafficked area, it might as well have been a large neon sign.

Annie held up her pistol, ejected the clip, slammed home a new one, and held the gun high, ready to shoot. She had been trained in how to secure a room, how to stay alive when entering enemy territory. She knew how to maintain focus, how not to succumb to fear, how to gain the upper hand and hold on to it.

She kicked in the door, crouched low, and swept her gun about the room—but there was no movement, only dark shadows cast by the light wash through the door. She took a step in. There was no mistaking the water on the floor, the wet footprints, but they only entered the room, they never left. Keeping her back to the wall, she inched along, clearing the corners. She checked the ancillary room, empty but for a single desk and chair.

She turned back to the main room, but as she rolled in, spinning around, gun still held high as a precaution, she never anticipated the attack. It wasn't from bullets or knives; it wasn't even from a person.

Annie stepped upon the carpet in the center of the room and it was as if a creature from hell had taken hold. She plunged through the hole, the carpet leading the way, tumbling down into an abyss.

She twisted and turned as she fell through space, her head hitting the ladder, her hands and feet scrambling for purchase, her eyes enveloped in darkness. The rifle on her back sparked as it scraped the wall, and she violently swung out her hands and feet, desperate to save herself. Suddenly, her left hand caught the rail, wrenching her shoulder, her body jolting to a stop, arcing downward, slamming into the ladder. She grabbed tight with both hands, planting her feet firmly. She caught her breath, closing her eyes to gain her composure, angry at herself for falling victim to someone like KC. Ignoring the pain, she descended.

It was farther than she imagined, but she wasn't sure if it was just an illusion from the darkness. She hit the water and grabbed the rifle from her back, holding it high, keeping it dry. She reached forward along the stock, flipping on the weapon's light. Shining it around, she found herself in the base of a well. She sloshed through the arched door into a small stone room, three doors facing her.

Pointing her rifle about, the bright weapon light casting its harsh white glow upon the stone, cavelike space, Annie looked for traces of KC, and soon found her wet footprints leading out of the tunnel to her left. For nearly one hundred paces she followed them until they gradually disappeared. She continued, the ceiling rising and falling, the smell of damp earth all about. She finally came to three tunnels and examined the ground, looking for disturbances, for any sign, but there was no indication of which way KC had gone.

Annie flipped on the rifle's laser sight and the small red dot danced on the far wall within the circular glow of the weapon's white light, like a shifting bull's-eye target whose pinpoint center meant certain death.

CHAPTER 40
THE VENETIAN

When Michael, Busch, Jon, and Carl boarded the elevator they found a large, silent guard standing there, his gun visible as he hit the button and the cab began its ascent.

"Do you know what happened?" Carl asked the guard in Chinese.

The man shook his head no, as if he were shaking off a bug.

"Well," Jon added, "I'm not getting stuck down here."

The guard turned his attention to Jon and pointed to the case.

"Yes?" Jon responded.

"Please, open your briefcase."

Jon stared at the man, annoyed. But he put the case down, flipped the lock, and pointed at the case. "Go ahead."

The guard reached down and lifted the lid to see the mess of papers. Without a word he closed the case. Jon relocked it.

"I'll be sure to let management know of your diligence," Jon said in Chinese. And though Michael and

Busch had no idea what he was saying, there was no mistaking the false anger in his tone.

The elevator doors parted and Michael and the others exited into the main floor staging area to find Shi standing there by his cart of gambling chips. Michael could see the worry in his eyes as a guard waved his wand over the cart. A moment later his screen displayed the expected amount and Shi was waved on.

SHI HAD FIVE stops to make: the Golden Fish, the Red Dragon, the Imperial House, and the Phoenix gaming areas. But his first destination was the private rooms, the high-stakes secluded suites where a single room could turn over as much money in an hour as the Red Dragon gaming area could turn over in a night. High-stakes games, with the wealthiest clientele, always came first in catering, drinks, amenities, comps, and availability of high-stakes chips.

Escorted by a guard, Shi wheeled his way along the outside edge of the Golden Fish gaming area. He walked at a steady pace, with the same demeanor he had every night he worked, his face never displaying the fear he felt for his daughter.

MICHAEL, BUSCH, AND Jon walked through the center of the Golden Fish area toward the central lobby. Michael kept Shi in his peripheral vision while Jon and Busch continued to talk and walk, all the while looking ahead so as not to draw attention.

They hung a left and arrived at the private elevator to the private gaming rooms. A guard motioned them to the waiting elevator just as Shi and his cart arrived. Michael, Busch, and Jon entered the elevator, but the guard motioned Shi to stop as he withdrew his wand and verified the cart's contents.

The three watched as the doors slid closed, cutting them off from their prize.

Within moments, the doors opened and they exited into the private area. It was a large, circular space, plush, the walls covered in silk, doorways and floors made of a deep cherry wood. They noted four hallways running off in various directions, numerous private rooms off each branch. There was a hush over the space, a near reverential silence for those who gambled millions.

A short man of mixed heritage stood in the center, impeccably dressed in a suit and a crimson tie; his countenance was firm but welcoming as he nodded to them. "What might your entertainment be for the evening, gentlemen?"

"Baccarat," Michael said. "But I will need to reload our chips."

Jon reached in his breast pocket and withdrew his billfold to reveal a large amount of bills.

"We'd be happy to accommodate you. A replenishment of chips is just arriving."

The man motioned them into a room where a croupier stood in wait at a small table covered in green felt. In the corner was a young woman with dark eyes and full lips, wearing a black cocktail dress. Her beauty surpassed that of any woman seen downstairs. She waved her hand at a well-tended bar, offering her services for whatever they desired.

Michael smiled and pulled out his BlackBerry, happy to see that his email had gone through. He typed a single word, left it in the queue to be sent, and tucked the phone back into his pocket. He pulled out the small electronic box; glancing at it, he saw the tiny red dot drifting away.

"We may have a problem," Michael said. But then they heard elevator doors open, and moments later, Shi, accompanied by the guard, pushed the cart through the open doorway.

"What problem?" Busch asked.

"Never mind," Michael said as Shi and the guard stepped into the private room.

THE SECURITY CAMERAS were well concealed. There were two in the lobby ceiling, two on either end of the hall, and two in either corner of the room they now stood in, positioned to capture the greatest breadth. It didn't take Michael much searching; he knew where he would place them if he were hired to protect the room.

There was a single blind spot. The two cameras were positioned in order to overlap each other's blind spot, but if a large object was in the way, the security view of the room would be obscured. Michael knew they couldn't bring in a tarp or any large object, but he didn't need to. The casino would accommodate his every need.

As the cart entered the room, it was like a well-rehearsed magic trick. Shi removed two cases of chips and handed them to the croupier. He turned the cart sideways, its placement by the corner now blocking the camera's view of the corner. He picked up his digital inventory pad and began entering data.

All eyes were on the croupier as he opened the maroon box to verify the contents of large-denomination chips. His hands obscured by the cart, Jon reached in and silently pulled out the metal case, lifted the lid of Michael's wide banker's briefcase, pushed aside the false top, and dropped it in. Covering it with the false top, he locked up the case.

It took all of two seconds, and then Shi turned the cart and pushed it out the door.

And immediately, the room flooded with guards, fifteen strong, all dressed in a uniform of blue blazer and gray pants. They were led by two men, both of mixed Asian heritage.

Michael reached into his pocket, wrapped his hand about his BlackBerry, and with no one aware of what he was doing, pressed the Send button, the programmed message instantly dispatched.

"I'm sorry, gentlemen, you need to come with us," the taller man said in perfect, unaccented English.

"What are the charges?" Jon said, as if nothing was wrong.

The second man took the briefcase from Jon, opened it, and removed the metal box. He laid it upon the table, examining it, turning it around. "I'll tell you what the charges are if you tell me what's in the box."

But Michael, Busch, and Jon remained silent.

"We can open it here or downstairs," the second

man said, running his hands through his salt-and-pepper hair. "Whatever you prefer. There is a reason the Venetian has yet to be robbed."

"No, we'll open it right here," the tall man said as he reached over, unhasped the lock of the metal box, and lifted the lid. The man took an unnaturally deep breath, his face a mask, his emotions concealed.

The team of guards stood in silent anticipation.

He finally looked up at his partner but was at a loss for words.

Michael and Busch exchanged a glance, confused.

The tall man slowly reached in the case, grasped its contents, and lifted it out as if he was handling a newborn child, a priceless artifact. But as he lifted it out, the entire room fell into shock. Some remained stoic while others averted their eyes; some out of shock, some out of respect.

He gripped it by its long auburn hair, the face pale, drained of life.

Busch was in shock, as he had seen the woman just hours earlier at McSorley's, her face brightly lit, smiling in anticipation of love.

"Oh, God," Busch said as he stared into the dead, vacant eyes. Her red hair was perfect, as if it had just been done, though her face was ghostly, her makeup in harsh, frightening contrast against the pale, drained skin.

The life was sucked out of the room; no one said a word as all eyes were drawn to the gruesome sight.

For they were staring into the dead eyes of Pamela Weiss.

CHAPTER 41
THE FORBIDDEN CITY

KC walked through the rocky tunnel, her flashlight shifting from the map to the passage ahead. While Jenna had marked the map with compass settings, she had no way to know which way was north. She knew she had to maintain focus, for if she was turned around even ninety degrees she would be lost.

"Do you hear me?" Annie's voice startled KC. It reverberated off the walls, seeming to come from everywhere. It was filled with a rage that was amplified not only by the rocky surroundings but by the darkness that lay just beyond the beam of her light.

"Do you hear me, KC? I know you do."

KC froze, turning off her flashlight. She crouched down against the wall, losing herself in the dark. She tucked her light into her bag, pulled her knees to her chest, and listened.

"You don't need to answer, just listen," Annie yelled. "The farther you run from me, the closer you are to death."

KC held her breath, unsure where Annie was, hoping the cover of darkness would hide her.

"I know about your headaches," Annie continued. "I know about your bloody noses."

Thirty seconds of silence filled the air, seeming like an eternity.

"They are just the beginning. Soon the infection will grow more painful, crippling."

KC inhaled, her mind clouded with fear and confusion.

"You are dying, KC, and the only way you can save yourself, and everyone else, is by giving me that box."

CHAPTER 42
THE VENETIAN

Lian hung up his cell phone and tucked it into his pocket as he walked out the main door of the Venetian. He stepped to the circular curb, where a sea of Mercedeses, Range Rovers, and BMWs lay in wait. There were no Lexuses or any Japanese cars, sentiment still running strong against their country of origin.

On his shoulder he carried his black satchel. It was creasing his freshly pressed Zegna jacket, but the money he'd made this evening helped to deaden his anxiety over his wrinkled appearance.

Several car attendants jumped to his side, offering him a ride, but Lian spotted the black Range Rover five cars away, the rear door held open by a driver who nodded at him.

Lian walked across the drive. The Range Rover's windows were blacked out and its driver was nondescript, he and the vehicle blending in with the dozens of other cars waiting to pick up their exhausted charges, who were more than likely drained both financially and physically from wrestling with the odds.

Lian stepped into the vehicle to find the man sitting alone in silence. He held up a three of spades, the card Lian had been told to look for to confirm his identity. Lian held his satchel close to his right side, concealing it from the man. Lian had been hired by Jon Lei, who'd contacted him twenty-four hours ago, in the middle of the night. The money was well above his normal rate and would settle a host of debts he currently held while leaving him with more than enough money for the coming months. His instructions were detailed and explicit.

He had picked up the high-end satchel with its metal case several hours ago. He'd never questioned its contents or what he would be stealing. At the age of thirteen, when he'd committed his first crime on behalf of the Black Dragon Triad, he had learned never to question the task expected of him. Whether it was stealing from a business, burning down a building, or killing someone, the less he knew of the details and motivations, the more clearheaded he would be while carrying out the deed and the less guilt he would feel when the task was done.

He had been given the room key, traveled upstairs, and slipped the key card into the door. But as he entered the suite, he didn't expect to be walking into the barrel of a gun.

He knew the gun, but more important, he knew the man who wielded it.

Gan Jie Kang was a cleaner, a fixer, someone who could make a crime disappear, be it evidence, witnesses, or bodies. He was always in high demand, not only for his success rate but for his thoroughness and speed.

But before he could react, before Kang pulled the

trigger, the gun was lowered and tucked away. Without a word, Kang disappeared into the bathroom.

Lian looked about the opulent suite and spied the bag on the desk. He entered the living room, opened the bag, and found the case already inside along with a loaded pistol and an envelope of cash.

He threw the bag over his shoulder and headed out. He wasn't sure why Kang was there, but he understood the older man's presence when he looked through the open doorway to the bathroom. The white tile was covered in dark blood, the wall marked with a thin streak as if it had been painted there with a fine, narrow brush.

A body lay in the center of the large bathroom; it was female. She was dressed in an elegant business suit, jewels upon her fingers, confirming it wasn't a robbery. She was Caucasian; her long legs left no doubt. She had been dead for several hours—the darkened blood on the floor indicated that. But it was the means of death that sent a chill through Lian. It was old-school, done by an expert. No one had used that method lately except for Xiao. And if he was involved . . .

Lian grabbed the satchel and left Kang to do his job alone.

LIAN HAD ARRIVED at the tables in the Golden Fish at 1:00 a.m., casually gambling a few thousand dollars away, knowing that losers always blended in at a casino, becoming invisible to all eyes. He sat at the furthermost blackjack table, nearest the service doors, his back to the wall, his gaze floating about. His mind kept jumping to the headless body. Truth be told, he had seen plenty of death, but this . . . This was different. It was a woman, a ritual killing meant to make a point, to instill fear. And if Xiao had committed it, Lian was in fear of his life.

Just after two, right on schedule, he spotted Jon and the two Americans coming down the main hall in their crisp new suits, looking as if they were going to a meeting. They met a casino employee and disappeared through the service doors.

Thirty minutes later, they emerged from the service door thirty feet behind a large cart filled with chips. Lian folded his pair of jacks, grabbed his now meager chips, and casually left the table. He stayed back, watching as Jon and his two friends took the outside route, the dark-haired American's eyes on his prize as it wheeled its way to the private elevator on the other side of the Golden Fish area that served the VIP gambling suites two levels up.

He made his move as Jon and the two men stepped into the cab and disappeared, leaving the chip-filled cart to wait for the next cab.

As the second elevator arrived, Lian stepped up to the guard and whispered his intent to kill him right there. The man had a choice: let him make a quick and simple exchange and leave or get killed and let the exchange take place anyway.

"The cameras will see you."

"The cameras don't see everything," Lian said. He had been told exactly where to stand, where all of the blind spots were. "Try to reveal what I am doing and you will surely die."

Lian pulled aside the two center maroon boxes of chips to reveal the metal case. He had been told it would be there, but seeing it still surprised him.

Suddenly the young man pushing the cart grabbed his wrist with a viselike grip. "I can't let you. You don't understand."

Lian looked the man in the eye. "Relax. I was told to tell you your daughter is fine and will be released in an hour. We don't have much time."

The younger man studied him for a moment and finally released his grip. Lian pulled the case from the cart, swapped it with the case he had, and tucked it back in the cart. He replaced the two boxes of chips and let the man enter the elevator.

As the elevator left, Lian slung the bag onto his shoulder, turned, and walked toward the main entrance. Halfway to the door, he pulled out his cell phone and dialed the number he had committed to memory.

"Venetian Security," the voice answered.

"Good evening," Lian said. "Sorry to trouble you, but there is a large robbery about to occur in the VIP section, the private gaming rooms. The three men committing it are armed and dangerous and will not hesitate to kill."

As Lian walked out the main doors, he closed his phone, tucked it into his pocket, and smiled at his deception.

The driver closed the door and remained outside as Lian took the three of spades and tucked it into his pocket. He reached into the satchel and pulled out the metal box, handing it to the man.

Lucas gave no acknowledgment, no thanks, as he placed the case reverently in his lap.

"Jon said I'd get the balance of payment COD."

Lucas ignored him as he thumbed back the hasps. He lifted the lid as if he were about to peer into the mysteries of God.

Lucas stared into the depths of the case for a moment before turning back to Lian, a tinge of anger in his voice. "Do you have any idea who you are dealing with?"

"No," Lian said in his accented English. "And quite honestly, I don't care. Just give me the money and I'm gone."

"You're joking."

"I'm not the type to joke," Lian said. "I'm sure Jon mentioned that when you hired me." Lian finally tilted his head and looked in the case and saw it was empty.

"What is this?" Lucas said.

"This was the box on the cart."

"And you didn't open it?"

"I don't care about your secrets, I just care about my money."

"You watched them come out of the service area?"

Lian nodded. "From that moment on, the cart never left my sight."

"You saw them all go upstairs? You sure?"

"Yeah, in the elevator."

"If they switched cases beforehand," Lucas said, "they would have just left the building."

"Unless they knew you were about to double-cross them," Lian said. "What was it supposed to contain?"

"What we are doing doesn't concern you—"

"Until I'm paid, it does. And if you think you're going to screw me over the way you are screwing over members of your team . . . I can promise you I won't tolerate it and Kang certainly won't tolerate it; he'll kill you for even thinking about not paying him."

"Who's—"

"Look." Lian's voice grew cold. "I don't care about what's in your box, what's supposed to be in your box, or how you screw your people. But—"

"Who's Kang?" Lucas interrupted him.

"What?" A dawning filled Lian's eyes. "Oh, shit."

"Who's Kang?" Lucas repeated.

"He was in the hotel suite when I picked up the case."

"Who is he?"

"He's a cleaner, he was dealing with the body."

"What body?"

"A female."

"What did she look like?" Lucas asked slowly.

"Not sure. Very well dressed, Caucasian—"

"I meant her face . . ."

Lian just looked at him. "There was only the body, there was no head."

CHAPTER 43

"Someone traded out the case," Busch said, doing everything he could to restrain himself. They were locked in an adjacent poker room while a dozen security agents dealt with the carnage next door.

"No shit," Jon said.

"It was traded in the elevator," Michael said.

"You don't know that. The case was out of our sight for close to ten minutes."

Michael shook his head. "No, the chip on our case, the one I've been tracking, came out at the lower level, it was in the casino and at the private elevator downstairs. I saw it move off-center just before the elevator arrived up here. I didn't question it."

"Maybe you should've," Busch said, his voice filled with anger.

"You want to tell me what's going on?" Michael said to Jon.

"How would he know?" Busch asked.

"Did you kill her?" Michael pressed.

"No," Jon said with disgust in his voice.

Michael had seen the shock on Jon's face when the head was displayed, but he had also seen anticipation in the man's eyes, something that shouldn't have been there.

"But you knew the cases were switched?"

"What?" Busch said. "You were setting us up? You son of a bitch."

"You knew the cases were switched, didn't you?" Michael asked. "But somebody betrayed you, too. How's it feel?"

Jon stood there, his face unable to hide his shock.

"You're a gun for hire," Michael said. "Make no mistake. Like you said, like the colonel said, whatever it takes, a few lives to save many."

"While everyone averted their eyes or stared at the face," Jon said, "I looked at the neck, the precision of the cut. It was pure, no tearing at any point."

"You speak with admiration," Busch said.

"No. I speak with respect, with fear. It was done with the finest of blades, a *jian* or katana, crafted by an expert swordsmith. Someone was sending a message."

"No shit, shaheem." Busch shook his head. "I think the message was clear."

"The message wasn't for you or me," Jon said. "The woman killed was Lucas's girlfriend, the woman he loved."

"I didn't think he was capable of that emotion," Busch said.

"Earlier this evening a man named Reiner, Lucas's assistant, was killed in the same manner, his head sent to the colonel."

"You could have mentioned that," Busch said.

"It wasn't a need-to-know thing."

"I think that's an everyone-needs-to-know thing," Michael snapped.

"Why don't they just kill the colonel and save us all from this nightmare?" Busch asked.

"Why does this Xiao want to torture Lucas?" Michael asked.

Jon was thinking, weighing his next words, until he finally spoke. "Xiao is Lucas's brother. He's taunting him, chipping away at his soul, at his life. You'd better hope he doesn't succeed, for if he does, if Lucas dies, he has a way of reaching out from the grave to kill you. He's the type to plan for every contingency, and who knows what Annie will do?"

The door opened and the tall security agent stepped into the room, followed by two more agents, their guns conspicuously drawn.

Jon stepped forward. "I need to make a phone call."

"In a few minutes you will be escorted down to the security level of the casino."

"We did not murder that woman," Jon said.

"What woman?" the agent said.

Jon fell silent.

"There has never been a murder in the Venetian." The man paused. "Or at least any evidence of one."

"What did you do with that woman's head? Where is her body?" Busch asked, his face growing red with anger.

"We wipe away unfortunate events such as this," the man said softly, making a point. "There will be no record she ever set foot in this resort."

"How?" Busch asked.

"In the same manner we will make the three of you disappear."

CHAPTER 44
THE FORBIDDEN CITY

Annie entered the stone cavern, her weapon light leading the way. The ceiling was low, a glasslike body of water on the far side, ten yards away, her light dancing off the surface, sending colored shards about the earthen room.

"That box is useless to you, KC," Annie said loudly. "You have no idea what it contains or what its function is."

"Shoot me and you'll never find the box," KC's voice echoed.

Annie spun about, her rifle held tight, its beam sweeping the room. But the space was empty. There was no sign of KC.

"I've hidden it," KC's disembodied voice said, "and you and your army and the Chinese and whoever else you want to enlist will never find it."

Annie spun around again, unsure where the voice was coming from. She walked about the cavern, shining the light into the corners, desperately trying to pinpoint KC.

She finally stopped a moment, removed the pistol from her waistband, laying it upon a rock. She unclipped the weapon light from beneath the rifle barrel, laid the rifle next to the pistol, and walked into the center of the cavern.

"You know those were my only two weapons," Annie said as she held up one hand while shining the light around her body. "Please."

KC stepped from the shadows, her back to the body of water; she flipped on her flashlight, shining the blinding light like a weapon in Annie's face. "What do you mean I'm dying?"

Annie stared at her, and for a moment there was an expression of compassion and sadness on her face. "It's a virus. I don't know the full deal on it, but it shows itself first with a bloody nose; the headaches are the second symptom. And it gets far worse from there. It will run its course in days."

"Where did it come from?" KC asked, ignoring her last statement, adjusting the neoprene bag that hung from her shoulder. "And how the hell did I get it?"

Annie pointed her finger at the ceiling. "The emperor who built the city. One of his admirals brought it back from some island six hundred years ago, but there is a cure. The piece within that red box will lead us to it. So you see, you destroy that box, you're killing yourself."

"Are you offended I'm stealing that pleasure from you?"

"Do you understand why I'm not concerned with your life?" Annie's compassion vanished.

KC stared at her.

"There's a man who possesses this virus, says he'll let it loose on U.S. military personnel. He infected Colonel Lucas as an example."

"Karma's a bitch, ain't it?" KC paused, digesting what Annie had said. "And how was I infected?"

"Back in New York, at the airport bar." Annie paused. "I infected you. One drop in your drink."

"So you killed me days ago." KC seethed. There was no self-pity in her tone, only anger. "You never had any intention of letting me live. Is Michael infected?"

Annie remained silent.

"Is Michael infected?" KC screamed.

"No. They're just going to shoot him. We infected you as leverage in the event you or he tried to run, like you did now."

"So," KC said, shaking her head, "why should I even think of giving you this box?"

"Because it will help us find this island where the cure is located."

"I could go and find your island myself and let your precious colonel die."

"No, you couldn't. You don't have all the pieces of the puzzle that the colonel has. But I'll guarantee, you give me that box and the colonel gets the cure, you'll get the cure, too."

"Bullshit. You poisoned me before you met me. You just tried to shoot me in the back—"

"You were running away with the case. Don't tell me you wouldn't have done any different if you were in my shoes. I need that red box, KC, I'm not about to allow hundreds of people to die—"

"No, only two: Michael and me."

"Would you trade two lives to save a hundred, a thousand?"

KC inhaled. As ruthless as Annie was, KC understood her logic: The needs of the many outweigh the needs of the few. But she was talking about Michael's life, and KC wasn't about to sacrifice him for this woman's story.

"You find me despicable," Annie said. "A woman with a gun, killing. Do you understand now? Do you understand why I have done what I have done?"

"You took pleasure in what you did long before you found your *profession*. And I understand that you and your colonel are so despicable that the only way you can get people to help you is by blackmailing them, by holding their lives over a flame."

"Are you going to help me?"

KC ignored her, lost in thought, trying to comprehend everything that had just been revealed to her. She had never dwelled on her own mortality, had never dwelled on death, always embracing life. But now, with the thought of having it ripped away—

Without warning, Annie reached behind her back, grabbed a pistol, and thrust it into KC's face. "Give me the box."

"And I thought we were friends." KC smiled, unfazed by the barrel staring at her.

"I don't have time for games."

"You've already poisoned me, now you're going to shoot me? I've got nothing to lose. Kill me now and you'll get nothing. It will be you who failed."

Annie grabbed the zipper on the neoprene bag that hung on KC's shoulder, violently unzipped it, and dug in, finding a dive mask, the hand-drawn map, a water bottle, and nothing else.

"I told you—"

"Where is it?" Annie screamed.

KC just smiled, taunting her, relishing her escalating rage.

Consumed with frustration and rage, Annie drew back her hand and slapped KC across the face.

KC's head snapped left.

"Give me the box!"

KC kept her focus, ignoring the stinging red welt on her cheek, and grabbed the barrel of the gun, twisting it upward. Annie had not seen KC violent, had not seen her aggressive, and was momentarily startled that she fought back, surprised at her strength. Annie grabbed the butt of her gun with two hands.

KC swung the flashlight up and hit Annie upside the head, stunning her. KC wrenched the pistol out of her hand, throwing it behind her, where it hit the water with a splash and vanished.

But Annie dove at her, knocking her to the ground. As KC scrambled to gain her footing to escape, Annie saw it, protruding from her pocket: the red box. She lunged at her, tearing it out of her back pocket.

Annie quickly turned and raced for her guns on the rock, scooping up the pistol and spinning about.

But KC was already running, heading for the water. She reached in the bag at her side, grabbed the mask, and zipped the bag back up.

As Annie fired a hail of bullets, the reports echoing in the confined space, KC hit the water and swam down, pulling the dive mask over her eyes and nose. Pressing her palm against the top while blowing out her nose, she cleared the water from the mask, and her vision opened up. The water was pure and crystal-clear. She shined the flashlight before her and swam down toward the single door ten feet down. The frigid water was already playing havoc with her muscles, sapping their strength.

In the rush of escape, she hadn't gotten the breath she wanted, but feared resurfacing, as Annie would surely be waiting to shoot her in the head. She continued down, clearing her ears as she went, the weight of her clothes pulling on her, impeding her speed. She pulled as hard as she could, deep, long breaststroke pulls and kicks, driving herself to freedom. The beam from the flashlight in her left hand spun about like klieg lights on the ancient room she swam through. She dived through the doorway, continuing as the map had indicated. The corridor ahead was stone, the ground smooth, carved from the granite; she had committed the route to memory and knew it was only another twenty-five yards.

But as she swam, she felt her lungs catch fire. She wasn't sure if it was from the shallow breath she had taken or the virus that she had just learned was slowly killing her.

The flashlight beam caught her exit, just up ahead, the rising corridor that opened into another room, a room that would allow her to leave this underworld.

She began to surface, her strength and breath renewed now that she was almost free of her watery confines—but her head hit stone. She shined the light up but it reflected back. She moved along the ceiling, realizing that something had collapsed, blocking her exit.

Her lungs on fire, she pulled as hard as she could, moving forward another ten yards, but again the ceiling seemed to continue. Dots appeared before her eyes. Her muscles burned, the cold water, the lack of oxygen sapping all of her strength. And the light fell upon an opening another ten yards ahead. With her heart pounding, her lungs depleted, she tried to find the strength to make it, kicking for her life, but it was too much.

And she blacked out.

As Annie caught her breath, she looked at the red box, smiling at KC's foolishness. She wanted to pursue her, but knew she was at a disadvantage, her swimming skills poor, a lack of ability that could kill her here.

She rubbed her head where the flashlight had hit her, the ache compounded by exhaustion. She had been going nonstop for three days now with minimal sleep, and could feel the toll on her body.

She tucked the small red box into her pocket, affixed the weapon light back to the base of the rifle barrel, and headed back the way she came . . .

. . . and caught sight of the blood. It had dripped on the back of her hand. She ran her fingers over the wound from where KC had hit her; it throbbed, but as she looked at her fingers, she saw no blood. She ran her hand across the tender area again, but still found no sign of blood.

She suddenly stopped in her tracks, took a breath, reached up, and touched beneath her nose . . .

. . . and felt the flow coming from her right nostril.

CHAPTER 45
THE VENETIAN

The tall man with dark hair stood outside the casino, his eyes fixed on the black Range Rover.

He had parked his car in the garage of the casino and had walked through the four gaming rooms for the last several hours, sampling tables, gambling casually. He was exceedingly good at it, though he believed more in fate than in odds. He was getting a feel for the ebb and flow of the clientele at this hour, making casual conversation. He had a gift for languages: He was fluent in all the Latin-based tongues, English and German, and Mandarin, which had made the last twenty-four hours far more manageable, not only in terms of conversation but in terms of reading various documents.

He had watched Michael, Busch, and the two Asians disappear through the service door and emerge thirty minutes later. He watched as they boarded the elevator to the private rooms, and as the chip cart behind them was held up for a moment by the man with the bag on his shoulder.

He knew full well what was going on, and followed the man with the bag through the Golden Fish casino.

As the tall man walked by the ornate trash receptacle by the elevators, he reached into his pocket, pulled out a wad of paper, and tossed it in.

He watched as the man ahead of him pulled out his phone and dialed, falling into a conversation as he headed for the exit.

Again the tall man reached into his pocket. Drawing out another wad of paper, he feigned wiping his nose and tossed the paper into the next receptacle.

Emerging into the front drive, he watched as the man with the bag on his shoulder entered the Range Rover. The tall man's phone vibrated; a message came through on his phone. He pulled it out, glanced at it, and quickly tucked it back in his pocket.

He waited five minutes, his eyes never leaving the vehicle. He had no need to fetch his car. There would be no chase, and he had no fear of the Range Rover's driving away.

He walked up to the vehicle and tapped on the rear window. The window slowly came down, revealing the two men.

"Good evening, Colonel," the tall man said in a subtle Italian accent.

"Who are you?"

"I understand your box is empty," the tall man said.

The colonel glared at him.

"May I join you?"

Without waiting for an answer, the man walked around the front of the Range Rover and got in the passenger side next to Lian.

"Since you know who I am," the colonel said, "who are you?"

"My name is Simon," the man said. "I'm Michael's

priest. We both know that the book you seek wasn't in that case."

"How do you know?"

"Because I have what was in that case, all three pages, telling me exactly where Zheng He's diary is."

Lian drew his pistol and pressed it to Simon's head.

"To begin with, I have no fear of death." Simon smiled as he looked at Lian. "But more important, kill me and the location of the book is lost forever."

"I just want my money," Lian said. "And it appears you're standing in the way of that."

"How did you get it?" Lucas asked as he reached over and pushed Lian's gun away from Simon.

"Michael gave it to me."

"I don't understand."

"And you won't. Now, as you have no doubt arranged, Michael and Paul have been taken into custody. I saw the security detail go upstairs for them and Michael sent me a message." Simon held up his phone. On the screen was a text message with a single word: COMPROMISED. Simon paused a moment, staring at the colonel, without a hint of fear in his face. "Now, I'm going to get them out of there and you're going to help me."

"Not a chance," Lucas said.

"Oh, there is every chance. You see, Colonel, if the Chinese find out the U.S. military was coordinating this robbery, you're going to have an international nightmare on your hands. At best, you'll end up rotting in some Chinese prison . . . Or maybe they'll just execute you, sweep it under the rug, and take the book and everything that goes with it for themselves."

Simon pulled out a small black box, a screen in the center with several colored buttons along the side, and noted the red blinking number 1 on the right of the screen pinpointing Michael's location.

"They're still upstairs, and the Venetian's security believes everything is under control. But in five minutes," Simon said to Lucas as he pointed to the main entrance of the casino, "people will be pouring out of those doors, fearing for their lives. I want this car door open and ready so your driver can whisk us all out of here. Understood?"

Lucas remained silent.

"And if you even think of harming Michael or KC, not only can you forget about ever getting your book, but dealing with the Chinese government will be the least of your problems."

CHAPTER 46

Simon stood in the central lobby by the Golden Fish casino, his eyes fixed on the private bank of elevators one hundred feet away, where three large security guards stood in wait.

As the elevator door opened, Simon watched Michael, Busch, and Jon step from the cab; four guards exited behind them carrying their bags. They were not restrained or handcuffed, but the three other guards waiting for them left them no chance of escape.

If they made it to the service area, down into the lower level, Simon knew they would probably never be seen again.

Simon reached into his pocket and wrapped his hand around the small black box. Michael had left it for him along with a few other trinkets in his hotel room; his friend's creative expertise never ceased to amaze him.

Simon had arrived by private jet twelve hours earlier. He followed Michael's email instructions exactly, remaining inconspicuous as he memorized the plan and then walked through it three times over. He knew what he was about to unleash, but felt no remorse; he would do anything to save his friend. So Simon ran his thumb over the box and pushed the blue button. There was no explosion, no sudden bang or event, but Simon knew that wasn't the case down below. In the bowels of the Venetian, all hell was breaking lose.

RENE CLAUGE, THE head of chip security, sat back in his chair, staring at the three monitors. The first reflected the 131 million in chips in circulation upstairs: 9.5 million within the three thousand machines, 103 million at the tables, 11 million at the windows, and the balance in people's pockets. The second monitor reflected a new gambling program he was working on, and the third displayed the movie *Casablanca*.

In Rene's eyes, no one was smarter than himself; no one had delivered more to casino management than he had. And over the last month he had concluded that he deserved more for sitting eighty feet below ground at three in the morning staring at a computer monitor. He had graduated top of his class at MIT, both undergrad and grad. His contract was all well and good, but he knew now he was worth far more. Come Monday, he'd renegotiate his contract with the Venetian or split and take his new RFID ideas with him.

A sudden alarm sounded on his computer. Rene stared at his monitor; he stared at the impossible. There was no question that less than a minute ago there had been 131 million in chips on the floor. But if what he saw now was true, then someone had not only cracked the algorithm on his chip but flooded the casino with counterfeits, an act that could cripple operations. For what he saw was the sudden circulation of more than $300 million in new chips.

And if that was the case, his plan to seek new employment come Monday wouldn't come to pass, not because his reputation would be in question but because he would be dead.

Without further hesitation, he hit the alarm.

FOR THE SECOND time that night, the lower level went into lockdown; elevators were recalled, fire stairs sealed. But this alert was much more urgent. The entire cadre of security personnel, 110 strong, flooded the casino floor. Three guards took up position at every exit, teams fanned out looking at the tables, listening for direction from central security on Sublevel Three.

And the drastic step of closing the exchange windows was taken. The staff assured guests that it would only be for a moment as a computer glitch was corrected. But a murmur had already begun among the guests and gamblers who held winnings. It was never the losers with empty pockets who went to the windows to cash out, only the winners, the ones on a high from beating the odds, from beating the house, that stood there all smiles with dollar signs in their eyes. And if their winnings were somehow negated . . .

SIMON WATCHED AS the cadre of guards exploded out of the service area across the floor. They fanned out to the tables, toward the doors, their eyes darting about, looking for suspicious people.

In his several hours of gambling, Simon had frequented tables in each of the four casinos—blackjack, poker, fan-tan, sic bo, roulette—staying long enough to lose a few hundred dollars, to make conversation, to affix one of the small self-adhesive RFID chips beneath the table. Wafer-thin, smaller than a dime, they were out of sight and inactive until he activated them with the blue button on the small remote. But Simon didn't just affix them to tables, he slipped them into pockets of unsuspecting gamblers as they spoke, as he bumped into them; he left a few in the bars and restaurants. He spread hundreds of the small electronic chips throughout the Venetian. Michael had made them, programmed in various large denominations, activated just moments ago, sending confusion to the monitoring world below. He couldn't help smiling at the thought that the control of the casino, its heart of operation, came from below as opposed to above.

Simon could see the seven guards escorting Michael, Busch, and Jon reach for their earpieces, listening to instructions. And suddenly, Michael, Busch, and Jon were each grabbed by a guard and shoved double-time into the service area.

A large *whoomph* came from the fancy trash canister by the elevator. Smoke began to billow, growing thicker, denser, rising to the exquisite ceiling before curling back down. The volume of smoke was enormous, obscuring the immediate area.

It took only seconds for the crowds to see it, for the

alarm to sound. All tables, all bets were frozen. Gamblers grew annoyed at the inconvenience, like children bellyaching at a school fire drill, until they caught sight of the smoke, until they began to cough and their eyes began to burn.

Panic began to take root in the Golden Fish Casino, quickly escalating. People scooped up their chips and made for the nearest exit. With alcohol dulling their senses, confusion filling the air, people charged the doors, turning toward any exit they could find.

As Michael, Busch, and Jon were rushed through the escaping crowd, they came within twenty feet of Simon, and as he saw their faces, he hit the red button on the box in his pocket again.

A second *whoomph* startled the already-terrified crowd, and equal amounts of smoke billowed forth from another trash receptacle, filling the air. The panic doubled, people coughing, rubbing their eyes, racing to find their way out.

In the resulting mayhem, Michael tore away from the guard holding his arm. Busch effortlessly spun out of his captor's hold and drove his large fist into the man's jaw. The two turned and ran into the chaos, instantly lost within the escaping crowds and smoke.

Within seconds, Jon dropped, spinning his right leg out, sweeping out the feet of his captor, racing in the direction of Michael and Busch.

Within the cloud of smoke, Michael stripped off his suit jacket, his tie and shirt, his head down, eyes squinting, running from the guards who were no doubt in pursuit, but as he could hardly see, he knew the same held true for them. And while the smoke obscured the sight of the panicked crowd, it also impeded the view of the security cameras. Though the crowd was in a panic, fearing for their lives, Michael knew there was no true danger. He had constructed the smoke bombs and left them for Simon; the chemical compound, made from sugar and a touch of crushed red pepper, was harmless. He'd wrapped the golf-ball-sized devices in tissue and left them along with the bag of tracking chips in a box in his hotel suite upstairs for Simon.

Michael was lost within the throng of panicked gamblers, moving with the masses, when someone snatched his arm, violently pulling him forward. Michael struggled to get away, but the grip was like a vise.

"Put this on," Simon said, holding out a blue shirt.

Without a word, Michael grabbed the shirt, slipped it on, and buttoned it up.

A herd mentality had taken hold, everyone following the pack, not knowing if they were heading over a cliff, into the fire, or to safety. But Simon knew exactly where they were going. He pulled Michael to the side of the crowd, Busch following right behind him, passing people and outrunning whoever was pursuing them.

And in all the craziness, they had not only lost their captors, they had lost Jon.

They burst out of a side door into the clear night air, a sea of people gathering, over a thousand strong and growing. Staying within the masses, they moved through the side parking lot to the north for one hundred yards until they arrived at a black Town Car. Simon clicked the key fob, they all jumped in, and Simon drove out of the lot past the stream of arriving fire trucks and ambulances.

"When the dust settles, that is going to be one pissed-off casino," Busch said.

"Yeah, along with your colonel friend," Simon said. "When he finds out that he is sitting there waiting for no one, he'll go through the roof."

"You're late. How long have you been here?" Busch asked.

"Long enough to save you from yourself," Simon said as he drove over the bridge back to old Macau.

"You know," Busch said, "you shouldn't be joking around, this whole thing is your fault—"

"Thanks," Michael said to Simon, interrupting Busch. "You got my emails, right?"

"Yeah." Simon held up his PDA.

"What the hell did those pages say?" Busch asked.

"It was a codicil to Marconi's will, about things he acquired recently that weren't in his original will. He left everything to his wife and kid."

Michael thought of the anguish on Marconi's face and in his scream, as he recalled the headless bodies on the floor of the man's castlelike estate.

"Xiao wasn't buying the diary," Simon continued. "He never had any intention of paying for it. He had always meant to kill Marconi and to just steal it."

"And do those three pages say where the book is?"

"They outline a number of recent transactions: Who owes him money, gambling debtors, things that weren't meant to be part of some public estate record. Along with the information about where the box that holds his most prized collection resides."

"Where are we going?" Busch asked.

"How's KC?" Simon asked Michael.

"I think she's sick . . ."

Simon looked deep into Michael's eyes. "Well, we're going to find her, and if she's sick, we're going to make her better, do you understand?"

The car fell silent.

"And, Paul, in answer to your question—you're not going to believe where we are going."

"How?" Lucas screamed at Jon. Any restraint that the colonel possessed had vanished. "You had them under escort . . . and they slip away with the contents of the case? I can't even begin to tell you what an unmitigated disaster this is." Lucas paused. "How the hell did they get the book out of there without you seeing it?"

"They don't have it."

"How do you know that?"

"Because the box we had was swapped out—"

"No shit," Lucas said as he threw the empty box at Jon. Jon flinched, blocking the box from hitting his face. "We were the ones doing the swapping. How then did the box you stole from Sublevel Six become empty?"

Jon was fighting to keep his emotions from escalating to Lucas's level.

"I got an empty box," Lucas said. "What was in the box you saw, that was opened up in the private gaming area?"

Jon was silent, not wanting to describe what he had seen.

"Say it!" Lucas shouted. "Say it! What was in the box?"

"A head . . ."

"Whose head?"

Jon remained silent.

Lucas pulled out his pistol and jammed it in Jon's face. "Whose head?"

"Pamela's . . ."

And Lucas lowered his gun. He caught his breath, composed himself. The moment hung there as he let the news sink in.

"You will find them," Lucas said. "You will find that book, or I will personally see to it that you are thrown in the deepest, darkest prison I can find, where you will die the slowest of deaths."

CHAPTER 47

Cemitério São Miguel Arcanjo sat in the middle of the city, an oasis of grief on a ten-acre parcel. Inside its walls sat the Chapel of St. Michael, built in 1875. It was surrounded by tens of thousands of graves, tombs, and family crypts.

Over the centuries, Macau had attracted a substantial Catholic population. When the Portuguese arrived in 1535, they brought with them their country's religion, and though they weren't seeking to convert the Chinese, the religion was embraced over the next four hundred years.

"I feel like a grave robber," Busch said as they walked among the tombstones, the realm of the dead bathed in darkness except for the light wash of the city that surrounded it.

"Well, that's good," Michael said. "Because you are."

They followed Simon, who walked at a fast clip, knowing exactly where he was going. In one hand he clutched a cemetery map, in the other his PDA, the three documents Michael had sent him on display.

They arrived at a small marble building, of Greek Revival design, with small white fluted columns supporting a marble overhang. Open-winged angels were carved into the eaves, while a crucifix with a lifelike image of Jesus was welded into the large patinated copper door.

"Why wouldn't Xiao look here, if this is Marconi's family crypt?"

"Because it's not his family crypt, it belongs to the Denola family. Gento Denola did legal work for him, was on a silent cash retainer. No one beyond Marconi and Denola was aware of their relationship."

Simon slipped the crowbar into the copper door and pried it open. The three entered, pulling the door closed behind them, sealing themselves in pure darkness and silence.

"Turn on the light," Busch said quickly.

It was a moment before Michael flipped on his flashlight, smiling broadly at Busch's fear.

"That's not funny," Busch snapped at him.

"It's funny on so many levels," Simon said to Michael.

Before them was a set of marble stairs, brass railings on either side. An earthy smell filled the air. On the wall was a marble plaque, carved with the names of the deceased, their dates of birth and death.

Simon led the way down into the earth, where they found a room twice the size of the structure above. In the center of the room were two benches; along the far wall was a small altar, a long leather kneeler before a crucifix. Upon the altar table were dozens of pictures, some aged, sepia-toned, of men and women in their prime, portraits to remind the grieving of their deceased relatives in better days. Candles abounded, while dead flowers lay crumbled upon the bases of glass vases.

Simon looked at his PDA, at the scan of the three sheets of paper, before finally looking back up at the right wall. Built into the left and right walls were individual crypts, twenty three-by-three endcaps per side, all but three of which were engraved with the names of those within.

Simon counted over and laid his hand upon *Maurice Denola—Born 1932, Died 1961.*

"You've got to be kidding me," Busch said.

Simon pointed at the white concrete grouting. "Does that look like it was done fifty years ago?"

Simon slipped the crowbar into the marble seam and pushed, but it didn't budge. He tried again but it was useless.

"Give me that," Busch said. "God forgive me."

And he leaned on the bar with all of his 230 pounds, all of his six-foot-four frame's muscle. He struggled, flexing, tugging, his face going crimson with effort until the seam finally popped, the cover loosening.

Simon grabbed hold of the cover and lowered it to the ground to reveal the coffin. Aside from a layer of dust, it seemed brand-new. Simon grabbed the end and Busch and Michael helped him slide it out, placing the seven-foot coffin on the ground of the crypt.

"This is wrong on so many levels," Busch said as he looked upon the coffin. "What if he's in there?"

"Why? You afraid he's going to wake up and bite you?" Simon teased.

Simon grabbed hold of the coffin's lid.

"Don't you want to bless yourself, say a prayer? After all, this is part of your job description."

"Believe me," Simon said. "What I have been doing

the last ten years isn't part of anyone's job description, especially a priest's."

Busch held his breath in anticipation as Simon lifted the lid to reveal a white silk interior. But there was no body, just a wooden box, three feet long, made of haphazard scraps of wood cobbled together. Simon lifted the hinged top and peered inside.

"Thank God," Busch said.

"Well?" Michael said.

"I need someplace to examine this," Simon said.

"I've got the perfect place," Michael said. "It's the last place they would expect us to go."

MICHAEL, BUSCH, AND Simon stood in the center of the safe house on the second floor of the brothel. Busch's eyes were glued to the monitors, which showed images of the front, rear, and secret basement door in and out of the bordello.

Michael had duped the key; the code was an easy crack. After all, they'd left him in here for countless hours. In point of fact, Michael hadn't dragged Busch and Simon there to hide. If he had any hope of finding KC in the Forbidden City, in Beijing, he needed a way to track her. She had no cell phone, no means of communication. But he knew the next best thing. Sometimes to track the untraceable you had to look for their escort. Michael had seen the file on Annie, had studied it, learning everything about her that he could, which was minimal at best. But he was sure she had a cell phone, and if she did, tracking it was child's play.

Simon removed the lid of the three-foot wooden box and looked into it.

"My God," Simon said as he reached in and pulled out a scabbarded sword, slowly unsheathing it from its black enameled case. It was truly exquisite, the blade etched in Japanese symbols and phrases.

"Do you know what this is?" Simon asked.

Michael shook his head.

"This sword is the legendary Japanese sword Kusanagi, more revered and mystical than Excalibur, only this one is real, not myth or legend. It's a revered artifact, part of the Imperial Regalia, the three sacred Treasures of Japan. It hasn't been seen in years, stolen from the Atsuta Shrine decades ago."

Simon continued digging, pulling out a katana, a jade fertility idol from Thailand, and a Shiva statue. "Recognize this?" Simon asked Michael.

Michael smiled as Simon laid the Topkapi Dagger on the table.

These items were valued at hundreds of millions of dollars, some would say priceless, all revered symbols of their countries and religions. But what Michael focused on was the last object in the box, as if it were the last present to be opened at Christmas.

It was wrapped in a maroon velvet bag, a golden drawstring holding it closed.

Simon removed it, placed it on the table, and unwound the tie, pulling out a six-inch-thick leather-bound book.

"Guys, time is at a premium here." Busch's eyes remained fixed on the monitors. "Michael, quit wasting time. We can look at the book later. You need to find whatever it is you need so we can get out of here with a chance of a future."

The book was exquisite, embossed with a ferocious giant tiger, fangs bared, in battle against a five-clawed dragon. The rendering was lifelike, seeming to jump out of the leather binding. Chinese lettering appeared along the side, and clouds and symbols filled the background.

Simon ran his fingers over the leather of the book, created more than a half-millennium earlier, marveling at the knowledge rumored to be contained within. It was like finding the Dead Sea Scrolls, the combined journals of history's greatest explorers, a warrior's diary of diplomacy and war, a codex of magic and science.

Simon flipped open the leather-bound book, each page a work of art in its own right. There were elegant writings, the Chinese characters graceful, sweeping, mysterious to those who did not speak the language. Artwork adorned most pages, in different styles, as if different artists had assisted in telling Zheng He's life.

There was a portrait of a large man, barrel-chested and strong, robust and handsome, with fierce eyes, dressed in a long, flowing white robe stitched with gold. He wore a long black cape and clutched a fearsome sword in his left hand.

"Admiral Zheng He was China's greatest explorer," Simon said. "Conqueror, diplomat, trader—he fit so many bills. He was a Muslim, a eunuch, a warrior, he was the greatest adventurer in Chinese history, yet few people outside China could tell you who he is.

"Zheng was born Ma He, a Muslim Mongol captured in his youth and placed in the household of Ming Dynasty prince Zhu Di. His name was changed to San Bao, which means Three Jewels. He grew to be a mighty soldier and one of Prince Zhu Di's closest friends and advisors. In 1402, when the prince staged a coup deposing his predecessor, San Bao was at his side. Zhu Di, now the emperor, christened his closest friend Zheng He.

"Zhu Di, known as the Yongle Emperor, the Son of Heaven, in an attempt to restore China's golden age of the Tang Dynasty, chopped down the forests of Annam—what is now north Vietnam—and built hundreds of massive treasure ships, making his friend Zheng He the admiral in charge.

"When we think of explorers, we think of Columbus, James Cook, Magellan, Marco Polo, but they all pale next to this man. His armada of giant junks was far larger than any of the fleets Columbus commanded, and that was one hundred years later. Zheng He's ships were five times longer, much faster, and more seaworthy. He had more than three hundred oceangoing vessels, and a crew of nearly thirty thousand men.

"Described collectively as swimming dragons, the ships had as many as nine masts apiece, with the largest ship holding one thousand people. They carried soldiers, doctors, cooks, interpreters, astrologers, traders, and holy men; there were equine ships for horses, repair ships, ships carrying gifts for tribute to other nations, water ships carrying a month's worth of fresh water. The senior captains were eunuchs. The expeditions covered nearly 186,000 miles—that's seven and a half times around the world. And remember, this was six hundred years ago.

"It was one of the greatest fleets ever assembled, rivaling the Spanish Armada and Japan's Pacific fleet. Zheng He's personal ship was a technological marvel, at 425 feet long and 190 feet wide. With nine masts, it was the largest wooden ship not only at the time but ever since. We're talking aircraft-carrier size."

"Who discovered America?" Simon asked abruptly.

"What?" Michael asked, entirely confused.

"Who was the first person to land his ships on North American soil?"

"Columbus landed in the Caribbean; is this some kind of trick question?"

"No trick . . . and you are wrong. Admiral Zheng He landed on the northwest coast of North America in the 1420s. He made seven historic voyages to far-off lands: Asia, India, the Middle East, Africa, the Americas. In his travels, he exacted tribute, bringing kings, sultans, and emperors to their knees. He opened up trade routes that brought Chinese porcelain, silk, and culture to the world. He brought giraffes, apes, camels, and elephants home to China; some say he brought back the unicorns of Chinese mythology.

"From India he brought back spices and precious jewels, riches beyond compare, silks and skins procured in trade, precious metals and stones stolen in midnight raids from villages that dared to attack his mighty fleet. There was food, wines the like of which the emperor had never tasted. And a coterie of people willingly returned with the admiral, men and women of all shapes, sizes, and colors, who wished to learn of China and its ways.

"During his journey a rebellious crew led by a sinewy, powerful man by the name of Shin Fin had seized one of his ships, killing its captain, attacking two other ships in the fleet before fleeing. But Zheng and thirty of his fastest ships recaptured the vessel during a storm in the South China Sea.

"But instead of killing the mutinous crew as an example, Zheng gave Shin Fin and his crew the opportunity for forgiveness, for redemption, if they could complete the simple task of surviving five days at sea.

"Snapping off the rudder of the ship, taking all of the oars and sails, Zheng left them adrift in the South China Sea. He had the ship's hold filled with food, water, and supplies, bade farewell to Shin Fin, and told the crew they just needed to survive for five days.

"Zheng pulled his fleet back to the horizon on all sides and for five days they watched. The activity aboard the ship never waned, all aboard moved about their daily duties, the ship's deck covered in activity throughout the daylight hours. At night, the torches, lanterns, and firepots glowed, their flames alive until dawn. The routine never changed; the days remained clear without rain or heavy seas. But it was on the night of the fifth day that it all changed. The glow of the torches snuffed out less than an hour after sundown; there was no glow from the lanterns, from the cooking fires. At dawn of the sixth day, Zheng confirmed his suspicions of lifelessness and sought a volunteer.

"Ruin Bai hailed from the southern tip of Korea. He

was the most fearsome of warriors and led Zheng's men on numerous excursions into unknown jungles and territories, successfully defending against and repelling attack too many times to count. When Zheng asked for a volunteer to face certain death, it was Bai who stood and demanded the assignment.

"Before he left, Zheng gave him a sip of fluid drawn from a red carafe wrapped in leather, embossed with the picture of a large majestic bird.

"Rowing alone across the five-mile distance, Bai boarded the ship and found everyone dead, their bodies contorted in agony, covered in sores, red pustules tinted with blackness. Their faces were locked in grim expressions of fear as if they had all been struck down at once by a force from hell.

"For five days Bai stayed upon the ship. He disposed of the bodies, weighing them down with cannon shot, tossing them over the side to sink to the depths of the sea. Bai remained onboard the ghost ship; he ate and drank from the supplies he had brought with him, clearing his mind, praying to pass the time.

"On the fifth night, he went to sleep with every expectation of awakening in heaven. But with the sunrise of the sixth day, he smiled, for despite his doubts, he awoke to a new morning, overjoyed to find a new day ahead. For ten days he did so, each night expecting to die, each morning surprised to be alive.

"Bai signaled Zheng, and within hours, men scampered about the ship, making her seaworthy again, hoisting the multibatten sail.

"For his bravery, for facing death without fear, Bai

was rewarded with something he did not think could be awarded by man, not even as great a man as his admiral. Bai was blessed with life, long life, far more years, it is said, than any man of that era. He was said to have lived far beyond one hundred years, but looked half his age. Bai finally disappeared when rumors circulated that he was possessed, that he was a demon. Something that only he and Zheng knew couldn't be further from the truth.

"For Bai and Zheng knew that there were two objects, out of legend, stolen from an island temple in the heart of a southern ocean. An island they had found and referred to as Penglai. That was where they had stolen the two liquids from.

"The first was called the Dragon's Breath. Its power had been confirmed; the tiniest of amounts mixed with the crew's food had killed them all.

"But Zheng did not just find death on the island, he had also found life, a way to counter the Dragon's Breath. He called it the Phoenix Tears after Fenghuang, the Chinese Phoenix that brought balance to the Dragon's Breath. It was a countermeasure to the darkness, but it did not just counteract the Dragon's Breath, it was an elixir that was rumored to cure disease, heal wounds, stop death."

Simon stopped his story and turned to the book, becoming lost in the text as he sought the details beyond his knowledge, his fascination blinding him to the others, who were waiting on his next words. He read through the book, turning pages, nodding his head. The book was much thicker than he had expected, hundreds of pages long, with fold-out leafs. There were descriptions of battles both on land and at sea, of diplomacy, of trade, of medicines and magic.

He kept flipping pages, fighting the temptation to read it all. And he finally arrived at what he was looking for. It folded out three times; its exacting detail exceeded his hopes. The map included all the continents, the Horn of Africa, the Middle East, the Red Sea, the Persian Gulf; there was North and South America, irrefutable evidence that the rumors of Zheng He's discovery of the continents nearly one hundred years before Columbus arrived in the Caribbean were true.

And on the opposite page was a near masterpiece of a painting depicting a mountainous volcanic island, bathed in lush green foliage, encased in a white sandy beach; an island that floated on the ocean mist, a river flowing out of a rain forest jungle, emptying into the ocean.

Simon read the captions beneath the painting; he studied the map and finally looked up.

"Well?" Busch prodded him.

"This is it, this is the map to what Zheng He thought of as Penglai. It describes it in detail. A mountainous island located in the middle of nowhere, a paradise, a place of unnatural beauty. Billions of spectacular flowers, trees made of coral that bear luminous pearls. The dew of eternal life flows from the rivers imparting immortality to those who are worthy."

"Eternal life my ass," Busch said. "You know how stupid you sound—"

"This book speaks of magic and legends," Simon cut

him off, ignoring him, "of the riches Zheng He brought there and the treasure that was there upon his arrival. It speaks of the origin of the Dragon's Breath and the Phoenix Tears, and how they are born of the island and not to be removed."

"Bullshit," Busch said. "There is no cure-all, no elixir of life, no legends and magic—"

"Hey, I'm just quoting," Simon said, "not verifying. But remember this, a lightbulb in the middle ages, your computer or phone to people in the age of the Renaissance would be considered magic, miracles of God, or perhaps the devil. One man's magic is another man's science.

"It's interesting: It describes the island as surrounded by a great undersea dragon that will pull the unworthy to their death, a guardian placed there by the gods."

"Great," Busch said. "Magic, legends, and dragons."

"You're forgetting treasure. Gold and jewels, untold wealth."

"KC is sick," Michael said abruptly, "I know it, I could see it in her face. And Lucas infected her somehow. It's all tied to that island."

"Michael, you can't tell me you believe—" Busch began before being cut off.

"If KC is sick, if she has been poisoned with something from that island, and a cure is there," Michael said, "I'll believe in anything."

"Shit," Busch said as he looked at the monitors. A man stood at each of the entrances to the brothel. All of them were heavily tattooed and dressed in black. And through the main door came Lucas, Jon, and three more Triad members.

"Dammit," Busch said. "I told you we should have left—"

Simon held up his hand, silencing Busch. He ran his finger over the edge of the map, following the perimeter, and became focused. He carried the book to the copier and Xeroxed the map and the island painting.

"What are you doing? We don't have time," Busch said as he watched the monitors. Lucas remained in the lobby as Jon came up the stairs with three large men, pistols in their hands. Busch looked at the doors of the brothel, each of them blocked by a gang member. "My taxpayers' dollars aren't supposed to go toward funding assholes like this to kill me."

Busch looked at the window, rapping on it. The bars were thick; the glass was bulletproof. "This is just great. What the hell are you doing?" he said to Simon.

Simon was tucking Xerox copies into an envelope and slipping the book back into the velvet slipcase. He passed the book to Michael, who tucked it in his black satchel.

Jon and his team approached the door. Busch and Simon grabbed their guns.

"Don't," Michael said. "I need to find KC."

"They're coming in here to kill us." Busch pointed at the book in Michael's bag. "They're going to shoot us and take that bag from your dead body."

Michael looked around the room, his mind working, searching for a way out, a solution.

He suddenly tore open the armory closet, grabbed

three hunks of C-4, and ran to the workbench where he had created the chips and tracking devices. It was still cluttered with electronics. He swiped up three chips with LEDs, jammed their protruding wires into the puttylike blocks, and placed them in plain sight around the room. He pulled the small black box from his pocket, the one he had used to track the chips, and placed his thumb on the side button.

"So, you're going to blow us all up?" Busch asked in shock.

Michael said nothing as Simon smiled.

Michael walked to the door and stood to the side of it; Simon and Busch aimed their weapons.

And they all watched on the monitors as Jon and his team pulled their guns, bracing themselves for attack.

Jon pressed his finger to the pad, punched the code into the door, and it released with a click.

Two of the gang members rolled into the room, firing their guns. Busch and Simon dove for cover.

From behind the metal door, Michael shouted, "Dead man's switch."

Jon's eyes fell on the scattered C-4 and he instantly understood, barking orders to the three gang members, who stopped firing, realizing they were within a trap. If Michael was killed, the button beneath his thumb would be released and the room would be torn apart, killing all of them.

Jon walked into the center of the room, looking at each of them. There was rage in his eyes for being outsmarted. He stepped toward the box of artifacts as each of three gang members squared off in front of Michael,

Simon, and Busch. No one lowered his weapon, the air thick with tension.

Jon looked at each of the artifacts, picking each one up in turn, examining it, smiling. He picked up the Kusanagi and it took his breath away as he recognized it, handling it as if he were holding an angel. He turned it about, swinging it in a large arc, feeling its power, revering it. He finally placed it back in the box and picked up the katana, far lighter, and far more deadly. He unsheathed it, cut the air with it, spinning it about in quick figure-eights, stabbing at ghosts. He turned to Michael and pointed the katana at him.

"Where's the book?"

Michael didn't answer.

Without warning, Jon raised the blade in the air.

CHAPTER 48
THE FORBIDDEN CITY

K C floated to the surface, emerging into a large open room. Her head throbbed, her body ached as she crawled from the water into the room. Her chest heaved and she coughed violently, expelling water. She rolled onto her back and shined her light about.

The room was large, appearing ancient, but the rusted compressor against the wall made her realize she wasn't the only person who'd been here in the last several decades.

Rising to her feet, she looked around and saw abandoned construction debris, shovels, jackhammers, and pickaxes scattered about. There was a single door, metal—again, rusted. She opened it and walked out into a large hall, which she followed, emerging into what could only be described as an enormous tunnel. It was as wide as a six-lane highway, nearly one hundred feet across, and the ceiling was over twenty-five feet high. As she shined her light down the passage, she saw the beam disappear into darkness, the tunnel stretching on for a straight shot as far as the light would carry. She turned and looked behind her, finding the same situation, a passage into permanent nighttime. There were lights strung from the ceiling, but all were dark.

She had no idea in which direction to go.

She pulled out the map that Jenna had given her and saw that the tunnel stretched on for over twenty-five miles into the foothills. It was the government escape route carved over fifty years ago to afford passage away from a nuclear holocaust. But as the years had passed and the Cold War ended, the route was no longer maintained.

KC noted a red circle that Jenna had drawn; it was a half-mile north, indicating an escape hatch to the surface. The only problem was that KC had no idea which way was north; the paths in front of her and behind her were nearly identical, with no direction indicators. But then she realized that those for whom the escape route had been intended would all be racing away from the city, and they surely knew what direction that would be.

But to her . . .

She reached into her pocket, pulled out the black silk pouch, and smiled as she opened it.

She wished she could see Annie's face as she finally got the red puzzle box open, watching as the triumph in her eyes faded into defeat, stunned by the sight of the empty box.

When KC had arrived in the cavern, she knew she needed to act fast. She'd pulled the red box from her pouch and examined it.

It wasn't about locks, hasps, or seams. All were internal, the six-hundred-year-old craftsmanship rivaling anything today. She had held the box close, examining the edges.

On the face of the small case was an etched drawing. It was Zheng He.

She placed her thumb on his chest and could feel the slight play. She turned the box over, looking at the yin and yang, small, elegantly carved. She pressed upon it, holding it down while turning the box back over and pressing Zheng He's chest simultaneously. The mast of the ship rose a quarter inch.

And the box popped open to reveal the black silk bag.

Looking upon it now, she reached in and pulled out a circular brass disk; in its center, and nearly the same circumference, was a polished, glass convex window. Around the brass case were markings, small and intricate: dragons, tigers, monkeys, and clouds, houses, ships, and graves. The arrow in its center floated about.

It didn't matter that it wasn't marked north, south, east, west. The needle didn't need to know in which direction to point; the magnetic poles took care of that. The ancient, elegant compass was meant to guide admirals and men of the sea. Today it would guide her to freedom. That which she had stolen would be her savior.

As she walked north through the tunnel, shining her flashlight about, she passed abandoned military vehicles, cars, and trucks of 1970s and 1980s vintage, windshields cracked, tires flat. She was amazed that the Forbidden City, created nearly six hundred years ago, had stood the test of time, but vehicles built by modern man couldn't last a quarter-century.

She finally came to the point on the map that Jenna had circled. The Chinese lettering was upon the wall; though she had no idea what it said, she knew what it meant. The long ladder that climbed twenty-five feet up into the ceiling made that clear.

The rungs were still sturdy, and surprisingly rust-free. She tucked the compass into its silk pouch and back into her pocket; she rolled up the map, slipped it away, and began her climb.

At twenty-five feet she disappeared into the concrete ceiling, a narrow tube that was obviously an escape hatch for fleeing the tunnel in the event things down there were worse than things up top. It was another twenty-five feet before she arrived at a circular hatch. A spoked wheel was centered upon it, like a submarine hatch.

She wrapped her legs around the uppermost ladder rung and gripped the wheel, trying to turn it, but it wouldn't budge. She reangled her body and tried again, but once more it was useless.

It was on her third try that it budged—it was as if something snapped within—and the wheel began to turn freely, unspooling its seal like a nut upon a bolt. As she continued to turn, she paused a moment and was quickly wracked with fear . . .

The wheel was turning by itself.

Unsure whether it was the design, momentum, or worse, she looked down, thinking to escape once more. But then she grabbed the wheel and its movement halted.

She took a breath and continued turning one more revolution, and the seal released with a gasp. She pushed against the hatch and it rose. Cautiously, she climbed out to find herself in a basement where a dark, foul odor filled the air. She quickly shined her light about, but there was no one there, and she was thankful that it was just her imagination that had made her think the wheel had been turning by itself. She walked out of the room to find herself in an old abandoned food processing plant. Animal bones filled dried vats, rusted machinery and racks lined the walls. And though the room hadn't been used in decades, the stench seemed like that of fresh death.

As KC turned around once more, the shadows came alive; she shined her flashlight in the corner, its beam glinting off the barrel of a gun.

"Hello, KC," Annie said as she stepped forward.

CHAPTER 49
MACAU

The katana in Jon's hand arced down, the blade invisible, its speed seemingly faster than light. Michael had no time to react as it split the air . . .

. . . And sliced through the gang member in front of him, cutting him down with a single stroke, the edge severing the arteries of his neck, continuing down through his chest. But Jon didn't stop: His balletlike moves carried the blade outward in a sweep, cutting through the gang member standing before Simon, piercing the man's belly, slicing him through, nearly carving him in half.

The gang member before Busch had the most advantage, he had all of a third of a second to react, but it was enough time for his finger to begin to squeeze the trigger. But Jon simply adjusted his attack, turning the blade over, modifying his arc to cut the man's hand off at the wrist. It fell to the ground still clutching the butt of the gun. Before the man could even gasp, before the pain ran through his nerves to his brain, the sword drove up into his chest, slicing sideways, cutting his heart from its veins and arteries.

Michael stared at Jon, at the bodies around them, the volume of blood like nothing he had ever seen before.

"We've got thirty seconds at most," Jon said.

Michael removed his finger from the button and tucked the box back in his pocket; there was no explosion.

"Nice ruse," Simon whispered to Michael.

Busch stared at Michael, confused.

"Those weren't detonators," Michael said, "just LEDs."

The four charged out the door and down the rear stairs, which led into the basement, Jon in the lead. The gang member at the door raised his gun, but hesitated as he saw Jon in front. And with his hesitation, the gang member died, as the blade silently slipped through his throat.

They emerged onto the narrow street.

"I don't know where KC is," Michael said. "I left Annie's file up there."

"We've got to move," Jon said. "Lucas has more men coming."

Busch grabbed Jon by the neck, slamming him into the wall.. "You are the type who would kill his own mother for a nickel, so tell me why slaying those men back there will wipe away your deeds of the last four days and make me trust you and convince me that you're not setting us up."

"Simple. Just as I was to execute you and Michael, I was to be killed after I slew you."

"Bullshit. This was a money grab for you, you're not the seeking-redemption type. Why didn't you just cut and run?"

"Because . . . where you're going, I can still get paid and disappear. You're right, it's a money grab, and you just became the highest bidder with the best survival rate. And I just became your best hope to find KC Ryan. So let's get the hell out of here before those guys coming around the corner start shooting."

Busch relented and they ran down the narrow streets, past the old locked and gated shops. Rounding a corner, Jon threw a set of car keys to Simon as they arrived at a silver Mercedes 500. They jumped in; Simon started the car and pulled out.

"Where were you planning on going?" Jon said.

"We've got a plane to catch," Simon said.

Jon took a moment, looking around, and a black Range Rover tore around the corner.

The street to their left was narrow and several cars were crawling along, their brake lights flashing intermittently. The street ahead was cordoned off, terminating at a wooden fence. There was nowhere to go.

"Through the fence," Jon shouted. "Go!"

And the gunfire behind them exploded.

Simon punched the accelerator as Michael ducked down in the front seat. Jon pulled out his cell phone, quickly barking an order as he looked at the approaching SUV behind them.

Simon exploded through the wooden fence to find himself faced with a metal guardrail that wrapped a long corner. He threw the wheel to the right and raced down the sidewalk, narrowly squeezing between the rail and the brick building on his right until the guardrail ended and he found himself in the middle of an open street, the roadway ahead clear of not only people but cars, bikes, carts, and any sign of life.

He hit the accelerator and pushed the Mercedes as hard as he could, the speedometer quickly climbing above one hundred miles per hour. The Grand Prix racecourse was wide open, the streets cordoned off for the first race at 7:00 a.m. Simon pushed the Mercedes to its limit. They were moving at nearly 120 miles per hour, the old buildings whizzing by, the explosive sound of spitting air reverberating every time they passed a small shop.

The Range Rover kept up its pursuit, coming through the fence, squeezing between the building and the rail seventy-five yards back, its engine straining as it began to catch up.

The sidewalks surrounding the temporary racetrack were empty at 5:00 a.m., but as they neared the grandstands, the pit stops and storage compounds for the race cars, they could see the beginnings of early-morning activity.

"Where the hell are we going?" Simon said as he pushed the car to its limit, past the fuel tanks, past the empty viewing stands, toward the sunrise, which was just beginning its glow over the water ahead.

"Just straight ahead. I've got a friend who'll help us."

"We can't run this course all day."

"Don't worry, we run out of track in thirty seconds."

And Simon could see the water ahead. They were bearing down on a bridge, the section of racetrack that ran over the water. The track took a sharp left ahead, but Simon could see the way was blocked by a large street-sweeping truck that was cleaning the track for the day's races.

The Range Rover was fifty yards back and closing fast.

Simon would be out of the roadway within ten seconds.

Jon rolled down the window, leaned out.

"That's not going to do any good—"

And Jon rapid-fired his gun.

A fuel tank to their right exploded, a huge fireball rolling up into the sky, the high-octane race fuel superheating the air. Michael could feel the heat on his face from nearly one hundred yards.

And the Range Rover skidded into a spin, trying to avoid the liquid inferno that spilled out on to the roadway, a wall of flame blocking its way.

Simon slammed on the brakes, the tires squealing on the bridge as they ran out of roadway. The street sweeper was completely blocking any hope for escape as its driver jumped out, staring in awe at the conflagration behind them.

"Great," Simon shouted. "You just blocked our only way out!"

They all jumped out of the car and looked back at the fire.

Without a word, Jon ran to the edge of the bridge and leaped over the guardrail. Michael ran up behind him and looked down to see a speedboat in the water eight feet below.

"Well?" Jon yelled. "Let's go!"

LUCAS WALKED INTO the safe house, barely able to control his rage. He was alone as he looked at the bodies, the blood everywhere.

And then he saw it, on the floor, a white envelope. He picked it up, opened it, and found a Xerox copy of the map of the island.

He pulled out his cell phone and quickly dialed.

"Yeah?" Annie answered.

"Do you have it?"

"I will in a moment."

"Good, then kill the woman."

"I thought we were—"

"Kill the woman."

CHAPTER 50
THE FORBIDDEN CITY

"How did you find me?" KC asked as Annie led her at gunpoint out into the China predawn.

"Where is the compass?" Annie asked.

KC stepped from the abandoned building, its parking lot peppered with weeds that pressed through the cracked concrete. "Wasn't it in the box?"

"Very funny."

"I'm impressed you figured out how to open it," KC said.

"Open it? I smashed it with the butt of my pistol. I'm not one for puzzles. Now, where is it?"

"How could you possibly have found me?" KC asked. "There are dozens of escape hatches along the way."

"You underestimate me." Annie led KC across the lot toward a white Town Car that sat in the glow of a lone streetlight.

KC smiled. "So says the woman who fell for the empty-box routine." But her smile quickly faded as they arrived at the car and KC saw Jenna tied up and blindfolded in the backseat.

"Let her go, she has nothing to do with this," KC said. "No one else has to die."

"That might be unavoidable," Annie said.

As KC looked at Annie in the glow of the streetlight, she understood how true Annie's words were; she finally saw the dark stains, nearly imperceptible against Annie's dark shirt; there was a hint of blood around her left nostril. "Karma's a bitch, ain't it?"

Annie said nothing as she held her gun on KC.

"How long have you been infected?"

"Give me the compass," Annie said.

"Why, so you can give it to your boss, the man who poisoned you?" KC said. "You don't strike me as someone who'd just roll over and die. You shoot innocent people in the back. What do you do to those who want you to die?"

Annie raised the gun to within inches of KC's face. "He told me to kill you now, not to wait for the poison to consume you, just end your life right here on the spot."

"So," KC said, "why haven't you? Why not just shoot me and take the compass off my dead body?"

Annie glared at her.

"Because the compass is only one piece of the puzzle," KC said, answering her own question.

Annie spun KC around, zip-tied her arms behind her back, and pulled the compass from her pocket.

"To save your own ass, you need me as live bait to lure Michael and the other piece of the puzzle here to Beijing," KC said, "here to you."

CHAPTER 51
MACAU

The Boeing Business Jet climbed high in the sky. It was the quintessential luxury jet, the largest of the private designs short of a full-body 737. The property of Steven Kelley, the jet had delivered Simon to Macau after picking him up in Rome.

A successful M&A attorney from Boston, Kelley had made his fortune long before he met the son he had given up nearly forty years earlier. Though Michael had been raised by Alex St. Pierre, he was the biological son of Steven Kelley, who had given him up when he was just hours old, upon the death of his birth mother. Unable to care for the child, with no financial means and just one step from the streets, Kelley helped to assure Michael's placement into a warm, caring family and had watched anonymously from afar as Michael grew up. They had only reconnected two years ago, thanks to Michael's late wife, Mary, but had formed a bond over that brief time that made it feel as if they had been close for decades.

Busch sat in the deep leather chair and stared at Jon, who sat across from him and Michael.

"The flight's only two and a half hours," Simon said as he emerged from the cockpit. "We should be landing by nine."

"How are we going to find KC in such an enormous city?"

"She's with Annie," Jon said.

"That gives me no hope," Busch said.

"I can find and deal with Annie."

"And if your ex-employer has tipped her off to your Benedict Arnold?"

"I'll find her," Jon said, annoyed at Busch's questioning. "I promise I'll help get her back to you."

"How sick is the colonel?" Michael asked.

"Nosebleeds, headaches—he's on some serious pain meds. He was adamant about finding that island by tomorrow. While he'd been after his brother for so long, wanting to stop this virus from getting out into the general population, everything changed when his own survival became an issue."

"And when was KC infected?" Michael asked almost clinically, barring his emotions.

"Four days ago, as she was leaving the States."

Busch stood up from his seat, his head almost hitting the ceiling as he walked to the back of the plane, doing everything he could to restrain himself.

"Listen, Lucas has no doubt that this antivirus, this treatment that is on that island, will cure him. He's a meticulous man, his reputation is no-nonsense, and he's not prone to believing in false hope. The cure is there. We get KC there, she'll be okay." There was sincerity in Jon's voice.

"Can I get you guys a drink?" Simon said as he walked by, Zheng He's book under his arm.

Michael and Jon shook their heads no as Simon continued to the back of the plane.

"And, Michael," Jon continued, "I'm sorry. I know it means nothing, but I am."

Michael stared at Jon, the moment stretching out. Jon got up and headed to a seat near the front of the plane.

Michael stared out the starboard window. The low-lying clouds on the horizon were splashed with pink as he watched the sun begin its climb, emerging from the China Sea.

Despite Jon's words, despite what Simon had read in Zheng He's diary, Michael was filled with fear. He had lost his first wife, Mary, to cancer, and it had torn him apart, unable to save her as she withered away. Now KC was sick, but this time he could save her, he could bring her the cure that he couldn't find for Mary—if Simon was right. But even if they could find the island, who was to say the Phoenix Tears would be there, and could be found? There was no pharmacy on the island, no one you could just call upon arrival to bring it to you. The only thing that gave him any glimmer of hope was that the Dragon Tears existed, someone had taken them from the island, and if the disease was there, then maybe, just maybe, so was the cure.

Michael felt his BlackBerry vibrate from within his pocket. He pulled it out and looked at it to see a new text message coming in.

Michael,

I know you're coming. 10:00 a.m. The Temple of Heaven. Alone. The map for a life.

Love, Annie

Michael looked down at the accompanying picture. The image of KC was from a car, at nighttime. He could see the blood on her shirt, around her nose, but despite her appearance, despite being held against her will, there was no mistaking the anger in her eyes.

CHAPTER 52
BEIJING

The black Town Car raced through the crowded streets of Beijing, Jon at the wheel, swerving in and out of traffic, knowing the roads as if it were his hometown. The business jet had skidded in fifteen minutes earlier, the Town Car on the tarmac fueled up and waiting for Michael, Busch, Simon, and Jon.

"This is not a good idea," Busch said from the backseat.

No one responded.

Michael looked at his watch: It was 9:30 in the morning.

Five minutes later, they pulled up to a large park on the south side of the city and pulled to the side of the road. Tourists and locals were coming and going through the main tree-lined entrance.

"I go alone," Michael said as he tucked an envelope into the inner pocket of his blue blazer.

"Not a chance," Busch said as he pulled out his gun and slammed in a clip.

"You can't go," Jon said to Busch. "Annie has seen a picture of you in your dossier, and with your size and hair color, you stick out."

"That's bullshit—"

"I'm not risking KC's life," Michael said.

"I'll go," Simon said. "She'll never know I'm there."

Michael shook his head as he opened up the door and stepped out of the car. "No, I need to do this alone."

"I'm not letting you or KC out of my sight," Simon said. "So just get over it. Jon can drop me off on the other side of the park. Annie's eyes will be on you, she'll never know I'm there."

"And we're just supposed to sit here?" Busch asked.

"No," Jon said.

Michael opened the trunk of the car, reached into his black duffel bag, and pulled out a small black book. He returned to the car and gave it to Busch.

"Time for you to embrace your true calling," Michael said.

MICHAEL WALKED TWO hundred yards down a tree-lined walkway. The morning crowds had begun to gather, groups of people doing tai chi, tourists walking at half-speed looking around the oasislike park in the city of Beijing.

Michael emerged into a large open courtyard. The Temple of Heaven was in fact a complex of temples and small buildings, with the complex centered on the Hall of Prayer for Good Harvests. Sitting upon a three-level marble base, the circular structure soared almost 120 feet in the air, capped in a three-tiered blue-tile conical roof, separated by intricately painted bands that were alive with images of dragons and mythical creatures.

Michael ascended the marble stairs, entered the circular temple, and was overwhelmed by the soaring, intricate ceiling. Constructed between 1405 and 1420—the same time as the Forbidden City—the Hall of Prayer was built upon twenty-eight pillars and didn't contain a single nail but had in fact been built using joints, laths, interlocking columns, and rafters. The ceiling was a stunning mosaic of artistry that was carried into the immense pillars and columns.

Every spring the emperor would travel several miles from the Forbidden Palace to offer sacrifices and prayers for strong, healthy crops, a tradition that fell into history with the last emperor.

In the center of the room was a large marble stone, and as Michael saw the small plaque with the English translation on the bottom, he understood why Annie had chosen this location. Known as the Dragon and Phoenix Stone, it was a symbol of harmony, of balance, of life and death.

And then he saw her on the far side of the room by the side door; KC stared back at him but didn't move. Michael smiled as he approached her. Her face had lost color; he could see exhaustion in her eyes. He looked around for Annie, but saw no sign of her as he arrived at KC's side.

"You shouldn't have come," KC said as she stepped into his embrace.

Michael took KC in his arms, unable to find the words as he pulled her to him, as he held her tight, inhaling her scent, rejoicing in the moment he'd thought would never come again.

"I'm so sorry," KC said as she hugged him, breathing him in, closing her eyes as the rays of the morning sun poured through the temple.

Michael leaned back, taking her face in his hand, resting his forehead against hers. "Are you okay?" Michael asked.

KC looked up into his eyes and nodded . . . And Michael knew she was lying; he knew she was sick, that she had been infected. And seeing her condition, his worst fears were realized.

"Did you bring the map?" KC whispered in Michael's ear.

"It's in my pocket," Michael whispered back. "But I've no intention of giving it to anyone."

"She's worried about you, Michael," Annie said.

Michael spun around to find Annie standing ten feet behind him, her short black hair and smile sending a chill through his heart. He had only seen her for the briefest of moments back in New York, on the elevator, on the street, when she had committed a cold-blooded murder, and then hours later when he'd watched her image on the iPad as she and KC were talking at the airport.

"What did you do to her?" Michael demanded.

"She's worried that I'm going to kill you," Annie said. "Did you bring the book?"

"No," Michael said. "It's too fragile, and besides, do you think I'm that foolish?"

"Do you think I'm leaving here without the map?" Annie said.

Michael cast his eyes downward and saw the gun in Annie's hand, concealed under her jacket.

"You would shoot her?" Michael asked.

"Actually, I truly like her, though I wouldn't hesitate to kill her to save myself, Michael. She and I are very much alike. It's funny, you have strong feelings for both of us, but they are opposite feelings. But this gun is not for her. The gun is for you. I told her I'd kill you if you didn't comply. But if you insist, you can watch me kill her instead."

Michael stared at Annie.

"May I have the map, please?"

"Why don't you just get it from Lucas?" Michael said. "He has a copy."

"I want it from you," Annie said.

"Going rogue?" Michael asked. "I don't think he'll take to that too kindly."

"I'm not too concerned with what you or he think."

"I need that compass, Annie," Michael said.

"And I need the map," Annie said.

Michael looked at KC, at the exhaustion in her face, his eyes finally returning to Annie. "She'll die."

"How about this? You can keep the map and I'll kill you now, or you can roll the dice, give me the map, and you and she can have a few more days together, be able to say your good-byes."

"Where's the compass?"

"For the same reason you didn't bring the book, I didn't bring the compass. Great minds think alike, right, Michael? Face it, I own you, just like I own KC, just like I own your friends who are in my hotel room right now, looking for it."

BUSCH AND JON tore through the hotel suite at the Crown Plaza Beijing, ripping open drawers, closets, flipping mattresses. Jon had known where she was staying; it was in the files at the safe house.

As Busch entered the bathroom, he heard a moan and turned to find a woman bound and gagged on the floor of the shower. He quickly leaned down, tore the zip ties from her wrists, and removed the rag from her mouth. She was bruised, incoherent, barely awake. Busch picked her up, carried her to the bed, and laid her upon the mattress.

"It's okay," he whispered.

"Shit," Jon said as he saw the woman.

"She's going to kill KC," the woman said as she softly wept.

"Don't worry, KC's in good hands."

"She said she'd kill me and anyone who enters this room."

"Believe me, no one is going to kill any of us," Busch said as he turned to Jon.

"Were you their guide?" Jon asked.

"Yes. I'm Jenna."

"You're safe now," Jon said as he turned back to Busch. "We don't have much time."

"What if she had the compass with her?" Busch said. He turned back to Jenna. "Did you see the compass?"

She shook her head.

"There is no way she brought it with her to her meeting with Michael. She wouldn't risk losing it," Jon said.

"Instead, she left it in the hotel room?" Busch asked.

"Where else in China could she possibly hide it?" Jon said.

"There's a room safe," Jenna said, "behind the media cabinet. I heard her use it."

Busch turned and opened the media cabinet, ran his hands around the edges, looking, and noticed a small hinge on the stereo shelf. He gave it a gentle tug and the entire shelf swung out to reveal a room safe, two feet square, with a keypad. Busch pulled out the small black book Michael had given him; he scanned several pages until he found the name of the room safe. It would be his first attempt at safecracking; he couldn't help thinking that this was the last thing he'd ever thought he'd be doing when he retired from the police force.

He quickly punched in the numbers of the override code and the door swung open. There was nothing but a single white envelope. And it was addressed to Jon.

"So she knew you'd be with us?" Busch asked suspiciously as he handed him the envelope.

Jon ignored the comment, opened the letter, and quickly read it:

> *I have the compass, tucked away and safe.*
> *Kill them.*
>
> > *Annie*

"So, IF I give you the map and you locate the island, how are you going to get there?" Michael asked Annie as they stood near the rear wall of the temple.

"Annie," KC said, "let's do it together. If we pool our talents and resources we can both walk away with another day."

Annie looked at KC, and the moment hung in the air.

"If you make a mistake," Michael said, "if Lucas catches you, he'll kill you."

"I'll be dead in days anyway. I want my life in my own hands, I want to control my future. I will not leave it up to anyone, especially those who wish me dead. I know what I'm doing."

And in a single motion, Annie pulled her gun, swiped her leg around, knocking Michael against the red wall, and drove the barrel into his cheek.

"Give me the map," Annie said, leaning into Michael, speaking in hushed tones.

KC looked at Michael, her eyes pleading. He subtly shook his head no.

Several tourists began to notice Annie and her gun, and silently began to move toward the doors, while others were staring up at the magnificent ceiling.

"I won't ask again," Annie said, pressing the gun into Michael's cheek as she flexed her trigger finger.

KC raised her hands to calm Annie, turned to Michael, and slipped her right hand into his pocket, pulling out the envelope. "I won't let her kill you."

"Don't," Michael said as he looked at her.

"I'm sorry," KC said, and she handed the envelope to Annie.

"Open it," Annie demanded as she continued to hold the gun on Michael.

KC tore open the envelope and drew out a large Xerox copy of the map, holding it up for Annie's inspection.

Annie studied it, her eyes racing over the images, and she finally snatched it from KC's hands.

But she left the gun pressed to Michael's cheek.

"We had a deal," KC said.

"I can't risk you trying to stop me."

A gun suddenly came to rest on the back of Annie's head. "We haven't had the pleasure." Simon stood behind her. "Please lower your—"

Without a word, Annie fired her gun . . . into the wall behind Michael, the explosive report echoing about the high ceiling.

The temple erupted in mayhem. The tourist crowd quickly scattered as if running from fire; there were no screams, just hushed whispers and racing feet as everyone moved for the doors, running for their lives.

And with all the confusion, no one noticed Annie, who had folded into their midst, disappearing with the map into the morning.

JON PULLED UP in the black Town Car. Busch hopped out and opened the door for KC.

"Hey, Paul," KC said, as she stood on her tiptoes and kissed his cheek.

"Hey, little lady," Busch said as he wrapped her in his large arms.

"Here to save me again?" KC smiled as she nearly disappeared in his embrace.

"When Michael mentioned China, I said, Hey, that's on my bucket list, you mind if I tag along?"

"Who's this?" KC said as she looked at Jon in the driver's seat.

"Jon," Michael said, waving his hand between them, "KC."

"Hi," Jon said, as he opened his door and leaned out.

Busch released KC and held up Annie's letter. "Jon-boy here was supposed to kill us."

"I figured I had to find a way into your good graces." Jon smiled.

"I don't know if you're there yet," Busch said, laughing, "but not shooting me is a step in the right direction."

KC smiled and melted back into Michael's arms. "Listen, there is something I need to tell you."

Michael looked at her. "I know . . . we're going to take care of you."

"But without the compass . . ." KC said, "we have no idea where it is."

"Oh, yes we do," Busch said as he reached into the car and pulled out one of Michael's chip-tracking black boxes.

CHAPTER 53

Annie pulled the paper out of the printer and placed it on the table; it was a map, an exact copy of the one she'd taken from Michael. She had her doubts about the authenticity of Michael's map, thinking he might trick her, just as he had done with Lucas, as KC had done to her in stealing the compass.

Lucas had a plane fueled and ready at the airport to whisk her back to him in Macau so they could unlock the secret of the map together. But Annie needed every second she could get . . . and as much as she didn't want to admit it, she would need Lucas and his resources if she hoped to get to the island on time. But once there . . .

Wasting no time, she pulled out the antique compass. Along its circumference were a series of ornate dragons and tigers that corresponded to a legend on the scanned image of the map. She placed the compass upon the legend, orienting the images until they matched up.

"Well?" Lucas's voice, coming over the speakerphone on the table, echoed in the small conference room.

"Give me a minute," Annie said, her eyes focused on the map. She read the coordinates in the map's corner that she translated from Chinese. She pulled out a ruler, measuring distances, drawing lines, jotting down notes.

She looked over at the black chip that had been in the envelope with the map, the one Michael had so cleverly hidden, the one that was allowing him to track her. Michael had always planned for her to leave the temple with the map, his ruse distracting her from his true goal of following her here.

And Annie smiled, thought of tossing the minuscule chip in a cab, down the drain, putting it on a train, sending him on a wild goose chase, but she knew the wall he was up against right now was filling him with a far greater frustration than she could manufacture, for she was in the one place in all of China where Michael couldn't touch her.

MICHAEL SAT IN the rear of the car with KC, Simon beside them, Jon at the wheel while Busch rode shotgun. They all stared out the window at the large compound.

"Son of a bitch," Busch said. "How the hell does she get protection like that?"

"Connections," Simon said.

"Connections, my ass. This whole thing stinks to high heaven."

"I can't go near there," Michael said. "I'd be arrested in a heartbeat."

"I wouldn't even know where to go once I was in," Busch said.

"Don't look at me," Simon said. "I'm Italian. We

wait for her to emerge. If we each cover a side of the building—"

"We don't have time," Michael said. "She could stay in there for hours. Maybe they'll give her an escort out and we won't get within one hundred yards of her."

"Are you sure she's in there?" Jon said to Michael.

Michael held up the tracker, the blinking red dot in the center of the GPS map. "Unless she found the chip and somehow slipped it up to the second floor."

"You sure it's the second floor?" Jon asked.

"This thing does altitude very accurately, and she's twenty feet above us right now."

Without a word, Jon removed his gun. Laying it on the seat, he reached down and took off the knife strapped to his ankle, pulled the extra clips from his pocket, gave them to Michael, and exited the car, slamming the door behind him.

They all stared as Jon walked across the street and into the U.S. Embassy.

JON JOGGED UP the walkway, past the large reflecting pool to the main entrance of the U.S. Embassy compound, a grouping of buildings filling an entire city block in central Beijing. A large eight-story office building at its center, it was surrounded by several shorter expansive structures that stretched along the entire block. Fronted by an open glass entry, it was modern, a far cry from the stone townhouse embassies in Europe.

Jon pulled out his passport and showed it to the four armed guards who stood at the main gate. A Marine in dress uniform nodded to Jon and escorted him in, leading him across the small plaza and through the large main doors.

They entered the marble lobby and it was as if Jon were back in America: flags hung conspicuously about, a large portrait of the president hung on the far wall. The lobby was a bustle of activity, all Americans, all speaking English as they hurried about their day.

Jon was escorted to the desk sergeant. "Good evening, Sergeant. Lieutenant Jon Lei, retired." Jon handed over his passport and a military ID.

The sergeant scanned both items, handed them back, and smiled. "It's a pleasure, Lieutenant. How can I help you?"

"I'm currently with the Tridiem Group under retainer to Colonel Lucas out of Camp Zama. I'm looking for a colleague by the name of Annie Joss."

"Of course. She's on the second floor, room 2112." The sergeant passed Jon a floor map. "You'll need to check your weapon—"

"No need." Jon smiled. "Left it all behind."

The desk sergeant pointed to the security checkpoint. "You need anything, just dial zero."

Jon nodded as he turned and made his way through the checkpoint, taking the stairs to the second floor, quickly finding the room and entering.

"Annie," Jon said as he walked into the conference room.

"I heard you turned sides," Annie said, not looking up from her map.

"Really, and whose side are you on?"

"America's." She finally looked up.

"You've been telling everyone that for so long, you've begun to believe your own bullshit."

"So says the man who always works for the highest bidder."

"Seeing we both work for Tridiem, doesn't that apply to you, too?" Jon asked as his tone grew serious. "Do you really believe this island exists? That it has what Lucas so desperately needs?"

Annie nodded. "It better exist, or I'll kill that son of a bitch before we both die."

"You're sure you aren't contagious?" Jon asked as he looked around the room.

"Positive. The virus needs to be ingested or enter the bloodstream. If this stuff was easily communicable, we could kiss a big chunk of the world good-bye. But you know what else I believe?"

"What's that?"

"That this island holds far more than the cure for this disease. Zheng He's treasures, the things he sailed with on his last voyage, are on that island: The gold the Japanese looted from China during World War II, Yamashita's gold—everyone says it's in the Philippines but I'll bet it's on that island."

"So, what, are you going to run off with Lucas to the island and think you can just steal it from him, take it from underneath his nose? He'll bring in forces, guaranteed."

"No, he's going in lean, I confirmed it. He's so afraid of dying, he can't wait for backup. Once we're there, I'll kill him."

Jon stared at Annie. "Give me the compass."

"Why? I already know where the island is." Annie pointed at her markings on the map.

"And if you're wrong, if you've missed something and rush off to the wrong location?"

"I'm right," Annie said.

"Always so sure of yourself. Are you willing to stake your life on being right? Because that's what you're doing. You will die if you're wrong. And if Xiao is out there with the Dragon's Breath . . . How many more will die?"

Annie paused a moment. She looked at the compass, finally picking it up off the table. She walked over to Jon and placed it in his hands.

Annie looked up into Jon's eyes. For a long moment, the air was thick between them. It had been days since he had seen her. He could see the exhaustion in her face but it didn't diminish her beauty. As far as he was concerned, nothing could.

And she kissed him, wrapping her arms around him, inhaling him as if he had been away for years. And he kissed her back, strong, hard, drawing her to him, reconnecting after too long.

"So," Annie whispered. "You take the compass and lead your little merry band of thieves to the island, and whoever gets there first wins."

"And what do we do when we get there, with the colonel, with St. Pierre?"

"We cure me, take what is rightly ours, and kill them all."

Annie grabbed Jon by the back of the head and pulled him in for another kiss.

CHAPTER 54

The compass was truly spectacular, the circumference ringed in an alternating succession of dragons and tigers, each unique, each squared off in attack. The central bulb was filled with liquid, the floating needle etched with a bird in flight among the clouds. Subtle hash marks underlined the warring beasts, corresponding to traditional compass points with varying degree of midpoints.

"This compass is backward," Michael said as he noted the needle pointing south.

"No," Simon said. "Chinese compasses point south. They invented the compass more than twenty-five hundred years ago. Chinese literature references it being used around 1050. Zheng He was the first person to navigate the seas with a compass, to truly use it in the modern sense, something that wasn't picked up by Europeans until much later. Though that compass points south, obviously the other end points north; the axis never changes."

Michael focused on the map page of Zheng He's diary. The page actually folded out three times, a map of the breadth of the world far more detailed than anyone could have imagined having been created in 1425. It showed not only India, Asia, the Middle East, and Africa in surprising detail, but also both North and South America. Each of the seas was adorned with magnificent dragons diving through the water, exquisite ships atop mountainous waves, sea creatures exploding up out of the depths.

In the lower right-hand corner of the page were a dragon and a tiger entwined in battle, the shapes of their bodies forming a yin-yang. As Michael looked around the map, he noted that along the edges of the pages were similar tigers and dragons in battle, chasing and attacking one another. He turned his focus to the images that ringed the compass and he realized . . .

Michael placed the compass upon the yin-yang, orienting it until the beasts on the compass matched their counterparts on the edges of the map. As they lined up, he watched as the needle began to subtly turn from the north-south axis.

He lifted the compass and watched as the needle spun back several degrees to its proper axis. Running his hand around the page, hovering the compass just above the surface, the needle danced and shifted, and he finally put it back in place on the corner of the map. He turned the compass around and, once again, as each of the beasts lined up, the compass point shifted several degrees.

"The paper." Michael smiled as he ran his fingers along its edge. "It's inlaid with some type of magnetic ferrite, a minuscule amount, very subtle, but when the compass is positioned according to the symbols on the compass's ring, it's enough to draw the compass off point."

Using the ancient compass, Michael looked at the grouping of islands to the south of the Philippines and computed the heading and location of Penglai from Zheng He's notes at the top of the page.

"Give me your compass," Michael said to Busch.

Busch pulled his father's compass watch out of his pocket, flipped it open, and handed it to Michael. Michael removed Zheng He's compass, placing Paul's in its place, orienting it on the north-south axis of the map. Using his calculations on Paul's compass, he quickly pinpointed a remote dot of an island in the South Pacific. He removed Busch's compass and replaced it with Zheng He's compass, orienting the modified axis in accordance with the line of the matching dragons and tigers, and smiled as the compass point pulled several degrees west.

"Anyone who tries to follow the coordinates on this map with an ordinary compass would arrive at a different island. They would think they'd found Penglai, patting themselves on the back, never realizing the true island was here."

Michael pointed to the open sea, where an ornamental five-fingered dragon dove through the waves. Busch turned to the large modern map and began calculating, finally writing out a group of coordinates.

Michael turned to see KC asleep on the couch, a trickle of blood dripping from her nose. Busch and Simon followed Michael's eyes, their faces filling with concern.

"We're running out of time," Michael whispered.

* * *

Jenna dropped Michael, KC, Busch, Simon, and Jon at the entrance to the private air terminal, returned their rental car, and boarded a plane for San Francisco. It was time for a career change.

The five hurried through the private terminal of Beijing Airport to Steven Kelley's jet, which sat in wait, engines running, ramp down in welcome.

"Your dad is going to be pissed," Busch said. "You're putting serious miles on his plane, and the cost of fuel—"

"I'll cover it," Simon said. "This is my fault."

"You got that kind of money?" Busch asked. "Pretty steep for man who took a vow of poverty."

Busch patted Simon on the back as they entered the plane, Busch being sure to put his left foot first.

Michael helped KC up the ramp. Though she could walk on her own, Michael could see the pain in her eyes. He never believed in any of this magic, hocus-pocus legend stuff, but he knew the disease was rooted in science, in nature. The Dragon's Breath was spoken of in history, referenced by Zheng He, by the Yongle Emperor, and so, too, was its antidote, the yin to its yang, the Phoenix Tears. The names would have made him laugh if the matter hadn't been so serious. Whether magic or science, history or legend, Michael would find it, he would believe in it, as it was the only thing that could save KC from her fast-approaching death.

"Got us a boat," Busch said as he closed his cell phone.

"What kind of boat?" Michael asked.

"The kind of boat that floats in the ocean. Reserved it with your credit card, didn't think you'd mind. I told the pilot where in the Philippines. We've got a twelve-hour boat ride southeast from there."

"What if Lucas gets there before us?" KC asked as she reclined her seat.

Michael smiled at her. "I wouldn't worry about that."

CHAPTER 55

Lucas sat in the bridge of the U.S. naval boat, the sixty-foot craft traveling at thirty-five knots through the relatively calm ocean. With a single phone call, the boat had been ready and waiting with a crew of three when he landed in the Philippines.

Lucas stared out at the blue ocean as he plunged a needle into his arm, injecting himself with a potent cocktail of painkillers and stimulants. The drug mix muted the pain, helped to sustain his strength, but couldn't forestall death, which was fast approaching.

Annie was in the bow with two of Lucas's men, her five-hour flight landing at nearly the same time as Lucas's. The boat was waiting dockside and not a word was spoken until they were safely under way, the course plotted to the coordinates that Annie had calculated with Zheng He's compass and map.

They were two hours into their eight-hour journey when Jon called her satellite phone, giving her the modified coordinates. Annie cursed herself, not just because she had gotten them wrong, but because Jon had been right.

They were two hours ahead of Michael and his team, more than enough time to make land. Now that they had all of the information, the race would be over, Lucas and Annie would arrive at Penglai first, not just because they had the intel but because Jon would ensure Michael and his friends would never get close.

JON OPENED HIS black knapsack, pulled out two 9mm Sig Sauers, three clips, and his knife. He loaded a clip in each gun and tucked them in his waistband at the small of his back; he sheathed the knife and strapped it to his ankle, concealing it under his pant leg. There were four aboard. Michael and KC would not be a problem, it was Simon who was the most skilled and would react the quickest, which was why he had to kill him first. There was no need to keep Busch alive. Jon could pilot the boat himself; he had driven too many boats to count back when he was in the Navy.

Dumping their bodies would be simple; he'd weigh them down and drop them to the seabed over a mile below before continuing to rendezvous with Annie at the island.

He took the narrow step up from the lower level into the salon, pulling his shirt over the protruding pistols in the rear of his waistband.

KC was asleep on a couch, her face pale, her breathing sounding labored. Michael was beside her, quiet and worried. Simon was on the opposite couch, his feet on an ottoman, trying to get comfortable.

Jon reached behind him—

"You guys have got to see this," Busch called out from the bridge.

Michael and Simon left KC sleeping on the couch and stepped into the bridge. Jon kept his hand on his gun and slowly followed, standing in the doorway with his three marks in front of him. Watching, waiting on Busch.

"Tell me what you see," Busch said, his hand about the helm.

They looked out the front window at the open sea; the water was clear and blue to the horizon. Turning their attention back inside, they saw that all of the instruments looked normal, the engine was running clean, its roar steady and powerful.

"What are we looking at?" Michael asked.

"I locked in a manual heading as soon as we left port, the autopilot maintaining a straight line as opposed to a compass heading. Like any good captain, I keep my eyes on the compass. Though I wasn't following a compass heading, I knew the heading of the island nonetheless." Busch tapped the large ball compass that sat upon the dash. "The compass has been drifting west by a little less than a degree each hour; it's been five degrees so far. If we were on autopilot, our course would have been changing to match the compass heading. This is why no one finds the island; it's like the island doesn't want to be found. Everyone is so reliant on a compass, and the shift of the compass is so subtle, no one would ever question it."

"What about GPS?"

Busch flipped a switch, and they all looked at the video screen. "GPS triangulates your positions off satellites, pretty simple algorithms. The big ships use it, the new sailors use it, but the old seadogs still rely on the compass. Since the island is not on the shipping routes it's not even thought of, but anyone looking for the island locks in the heading on their GPS and this is what they find."

Busch pointed at the screen. It said *Searching for signal*.

"There are seven sats to pull from, you need three to triangulate position, but this GPS never finds more than two—the magnetic field is somehow interrupting the signal."

"So the island, by virtue of this magnetic field, is invisible?"

"No, not at all, just invisible to technology, and since man relies on technology so much, we've blinded ourselves to this world and who knows how many other places."

Jon removed his hand from his pistol and pulled the shirt over it.

"What do you mean it's not there?" Lucas demanded.

"I mean there is no island at these coordinates, sir," the young Navy lieutenant said.

Lucas looked at the GPS screen, which was blank. "That's not even working."

"We've been riding the compass for several hours. The GPS signal has been weak at best."

Lucas spun around and faced Annie, his eyes bloodshot, his face gray and fatigued. "You screwed up."

"Absolutely not. I did the calculations; they were based off a glitch in the Xeroxed map. I spoke to Jon a few hours ago and gave you the modified heading that they are following; theirs was based off the diary and the compass, and they didn't make a mistake."

"Well, the island is not there. You care to explain how Jon was right?"

Annie pulled out her sat phone and hit Send. She waited thirty seconds before doing it again, but there was no signal.

"Turn the boat around," Lucas shouted.

"Where?"

"To someplace where we are not lost," Lucas shouted. "Take us back to the point where we have a GPS signal."

Lucas drew his pistol and pointed it at Annie's head. "You better pray we find that island in the next three hours, because if we don't, the last thing I will do before I die is kill you."

CHAPTER 56

The island appeared on the horizon as a small dot.

As they approached the designated coordinates, Busch could see the point of the compass shift two degrees, an infinitesimal amount, one that a ship's autopilot would immediately correct for, and they would have missed the island. But he maintained his original course, and within an hour, it was there. It was just a blip, a small dot on the horizon, easily mistaken for a distant ship or mirage, but as they continued closer, it rose out of the sea, slowly climbing into the air until it loomed ahead.

Unmistakable, it was larger than Michael had expected, a volcanic island, its mountainous cone climbing several thousand feet, the entire expanse green and lush. Busch kept one eye on the depth gauge and one on the copy of the map.

"You sure about this?" Busch said.

"Without question," Simon said.

As they got closer to shore, Busch could see the change in the sea. While the waters he currently rode were calm, those surrounding the island appeared far more agitated; heavy waves and cross currents ringed the island despite the blue skies above.

At five miles out, Simon flipped open Zheng He's diary, tore out the ancient Chinese drawing, and taped it to the side window. The painting was intricate, detailed, reflecting topography, the rise and fall of the hills, the clipped edge of the volcano's cone. Busch turned the boat to port and began to circle the island in a clockwise fashion, cutting his speed to fifteen knots as he kept one eye on the painting and the other on the island. He had no idea whether there had been an eruption in the last six hundred years, something that would surely have changed the appearance of the island.

Busch kept the boat steady, staying five miles out from shore just as the diary had described. Simon and Michael hung over his shoulder, staring at the island as they circled, all silent in anticipation.

And then, as if in some child's game, they saw it. The image of the island was a near perfect match to the picture: the rock outcroppings, the far west cliffs, the sharp drop off the cone's eastern flank.

"Son of a bitch," Busch mumbled.

"Told you," Simon said.

Busch couldn't believe it as he turned in toward shore. He pulled the painting from his side window and affixed it to the windshield in front of him, making sure the two images before him matched.

"Zheng He said there was but a single approach to the island, a narrow channel laid by the gods to keep the unworthy out. He described the reef as an enormous water dragon that ringed the island, protecting it, waiting to snatch the unworthy into the depths."

At four and a half miles out, the seas grew from a

light chop to a heavy swell. Though the sky above was clear and the winds out of the southwest were only at five knots, the waves were becoming stormlike.

"The water we were over was three thousand feet deep," Busch said, "but for the last hundred yards, we've been at 150. If it was land, it would appear like a half-mile-high wall."

It was the base of the island, thrust up thousands of years ago, the lower base of the volcano that leveled off for four miles until reaching the island, where it climbed again.

The coral reef that surrounded the island rose to just feet below the surface for the entire circumference except for the two-hundred-foot section Busch was heading through now. And as he slowly motored in, he realized there was a second ring, which appeared to be volcanic, with several subsurface channels that cut through the lava rock.

The inflow of water through the channels exceeded what the outflow over the two reefs could handle, creating a pressure where the waters were churned up, proving nearly impossible to navigate. With the shallow reefs, ships were thrust upon the sharp rocks and coral, their hulls compromised, sending them to the depths. It was for the same reason Bermuda had nearly four hundred sunken ships ringing its island, captains unaware of the forbidden beauty that lurked just beneath the blue waters.

Busch understood why the island had remained uncharted. The compass correction sent people away from the island while those who sought it out or happened upon it were soon shattered upon the rocks and coral, pulled to the depths, dying before they had the chance to tell their tale.

Busch held tight to his course, ensuring the picture and the image of the island remained lined up. Watching his depth gauge, he could see the ocean floor climbing, while on the side-scan radar, images of the deadly coral reefs loomed on either side, seemingly in wait to tear open the hull.

Busch held tight to the wheel as the heavy seas tossed them about, desperately trying to force them toward death.

A half-mile from shore, the seas began to calm. Busch checked his gauges and turned the ship hard to port, circling about the island again. It was like a rat's maze as he weaved through the hazards.

He finally made the other side of the island and could see the mouth of the river ahead, a natural channel carved from the depths, the river's flow dredging away the silt and buildup. The waters again grew rough from the delta, where the ocean and fresh water met.

Busch pressed the throttle and muscled the boat toward the mouth of the river.

IT WAS TRULY a jungle, like something out of an adventure story: a rain forest thick with vegetation, dense trees, heavy foliage, bushes, and vines. The sound of wildlife filled the air, the songs of birds, the screech of mammals.

The river wound through the jungle, the lone roadway

to the heart of the island. It flowed outward at a gentle pace, the crystal-clear waterway teeming with fish. Suddenly, a heavy downpour turned the river into a boiling froth, the air into flowing sheets of water that prevented them from seeing past the bow of the boat. But as quickly as the rain had come, it ended, the humidity level surging. Steam poured off the rocks and trees as the river seemed to swell.

Shots rang out, strafing the side of the boat. Jon dove for cover behind the bulkhead, peering out to see the shooter lying prone across a tree branch at the river's edge. Michael, Busch, and Simon grabbed their guns but were waved off by Jon as he crawled back to the pilothouse, grabbed his rifle, and climbed the interior ladder to the second deck.

Jon lay out on the deck, propped his rifle up in front of him, and peered through the scope. The man, dressed in black pants and a black T-shirt, lay there, no doubt, believing he was protected by the jungle, clutching a Heckler & Koch PDA rifle, military issue. And as the man leaned forward, placing his eyes against the sight, it was too late.

Jon pulled the trigger and the right side of the man's head exploded, his body tumbling from the branch to the jungle floor.

LUCAS'S SHIP THREADED through the needle of the narrow channel, cutting through the waves, the front- and side-scan radar illuminating the precarious passage. Finally making it to calmer waters, they began to loop around the island.

Lucas had summoned Annie out on deck, and they watched in silence as the ship rode around the island, neither saying a word until . . .

"Were you planning on killing me now or after we got to the island?" Lucas said suddenly to Annie.

Annie stared at the island, doing everything she could not to give herself away. "I don't understand."

"Oh, yes, you do. You and Jon are lovers—that is not a secret. The reason he left me was out of fear, and the reason he is now with them is money, treasure, the things that are rumored to be here. And his radioing you? That was to keep you safe, to ensure your arrival on time so he could get you cured."

"You hired me, I shot that young man on the streets of New York, putting myself in danger. I kidnapped KC Ryan, persuaded her to help me in Spain, ensured her compliance in the Forbidden City, killed others along the way. I even stole back the compass to decode your map—"

"Which you failed at—"

"I've done everything you hired me for. I've killed, stolen, put my life in danger, and yet you poisoned me."

"A dying man—or in your case, woman—becomes more than resourceful. I needed someone who shared my motivation," Lucas said. "When time is ticking and death is seconds away, one pulls rabbits out of hats every time. Wouldn't you agree?"

"You tried to kill me."

"Oh, no, not tried," Lucas said. "Shortly, I will succeed unless you share in what I'm about to retrieve."

Lucas paused. "How's the pain, by the way? I don't know about you, but it's crawling up my spine."

"You're a son of a bitch."

"That I am, so if you want this son of a bitch to save you, tell me how you were going to try to kill me. What was it going to be, gun, knife, tossing me overboard, or something more elegant?"

Lucas opened up a large duffel bag and withdrew a black-scabbarded *jian*; he folded his hand about the leather-wrapped hilt and withdrew it, turning the polished double-edged blade over in the air.

And without warning, Lucas snapped the blade like a whip, stopping its point upon Annie's heart. "Elegant, wouldn't you say? But you prefer other means, I know, so what was it going to be?"

Lucas pushed the point slightly forward, cutting through her shirt, nicking her skin.

"A bullet to the head," Annie said. "Dump you overboard."

"Clean, no body." Lucas nodded in approval. "Now, tell me, how would you like to die?"

BUSCH DROPPED ANCHOR by the right bank of the river.

"Look," Jon said as he peered through binoculars from the upper deck at the front of the boat.

Busch put his own field glasses to his eyes and focused them upriver toward a wide lagoon. It was large, but the edge of a dock could be seen to the right, though it was mostly obscured by jungle. In the distance, beyond the white beach, were the footings of a large building.

"Look left, by the edge of the river," Jon said.

Busch scanned the area, finally seeing a lone man, shirtless, sitting in the sun. His hair was dark, and there was a hint of Asian heritage in him—then suddenly he turned, almost looking directly at Busch.

"Holy shit," Busch whispered.

Michael and Simon crawled up on deck beside them.

"Who is that?" Michael asked. "Xiao?"

"No tattoos," Jon said.

"Lucas?" Simon said.

"How the hell did he get here before us?"

Jon continued to study him through his binoculars. "Oh, my God."

LUCAS STOOD ON the bow, wiping a trickle of blood from his nose as he unbuttoned his dark shirt.

Annie stood behind him, leaning against the wheel-house.

"Do you want to live?" Lucas asked Annie, though not turning her way.

Annie remained silent. Her body was beginning to ache; her head pounded with a headache like she had never known. And while the symptoms would subside, she knew they would come back stronger, again and again, until she could no longer stand it, until it finally consumed her and she was released into death.

She thought of her mother, of the pain she had endured, of her sister and grandmother, of all the women in her life dying before the age of thirty. She thought of how she herself had feared death all of her life, had made herself hard, strong, seemingly invincible. And now, months shy of her thirtieth birthday, her once healthy, strong body had been poisoned by this man. She thought of fate and how no matter what she did she couldn't escape it . . . Staring her demise in the face, she broke. She would do whatever it took to save herself, whatever it took to overcome the curse that had befallen all of the women in her family.

"Yes," Annie said. "I want to live."

"And you will do what I ask when we arrive?" Lucas removed his button-down shirt, revealing a white long-sleeve shirt beneath it.

"Yes," Annie said.

"Then I will let you live." Lucas removed his undershirt, baring his torso. It was a tapestry of color, an enormous demon dragon, its teeth bared in attack, its bloodshot eyes filled with death, that horrifically wrapped his torso, shoulder, and arms. Bloody gauze dangled from his muscled stomach, revealing a large burn at his waist; fresh, raw scar tissue melted his skin, corrupting the tattoo into a vision that terrified Annie.

But not as much as the realization of whom she had been working for, answering to for the last several days. She'd thought she had been hired by the colonel and was working with the support of the U.S. government on a deep-cover mission, but it had all been a ruse. She knew they were brothers, knew the death wish they had for each other. She had simply thought she was working for Isaac Lucas, not his brother. She'd thought she was killing for a noble cause, not for some vainglorious head of a Triad, a ruthless man who was far more lethal than she was.

He reached in his duffel bag and withdrew a black box. He laid it upon the deck table in front of Annie. It was etched with a dragon entwined in battle with a snarling tiger, the black lacquer finish dazzling in the midday sun. He ran his fingers over the design and the lid popped open to reveal a black porcelain bottle.

"So small, yet so deadly," he said, holding up the small bottle. "Something we can both attest to. Selective extermination. Dropped into the food stores of a military base, devastating; poured into a city's water supply . . .

"And yet the virus brought on by the Dragon's Breath is not contagious; mother nature at her finest. Once we arrive at the island, once I have the Tears of the Phoenix, I will hold the power of life and death in my hands. The power of gods and emperors."

Jacob Lucas finally turned and stared out at the open sea.

Annie had been told he was dead, had never heard anything to the contrary; she'd heard he had burned to death while going down with a ship. But the news of his death had been premature. For the man known as Xiao was standing before her, and she had just pledged herself to him.

CHAPTER 57

"You've been working for the enemy, a terrorist," Busch said as he laid his gun down beside him. He was huddled in the back of the boat with Michael, Simon, and Jon.

"I had no idea," Jon replied.

"Really?" Busch snapped.

"He fooled us all."

"How?" Michael asked.

"Does it matter?" Simon asked.

"I don't care who he is," Busch said. "It doesn't change the fact that he wants us all dead."

"Xiao isn't just looking for a cure for himself," Simon said. "He's looking to master the Dragon's Breath. And there's plenty more of that here. In the hands of someone like him—"

Busch picked up his gun and said to Simon, "It doesn't change the fact that when I see him, I'll kill him."

MICHAEL STOOD OVER KC, who was slowly waking; her skin had gone pale, taking on a gray hue as life slipped from her body. Her deterioration was accelerating;

Michael could see the pain in her eyes as she struggled to move. He rubbed her head, her shoulders, did whatever he could to comfort her.

"I'm so sorry," KC said, forcing a smile.

"Hey, nothing to be sorry about," Michael said as he handed her a mug of hot tea.

She wrapped her hands around the warm mug and struggled to sit up.

"Stay where you are. You need to rest, conserve your energy."

"I'm fine," KC said. She looked Michael over, noting he was dressed in black, a pistol in a shoulder holster, his knife at his side. "Going for a moonlight stroll without me?"

"I need you to stay here, sit tight, no lights. I'll be back in a few."

Michael kissed her warmly, slowly, letting his feelings pour into her.

"I look awful," KC whispered, inches from his face.

"Not to me," Michael said.

"Where are you going?"

"I'm going to do what I do best." Michael smiled. "I'm going to go steal your life back."

NIGHTTIME HAD FALLEN over the jungle. Michael and Simon moved up the right bank of the river while Busch and Jon came up the left. They were well armed, guided by moonlight, radios in their ears.

"Tell me we have a plan," Busch said through his ear-mounted radio to Michael. He adjusted the sniper rifle strapped to his back and patted the pistol at his side, a force of habit from his days as a cop.

"Yeah, to find the thing that is going to save KC," Michael whispered.

"Okay, just two more questions. How and what is it?"

"We're doing the how, and I have no idea what 'it' is."

They quietly walked in parallel on either side of the river. A quarter-mile up and around the bend, the river opened into a large lagoonlike lake. On the east side, a large waterfall cascaded into the lagoon, carrying water from the volcanic mountain above, churning up the water before flowing out to sea.

Jon and Busch arrived at the jungle's edge, a white sandy beach before them. The embers of a fire still glowed where the real Colonel Lucas had been sitting an hour earlier.

As they looked across the beach, they saw a large temple upon a white dais, set back fifty yards from the water's edge, its windows flame-lit from within. Though it was covered in the shadow of the mountain behind it, there was no mistaking its Chinese heritage: its multitiered sloped roof, its red hue, the small dragons resting upon the eaves.

But their attention was quickly drawn to the ship in the dock. It was a naval vessel, seventy-five feet long, brilliantly aglow in a wash of halogen light. There was a single sentry on the bow, his feet up on the rail as he read a book.

But then they saw the ships in the surrounding docks and their collective breath was taken away: It was a collection of oceangoing vessels worthy of any sea museum.

An enormous Chinese junk with furled sails; a Spanish galleon torn from history. A paddlewheel steamer that looked like something you'd find Mark Twain upon, an old merchant ship, and a Japanese war boat from World War II.

"Did you get a load of these boats?" Busch said into his microphone.

"Yeah," Michael answered back from the other side of the river.

"That Chinese junk is nearly six hundred years old," Simon said. "It doesn't stay in shape like that without someone maintaining it."

"You see the sentry at the bow?" Jon asked.

"Yeah, one more at the stern," Simon said.

"Do you want me to take them?" Jon asked.

"No, no need to kill anyone unless we're in danger," Simon said. "I'll deal with them. We need to figure out how many more are here."

"We've got movement on the junk," Jon said.

"Can't see it from here," Busch answered.

A shadow came down the gangplank onto the docks.

"I don't think that is one of Lucas's men," Busch said.

A large Chinese man walked across the moonlit courtyard, his black hair pulled back in a ponytail. He was barrel-chested and commanding, dressed in a loose-fitting black robe.

"That's impossible . . ." Jon whispered, looking closely.

"What's impossible?" Busch said.

"That's Zheng He."

CHAPTER 58

The gun's muzzle landed at the back of the sentry's ear, startling him.

"We're not here to cause problems," Simon whispered, urging the man to stand up from his chair at the bow of the naval vessel.

The soldier was young, tanned, relaxed, and foolish. Simon took the gun from the holster at his waist and guided him to the back of the boat, where Michael had the other soldier.

Simon led them into the ship, staying three feet back, out of their range of counterattack.

"How many are on the island?"

The two soldiers remained silent as they kept walking.

Simon directed them down the stairs to the engine room and forced them through the open door. "We'll be back soon," he said as he closed the door behind them, spinning the wheel lock tight. He pulled a strand of rope from the bag at his side and secured the wheel lock from spinning.

MICHAEL AND SIMON stepped up on the deck of the Spanish galleon. Her deck was clean, as if ready to head out to sea, her sails furled, the stitching of numerous patches evident on her canvas.

The ship was smaller than images Michael had been bombarded with all his life and was dwarfed by the Chinese junk in the neighboring slip, but nonetheless was spectacular in its detail and craftsmanship, seeming to jump out of some painting of the Spanish Armada.

Busch came from belowdecks. "Follow me." And he turned back down the stairs.

"You found Lucas?" Michael asked. Simon was right behind him.

"Yep," Busch said as he squeezed down an impossibly narrow stairway into a hold, his head scraping the ceiling.

Michael came down the stairs, focused on Busch, Simon taking up the rear. "What the hell is he doing down here?"

But Busch didn't answer; he merely turned and looked across the room. Michael and Simon followed his line of sight and inhaled in shock.

Before them were twenty chests, five of them wide open, overflowing with pieces of eight, gold ingots, sparkling jewels. "Do you realize what this is worth?"

Michael turned to him. Though he was amazed at the find, he was focused on saving KC. "This is great, but where's Lucas?"

Busch nodded and led him back up the two flights of stairs to the main deck. "There's a lot more going on on this island than I think any of us suspect."

"Yeah, like what is a Spanish galleon doing in the South Pacific?" Simon asked as they walked along the deck toward the stern.

Busch opened the door to the captain's quarters and ushered Simon and Michael in. The suite was small, though larger than any other space on the ship. It was well appointed in dark wood and thick, aged carpets; a large bed abutted the port wall, while a teak table sat in the middle of the room with several goblets and pewter plates filled with fruits.

Leaning against the far wall was Jon, his gun pointed at the man standing at the large span of ornate windows that overlooked the jungle.

It was Lucas, but not the same Lucas who had captured him, who had used him, who had poisoned KC; there were subtle differences in his posture, in the wrinkles at his eyes, the stresses of life etched just slightly differently on the same canvas.

"Colonel Lucas?" Michael asked.

"Yes," Lucas said. His voice was deep, matching the voice that Michael had come to know over the last week.

"My name is Michael St. Pierre."

"Where are my men?"

"They're safe, locked in the engine room of your ship, though they're feeling a little embarrassed," Simon said.

"We don't mean you harm," Michael said. "But someone very close to me is dying, poisoned by your brother."

The real Colonel Lucas nodded. "No offense to you or them, but why should I care?"

Busch pulled out his pistol and held it to Lucas's head. "I take extreme offense at that—"

"Besides our holding you at gunpoint," Michael interrupted Busch, "you should care because your brother is on his way here to kill you."

Lucas smiled.

"I'm glad you find that funny."

"If he's on his way, it means he's dying."

"The same poison in his veins is in my girlfriend's."

Lucas considered Michael, unfazed by the guns pointed at him.

"Is there a cure?" Michael asked.

"Yes," Lucas answered without delay.

"It's here?" Michael asked, an urgency in his voice. "You know it works?"

"Of course."

"How do you know?" Simon asked.

Lucas paused before his tone changed. "Because I'm standing here alive."

Busch lowered his pistol.

"Please . . ." Michael looked into Lucas's eyes. "I can't let her die."

Lucas turned and looked back at Jon, who still aimed a gun at his back. "You can lower your weapon."

Jon looked at Michael and let the gun fall to his side.

"You know your brother assumed your identity?" Jon said. "I thought I was working for you, as did a number of people."

"I didn't know," Lucas said. "The son of a bitch left me for dead."

"On the *Gentlemen's Den*?" Michael asked.

"Yeah, how did you know?"

"Because I was there," Michael said.

"Really? Were you the one who cracked the safe?"

Michael nodded.

"That pissed my brother off something awful."

"But I saw you tie him up; I saw you pilot your boat away."

"You sure?" Lucas asked with a turn of his head.

Lucas looked at Michael for a moment. "Imagine the shame, the embarrassment of an army colonel having a brother who is a gang lord, a terrorist. No one ever suspected; Interpol, our government, everyone had him down as full-blooded Chinese.

"Over the years, when time allowed, I looked for him without success. A month ago intel started to percolate that he was planning something international, something to do with me, Zheng He, and a book. When I heard that, I suspected it concerned something our father had found. A diary and this island and something called Dragon's Breath. I had a team looking for him and picked up his trail ten days ago.

"He knew we were behind him that night in Italy; he knew I had no intention of bringing him back alive. And on reflection, I realized he leaked the intel on himself to draw me there, to draw me to him, so he could steal the book and take my place.

"I captured him, his men were dead. He knelt on the floor before me."

Michael remembered it all, how he had watched as Lucas slipped the bag over his brother's head.

"But then how did he escape?"

"I had my gun held on him, and I approached him from behind to tie his hands. I was foolish; I should have just shot him dead.

"Though we are identical twins, his training is far superior—martial arts, swords, exotic weapons—he possesses an almost inhuman speed. My arrogance blinded me.

"As I leaned down over him, he attacked. Though he was blindfolded, he knew exactly where I was. He struck out, hitting me in the throat, swiping out my legs. He ripped the bag from his head and stood over me.

"He pulled out the black Chinese puzzle box and, running his fingers around it, opened it, extracting a black porcelain bottle, sealed within the puzzle box for centuries.

"He grabbed my jaw with his powerful hand, squeezing my mouth open, and poured in a single drop. It tasted like nothing; I wasn't sure if it had actually entered my mouth. He placed the small bottle on the table.

"He stood above me, all proud, in the same manner as I had with him. And I jumped up, driving my head into his jaw, the force knocking him back and nearly out.

"I grabbed his sword from the deck; I dipped the tip in the black bottle on the table, coating it. I raised it above my head, bringing it down, but somehow he caught the blade in midflight, his hand wrapped in his shirt slapping the sword, trapping it between his flattened palms . . .

"Ripping the sword from my hand, he twisted me to the ground, trussing my hands in front of me.

"Then he saw the wound on his hand. It was just a nick, a barely visible cut, but he knew he'd been poisoned. And he smiled. It was as if the plan blossomed in his mind right there. He took his sword and cut off his ponytail. He stripped the shirt from my back; he put on my hat, picked up my gun, and stole my identity.

"He threw the bag over my head and left me to die. He wasn't about to wait for the poison to work its way through my system; he was going to blow me up with the ship.

"He carried my dead crew to our boat, silent witnesses whose presence, combined with his identical appearance, left no doubt to command that he was Colonel Lucas. I struggled out of the hood, but was unable to free my bound hands. I leaped into the sea moments before the ship exploded. I nearly drowned before freeing my binds. Finally made it to shore. I didn't have much time to find this island and find the cure."

"But you never saw the compass or the book," Busch said.

"My father had a copy of the map and pictures of the island. He sailed for countless years searching for the island where he had been stranded so many years before, never knowing the island would always elude him."

"How did you get here?"

"I don't care how mysterious this island is, how it can hide from a compass, disturb radio signals; it can't hide from a satellite. I had a computer extrapolate the aerial image, matched it up to reconnaissance photos, and plotted a course. It took me three days to find it; I missed the island by fifty miles the first time, seventy the second, before I realized the compass problem.

"Zheng He's diary was stolen from this island over five hundred years ago along with the red and black puzzle boxes containing the compass and the vial of Dragon's Breath. It was taken from here by an assassin, one of Zheng He's most trusted men, who thought it would sustain China's greatness.

"Arriving back in the Forbidden City after ten years, he told the world that Zheng He had died at sea, his ship lost to the depths.

"He delivered the diary, the compass, and the Dragon's Breath as proof of the island's magic to the child emperor, Zhu Qizhen, known as the Zhengtong Emperor, the great-grandson of the Yongle Emperor. But as the emperor was all of sixteen, having assumed the throne at eight, he was advised by a very wise eunuch by the name of Wang Zhen.

"Fearing the book and the poison might fall into enemy hands—and in the state of the young emperor's court at that time, anyone could be an enemy—Wang Zhen sealed the three items in a textile box in the bowels of the Forbidden City, hoping they would be hidden away forever.

"Of course, sadly, forever is not that long a period of time." Lucas paused a moment, reflecting. "And here we all are. I was near death when I arrived here."

"You look pretty good to me," Busch said. "So where is this bottle of liquid life?"

"It's in the temple. You're going to have to take your girlfriend there and convince the man within the temple to save her." Lucas changed his tone. "You say my brother is on his way?"

"He's off course," Michael said, "but I don't doubt he'll figure out the route."

"Well, then, perhaps it would be a good idea to let

my men go," Lucas said. "And we'd better take care of your girlfriend before my brother, Jacob, shows up with guns blazing."

A LARGE TILED courtyard led from the deep lagoon to a white dais, upon which sat a building from the past. The deep red structure was capped with a two-tiered sloped roof of yellow tile. Light blue and yellow accent bands wrapped the arches and the molding between the first and second roof lines. It was as if the building had been plucked from the Forbidden City and positioned according to feng shui right in the middle of the jungle, the body of water in front, the mountain to the rear.

"This design is ancient," Simon said to Lucas.

Lucas nodded. "That's not the half of it."

As the two stepped inside, it was as if an echo manifested: The interior space was open and grand, dozens of red columns supporting the roof. Looking up, Simon saw a coffered ceiling, intricately designed, again with blue and gold accents, an individual dragon within each panel, meticulously done by hand. There were multiple rooms surrounding the central great room, ancillary living spaces.

And to the rear were three large doors, the two outer doors closed while the central one was open, revealing a dark, flame-lit tunnel.

Lucas turned to the right and led Simon down a long hallway, the walls decorated in Chinese silkscreen, images of cranes and rivers and the fairytalelike mountains in Guilin and Zhangjiajie, until they arrived at a dark red door.

With a simple knock, Lucas opened the door and directed Simon inside. Four middle-aged men, dressed in loose-fitting dark clothes, their Asian faces hailing from different regions of the continent, sat at a table. Their conversation abruptly halted as Simon and Lucas entered.

Sitting at a large table was a Chinese man painting an intricate oil landscape. He was large, wrapped in a long dark robe, his long black hair pulled into a ponytail. Around his neck was an ornate square piece of ivory, a dragon and a tiger entwined in battle etched into its face—a symbol Simon had seen frequently throughout Zheng He's diary.

But what Simon recognized even more clearly was the face of the man; he had seen it countless times throughout the diary. The orange peel–rough skin, the deep, piercing eyes, the broad cheeks.

As impossible as it was, he was looking at Zheng He.

CHAPTER 59

The small Zodiac rode down the dark river, cutting through the night as Busch manned the outboard engine; the jungle was alive with shadows and calls of the wild as shafts of moonlight pierced the canopy. Jon sat next to Busch while Michael was on the center bench, a sense of relief growing in him that KC would live. Despite his words of confidence, the optimism he tried to impart, he had feared her death; he had feared he would lose her just as he had lost Mary. But now . . . knowing Lucas had survived, his hope was renewed.

Lucas's men stood on the bow of the naval boat, watching as they headed downriver. Michael had released them from the engine room with apologies to both of them and to Isaac Lucas; though they understood, residual anger still hung in their eyes at being captured by a man twice their age.

"The Japanese ship?" Jon said.

"Yeah," Busch answered as he looked around the passing jungle.

"I bet that's Yamashita's gold."

"Family friend?" Busch joked.

"He was a Japanese general," Jon said. "He was the

first convicted of war crimes and executed at the end of the war. But the boat carrying his namesake treasure was lost. Men have spent fortunes in search of it."

"Well, if you feel like driving that boat out of here when we leave, I have no problem with it," Busch said.

"Seriously?" Jon asked with a half-smile.

"Fine with me," Michael said. "As long as KC's okay, I don't care what happens to any of the ships."

It was less than four minutes before they spotted their boat up ahead, unlit, looking more like a large outcropping, but as they got closer, pulling adjacent to the ship, Busch's eyes filled with concern. "Oh, shit."

And that's when they saw the second boat directly behind it, at anchor.

Michael leaped from the Zodiac, Busch behind him, guns drawn.

Michael scrambled up on deck and ran through the doors, through the salon down into the stateroom, but KC wasn't there.

"KC?" Michael called out.

And as the seconds ticked by, dread began to fill his heart. He raced around the lower level, up to the main salon, but there was no one there.

KC was gone.

"Nǐ hǎo. Wǒmen de yìsi shì nǐ de shānghài," Simon said in Chinese, greeting the large man and his companions, telling them he meant no harm.

The men didn't respond, the tension in the room palpable. Their eyes turned to the large man who was painting.

"If you meant no harm," the robust man responded in Chinese as he pointed to Simon's holstered pistol, "why do you come bearing weapons?"

"Protection from the unknown," Simon answered.

"Are you afraid of the unknown?" The man laid down his brush.

"No, just cautious, prepared."

"Your friend beside you arrived two days ago." The man stood from his chair; he was nearly as large as Busch. "He said he meant us no harm, yet one of his men killed one of our friends."

Simon looked at Lucas. "He said a member of your team killed one of his men."

"It was an accident." Lucas bowed his head in contrition. "You can tell him that the man who committed the act has died."

"How?"

"He was the man you shot from your boat when you sailed upriver."

Simon turned back to the man and continued in Chinese, "I'm sorry, as is Colonel Lucas. He wants you to know the man who killed your friend is dead."

"An exchange of death should give no man comfort." The large man shook his head.

"My name is Simon."

"San Bao." The man's robust voice echoed in his chest.

"Are you a man of faith?" Simon asked, looking at his mode of dress.

"I believe in many things, if that's what you mean." San Bao smiled. "Are you a man of faith?"

"I am a priest."

"Yet you travel with a gun."

Simon nodded. "I never said I was a saint."

San Bao smiled broadly, his face relaxing, which seemed to ease the tension of the other men in the room.

"Is your name truly San Bao . . . ?" Simon asked.

The man shook his head and smiled. "Your friend who has no idea what we are saying asked the same question."

"Are you a monk?"

"Just a man."

"You've been here a long time?" Simon looked around the room. It was simple: Shelves lined the wall, porcelain jars dotted with various inks and paints covering their surfaces. There was a large window facing the waterfall, the image seeming like something out of a dream.

"I've been here the majority of my life."

"Then you know this island better than anyone who's read a book."

"Depends on the book."

"Is this Penglai?" Simon asked.

"Ah, children's books. For a man of the cloth you sound like you believe that the legends are reality as opposed to allegory. You are a Christian?"

"Yes."

"If you found a beautiful garden with an apple tree in the middle and a snake within its branches, would you assume that was Eden?"

"Point taken," Simon said. "A woman with us is infected by the Dragon's Breath."

"For how long?"

"Five days. She is dying."

"Life is finite," San Bao said.

"Is it?" Simon said as he looked at the man, allowing the question to linger. "There is someone else coming to this island, and he is dangerous."

"It's getting very crowded on this island."

"That man is also poisoned and seeks the cure you used on this man, but I'm afraid his methods of procuring it will be violent."

San Bao stared at Simon. "There is a cure, but only enough for one, it is all that remains. Your friend arrived infected, came with guns, demanded to be cured, and as I just told you, one of his men killed my friend before we cured him. He is a man of war; when he leaves this island, will he be bringing death to others? Imagine when a man of medicine saves a murderer, and that murderer kills again. Is the man of medicine culpable? Does he have blood on his hands because he saved an agent of death?"

"This woman is innocent," Simon said, "as kind and giving as anyone I have ever known. By saving her, you will make the world a better place. I will not take this cure from you, but I will beg you . . ."

San Bao stared at Simon.

Outside, in the distance, gunfire erupted.

BUSCH TURNED THE Zodiac around and drove upstream; no one said a word as they tied up to the dock and cut the engine. The world around them was silent; the sounds of jungle wildlife had disappeared as if something dangerous, more vicious had arrived. And then shots rang out, bursts of gunfire, coming from the deck of the naval ship, shattering the night.

Michael ran up against the hull of the naval boat, taking cover as Busch and Jon raced for the woods.

And as quickly as the gunfire had started, it stopped. There was no movement, no voices, just the lapping of the water against the hull of the boat. Michael held tightly to his gun, craned his neck up, and peered onto the deck to see nothing but death.

Lucas's men lay motionless on the steel-gray deck, a pool of blood forming around them, their heads lying at their sides, separated from their bodies.

"He's here," Michael whispered into his microphone as he ducked back down.

But Michael fell to silence when he saw Simon and Lucas emerge from the temple, guns at their backs, stripped of their weapons, escorted by two men. And he heard the footstep behind him.

Michael turned to see a large Asian, dressed in black, two-fisting a Sig Sauer at him.

FLAMES DANCED TO life aboard the Chinese junk, their orange glow painting the night, casting enormous shadows along the water.

Xiao sat in a large ornate captain's chair, his shirt off, the horrific tattoos on his body seeming alive in the glow of the dancing firelight. Behind him, lying upon the deck, was KC, her eyes closed, her body shivering. Annie stood above her, her eyes bloodshot and sallow as she pointed her pistol at KC's head.

Michael, Simon, and Lucas were forced across the deck at gunpoint by Xiao's three men.

Xiao and Lucas locked eyes, a world of hate flowing between them.

"You look a breath away from death," Isaac Lucas said.

Xiao stood up and circled his brother. Though his face was pale and blood was encrusted about his nostrils, he showed no sign of pain in his movements. In his left hand dangled his *jian*, which he held close to his side as he appraised his brother. "Despite your survival, I think you're closer to death than I."

"Maybe, but you won't be far behind me." Lucas smiled.

"Was there anyone else in the temple?" Xiao said to his men, who silently shook their heads in response.

"Well"—Xiao turned back to Lucas—"seeing your condition, it's here and you didn't just find it on your own. So, before you make me resort to the things that bring me pleasure, why don't you tell me where the Phoenix Tears are?"

Lucas shook his head. "Not a chance."

"Oh, there's every chance—"

Without warning, two gunshots exploded from the jungle and one of Xiao's guards fell dead upon the deck.

BUSCH AND JON were at the jungle's edge, Busch's eye tucked in the scope of a rifle, Jon holding tight to his HK.

They had leaped from the Zodiac when the gunfire erupted on the naval ship, splitting off from Michael into the jungle only to emerge and see Michael, Simon, and Lucas being escorted across the dock and up onto the Chinese junk.

They quickly took up position fifty yards away under the safety of the jungle canopy, Busch kicking out the legs of the sniper rifle, adjusting the scope as Jon called out the targets.

"Three guards."

"One down." Busch lined up his sight and with a single bullet took the man down with ease.

Busch spun the gun sight onto Annie, who was ducking down, scanning the jungle, her gun still pointed at KC. "Smile for me, you bitch—"

And out of the corner of his eye, Busch saw Jon turning his gun on him. Without a thought, Busch let go of his rifle and grabbed the barrel of Jon's gun, thrusting it upward as he drove his fist into Jon's face, crushing his massive weight into the blow, sending the younger man to the jungle floor. Busch was enraged that Jon had used them, pissed off that he hadn't listened to his instincts and dumped him back on the mainland.

But Jon quickly recovered, rolling back. Though he was dazed, his left foot snapped out and caught Busch in the ribs, a loud crack echoing through the jungle. He spun in and delivered a quick series of jabs and strikes, pummeling Busch's head and torso, quick, precise, each blow placed to slowly take the larger man down.

Busch hated martial arts: the elegant dancelike moves, the philosophy behind each kick or punch. He preferred street fighting, boxing, and brute force. Now, he unleashed it all, his fury pouring through his fists. He drove Jon back, pounding upon him with blow after blow. And though Jon was able to block every other punch, it didn't matter, for Busch's six-foot-four size leveraged through blows that made contact, weakened him, driving him back into the ground.

"You son of a bitch," Busch said as he stood over Jon, catching his breath as he stared down at the bloodied man. He looked up to see the deck of the Chinese junk empty except for the dancing flames; everyone had run for cover.

And as he looked back down, he cursed himself for not listening to his instincts, for allowing his judgment to be clouded—and cursed himself again, for Jon had slipped away.

XIAO GRABBED KC by the hair and hoisted her up into a headlock, his other hand holding the *jian* to her throat. He dragged her across the deck, her feet struggling to keep up.

"If your friend takes one more shot, she dies."

Michael turned to the woods, held up his hands, and shook his head. Annie and the two surviving guards were ten feet behind Michael, Simon, and Lucas, their guns forcing them to follow Xiao down the gangway.

Jon appeared on the dock, his face bloodied as he walked past everyone to Annie. "Are you okay?"

Annie shook her head, her once-dark eyes fading, her face filled with pain.

Xiao stared at Jon. "You've betrayed everyone: me, them, even Annie. I think your death is the one thing we could all agree on. But . . . not yet."

"Isaac," Xiao said. "Please take me to the man who cured you or I will start killing these people, starting with this lovely blonde."

CHAPTER 60

They walked up the white walkway and entered the temple. Xiao's two guards and Jon fanned out down the halls in search.

"Incredible," Xiao said. "A monument to the past, how touching."

Moments later, the guards led four Chinese men through the central chamber to Xiao.

"Which of you controls the Phoenix Tears?" Xiao asked in Chinese.

The four similarly dressed men stayed silent, eyes cast down.

"None of these is the man in charge," Xiao barked at his men. He turned to Lucas and switched to English. "Where is he?"

"I have no idea," Lucas said.

"We searched every room," one of Xiao's men said.

"Except that one," Xiao said as he pointed at the three rear doors and began walking, everyone following him. Unlike the palaces within the Forbidden City, the rear doors of the structure did not open to another courtyard; they led to a flame-lit cavern, a tunnel that crawled back into the volcanic mountain.

As they passed through the center doorway into a dark tunnel, it became clear the passage had not been excavated but rather had been there for hundreds if not thousands of years. It was a volcanic vent, the walls and ceiling like black glass, made of rapidly cooled lava. The torches reflected off the black obsidian like a mirror, refracting about the space in an eerie manner.

As Michael looked up, he could see stars in the ceiling sparkling, winking at him. And he knew what he was staring at; this being a volcanic vent, a passage into the depths of the planet, it was dotted with diamonds, like the great mines of Africa; it was within the tubes of volcanoes where the rich man's crystal was carried up from the depths.

They continued forward until the tunnel opened up into a large cavern, a dead end where a clear pool of water rested on the far side, smooth as glass.

"You've got to be kidding me," Jon said. "So, what? He just swam away?"

"Who?" Xiao asked.

"Zheng He."

Xiao didn't react as he released KC. Michael raced toward her, but the guards held him back as Xiao walked about the cavern.

Isaac Lucas looked at Annie. "You're infected, too?"

Annie stared at Lucas but remained silent.

"Did you think you were working for me, for the U.S. government?" Lucas asked in a whisper.

Annie's silence answered his question.

"He used you, manipulated you," Lucas said, trying to get Annie to react. "And he's going to kill you. I know the pain you are in; I was infected. The pain gets far worse. Look at her."

Lucas pointed at KC, who lay on the rocky ground next to them, shivering, her face pale.

"You should both know that the Phoenix Tears exist, but there is only enough to save one life, and my brother has never been very good at sharing."

"Isaac," Xiao shouted from across the cavern as he stood before the pool of water. "Is that where he went?"

"That pain's feeling real good," Isaac replied. "I can hear it in your voice."

"You decide who you want me to kill first," Xiao threatened.

It was a long moment as everyone looked at Isaac.

"Yes," Lucas relented. "That's where he went."

"I'll go," Jon quickly volunteered.

"No, you get back to the entrance and make sure no one else comes in here," Xiao ordered, then looked at Simon. "You, priest, you're going. You and St. Pierre. You find this man Jon thinks is Zheng He and you bring him back with the Phoenix Tears or I'll start killing everyone, starting with her." Xiao pointed his sword at KC.

"And in case there is any doubt . . ." Xiao grabbed one of San Bao's men from behind and drove his blade through his back, its bloody tip exploding out of his belly. Xiao withdrew the *jian* and kicked the dying man into the water, blood spilling around him. "Just in case there is any doubt how I will do it."

Michael muscled past the guard, trying to get to KC, but the guard grabbed him violently about the neck.

"Let him go," Xiao barked. "Let him speak to her, she's his only motivation."

Michael tore out of the man's grasp and knelt at KC's side. Her eyes were at half-mast, her body shivering. "Hey."

"Hey back," KC whispered.

"You need to hold on, I'll be right back."

KC's eyes opened fully and she forced a smile. "Don't be late."

"I don't think I need to emphasize the urgency," Xiao interrupted. "And be sure he brings a vial of whatever cured my brother. If not, you might as well stay on the other side."

MICHAEL AND SIMON stripped off their shoes, socks, and shirts; the pool was nearly fifty feet wide and seventy feet across. The cavern ceiling sloped down sharply on the far side, descending until it met the surface. Reflections of torchlight danced along the water, reflecting up to illuminate the black volcanic rock, creating an eerie glow that portended something dark on the other side.

They had no idea where they were going, how deep, how far, or if the pool would just lead to an airtight pocket where they would drown.

Michael flipped on his flashlight, dipped it in the water to confirm it was waterproof, and began swimming out. Simon was behind him as they approached the far wall.

"How're your lungs?" Michael asked.

"Nothing like yours, but they'll hold."

Michael ducked his head underwater and shined the light around. The pool was far deeper than he had imagined, at least seventy-five feet down, its bottom a black mirror image of above, with the sparkle of diamonds refracting the light's beam. He swam down ten feet and held his position; the water was cool, fresh, and crystal-clear. He looked about, studying the wall until he found it.

"Okay," Michael said as he surfaced. "There's a tunnel, more like a tube, about fifteen feet down. You ready?"

Simon nodded as they both began to hyperventilate, clearing their lungs, expelling as much CO_2 as they could, inhaling air in gulps, and with a final intake, they dived down.

The beam of Michael's light pierced the water as they descended. Simon was a body length behind Michael, following as Michael disappeared into a narrow tunnel. It was no more than five feet in diameter, an old lava tube, and it felt like swimming through someone's dark nightmare. The tube went on and on, twenty-five feet, fifty feet . . . seventy-five. Michael's light danced about as he pulled and kicked through the water, unable to keep the beam pointed straight. At one hundred feet, Michael began to feel the burn in his lungs; it was low, but he knew it would grow quickly and would spread to his head. But Michael was not concerned for himself. Simon was at least ten years his senior, and while he was in great shape, swimming was not his strong suit.

Michael pulled and kicked with everything he had, but there was no end in sight, the tube seeming to go on forever. And it suddenly occurred to him: What if there was no other passage, what if they were swimming to nowhere? As the fire in his lungs began to burn and dots appeared in front of his eyes, he knew they were past the 150 mark, there was no chance of turning back—and if an exit didn't appear soon they would both drown.

XIAO TURNED TO his two guards. "Keep your eyes on the water. As soon as they surface, kill St. Pierre and the priest, but be sure not to harm the man they bring," Xiao said.

"No," KC screamed, her anguished voice filling the cavern.

"Get her out of here," Xiao said to Annie. "Toss her in one of the rooms to die, and come back here."

"What if she tries to escape?" Annie asked.

Xiao looked at KC in her weakened state, her eyes barely open. "She's having enough trouble just trying to stay alive."

"No, Michael," KC screamed as Annie took her by the arm, pulling her to her feet, and dragged her away.

AN ORANGE GLOW appeared up ahead. With his lungs on fire, Michael wasn't sure if it was an illusion or the manifestation of his pain. He dropped the flashlight and kicked and pulled with everything he had, emerging from the tunnel into another open pool, and made for the surface, his head breaking the water, gasping, coughing, and relishing the air. Two seconds later, Simon burst to the surface.

"My God," Simon gasped. "And we have to head back the same way?"

As Michael crawled out of the water, he couldn't believe his eyes. The cavern was lit in flame: Torches lined the walls, their orange light dancing about the large open area. The ceiling was nearly fifty feet high, and on the rear wall was another temple, smaller than the one outside but equally exquisite, with sweeping roofs and dragon-capped corners, its red walls appearing like fire under the torches' glow.

As Michael and Simon climbed up out of the water, San Bao emerged from the building. He was dressed in loose-fitting black pants and a shirt.

"They have your men," Simon said quickly in Chinese.

San Bao nodded.

"They have killed one already. He said if we don't bring you back with the Phoenix Tears, he will kill the rest of them and our friends."

Without a word, San Bao walked into the small structure and emerged with a small white porcelain jar.

"As I said, there is only enough for one," San Bao told Simon.

"We'll have to worry about that when we get to the other side," Simon said.

BUSCH STOOD OUTSIDE in the nighttime shadows of the Chinese junk. He had watched helplessly from the jungle as his friends were marched into the temple and disappeared.

With his rifle on his back and a Sig Sauer gripped

tight in his hand, he had slipped into the temple and had gone from room to room, but found no one there. The echo of voices came through the black tunnel that sat at the back of the temple; he approached but knew it was certain death to enter, coming up against who knew how many bullets as he emerged on the other side.

So he had gone back up to the ships to formulate a plan.

Suddenly Jon appeared, emerging from the temple door, his gun held high as he began to look about. Busch stayed in the shadows as he watched him walk across the courtyard, along the dock, and up the plank onto the Japanese warship. Jon looked over the rail, shining his flashlight around before slipping below deck.

Busch quietly boarded the ship, and with his gun held before him, made his way across the deck. He removed the rifle from his back, tucking it behind a deck storage box, and followed Jon into the ship. Busch did everything in his power to resist shooting the man, as he knew that somehow there was a way to use him to his advantage.

Noise resounded from the forward hold. Busch made his way down the hall and peered inside to find Jon removing the lid from a large wooden crate, the sixty-five-year-old nails groaning in protest. Jon laid the wooden lid on the ground, and as he shined his flashlight inside the crate, the room exploded in light, the beam refracting off bars of gold. Busch could see Jon's smile in the golden light, his body filling with excitement as he moved from box to box, lifting the lids to find the same sight. There were hundreds of similar crates, filling the entire forward hold.

"This was all about the gold for you," Busch said as he aimed his gun at Jon. "Convincing everyone you were pro-America, convincing your girlfriend you were trying to save her, convincing us you had switched sides."

"Do you know what this is?" Jon said as he kept looking through the boxes, never looking Busch's way. "This cache was one of those military legends of lost riches like Hitler's gold, Alexander's tomb—the only difference is, this is real."

"And you and Annie, you've been together all along?"

"Help me kill Xiao and his men and I'll give you as much of this as you can cart out of here," Jon said as he turned and looked Busch's way.

"What about Annie?"

"What about her?"

"You stopped me from killing her; I saw the two of you together. She looks as sick as KC."

"And she is, but there is only enough cure for one. Help me kill Xiao and you can have the cure for KC, you can save her."

"You'd give Annie up that easily?"

Jon looked at the crates and nodded.

Busch stepped back into the hall as Jon came out of the hold.

"Keep your hands out," Busch said.

"Don't you trust me?" Jon said as he pointed the flashlight at Busch while keeping his other hand open and away from the gun in his holster.

"Never have," Busch said as they emerged on the ship's deck. "Never will."

"Smart," Jon said as he hurled his flashlight at Busch, startling him. Jon immediately leaped into a roundhouse kick, his foot catching the distracted Busch in the hand, knocking his gun from his grasp. Jon spun around, but instead of striking Busch, he drew his own gun, swinging it up as his finger wrapped the trigger.

But Busch was ready, his hand reaching out and grabbing the barrel, twisting it away, tearing it from Jon's grasp. And in a single motion, Busch continued his momentum, picking Jon up, hoisting him over his head. And he threw him over the rail into the lagoon twenty feet below.

Jon hit the water and immediately scrambled for shore, swimming as fast as he could.

Busch turned to the storage locker and grabbed his rifle. He flipped out the legs, resting them on the side rail.

Jon emerged from the lagoon, looked back to see Busch prepping his rifle, and raced toward the temple, running as fast as he could, running for his life.

But this time, Busch stuck with his instincts; there was no hesitation. He rested his eye in the gun sight, quickly focusing on his target; he held his breath and pulled the trigger.

THE BULLET CAUGHT Jon in the left side of his chest, heart-high, a perfect kill shot, the force of the bullet driving him back against the red wall of the building.

And as he crumpled to the ground, unable to move, the world slowly began to fade. There was no epiphany, no sudden understanding of life or ironic moment when the meaning of it all became clear. His thought was the irony that he had found the treasure his Japanese father, the man who had raped his Chinese mother, had helped amass during World War II, and that no one would ever know he had found Yamashita's gold.

SAN BAO ENTERED the water as he tucked the white vial in his pocket.

"We need to catch our breath before we go again," Simon said in Chinese.

"I will meet you on the other side," San Bao said.

"Can you do me a favor, though you owe me nothing?" Simon asked. "Can you not give him that medicine yet, at least wait until we arrive?"

San Bao nodded as he took a single breath and dived under the water.

CHAPTER 61

As Annie and KC walked out of the tunnel and into the temple they heard the single gunshot and saw Jon fall down dead by the door.

Annie charged for him, but KC, despite her condition, grabbed her by the arm and pulled her back.

"You stick your head out that door, it's going to get blown off."

Annie stared at Jon's body and relented.

With no more energy, KC collapsed in the center of the temple's hall. Her body was wracked with pain, every movement was agony, the feel of the air against her skin like a raw fire, the sound of voices like deafening thunder in her ears.

Annie sat down beside KC, staring out toward the door where Jon lay dead. Tears formed in her eyes, which she quickly wiped away, trying to keep KC from seeing them.

"How can you align yourself with Xiao?" KC whispered. "How can you defend him, his false promises? You know we are both going to die. You heard what Lucas said, there is only enough for one."

Annie stared at KC.

"Does that mean Michael has to die, too? Please." KC looked into Annie's eyes.

"Jon is dead," Annie said, more to herself than to KC.

"I know, I'm sorry."

"I just thought . . ." Annie said. "I so wanted to live."

"Me, too." KC nodded, struggling to breathe. Taking a moment to focus. "So after we die, how do you want to be remembered?"

The moment hung in the air, and Annie laid her gun on the ground.

"I'm sorry for what I have put you through," Annie said with her head bowed. "In another life, if things were different, I think we could have been friends."

"Well," KC looked up at Annie, "we're friends now."

Annie looked at KC.

"Will you save Michael?"

ANNIE EXITED THE tunnel to find Xiao in conversation with his brother. San Bao's men were sitting quietly against a wall while the two guards stood at the water's edge, their guns pointed, ready to shoot.

"Is she dead?" Xiao called out.

"Not yet," Annie said.

"Jon's in place?"

"He's at the door." Annie's words were not a lie.

There was a sudden rippling of the water and the two guards held their guns tighter, their fingers going to the triggers.

Annie white-knuckled her pistol, looking around to see everyone's eyes glued on the water, and slowly began to raise the gun.

And San Bao broke the surface, quickly climbing

out of the water, his breathing remarkably under control for a man who had just swum so far.

The two guards' eyes scanned the water, both waiting in anticipation as if it was a contest to get the kill.

Annie kept her gun ready, but Michael didn't surface.

XIAO STARED AT the large man. "You've brought what I've asked?"

San Bao held up the porcelain vial.

Xiao held out his hand. "Give it here."

San Bao was hesitant, looking down at Xiao, unmoving.

And then Xiao whipped his sword up, stopping it an inch from the larger man's throat. Xiao held out his hand again, and this time San Bao complied.

Xiao turned to his brother.

"You just drink it?" Xiao asked.

"Why?" Isaac said to Xiao. "Everything you've done, why?"

"I was stolen away by our mother, thrust into an alien world while you grew up with our father, with the privileges of America."

"You were raised by our mother; you mean to tell me—"

"She was a haunted shell. Your father . . . our father sucked the life out of her and then had her killed."

"So you killed him," Isaac said.

"I merely delivered his deserved fate."

Xiao looked at the white bottle, unsealed it, and

drank the few drops from within. He waited a moment, expecting to feel something. "How long does it take?"

"You stole my life!" Isaac yelled at his brother.

"You have no idea how it repulsed me to wear that uniform. Which reminds me." Xiao reached into his pocket and pulled something out. He held it out for his brother to see.

It was the jade and ivory comb their mother had given to Isaac when she had abandoned him as a child, the one he had given to Pamela, which she always wore.

Isaac's face filled with rage as Xiao held up his sword.

"Despite my wearing your suit, your haircut, she knew instantly, as soon as that elevator door opened. I could see the fear on her face. Have you ever watched someone's eyes as the life escaped them?"

"You son of a bitch." Isaac leaped at his brother, but Xiao was quicker, with the reflexes of a man half his age. Isaac scrambled to grab him, but Xiao simply toyed with him, swinging the *jian* in large graceful arcs.

"Are you done?" Xiao asked as he stopped in his tracks.

"Not in the least," Isaac gasped as he finally got close to his brother.

"Yes, you are." And Xiao swung the sword, cutting off his brother's head.

GUNFIRE SUDDENLY ERUPTED, bullets skipping across the water, the guards furiously shooting.

And without hesitation Annie raised her pistol and

shot both guards in the back of the head. They fell down dead at the water's edge, their guns still clutched in their hands.

Xiao's head snapped around at Annie. "I thought you wished to live?"

"You just drank all there was, so fuck you."

Xiao held up his sword. "Do you think you're quicker than I? Do you think I couldn't make the ten-foot leap and slice that pretty head from your shoulders before you could shoot me down?"

Annie smiled. She knew the answer, but her smile was for something entirely different. She was okay with not living to thirty, joining her mother and sister in death, knowing that the last thing she did was to save the life of the man her friend, KC, loved.

Annie raised her gun, her finger wrapping around the trigger; she much preferred this to the harsh suffering she knew would soon be upon her infected body.

And from his side, Xiao's other hand snapped up and fired a single shot from the gun he held. The bullet caught Annie's forehead. She was dead before she hit the ground.

BUSCH SLOWLY ENTERED the temple to find KC in the middle of the room, unconscious. He scooped her up from the floor, cradled her like a child, and ran out of the building. Down the courtyard and across the beach he ran, up the gangplank of the closest ship, onto the Chinese junk, and to the captain's cabin, kicking in the door.

He laid her on the bed, wiping her blond hair from her face.

"KC," he whispered. "Come on, kiddo, you've got to hold on. You can't leave Michael alone. Don't you dare do it, dammit. He's counting on you."

Busch prayed, he begged, he wished with every part of his being for a miracle. He called on his karma, and his dead father, and every possible intervening force he could think of. And then he realized that he had broken his one rule in life: He had boarded the ship with his right foot. He hoped it wouldn't destroy the chances of his friend's survival.

XIAO TURNED TO the large man who sat silently on the rock.

"My name is Xiao," he spoke in Chinese.

"That is not your birth name," the large man responded in the same dialect. "That sounds like a name a child would dream up."

Xiao suddenly doubled over, wrapping his arms about his tattooed stomach. "Is this how the cure works?"

San Bao stared at him.

"What have you done?"

"You take life; you kill your own brother. And why? What purpose does it serve? Your country, your king, your emperor, your god? None of that. It serves only you. And a man who serves only himself is undeserving of salvation, not only of life on this plane but of life in heaven.

"Your heart is twisted. I'm sure it is filled with pain from some injustice in your childhood, but men overcome those things, they don't blame their circumstances on others—on parents, gods, or fate. Men play out the life that is placed before them, overcoming fear, overcoming shame and adversity." San Bao looked straight into Xiao's eyes. "You are the last person I would give the remedy to."

Xiao exploded with rage, raising the sword above his head. "Give me the cure!"

"I have lived my life, longer and fuller than you could ever dream of doing; I have friends and family awaiting me on the other side. Who awaits you?" He paused. "For you will be dead within minutes from the poison I just gave you, and I believe there is no one awaiting someone like you. You will walk eternity alone."

Xiao brought the blade down, flames dancing off its swiftly moving edge as it hurtled toward San Bao's neck.

But before the blade made contact, a gun exploded. Xiao was hurled back; the *jian* skittered out of his hands, his tattooed chest blossoming with blood.

Michael crawled from the water, gasping for air, clutching the still-smoking gun of the fallen guard who lay by the water. His eyes locked with those of Xiao, who lay upon the ground as his life poured out of the horrific tattooed beast upon his chest.

Simon emerged moments later to see San Bao walking toward his three surviving friends.

And without a word, Michael climbed to his feet and raced out of the cavern.

CHAPTER 62

Michael charged up the gangplank onto the enormous Chinese junk, heading straight into the captain's cabin to find KC upon the bed, Busch at her side. As he looked up at Michael, his eyes said the words his lips couldn't, and he stepped back.

Michael fell to his knees beside her. KC lay there, her breath shallow, her face pale.

"Hey," Michael said, forcing a smile.

"Hey back," KC said, pulling the blanket tight around herself. "I'm so sorry . . ."

Michael placed his fingers to her lips. "Shhh . . ."

"You filled my heart, Michael, you made it whole. Our short time of love was like a lifetime." KC paused, breathing deep. "I will love you, always and forever."

Michael looked down at KC, shocked at her deteriorating state. The color was gone from her face, her once-vibrant green eyes dull like slate, but his love didn't diminish, for it was her heart that he loved, her warmth, and her unselfish ways of putting others first, of filling a room with laughter and smiles when she entered.

"I've been meaning to ask you something," Michael said softly.

KC smiled.

"I meant to do it weeks ago, but I was scared."

"And you're not scared anymore?" KC whispered.

Michael shook his head.

"Will you marry me?" Michael fought back his tears.

"I love you, Michael. My heart is already married to you." KC smiled. "Yes, with all of my soul, yes."

Michael turned to Simon, who simply nodded and knelt beside them. Busch quietly walked over, knelt beside Michael, and placed his large hand on KC's shoulder.

"KC?" Simon began. "Do you take Michael to be your lawfully wedded husband, in good times and bad, in sickness . . . and in health"—Simon took a breath—"till death do you part?"

KC looked at Michael. "With all my heart, I do."

Simon turned to Michael and laid his hand upon his shoulder.

"Michael," Simon said. "Do you take KC to be your lawfully wedded wife . . . in sickness and health, through good times and bad, till death do you part?"

Michael looked deep into KC's eyes, taking both of her hands in his. "With all of my heart, with everything I am . . . I do."

"I now pronounce you man and wife . . ."

Michael leaned over and kissed KC with every ounce of his being, and she kissed him back, warm and sincere, their hearts and souls entwining, consummating their love.

"I'm sorry," KC said. "I didn't mean for this to happen."

They smiled at each other, their eyes looking within each other's soul.

A final breath escaped KC's lips . . .

And she died.

CHAPTER 63

Michael was alone. Simon and Busch gave him privacy as he held KC's limp body, his heart shattered once again. He stared at her face, her vacant green eyes. He swept his hand down her forehead, across her eyelids, gently closing them.

"I love you, Mrs. St. Pierre."

And he wept.

AT THE DOORWAY, San Bao appeared, stepping into the cabin. He looked at Michael and leaned down, nodding his head. He gently picked KC up from Michael's arms, carrying her as if she were a child, laying her upon the floor of the captain's quarters, and reached up to the white ivory square that hung from his neck. He pressed the dragon's head and the tiger's tail at the same time and a small door released on the side; from it he removed a thimble-sized porcelain vial. He removed a small cap, and with supreme focus, he tilted it toward her lips. The liquid flowed into her mouth, a single drop spilling on her lip.

Michael stood back as San Bao laid the bottle to the side and ran his fingers through her hair, rubbing her head, tilting it back. And he began to whisper, in a soft cadence, in a language Michael didn't comprehend.

The moment hung there, Michael wracked with grief, not comprehending what was happening.

And suddenly, a violent gasp exploded from KC's lips, as if she had risen from the sea, snatching a desperate breath of air. She coughed in fits and starts, her body wracked with the involuntary contractions . . . And then she finally calmed, her breathing easing, returning to normal.

San Bao stepped back, looked at Michael with serious eyes, and nodded. And without a word, he left the room.

Michael leaned over KC, running his hands over her warm pink cheeks, trying to catch his breath.

KC's eyes slowly opened and she looked up into Michael's. "Hey," she whispered.

"Hey back." Michael stared at her, not questioning what had happened, what the man had done. He was just thankful, thankful that fate had somehow been postponed.

"Did I . . . ?"

Michael tilted his head in question, unsure how to answer her.

"Does this mean we are still married?" KC said.

"You mean the 'till death do us part' thing?"

KC nodded.

"You're looking pretty alive to me, Mrs. St. Pierre."

CHAPTER 64

Simon handed the diary and the picture of the island to San Bao.

"Thank you," Simon said in Chinese. He then passed him the black puzzle box with the Dragon's Breath inside that he had removed from Xiao's boat.

"Thank you for letting the world forget about this place," San Bao said as he looked at the book. He opened it and stared at the picture of the large admiral and flowing robes . . . and he smiled.

"The Tears of the Phoenix . . . ?" Simon asked.

"Would you like to know its provenance?" San Bao nodded, knowing what Simon meant. "This island is filled with many mysteries." San Bao patted the black box. "If you would like, I will share them all."

Simon took a moment, thinking, understanding the dangers of full knowledge, and finally shook his head. "No, it would only be for my own vanity."

Simon turned to Michael and KC, who stood dockside staring up at the ships. "Do you want to ask about the ships?"

"No," Michael said. "I like a world with mysteries in it."

Simon smiled.

"We've still got a problem," Michael said. "Xiao had a file on KC and me."

"Xiao did, not the military," Simon said. "While he may have invaded his brother's world, he never made them aware of his."

"Okay, even worse. Where did he get it? How could it be so thorough?"

Michael and KC boarded the idling boat.

"Relax, we'll figure it out," Busch said as he climbed on board. "Have you guys thought about where we are going on your honeymoon?"

Michael and KC stared at him, confused.

"I think it's only fair that Simon and I get to tag along; we tag along on everything else. Besides, I'm really going to have to dig my way out of another hole with Jeannie and the kids."

Busch took the helm and turned the boat down the jungle river, heading back out to sea.

CHAPTER 65

The man sat in a large library made of stone and post beam, a warm English-style room out of the past. A fire blazed in the fireplace as he looked out at the snow-covered mountains, gathering his thoughts.

He pulled out the files on Michael and KC and placed them on the table. Compiled over the past year, they began with his knowledge of their dealings in Istanbul, and the intimate knowledge he possessed from when he had trained KC in her teen years, but Michael's history had proven to be harder to crack. He had pieced the dossier together based on what he had heard from KC, a ferocious memory, and very detailed research of the major unsolved thefts that he himself did not commit.

He looked at the clear plasticine folder and the set of fingerprints within. There was a portfolio of pictures compiled over the past fifteen months. Pictures of Michael at work, KC playing tennis, the two of them out at dinner . . . and intimately at home. Thousands of surveillance pictures, as if someone had invaded their hearts and souls.

The orange glow from the fireplace lit the man's burned face, which had been horrifically scarred fifteen months ago, when Michael and KC had left him for dead in the depths of a mountain in India. In the aftermath, he had lost his most prized possessions. He had lost the paintings he had stolen over the last twenty years, he had lost all of his money when his accounts were raided, when the authorities cracked open his safe and took nearly $75 million in diamonds.

He loathed Michael, not just because of what he had done to him, not because he was a rival thief whose actions in Istanbul and India a year earlier had destroyed his world, but because he had taken the one woman he had ever truly loved.

It had been a month since Xiao, a man he had done work for in the past, had contacted him, telling him he needed an expert thief to steal something from the bowels of the Venetian and the Forbidden City within five days. He had considered taking the job but knew it would require two experts.

Xiao had paid him $5 million in gold for copies of the dossiers and a guarantee of the couple's qualifications, with a penalty of his death if they failed. The man liked the odds, and though he hated St. Pierre, he knew he would succeed. They had arrived back at their home in New York two weeks ago seeming no worse for wear, though Xiao had seemed to disappear from the face of the earth.

Iblis looked once more at the files of KC and Michael and smiled, for they had no idea of the hell he was about to put them through.

AUTHOR'S NOTE

I love research, I love learning, I love feeding my curiosity. Imagine, before you begin a novel you get to indulge your interests and weave what you find into a new story, drawing on the past, on worlds long forgotten, bringing light to ancient mysteries, truths, and legends.

The Thieves of Legend started not as a novel but as a distraction. I was in the North Castle Library researching something about London, soon finding myself in the section on China, and before I knew it, I was lost in a textbook about the Forbidden City. The more I read the more excited I became. I found myself in a world digging past the headlines and common knowledge, getting lost in the forgotten details and wrapping myself in mysteries that have escaped the notice of so many.

And that's when I stumbled across Zheng He.

While the story of Michael and KC is fiction—except those parts that come from my life and those crazy things I do—much of the history of Zheng He is true. He was a man who sailed the seas upon enormous vessels—that would still be considered giant today—commanding a fleet of more than two hundred ships that sailed the world gathering riches, animals and beasts, spices and textiles, and returning them all to the emperor for his glory.

After finding his connection to the emperor who built the Forbidden City, learning of his voyages to Africa, the Middle East, India, and North America long before Columbus, and most particularly the fact that he disappeared after his seventh voyage, *The Thieves of Legend* exploded in my mind.

To learn more about Zheng He, the facts behind the fiction, and the inspiration for my characters, be sure to visit me at richarddoetsch.com.

ACKNOWLEDGMENTS

Life is far more enjoyable when you work with people you like and respect. I would personally like to thank:

Gene and Wanda Sgarlata, the owners of Womrath Bookstore in Bronxville, N.Y., for their continued support.

Sarah Branham for keeping it all in tune and being my advocate in this world of publishing. Peter Borland for your encouragement, insight, and that amazing ability to understand what I'm trying to say. I'm truly blessed to not only have you as my overseer but as my friend. Judith Curr, the most forward-thinking professional in the publishing world, and Louise Burke, for her unwavering support and belief. I could not be in better hands. Alexandra Arnold for keeping it all together; Dave Brown for getting people to sit up and take notice; and especially Joel Gotler, my Obi Wan guide in the West Coast cinematic world.

And head and shoulders above all, Cynthia Manson. First and foremost, your continued friendship is something I truly treasure. Thank you for your innovative thinking, your continued faith in the face of adversity, and your unlimited tenacity. Your inspiration, guidance, and business acumen are exceeded by no one.

Thank you to my family:

To my children—you are the best part of my life. Richard, you are my mind, your brilliance and creativity know no bounds; Marguerite, you are my heart, constantly reminding me of what is important in life; your style, grace under pressure, and sense of humor are an example to all. Isabelle, you are my soul; your laughter and inquisitive mind keep my eyes open to the magic of this world we live in.

Dad, for always being my dad and the voice of wisdom that forever rings in my ear. Mom, you were always my champion on terra firma and you no doubt still are; how else can I explain my good fortune since your passing.

Most important, thank you, Virginia. Even in the darkest moments, you fill my heart with hope, opening my eyes to the joys of life that can become so obscured by the trials, tribulations, and tragedies in this journey.

I love that you greet every day with a smile and end every night with a kiss; that you dance with such beauty, grace, and passion; I love your never-say-die, hate-to-lose competitive spirit, and how it infects all around you. I love your heart, your warmth, your beauty, and your dark eyes that reflect your soul; I love the way you put everyone else first and then revel in their success, I love the way you fill a room with laughter and smiles when you enter and how the party is always over when you leave.

Thank you for being you, for being mine, for being everything that's good in my life, I love you with all my heart.

Finally, thank you to you, the reader, for taking the time to read my stories, for reaching out through your notes, tweets, letters, and emails. Your kind words inspire and fill me with the responsibility to never let you down.

Richard

Pick up a blockbuster thriller
from Pocket Books!

Available wherever books and eBooks are sold.
SimonandSchuster.com